"Over there . . . more of them!" Vil shifted Martine's attention to the west side of the bowl. The Harper was distracted as another spear arced over their heads to tunnel into the snowdrift behind them. "Blast their mangy hides! It looks like a war party!" the former paladin cursed.

A baying rose from the woods in the direction where Vil pointed. Surging from the trees was a lanky line of fur-clad, snowshoe-shod gnolls, wreathed in a swirl of white snow. Yipping and howling, the beasts charged in ragged waves, some breaking stride to let fly steel spears. As the six-foot shafts hissed through the cold air, a screech of anguish proved one had hit its mark. Suddenly the air was filled with spears that flew like lightning at the tightly packed gnomes. One scream became a chorus as a full score of the Vani fell under the iron-tipped bolts.

"Jouka, fall back—now!" Vil bellowed.

THE HARPERS

A semi-secret organization for Good, the Harpers fight for freedom and justice in a world populated by tyrants, evil mages, and dread concerns beyond imagination.

Each novel in the Harpers Series is a complete story in itself, detailing some of the most unusual and compelling tales in the magical world known as the Forgotten Realms.

THE HARPERS

THE PARCHED SEA
Troy Denning

ELFSHADOW
Elaine Cunningham

RED MAGIC
Jean Rabe

THE NIGHT PARADE
Scott Ciencin

THE RING OF WINTER
James Lowder

CRYPT OF THE SHADOWKING
Mark Anthony

FANTASY ADVENTURE

SOLDIERS OF ICE

David Cook

TSR Inc.

SOLDIERS OF ICE

First printing: December 1993
Printed in the United States of America
Library of Congress Catalog Card Number: 92-61105

9 8 7 6 5 4 3 2 1

ISBN: 1-56076-641-7

TSR, Inc.   TSR Ltd.
P.O. Box 756   120 Church End, Cherry Hinton
Lake Geneva, WI 53147   Cambridge CB1 3LB
U.S.A.   United Kingdom

To Jim Lowder for guidance
and Helen for patience
—D.C.

Prologue

 It was a bad day for hunting. Old Wolf-Ear knew it would be fruitless. The sun was already too bright and too high, and the pack was too far from the ragged darkness of the woods. There wouldn't be any game in this flat snowfield between the forest and the icefall at the glacier's base. The hunter knew all this even before it wrinkled back its muzzle to sniff the cold, sterile scent of pine and ice.

The air carried none of the tingling warmth of deer musk or rabbit scat, only a suggestion of newborn mice buried deep beneath the snow. The grizzled stalker toyed with the idea of digging them out, but the tiny morsels weren't worth the effort. Besides, Wolf-Ear was with a pack and had to uphold the old gnoll's reputation as a hunter. So instead of digging, Wolf-Ear growlingly spat into the snow to cleanse out the lingering scent.

"No more hunting. Back to village," Wolf-Ear barked, glaring at the three whelps accompanying it, keeping its

1

one strong eye on them. Two of the three younglings properly lowered their heads in submission to the old cur's judgment. The third, though, glared back defiantly. This one stood slightly taller than the old hunter, the older gnoll being stooped and bent.

"I go back to camp with a kill." The challenger sneered in disgust, the blackish lips of its wolfish muzzle curling back to show dirty yellow fangs that hung over the lower gums. The younger gnoll shifted its rag-wrapped feet slightly forward in the churned snow to assert its challenge.

Old Wolf-Ear's neck hairs bristled at the move, and its good ear twitched under the coarse, greasy rags that wrapped its head. The old gnoll caught the warning snarl building in the back of its throat. As it kept its good eye unerringly fixed on the upstart whelp, Wolf-Ear unexpectedly lashed out with its spear to lay on a blow like a schoolmaster caning a boy. The suddenness of the vicious roundhouse swing left the younger gnoll defenseless, and the spear shaft delivered a bruising wallop alongside the whelp's ear, where luckily a thick, matted scarf cushioned the blow. Even with the cushion, the youngling still reeled, its vision wavering.

Before the stunned gnoll could plant its feet firmly on the slippery ground, Wolf-Ear almost casually struck again with a chopping whack to the knee. The youngling dropped like a felled tree into the drift behind it, cracking the ice crust to flounder in the powder beneath. Old Wolf-Ear stepped alongside it, and with a quick jab pressed the spear's point against the challenger's chest. Feeling the tip prick through all its layers of leather and fur, the whelp stopped floundering. Its attention gained, the old hunter snarled out, "I lead this pack. Do not challenge me, pup." Even as Wolf-Ear spoke, the grizzled gnoll made sure it knew where the other two cubs were.

"You lead, Wolf-Ear," the young cub mumbled, turning its

face away. Winter steam formed thick clouds from its muzzle as its mouth hung open slackly, showing a purplish red tongue.

Satisfied, the old hunter pulled back its spear and turned to glare at the two other younglings. They stood there, eager to watch a fight, while the wind flapped their greasy wraps of cloth and hide. Taken from some unfortunate traveler, the once-rich cloth they wore was tattered and stained, and decorated with tassels of animal fur and bits of bone.

Wolf-Ear growled at them just in case they had any ideas. The old gnoll hated working with the cubs, for they were too eager to impress the females of the lodges. Some more hard work would serve them right.

"Youngsters want a kill," Wolf-Ear snarled sarcastically. "Then we hunt on the tall ice." With that, it extended its spear toward the north.

The pack looked up at the great ice wall Wolf-Ear pointed to. It was the forward edge of the glacier that capped the northern end of their valley, a tumbled wall of rock-encrusted ice that had been there since before the gnolls had arrived. The broken wall, less than a half-mile away, stood about three times taller than the tallest trees at its base. The gray-black barren peaks of the mountains were its grim supporters at either side.

"To the top. We spot our kill from there," Wolf-Ear pronounced with grim glee. There was no game up on top of the wall, but the climb and cold would sap some of the fire from the young hunters. It they were smart, they would watch Wolf-Ear and learn how to survive on the ice. Otherwise—well, whatever happened they deserved. No one in the pack would mourn for weaklings.

In the hour that passed as the group clambered over the loose moraine and onto the angular face of the ice, Wolf-Ear watched with malevolent pride as the young hunters struggled. The climb was an ordeal for them, and their hands quickly became matted with frozen blood from the cuts of jagged stones. "Climb!" Wolf-Ear barked whenever one of them lagged behind, particularly the tallest one, and they scrabbled harder at the old gnoll's snarl, determined not to show their pain. Wolf-Ear hoped the climb hurt, for pain would teach them much more than the veteran hunter could.

As they neared the top, where the rim was a serrated barrier of upthrust plates pushed out by the glacier's relentless pressure, Wolf-Ear steered them toward a cleft in the wall. It was an old trail along the bottom of a narrow crevasse, one that tapered gradually to the top of the ice field. The going was easier here, and the pack made rapid progress toward the top. At last the old hunter called a halt and watched, amused, as its charges, bloodied and exhausted, sagged against their bows. Over and around them, the glacier groaned and creaked like a protesting spirit upset at their presence.

A grinding squeal shivered down the narrow walls of the canyon, rousing the group. Old Wolf-Ear had never heard a sound quite like that. It wasn't the rumbling thunder of an avalanche. Instead, it reminded the gnoll of spring ice breaking up on the river, the floes grating and shifting against each other, but up here that was impossible, for there were no rivers and the ice never moved. Curious, the old gnoll motioned the others to follow.

They hadn't gone five steps before the squeal swelled into a shriek. The crevasse echoed with shrill grinding as the crystal floor began to shake. Ice overhanging the lip of the top fell in shivering chunks and cascaded down, smashing against the sides, stinging the gnolls with frozen shards.

And then suddenly, the source of the noise came into view, rushing down the cleft straight toward them.

Avalanche, Wolf-Ear thought blindly, but the gnoll knew

it wasn't an avalanche even as it came into view. It was a wave of solid ice that flowed like water down a streambed, crashing over the broken snow blocks and splashing against the side of the crevasse. Icicles sprayed like froth in the flow's advancing flood.

"Run!" the old hunter barked, fear finally uncovering the compassion Wolf-Ear really felt for the kits. Its urging was hardly needed. The younglings were already scrambling, casting their bows and spears aside in haste.

Wolf-Ear wasn't so quick, and before the old gnoll could pivot, the rushing flood swept over it. The ice flowed over its body like water and swept it, floundering and gasping, along with the current.

The tallest of the younglings seized the lead, covering huge strides with its long legs. Behind it, the other two vainly tried to keep up, jostling each other in their panic. There was a thud and scream as the inundation swept the pair under. Realizing it couldn't outrun the flood of white, the surviving youngling desperately leapt for a jutting ice shelf. It was almost out of reach, but the young gnoll's strong fingers gained a crumbling purchase on the rotten ice and snow. Fueled by terror, the kit hoisted itself over the lip, the churning ice splashing on the creature as it surged past.

Panting on its belly, the gnoll peered over the edge and watched Wolf-Ear's frozen body flow down the crevasse until it disappeared over the icy waterfall as the bizarre river plunged toward the valley below.

One

 "A mug of ale, Jhaele," the small black-haired woman ordered as she strode through the door and plopped herself astraddle the hard bench of the great trestle table in the center of the taproom's commons.

"Aye, Martine," the landlady echoed. Her long platinum tresses gleamed in the light from the open door.

"No, wait. Best make it tea," the young woman called from the table. She drew her sheath knife and began to fidget with it, idly poking the tip into the tabletop.

The landlady nodded and sighed. "Tea, then." Wood tapped metal as she scooped a ladleful of water from the pot that hung over the fire. "Now, what's troubling you, dear?" the landlady asked kindly, looking back toward the other woman.

"It's—Jhaele, how did you know I'm upset?" Martine blurted.

The hosteler ambled over to set a steaming mug on the

table with a solid thump. "For one thing, you haven't been in here a minute, and already you've got that knife of yours out. If you spent as much time hunting as you spend carving at my furniture with that knife, you could be dangerous." Martine was suddenly conscious of the small blade in her hand and the lines she'd been absentmindedly etching on the unvarnished tabletop.

"Sorry."

"It's a tavern table. It's seen worse." The older woman dismissed Martine's worries with a reassuring pat on her shoulder. "So what troubles you?"

"It's just that Jazrac wants to see me."

"Harper business, eh?"

Martine almost gave a start until she remembered how everybody in this dale seemed to know everyone else's business, even secret business such as that concerning the Harpers. "I suppose," she allowed. "He's been my sponsor, vouched for me, and I'm still not a full member, you know."

I'm saying more than I should, the woman realized even as she said the words.

"Ah, I didn't, but that helps to explain things." Jhaele gave a wry smile that only someone who has heard countless secrets could do. "Don't you worry. He's a hearthlover, a stay-at-home. He probably wants you to do some legwork for him while he hovers around Elminster."

"Maybe," Martine allowed tentatively as she took up the mug. "But his message said he had important news for me."

"Hmph. With wizards, everything is important," the landlady chuckled as she turned to tend the fire.

* * * * *

Jazrac was waiting for Martine on the footpath that led to the mill. He looked old, but not so old as to be grandfatherly, nor was she so young by comparison. The wizard met her with a sweeping bow more showy than polite, his seasoned head bent till the sharp tip of his salt-and-pepper goatee brushed against his chest. The rich velveteen cloth of his robes, impractical dress given the rustic surroundings, rustled as he rose to his thin, imperious height.

"Greetings, Master Jazrac," Martine said with a schoolchild's nervous courtesy and a small bob of her body, as much of a curtsy as anyone would get from her. In her buckskin trousers and fur half-cape, such niceties were lost anyway. "You have news for me?"

"Indeed, great news. Come, let's walk," he offered and said nothing more. The wizard deftly steered her onto the mill path, clearly relishing the air of teasing mystery he was creating. Martine bit at her lip and followed, since there was no other choice. Jazrac was born to be overly dramatic, she knew. It was one thing she had learned in the several years she'd known him. He could have been a thespian had his magical talent gone undiscovered.

Though she was bursting with curiosity, Martine followed the older man into the faded brown woods. Behind them was Shadowdale, a collection of thatched houses clustered around a muddy crossroads. The curling spire of the Tower of Ashaba rose above the rest and was just visible through the branches of the trees. Jazrac led the way by half a step. Martine cocked her head to look up at him, dark bangs of bobbed hair spilling sideways across her forehead.

"Martine, my dear, I know it seems as if you've been doing nothing but playing messenger ever since you joined the Harpers." The huntress bristled at the condescension in his tone. "Certainly you've been kept busy. In fact, some of the others wondered if you might be in need of a rest. Four months trekking in the wilderness is more than enough time with no inns, no baths—barely even a bed, I imagine."

Rest? I don't need any rest. What have I done wrong? Martine thought. Her eyes flashed with alarm even as she strove to keep her expression calm.

Jazrac didn't notice any reaction, or at least paid no mind. With a muttered, twisted phrase, he made a pantomime sweep of the path ahead, velvet sleeve aswirl. The light breath of wind in the barren treetops suddenly arched and swirled down at his command, blowing the dead foliage into the woods till the leaves caught their sharp corners along the bank of the nearby millstream.

Martine barely glanced at the tattered shapes as they swirled away, unwittingly drumming her fingers on her thigh while waiting for her companion to continue. She was accustomed to Jazrac's little magical displays. She fearfully guessed his next words—praise for jobs well done, a suggestion that she needed more time or more guidance, then an offer of a mission suitable to her talents. Undoubtedly it would be another package to deliver or a fellow Harper to accompany on a mission, all so she could watch and learn. Only a few more such as these and surely they would advance her. A little more patience and seasoning were all she needed. In all this, Jazrac meant well; the wizard had generously watched over her career up to now. Martine's thoughts madly raced to review the scenario she was certain would follow.

The wizard interrupted her reverie. "Anyway, I want to tell you how pleased I am—everyone is—with your efforts. You seem to have . . . well, that Harper stuffing in you. Rare thing, too. So if you want to take a rest for a month or two, you deserve it." He looked down at her with the best consoling gaze his thin, creased face could manage.

Martine stopped walking and was about to give a not very carefully worded protest when Jazrac continued.

"Or," he said ever so slowly, the corners of his mouth

curling up in a tiny smile, "you could take on another mission—a solo job, a chance for you to really show your mettle. Are you interested?" Taking a slow breath of the bracing autumn air, Jazrac paused and then added, "It could be the big break you've been waiting for—a chance to prove you really are a full-fledged Harper." The wizard waited for some reaction from his protege.

For a moment, Martine kept silent, surprised by Jazrac's offer. The stream and skittering leaves sounded a soft background to their walk, underscored by the creaking and scraping of the aged waterwheel driving the grindstone at the miller's nearby.

"I don't need rest!" the slight ranger blurted, her alto voice rising eagerly. "Tell me about this mission."

Jazrac smiled with smug satisfaction at his protege's response. "Do you have any idea just how thin we Harpers have been spread of late?"

Martine's reply was a quizzical look.

He caught her hand, and with his sharp, bony fingers gently recited the litany. "Waterdeep, Impiltur, Thay, Chult, gods know where else. It seems as if every distant land has some problem that needs solving. Now something's happening in the north, up past Damara. There's been some kind of eruption, and we want you to investigate."

"Some kind of trouble in Damara?"

"I said an eruption, my dear. North of Damara, on the Great Glacier. A volcano of ice." Jazrac shivered slightly in the autumn cold and turned back toward the houses and fields of Shadowdale. Martine fell in step alongside him.

"An ice volcano? You're teasing me." The idea sounded too incredible to believe, even from a wizard.

"You should know me better than that, Martine," the wizard chided, head tilted till his goatee seemed to point at her. "This is Harper business. I'm serious."

Martine flushed.

"As I said, we're dealing with a volcano of ice. It happens sometimes, my dear—a rift in the walls between the worlds. Elminster and I have been tracking this one. It looks like an opening to the para-elemental plane of ice."

"The what?"

"Sorry. Wizard talk."

"Oh."

"It's an opening to another—um—plane. You know about the elemental forces—earth, air, fire, and water. Perhaps you aren't aware of it, but there are others, such as the para-, the quasi-, and who knows what other elemental planes, not as strong or important, and ice is one of those."

Martine listened avidly. She'd heard of the existence of the planes and knew about the four elements, but the rest was new to her. She hurried to stay alongside him, kicking away the leaves that had already blown back over the path.

"Anyway, sometimes the barrier between our world and one of these planes weakens until a hole opens, spilling elemental matter into our world," Jazrac continued, warming to his subject. Scholarly research was his meat and cheese, and he could quickly forget that others did not share his enthusiasm. "Geysers and volcanoes could indicate the planes of steam and magma. Yurpide of Impiltur, I think, even theorizes that rainbows and lightning storms have their origins in—"

"I get the idea. What I don't understand is why this is so important." Martine wanted to get the conversation back to her mission. "It sounds as if you know everything already."

"Ah, yes. Well, there is a danger, you see."

Her neck tingled with excitement. "What?"

The path reached the edge of the fields that bordered Shadowdale. A cold wind was rising out of the west, pushing in a bank of flat, gray clouds over Old Skull, the barren granite mount that overlooked the village. The wizard looked up and shook his head, perhaps at the prospect of bad weather coming. "Sometimes things cross over and enter our world. If it's only one or two of these elemental creatures, it's not much our concern, but if the rift should expand, it could prove to be a danger. You're going to go up there and seal it."

Martine couldn't resist a joke. "Suppose I brick it up?"

Jazrac turned his attention back to her with a vexed scowl. "Very funny. As a matter of fact, that's what I've been doing for the last few weeks—preparing the seals. Now that I've finished, it's time for you to put them in place. The frigid north is not one of my favorite places."

"So that's my big break, eh?" the woman deduced, adding a flip of her bangs to give just the right touch of sardonic nonchalance.

"If it all goes well," Jazrac said with pointed emphasis.

Martine realized her flippancy was wasted on the humorless wizard and assumed a serious expression. Still, her earlier nervousness was gone, and she felt the need to celebrate somehow. Wrapping an arm around the older man's waist, she tugged him toward the town before he could resist. "I promise not to fail you. Come on. It looks like snow. You can buy me an ale at the Old Skull and give a toast to my success."

"For that, I'll have to buy you a bucketful of ale, my eager young tyro," Jazrac protested as he allowed himself to be pulled along. The last summer songbirds scolded loudly at the approaching storm as the two hurried across the fields for the warmth of the thatched-roof inn.

Over mugs of spiced ale that warmed away the chill, Jazrac outlined the mission in detail. He spoke softly, for there were a few others in the taproom, and Harper business was none of their concern. From his pocket, he produced five stones, polished and smooth. They glittered like ice with blue fire at their cores. "Opals from the south," the wizard explained once he noted Martine's interest. "You'll have to set them around the rift like this. I assume it will be a crater." Jazrac spread four of the stones in a circle, deftly tracing the points of a star with his thin fingers, leaving one point empty. "Exactly equal from each other. Don't worry, the stones will glow when they're in the proper position." He nudged the fifth stone into place, and suddenly five points of blue luminescence glittered before Martine's eyes.

"That's it?"

The wizard broke the ring before the tabletop glow could attract the attention of Jhaele or the beet-faced Dalesman who sat near the fire. "Not quite." He produced another stone from a separate pouch. "This is the capstone. Touch it to each stone as you put it in place. That activates the seal."

"Okay," Martine nodded, taking the stone from his fingers. It looked like a fading ember, dull red and pitted, rather than a powerful magical artifact.

"Be careful. Keep it separate from the others. You don't want an accident triggering the seal while you're traveling."

"Is it dangerous?" The woman looked at the stone with new respect as she prudently set it back on the table.

Jazrac shook his head as he swept the opals into a pouch. "Not very—but an accident would ruin all my work." The words reminded Martine that Jazrac, at least, considered her journey important.

"Another thing. The red stone is a temporary fix. You have to bring it back so I can cast the finishing spells. Be careful not to bang it around too much. It's not as solid as it looks. Once the seal is activated, if the stone breaks, the seal breaks. So be careful and bring it back with you. Understood?"

Martine nodded. As she took the pouch of opals, the stones rattled softly in her hand. "Sounds clear enough," she added to cover a sudden twinge of nerves. Her first important mission . . . It seemed simple enough, but she couldn't help but worry whether she was up to it.

Across the table, Jazrac smiled, his goatee making him look cheerfully fiendish. "Good. Now, I want you to stay in touch with me while you're up there."

"How?"

"I'm a wizard, my dear, remember?" the older man chortled, letting a tone of condescension slip back into his voice. He tipped back in his chair. "I'll use my crystal ball. I can't hear you or talk to you, but I can see you through it."

Martine wasn't sure she liked the idea that Jazrac would be checking up on her. She hastily took a sip of her ale to cover a grimace.

"I'm not spying on you. If you write a letter, I'll be able to read it through the ball. Take this. I'll need an object to focus on, something to track you by." From deeper still in his pocket, Jazrac produced a small dagger. "I know your fondness for knives. All you have to do is pin your letter up with this dagger. That way I can find it with the crystal ball. I have to know what I'm looking for, after all."

Still uncertain, Martine took the knife and turned it over in her hands. It was a decorative knife with a carved bone handle and a red garnet set in the hilt, but the blade was short, hardly practical. A typical wizard's choice, she noted somewhat contemptuously. "If you insist."

Her sponsor ignored the reluctance in her voice. "That's it, then. How soon can you be ready?" he asked, elbows on the table, leaning forward till the tip of his goatee brushed his tented fingers.

Martine rolled the knife in her hands, letting the light from the inn's fire play off the blade. "A day or two, I'd guess. Three at the most. It depends on how long it takes me to get supplies. Astriphie's fit and ready for travel." Indeed, her mount was growing restless in the stables.

"Excellent. The less time wasted, the better. Here's to a safe journey and a successful mission, my dear." With tankard raised, Jazrac toasted her success.

The next day Martine, suffering from a slight hangover, set to work preparing for her departure. Shadowdale wasn't a large city, nor even a border town where outfitters thronged, so it took only the better part of the day to gather all that was needed—flour, salt, jerky, dried fruit, flatbread, sugar, lard, arrowheads, oil, extra bowstrings, needles, thread, and more. She especially wanted soap, since she had no desire to do without the luxury a bath might offer, even in some glacial lake. By nightfall, as she stretched her legs before the fire at the Old Skull, the ranger was relieved to be through haggling with the village's only trader, the irascible Weregund. Her status as a Harper, which it seemed everyone in town knew about, didn't make much of an impression on him, and every purchase had been a battle. Her supplies were finally complete, though, even the soap, and tomorrow she and Astriphie could hit the trail. As she gingerly sipped at her ale, she toyed with Jazrac's little knife, playfully refracting the flames of the fire from its blade.

"You'll be leaving us tomorrow, then?" Jhaele asked, her hair the bloody color of a hunter's moon in the blazing firelight. Pot in one hand, she offered up a fresh ladle of ale. "Old Weregund told me you were at his place buying supplies."

Martine nodded, tossing back the dregs of her mug. The innkeeper sloshed another round into Martine's cup. "This one's on the house."

"Well, thank you, Jhaele." Suddenly flustered by the landlady's kindness, it was the best Martine could manage.

"Call it a traveler's blessing. May Tymora's wheel turn in your favor."

"And may your house know the joy of Lliira's smile," Martine replied. She reluctantly raised her mug to Jhaele, unwilling to get into another night of toasting.

"Fair enough. Here's to the ladies of luck and joy." She raised her ladle to match Martine's toast. Draining it in a long draught, she wiped the foam from her chin and looked down with a kindly expression at the younger woman, still stretched in the chair. "I'll see that the stableboy has Astriphie fed and ready in the morning. You'd better rest up for tomorrow."

"Thank you, Jhaele." The landlady was already leaving as Martine spoke. Left again to herself, Martine settled back into the small firelit cocoon that surrounded her chair. The knife blade resumed its flashing in the light, somehow less playful than before.

Although she'd only been staying at the inn for a few weeks, Martine hadn't expected the farewells to sting so much. After all, besides Jhaele and Jazrac, there were few people she really knew here. She'd been pointedly avoiding most of the Dalesmen with a Harper's natural instinct for secrecy. Now, slightly tipsy and pleasantly tired, she felt a poignant stab of regret at the prospect of leaving the sleepy little hamlet. The flowing river, the winter-stripped trees, even the cracked, barren slopes of Old Skull seemed somehow homey and comforting. I could live here as well as anywhere else, the Harper thought idly, but she knew she wasn't ready to settle anywhere just yet. I'll be back, she told herself before draining her mug and trundling off to bed.

The dawn came with Martine feeling ill-rested and anxious. Journeys always do this to me, she noted irritably as she climbed out of bed. She could never sleep soundly the night before a trip, always waking up at hours only marked by their darkness, always jittery with the hopes and the tensions of wanderlust.

Astriphie's shrill cry from the stable yard got the ranger's sluggish blood moving. It was time to shake off the numbness of town and return to the wilds where she really belonged.

After a quick splash of chill water that passed for a rinse and a struggle with her traveling clothes, Martine clomped down the worn wooden stairs and into the yard. The pale morning sun washed over the cobblestones, the light having yet to reach the full richness of the day.

Martine was greeted by a harsh birdlike shrill that turned to a whinnying squawk. "Astriphie, keep still!" she shouted as her mount reared back, tossing its head so that it threatened to swing the goggle-eyed stableboy clinging to its halter clean over the yard fence. Astriphie was no ordinary steed, but a hippogriff, with the forequarters an enormous bird and the hindquarters a sturdy horse, the juncture between the two marked by a pair of golden-feathered wings. The beast clicked the bill of its eaglelike head, threatening playfully to snap the stableboy's arm like a dry splinter. The lad trembled, almost dropping the rope in abject terror, not being able to distinguish the hippogriff's playfulness from hunger.

The Harper hurriedly took the reins, and the boy scrambled to safety behind a stable door. "Astriphie, stop!" Martine commanded, punctuating her words with a quick falconer's whistle as the hippogriff reared up again. A sharp tug brought the creature back down, its front talons scrabbling on the stone while its rear hooves beat out an irritated tattoo. It craned its feathered head around to fix one blinking eye on Martine and then clacked in disapproval until she reached up and stroked the feathers of its massive wings soothingly. The long equine tail flicked against its haunches as if to point out where to scratch next.

"Good girl, Astriphie," the Harper said softly as she automatically ran her hands over the saddle straps, checking their fittings, making sure her packs and saddlebags were secure. High above the forests was no place to discover a loose girth.

Golden-pinioned wings beat the air in a gentle *whoomph* that swirled a maelstrom of dust and straw. The saddle slipped as the mighty trapezius muscles of the flying beast rippled under the leather seat, but the straps held tight. Satisfied, Martine tossed a coin to the boy. By now he had recovered enough to venture out from behind the door. Martine led Astriphie out into the road and lightly swung into the saddle. The stableboy ran to the fence to watch as the pair trotted, then galloped down the road, until at last, with a muscular heave of its great wings, the hippogriff lifted from the earth and sailed away over the top of the brown-leafed forest.

All day they flew east, soaring over the forest, the coast of the Moonsea barely in sight to the north. With only the briefest of stops for rest, they pressed on the next day and those that followed, until on the fourth day, they passed the vulture-haunted spires of Hillsfar, then three more to carry them past the streets of Mulmaster tumbling down the mountain slopes, and farther east to where boats could cross the Moonsea to the rocky shores of Vaasa. Here Martine nosed Astriphie northward and piloted the hippogriff over the stormy waters of the Moonsea until they sighted the northern coast, where they rested in a village of fishermen too poor to be suspicious of such a strange traveling pair.

After a few days of dining on fish while Astriphie took a well-deserved rest, the pair resumed their northerly course, following the trails up passes winding through the mountains that isolated the north. They flew over the northern stretches of Vaasa, where people thought all strangers were Damaran spies, and beyond to the plains of Damara, where villagers spoke in whispers of her supposedly Vaasan looks. Mindful of these animosities and suspicions, Martine kept her questions few and short when she stopped in villages, passing herself off as a merchant's agent looking for new markets for her employer.

By this subterfuge, Martine passed through Damara and found herself at last flying over the snowbound ridge of an isolated valley, the last before the walls of the Great Glacier itself. Samek, it was called, home to a village of gnomes, or so the garrulous frontiersman farther south had claimed. "Be the last outpost afore the wilds," he swore. "Mebbe they can guide you to the glacier, though 'tain't a harder-headed batch than them little folk. 'Tain't got no trade, an' they put up with no truck at all from outsiders, big folks especially."

The tracker's gloomy prediction came to mind as the Harper steered Astriphie into a gentle dive that would carry them over the valley's heart. At its widest, Samek was no more than a few miles across, pointed like a narrow slot north and south. The sides of the valley were ringed in by mountains already deeply cloaked in snow, the treeless peaks mottled with frozen white. Tall pines dressed in the dull greens of winter lined their slopes, the dour monotony broken on the higher reaches by cracked outcroppings of collapsed rock. Natural cathedrals to the gods was how Martine thought of these spectacular mountain peaks.

They swooped lower over the valley, and Martine turned her attention away from the peaks to scan the forests and meadows below, watching for the village. Since the valley was inhabited by gnomes, she didn't expect to see houses, barns, or the patchwork patterns of fields. The little folk didn't build their towns as humans did, she knew from experience. They liked to hide their dwellings in the bases of trees, in hillsides, or among the reeds along the river. Still, she hoped to spot a trace of smoke or a winding trail she could follow.

In her first two passes over the valley, Martine noticed the meandering track of several game trails, mountain streams reduced to waterfalls of ice, and the grass-tufted snowfields of frozen bogs, but no sign of a village. It was on the third pass, as Astriphie banked into a turn that tilted the saddle to a dizzying angle, that Martine caught sight of a wisp of smoke rising through the thick-growing trees. With a quick series of whistles and a hard pull on the reins, the ranger swung the hippogriff in a broad loop that came to bear straight toward the smoke. Black-green branches flashed beneath her feet as she urged Astriphie lower until her mount's hooves scraped off the branches of the uppermost pines. Martine strained in her saddle to peer over the hippogriff's side while its wings rose and fell in massive beats. Bearing straight on, they closed on the column of smoke that was their guide.

Flying almost too fast, the pair shot over a small clearing and straight through the rising plume of smoke. Martine instantly noted it had the tang of woodsmoke. Whipping around in her saddle, she caught a glimpse of a cabin and a man on the ground, staring up, with an axe in his hand. Not pausing to consider the consequences, she yanked back on the reins and shouted, "Down, Astriphie! Land."

The hippogriff plunged toward the nearest clearing, a smooth meadow along the banks of a stream. The beast hit the snow with a running bounce that jarred the ranger in her saddle and engulfed them in a blizzard of white powder. Martine wasted no time unbuckling herself and dropping to the ground, catfooted and ready, her sword already in her hand. "Stay, Astriphie," she commanded, leaving the hippogriff unhobbled just in case something dangerous happened by. The mighty steed flexed its wings contentedly and seemed to chirp back in understanding.

Once she was into the woods, the snow was far deeper than Martine had expected, and it was with considerable difficulty that she floundered through the heavy drifts. By the time the Harper reached the clearing she had spotted from the air, she was panting and sweat-soaked. She didn't try to scout out her goal, but stepped through the screen of underbrush boldly and stood in full view of the axeman. At first glance, she guessed the cabin's owner was at home in the woods like herself, a man who chose to live out in the wilds, and so she placed her faith in the usual frontier hospitality.

The man was standing near a stump where he had been chopping wood. There was a neatly piled stack of waiting logs on one side of him and a jumbled heap on the other. Behind him stood a small cabin built of solid pine logs. A rickety stone chimney clung to one side of the house, and a little shed that looked like a combination storehouse and entrance jutted off the front. The substantial walls were broken by one small window, heavily shuttered. The yard around the cabin was cluttered with snow-mounded piles of cordwood and what she could only guess were the half-finished projects of every frontiersman.

Despite the chill, the man wore no coat or gloves, and his tasseled woolen cap was pushed far back on his head. His hair was dun gray and short, cut carelessly so that it cropped out over his ears. Dark stains of sweat marked the heavy smock he wore.

As Martine stepped out of the woods, he hefted his axe in one hand, and she noted he held it the way a warrior would, rather than a lumberjack. He was a big man and older than Martine. She guessed his age at forty or perhaps fifty, her father's age, at least judging by his graying brown hair and the slightly stiff way he moved. His nose was crooked, as if it had once been broken, and a thick stubble grew on his chin, the look of a man who had few guests. His expression showed no surprise or emotion beyond the wariness that filled his eyes.

"Greetings," he said with the same hospitable caution she had shown. The stranger's voice was deep, and when he spoke, haggard lines flexed across his face as if his weatherbeaten cheeks were unaccustomed to shaping words. "I am Vilheim, son of Balt." He stopped, offering no more information about himself, although his sharp accent was like those she had heard along the Chessentian coast in the south.

"My respects to you, sir," Martine offered deferentially, taking care not to move any closer. "I have traveled a long way to see the gnomes of this valley. Do you know of them?"

The man swung his axe with a casual stroke and sank it into the stump. The sharp *chunk* of the blow echoed dully through the snowy woods. He spread his hands slightly, as if to show that he was unarmed, though Martine noted he never stepped out of arm's reach of the axe. Again there was a long silence that neither seemed eager to fill.

"Gnomes, eh?" he finally intoned. "You came here to talk to gnomes. That was you flying overhead, right, Miss . . . ?"

"Martine. Of Sembia." She shifted from side to side to keep her feet from freezing inside her boots. "I'm hoping the gnomes will guide me onto the Great Glacier."

The man's weatherbeaten face almost broke into a grin at the relish of some private joke, and then his stoic face regained its composure. "Forgive me, I have forgotten my manners," the woodsman quickly said, his voice apologetic. "I fear you have come a long way for naught, Martine of Sembia. The Vani are not friendly to strangers."

"The Vani?"

"The gnomes of Samek." He spoke in strained tones as he stiffly picked up his coat, a heavy parka of fur and leather, from the ground and brushed away the snow that clung to it.

Martine persisted, stepping forward to press her claim. "I still would like to try. Can you guide me to them?"

He stopped and suddenly scrutinized Martine, looking at her and beyond her into the gray woods, as if searching for any others who may have accompanied her. His gaze was startlingly sharp and intense, far more than she expected from an ordinary frontiersman, and it made Martine wonder if she had done the right thing by showing herself so abruptly. This simple woodsman wasn't what she had expected, and that made her nervous.

"Are you alone?" he asked.

"Yes. Are you?" She felt her hand inch unconsciously toward the sword that dangled from her hip.

Vilheim flicked his eyes between the sky and Martine until he finally seemed to compromise and gazed at the trees behind her. He rubbed at the thick stubble of his cheek tentatively. "Alone? Yes . . . I'm alone." Martine thought she detected a trace of sorrow in his voice.

The man met her gaze evenly. A shiver made her legs tremble, and she was suddenly aware just how cold it was as the dry breeze swirled up motes of ice between them.

"You'll freeze out here tonight," the woodsman said abruptly, a smile finally breaking across his face. "I can offer you a hot meal and a place to sleep. You are welcome to stay, although you may find me a disappointing cook. Your search for the Vani might best be done tomorrow when there is more of the day."

Martine accepted Vilheim Baltson's sudden hospitality at face value. She sensed a basic decency in the man. It wasn't just intuition, but also trust in the simple ways of the frontier. Visitors were too few to be abused or driven away. Martine seized the opportunity, thankful for the offer of warmth and comfort. "Much kindness, Master Vilheim. As soon as I've tended to my hippogriff, I'll gladly accept what I'm sure will be considerable improvement on another meal of boiled jerky and biscuit."

"I wouldn't be so certain," Vilheim warned as he pulled the axe free from the log to take it back inside. "Bring your animal up and come inside when you're ready. I'll straighten up the place a little."

Martine trudged back through the snow to fetch Astriphie. The hippogriff was crouched in bloodstained snow, tearing at the carcass of a deer, forcing the ranger to wait until the meal was done. Finally she was able to remount the hippogriff safely and fly to the cabin. After making a quick bed of pine boughs for Astriphie, she knocked at the cabin door.

"Come in," Vilheim called from the other side.

With one hand close to her sword, just in case, she opened the door and was instantly assaulted by an outrush of steamy warmth. Compared to the cold dryness outside, the cabin was like the tropics, and after days of camping in snow, it was a blessing.

"Come in quickly and close the door, or there'll be more wood to cut," her host chided from the fire. He was already ladling bubbling stew into two thick, wooden bowls. "Sit at the table. Please."

Martine didn't require more urging and pulled up one of the two rickety chairs she saw. The whole cabin was a single, sparsely furnished room—one wobbly table, two chairs, a bed heaped with comforters, and a chest. A well-polished, dented breastplate hung from a rack by the door, along with a battered war helm, several spears, and Vilheim's coat. The crudely tanned bear rug on the smooth wood floor in front of the fireplace was testimony to her host's prowess with bow and sword. These two weapons hung over the log mantel, both unpretentious but well made. Aside from these martial touches, the rest of the cabin's furnishings were purely functional—pots and pans, lamps, dishes, and the like. Overhead, the scarred wood rafters were carelessly decorated with leather bags hung from pegs and, in one case, a bent-handled dagger driven into the wood. Above the rafters, cobwebs glowed in the flickering light. There was one other door, which Martine had little trouble guessing led to an attached privy.

She had barely settled in before her host quickly set the table with bowls of hot stew, great brown rounds of bread, and a pot of fresh cheese. The aroma of grease, fried onions, and salted venison belied the threat of bad cooking. After Vilheim pulled up the other chair and mumbled a grace, Martine set to eating with a vengeance. She ate greedily while Vilheim observed silently.

After both had pushed their bowls away and Martine profusely thanked her host, the talk gradually turned to news of the outside world. They talked about trivialities—who ruled where, and what new wonders had arisen. He was particularly interested in how the land's faiths fared, and although she wasn't very religious, she told him what she knew. As the conversation continued, Martine came to call him "Vil," and he in turn managed to drop the formal "of Sembia" from her name.

Yet throughout their conversation, Vil revealed but little of himself. He was from Chessentia, as she had guessed, and had been living in the valley for about three years. He had settled here for privacy, he explained, and it was as good a reason as many she had heard.

She offered little more about herself. No mention was made of her role in the Harpers or of her current mission. It wasn't wise to carelessly advertise one's allegiance. Her host seemed satisfied to let her keep her secrets.

At last the Harper broached the subject of the gnomes.

"I know them," Vilheim allowed. "I've been their neighbor for three years now—but a short time, in their estimation. They're good enough neighbors, but in their own way." Vil paused and sucked on his lip as he tried to think of the right words. "They prefer their privacy."

"Do you think I could meet with them?" Martine tried not to sound too eager. Unconsciously her fingers started playing with her table knife, spinning it back and forth. "Or could you guide me to the Great Glacier?"

Vil leaned back, considering the young woman's question. "Better you try the Vani first. I usually stay away from glacier country. Tomorrow I will take you to see them, and you can ask for yourself."

Two

 Wakefulness came slowly to Martine the next morning. Sunk into the depths of Vilheim's feather bed, which he had insisted she occupy while he slept on the floor, Martine had no desire to rise. The Harper lay staring upward at the semidarkness, listening to the bleak, cold wind that moaned outside the window. Gradually the dim outlines of the rafters and the black roundness of a hanging venison haunch took shape over her, illuminated by the dying glimmers from last night's ash-banked fire.

What time she woke and how long she lay there, Martine could not say. Wake and sleep blurred together, one coming, the other going, in repeated cycles. Finally the dim shapes overhead lightened and filled as the eastern sun cleared the distant ridge and sent its rays through the gaps between the window shutter's slats, followed by the clank of cooking pots as Vilheim prepared breakfast.

With a sigh, Martine clawed her way out of bed and groped her way through the worn blanket divider, another thing her host had insisted upon last night. Instantly cold air swirled around her bare legs, reminding her of where she stood. She pulled her tunic closer to her for warmth. "Morning," Vil called out as he ladled water from a barrel and into a pitted old pot.

"Good morning to you, and thank you for the bed. Did any woman ever tell you you snore?" Martine cheerfully tweaked him as she rummaged through her clothes at the foot of the bed. Finding the warm leggings she sought, Martine pulled the curtain closed to get dressed.

"You're the first," Vil shouted over the makeshift wall. "Rose hip tea or hot goat's milk?"

Goat's milk sounded revolting. "Tea—" Martine began, only to suddenly awaken to the implications of the man's words. "Wait . . . am I the first one to tell you you snore? Surely you're jesting me." Even as she said it, Martine realized it was none of her business. Damn, she chided herself. I've really stuck my foot in my mouth.

There was a cough from the other side of the curtain. "I meant that you are the first—umm—woman to tell me that. Although the arrangements were always . . . well . . . pretty much like last night."

Martine remembered to think this time and decided not to ask any further questions. She was surprised her host hadn't taken offense, especially since the man seemed possessed of a decided puritan streak. Perhaps he was trying to reassure her of his own intentions.

"Well, you don't snore much," she lied, hoping that would end the subject. She straightened out her tunic and stepped back into view.

Vil had just finished hanging the pot on the claw over the fire and was leaning against the mantel, carefully prodding the coals into life with a poker. A small swirl of embers rose from where Vil poked the ashes. "Ready for breakfast?"

"Mm-hm. It smells wonderful in here." She wasn't

exaggerating; the air was tangy with the aroma of fruit and herbs. She took down the curtain to clear space for both of them at the small table.

"Cured venison, fresh cheese, whey, berry jam, and hardtack; tea or milk, as you prefer. I have a chance to make up for the meager table I set last night." He laid out a simple meal for the pair, unwrapping cloth-bound packets of soft, fresh cheese and dry biscuits, followed by pots of thick jam and translucent whey. With a final flourish, he set a marbled haunch of meat in the center of the small table so that one leg wobbled perilously under the weight.

"Good meal, indeed!" Martine gaped. Pulling over the two chairs, she waited for him to say a blessing and then dug in. Eagerly she ate chunks of hardtack smeared with buttery goat cheese and red jam and topped with slivers of venison. Even the fresh goat's milk, which she tasted dubiously at first, was refreshingly welcome after drinking only cold water and birch tea on the trail.

After a bit, when the silence made it apparent that Vil was rusty as a conversationalist, Martine asked, "Are you known among the gnomes?"

"We are . . . good neighbors, as I said last night." Vil shaved off another piece of venison. "I respect their ways, and they tolerate me." Behind him, the rekindled fire gave a popping sound as a pocket of resin ignited. "When I first came up here, I didn't see a gnome for a year. I think they hoped I would go away. It was only after I built the cabin that any of the Vani came by."

"Three years ago?"

He nodded as he finished his tea. "Don't worry, you won't have to wait that long. If we leave after breakfast, they should still be in council when we get to the warren. With any luck, they'll see you today."

This suited Martine just fine. She hurriedly finished her breakfast, only to have to wait until Vil finished eating. After

helping him scrape the dishes and clean the table, Martine
struggled into her coat and stood by the door, waiting.

"Have you ever been on skis?" her host asked as he laced
up his coat, refusing to let himself be hurried.

"Yes." Twice . . . and the first time was when I was ten,
Martine thought.

"Good. It's time to go."

Outside, in the morning shadow cast by the mountains,
Martine, with Vil's paternal advice, laced the ungainly
boards to her feet and set out to follow him across the
snowy hummocks, wobbling along, barely steadied by her
poles. The route he followed led through an icebound
world of alternating light and dark. Where it could penetrate the forest branches, the dawn sunlight turned the soft
snow-clad outlines of trees and roots into a dazzling domain
of white. Elsewhere, deep shadows quickly closed in and
clothed the landscape in darkness.

The air was rich with the scent of pines. Martine's skin
prickled from the cold. The trees loomed over the pair,
their white-dressed boughs locked so close together that
the bottom branches were hidden permanently from sunlight, leaving them scraggly dead sticks occasionally tufted
with needled clusters. The great trunks stirred with the
wind till the forest echoed with muted popping and creaking sounds. Winter birds confided secrets to each other
and warned of the passing strangers.

After they had pressed on for an hour or so, judging from
the rise of the sun over the eastern ridge, and Martine was
lathered in a fine sweat despite the cold, they struck a narrow path that twisted round gnarled roots and tunneled
through arched brambles. The path was clearly meant for
creatures much smaller than even the petite Martine. She
and Vil ducked, bobbed, and pushed their way through the
tangles until finally Vil pulled aside the last thorned branch
and slid easily into a small clearing at the base of a steep

knoll. The hillside was a tumble of granite shelves and trees clinging precariously to the slopes, all draped with snow.

The trail they were following led to the very base of the mound and then vanished—or so it seemed to Martine at first glance. In truth, the path ended at a cunningly concealed arch, shaped to match the jutting rocks that framed it. Set back deep in the opening were a pair of squat wooden doors of weathered gray pine, cleverly carved with vines and rocks so that their shadowed surface mimicked the summertime slope of the hill. Together the doors were almost as broad as they were high.

With the tip of his pole, Vil rapped at the snow-dusted doors. The sound hollowly reverberated from the hillside.

Barely a moment passed before Martine heard a muffled scraping from inside the hill. With a creak of wooden peg hinges, the doors swung inward, releasing a wisp of steam. The weak eastern sun reached through the slim gap and etched a thin line onto the polished floorboards beyond, the hint of snowy tracks marring the perfect smoothness of the wooden floor. The creaking stopped as a shadowy face peered through the crack, scrutinizing the visitors.

Apparently satisfied, the doorkeeper nodded briefly. "Welcome Vilheim, friend of the Vani," croaked a brittle voice as the gnome swung the door wide.

"Greetings, Tikkanen. We have come to see the council. Are the elders in session?" Vil bowed as best he could in his thick winter coat, and Martine followed suit.

The object of their courtesy was a little man who stood no taller than Vil's waist, stocky of build and buried in a thick cream-colored cloak that covered him to the very bottom of his chin. Despite his stocky build, Martine knew the little man was actually lean for one of his kind. Airy strands of long white beard escaped from the top of the collar and swayed like cloudy wisps in the breeze. The gnome's face seemed ancient, reminding Martine of a shriveled apple.

The doorkeeper's rheumy red eyes were barely noticeable behind his bulbous nose, a pronounced characteristic of his race. Tikkanen's nose was limned with thin red veins and colored with age spots.

"The council sits today, it is true." The old gnome cleared his throat and then pointed at Martine. "Before you enter, Vilheim, will you testify for your companion, swear that she will abide by the laws and customs of the Vani, that she brings no evil to this warren, bears not the mark of a blood feud, and carries no curse upon her?"

Martine's and Vil's eyes met for a moment. She was uncertain just what he would say. After only a slight hesitation, he answered, "I swear this upon the honor of great Torm."

The god of loyalty seemed an appropriate choice for such an oath, Martine decided, feeling relieved.

"Then enter, Master Vil and companion." The gnome stepped aside with a grave nod, and the two visitors clomped into the small pine-floored antechamber. Vil had to stoop to avoid hitting his head on the low beams. Martine was thankful for once that she was short. Behind them, the old gnome eased the outer doors shut to seal out the cold. In the guttering light of a candle, the pair undid the bindings on their skis. Tikkanen waited stiffly near the inner doors.

"Are they all this formal?" Martine whispered as she crouched down to unknot the snow-crusted lacings.

"Tikkanen follows the old ways," Vil whispered back. "And he is not deaf." Martine bit her lip and spoke no more.

"Leave your things in my care," the gnome instructed when they were ready. "The council will see you at the first convenient opportunity." He pulled open the inner doors, which were painted with ferocious-looking badgers. Vil bent down to pass through the low threshold, and Martine followed, ducking her head. Beyond the door, the hall was high enough for them both to stand up easily, although her companion's head barely cleared the ceiling. Old Tikkanen closed the doors behind them, shutting out the remaining chill.

Here inside the warren, the hall was filled with light from a pair of wall sconces that held carved wands glowing with magical light. While Tikkanen clicked the door bolts into place, the humans brushed the snow from their leggings. Eventually the ancient doorkeeper shuffled past to lead them down the corridor into the heart of the underground warren.

This was Martine's first visit to a home of the little folk. She had never been inside the dwellings of either dwarf or gnome, so she was fascinated by every detail. She had expected to see stonework and dank moss like a dungeon or cellar, or wooden beams like a mine, but not the bright wood paneling that covered the walls, ceilings, and floors. Far from dank and dark, it was bright and warm, with an airiness that Martine found welcome, for she had never been fond of the constricting quarters of caves.

Their path led them through another set of doors. These were intricately carved with stylized patterns of birds, trees, and entwined vines. This third door sealed in the warren's humid warmth, and beyond it they smelled the rich scents of pine, varnish, caraway, and baking ovens. As before, the way continued to be lit by magical sconces. Their route twisted deeper, past intersections and other doors embellished with carvers' art, until at last Tikkanen ushered the pair into a small room, undoubtedly large by gnome standards. In the center of one wall stood a door studded with brass medallions.

"The council is inside. You must wait for them to summon you," the doorkeeper explained before leaving.

Apparently used to this arrangement, Vil settled into one of the high-backed benches against the wall. Carved for gnomes, the seat wasn't more than a footstool to the lanky human. "Sit," Vilheim suggested.

"I think I'll stand." Martine couldn't look at the man, trying to maintain his dignity while his knees were tucked up practically under his chin, without feeling the urge to laugh.

"It could be a long wait," her companion cautioned.

Martine regained her composure by feigning great interest in the bare chamber. "I've been still too long."

Vil was right. The wait quickly became interminable. Bored, Martine eventually perched awkwardly on another bench, idly flipping the little silver knife Jazrac had given her. "What do you suppose is taking them so long?" she muttered.

"They're gnomes," Vil answered coolly. Thinking he'd been asleep, Martine jumped at the man's voice. The blade slipped between her fingers and stuck into the floor next to her boot with a quivering *thunk*. "The Vani have their own sense of time. You'd better get used to it. I've never seen anything hurry them," he mumbled drowsily.

"They can't have that much to do. It's only a little valley."

"The Vani have their own sense of what is important," commented Vil, making idle talk as he shifted his legs to a more comfortable position. "They are important. This valley is important. I doubt anything else is. Certainly you and I rank low in their priorities. The elders are probably inside having birch-bark tea while they try to decide the fair price of a goose that was accidentally killed, or something like that. It's the right way to do things as far as they are concerned."

None of this sounded particularly encouraging. It galled Martine to be stalled so close to her goal, even though she knew a few hours, even a day or two, would make little difference. It's the same old me, wanting everything to go just perfectly, she reminded herself. I just need to relax. Trying to keep that thought in mind, she sank back into the seat.

The time stretched on and on, although the boredom was

occasionally broken by visits from passing gnomes. A few even stopped long enough to give Vil an awkward greeting. They spoke with such thick accents, their *r*'s heavily rolled and their vowels sharply clipped, that it was almost impossible for Martine to understand them, but Vil apparently did not have any trouble. He carefully responded to each by name, occasionally asking about the health of a wife or child.

Several times Martine caught glimpses of little gnome housewives with blond-brown hair bound up in a bun. Two of them peered into the room for a peek at the human woman. After a brief look, they stepped out of sight to gossip and cluck in whispered voices. Martine decided not to disrupt their women's game and kept her eyes almost closed, feigning sleep. If they weren't so short and broad, Martine decided, they would be like housewives everywhere. Here they dressed in red and blue dresses and embroidered white aprons. In other lands, the clothes might be different, but the gossipy curiosity was unchanged.

Sometimes children, more honest in their curiosity, accompanied the women. They stood staring long after their mothers stepped away in embarrassment. Martine noticed that Vil generated no such attention. Perhaps he was a familiar guest and therefore not worthy of note. "I must be pretty unusual, eh?" she finally said to Vil. She was growing tired of watching others watch her.

The man yawned and nodded. "Well," he finally allowed, "they've seen humans before—me, mainly—but you're the first human woman and, by their standards, not a particularly ladylike one."

"Thank you!"

"I meant ladylike in their eyes. Fighting is a man's job among the Vani. Women raise the children and rule the home. Men hunt, farm, and deal with outsiders. You're different. You go against their expectations."

"The council's in for a big surprise, then." Gods know what they might think if they learned I'm a Harper, too. The thought became the flicker of a mischievous grin on her face.

"I guess they know already," Vil commented as he stretched his cramped legs yet another time.

At last the brass-bound council door swung open. Standing in the doorway were two gnomes in blue robes girdled with sashes embroidered in red and green. Both were young gnomes, hardly elders, Martine noted. The first had close-cropped, curly black hair and a contrasting full beard. The other looked a little younger and had more belly on him; his face didn't look as weather-beaten, either. His hair and beard were both black, long, and braided, the tips of his chin braids just brushing his chest.

Vil rose to meet the gnomes. "Greetings, Jouka Tunkelo," he said to the leaner of the two. "And to you Turi Tunkelo."

"Greetings to you," the short-haired Jouka answered with a curtness that discouraged further conversation. "The council invites you to come inside." As she followed the gnomes into the chamber, Martine wondered whether the last was said with disapproval or whether it was just colored by his dour accent.

The council chamber was a small amphitheater, square in shape and higher-ceilinged than the other room. The spacious height was necessary to accomodate three tiers of benches on three sides of the hall. A scattering of gnomes, all of them old, wrinkled gentlemen, sat in every posture on the seats. One, bent with age, leaned forward on a gnarled cane until his long white beard brushed the floor. Another seemed to doze, his bald head wobbling sleepily as he leaned back against the next tier. Others sat clustered in little clumps, serious little bearded men sipping at cups of tea. Judging by their beards, not a one of them, discounting the two ushers, did Martine guess to be less than a great-grandfather. At the same time, she knew the appearance was deceptive, for gnomes had life spans of two hundred or more years. These might be great-great-great grandfathers, for all she knew.

At the very center of the benches, in a seat of obvious authority, sat a most singularly dressed elder. While the others wore pants and jackets of linens and wool, the old gnome in the high seat wore a knee-length tunic of buckskin. This alone was not singular; several other gnomes wore items of buckskin, Martine noted. What made it notable was that the elder's tunic was festooned with iron charms that hung from leather thongs, so many that the gnome clinked and rattled with every move. The charms, which seemed to be mostly crude sigils and icons, swayed against his stout chest, sometimes tangling themselves into his curly white beard. His thick silver hair was carefully held in place with a birchbark cap, more ornamental than functional. From his dress and the position of his chair, Martine figured the gnome to be the warren's priest, although of what god she could not possibly say.

When the two humans reached the center of the chamber, the white-bearded priest rose to his feet, age and formality making his movements rigid. His charms swayed on the ends of their thongs, and their harsh tinkling signaled quiet to the rest of the audience.

"The Council of the Vani greets Vilheim, son of Balt, and his female companion."

"Gracious is the council, wise Sumalo," Vil replied.

"Kind it is to be so generous with its time," Martine added. Vil's look, seen from the corner of her eye, told her she had said the right thing.

The gnome priest nodded slightly in approval. "We grant you the right to present your case." There were a few murmured grumbles at this point, although Sumalo, perhaps hard of hearing, paid them no notice. "May Gaerdal

Ironhand bestow on us eyes to see through falsehood, ears
to hear the truth, and tongues to speak with wisdom." The
priest picked up a peeled birch rod from the seat beside
him. Pressing it to his lips, he murmured a phrase incom-
prehensible to Martine. Sumalo held out the rod toward the
humans. Vil hesitated, then accepted the branch and kissed
the wood lightly. "Forgive me, Torm," he whispered.

Feeling no religious compulsions, Martine took the rod
and performed the ritual to satisfy her audience. "May your
god guide me," she invoked, figuring it did not hurt to ask,
before passing the rod back to the priest.

"The bond is now forged," Sumalo pronounced as he
held the rod aloft. "Let the outsider speak."

Until this moment, when every gnome's face was turned
toward her, Martine hadn't expected to be the center of
such attention. The ranger had never been one to get up
before a crowd and speak; in fact, she had always preferred
the isolation of the forest. Now she could feel her face
flush; it felt as if a cold fist were squeezing the pit of her
stomach. The speech she had rehearsed in her head all
morning evaporated from her memory. "Uh—elders," she
stammered, "I am Martine of Sembia, a huntswoman by
trade. I come to you with a simple request. I'm bound for
the Great Glacier and was . . . uh . . . hoping that someone
here could be my guide." It was all sort of blurted out as
she hurried through a considerably shortened version of
what she had intended to say.

With her speech finished, Martine waited for some reaction. The gnomes on the benches waited, too, not accustomed to such brevity. Finally, after a long, awkward
silence, the Harper felt compelled to say, "That's really all I
came to ask."

With slow understanding, the councillors came alive with
a wave of murmuring. Within moments, they were deep
into their discussion, seeming to forget the humans

standing before them. Martine watched with puzzlement the seriousness the elders displayed over her simple request and the vociferousness of their debate.

"Gnomes . . . I told you so," Vil whispered over the ranger's shoulder so only she could hear. "Never a simple answer. There always has to be a debate."

"Do you know it's winter?" demanded one of the younger elders.

"Soon," she corrected.

The first question broke open a floodgate of others, and Martine found herself besieged on all sides. She couldn't understand many of their questions, posed in thick gnomish accents, and often had to look despairingly to Vilheim for translation. With every answer, she did her best to choose her words politely and carefully.

"How do you plan to get to the Great Glacier?"

"Fly."

"Are you a wizard?" That question raised a worrisome buzz from the council.

"No, I have a hippogriff named Astriphie. We could ride him."

"What business do you have on the glacier?"

"My own, good sir."

"Why do you come here?"

"In truth, for no more than I said—to hire a guide."

After how many minutes and how many questions she did not know, the hollow thump of the priest banging the birch rod on the floor interrupted the interrogation. "Enough talk," Sumalo announced. "Brothers, we will vote."

Standing in the center of the floor, Martine wondered if she should sit or leave the room. She looked at Vil, but he only shrugged to show he was as perplexed as she.

Mumbling, the old gnomes settled back into their seats, their white heads bowed. Slowly, one after the other and in no particular order, each raised his head and looked at the priest. At first Martine wondered if it was some kind of thought speech, until finally she started to notice the almost imperceptible gestures each made. Finally the gnomes were finished and once again looked at her. Standing to his full, short height, Sumalo spoke. "Our answer to you is this: Come back in the spring, Mistress Martine of Sembia, when the weather is good for travel. Now is the season of the hearth, the time of rest for our people. It is bad luck to stray far from the warmth of the fire. Spring is the time to begin journeys, when good luck will be with you. Go now and return when the sap flows in the maples. Let your gods guide you wisely."

Martine's shoulders sagged, crestfallen. Struggling to hold back bitterness, she somehow managed to find the composure to speak. "I thank the council for hearing me, but I cannot wait for spring. I must reach the glacier now." The Harper bowed slightly to all assembled.

After Vil said his good-byes, the two departed. Outside the council doors, Tikkanen met them and guided them back to the outer doors. Once they were bundled and had their skis on, the two humans set out through the woods. Martine set a punishing pace until finally, exhausted, they reached the woodsman's lonely cabin.

Once inside, Vil built a fire while Martine squirmed out of her bulky gear. Freed of its weight, she collapsed into one of the hard-backed chairs, exhausted and discouraged.

"What will you do now?" Vil asked while adding bits of tinder to the fire.

The woman shook her head in resignation, her short, sweaty bangs clinging to her forehead. "Go on to the Great Glacier, of course. I've got a job to do." With a groaning sigh, she considered just how much she had banked on the gnomes' help to accomplish her mission. Now, without a knowledgeable guide, the chance of quick success was almost nonexistent. The same was true of her opportunity to impress the other Harpers with her efficiency.

Her fingers brushed Jazrac's knife, and then it was in her hand. Weighing the dagger in her palm, she thought about writing to Jazrac for advice, an idea she quickly discarded. Without thinking, she twirled the blade between her fingers effortlessly and flipped it point first into the tabletop, where it stuck, quivering.

Vil rumbled in disapproval.

Martine quickly whisked the blade back to its sheath. "Sorry. Nervous habit. If you'll have me as guest one more night, I'll be gone in the morning." She rubbed her hand on the table to smooth out the nick.

"Of course." Vil stood to his full height. "You're determined to go north, then?"

The Harper nodded.

Vil hung a pot of water on the firedog and swung it over the flame. "If you're willing, I could guide you," he offered almost casually.

"You?" Martine asked, realizing how she sounded even as she spoke. "I mean, I know you could, but aren't you—"

"Too old?"

"—too *busy?*"

Vil chuckled. From him, it sounded strange. "In wintertime, there's hardly a thing to do but split wood and hunt up here, and I can hunt at the glacier. I admit I know less about the north than the gnomes do." The old warrior sat on the hearth and still managed to be taller than Martine in her chair. "But I know more than you."

"You don't have to do this."

"I want to help."

Just as she was about to voice another protest, Martine reconsidered Vil's offer. There was no mistaking the earnestness in his eyes.

"How soon can you leave?" The question was cautious, designed to still give him an excuse to say no, but Martine could only remember Jazrac's old advice about allies—that no one ever helps without a good reason. What was Vilheim's reason? She wondered if the old wizard would have agreed to let him accompany her.

"As soon as you're ready. Tomorrow?"

"Seriously?" It was Vil's turn to nod. "Then tomorrow it is," Martine agreed, still not comfortable with her choice.

* * * * *

The next morning found the pair airborne as Astriphie labored under the double weight of two riders. Vil sat behind Martine's saddle, bloodless fingers clutching the saddle's angled back. Although the wind was bitter at this height, it was more than the cold that made him shiver. Even with a rope lashed around his waist, the man clearly did not feel safe. Martine tried to distract him, but between the wind's howling bite and the hippogriff's labored pants, it was only possible to communicate by shouting. After a few minutes of that, Martine knew she had to stop or lose her voice.

Nonetheless, the woodsman's ability to guide from the air impressed the ranger, considering that common landmarks seemed to transform themselves from a height of a thousand feet. At Vil's direction, Astriphie was making a straight course for a low gap in the mountains to the north. Unlike the pass at the southern end of the valley, which had been a smooth, open snowfield that stretched above the timberline, the northern pass stood out dark green as the trees marched right up and over the crest of the ridge.

To the left and right of the gap, the mountains sloped down like weak shoulders till they joined the curve of pass. Below them, Vil pointed out the river that flowed from the pass, a churning white ribbon that cut though the green foliage. That, he shouted, was their path until they crossed over to the north ridge.

Gradually, pulling higher with each beat of Astriphie's wings, the trio passed over the ridge, crossing from the gnome-occupied woods of the south to the cold and feral north. Beyond the ridge lay another valley penned in by mountains. It stretched out like a narrow finger to the north until it abruptly ended, truncated across its length by a sparkling wall that at this distance seemed to flow from between the mountain peaks like frozen treacle. In the morning sunshine, the distant glacial ice looked like a diamond set in silver. The wall's many facets glittered and glowed, beckoning them forward.

"Amazing!" Martine leaned back as she shouted so Vil could hear. The Harper had never seen such a great wall of ice before. The jewel-like glacier rose over a bed of dark, brooding green, a virgin forest that seemed to shrink before the ice's advance. The glacier towered over even the tallest trees and then stretched backward into the mountains until everything disappeared in a tangled horizon of smooth ice rivers and rock.

"Where to now?" Vil bellowed.

Martine realized she didn't actually know what she was looking for. Jazrac had been long on explanation about his elemental rift, but the wizard had never really told her what to look for. He had said it was on the glacier, but that was all. Martine didn't realize then how vast a glacier could be. Still, she couldn't admit not knowing what to do after dragging her host this far into the wilderness.

"When we get there, look for some kind of a disturbance, something unusual on the glacier." Although her answer seemed a safe bet, she was thankful that the yelling effectively hid any doubt in her voice.

"How long?"

"What?"

"How long for your mount to get us there?"

"An hour, maybe less," the Harper answered as she scanned the valley floor, trying to gauge their distance to the ice wall. Just then she thought she spotted something below. "What's that down there?" Used to traveling alone, Martine pulled Astriphie into a quick dive, prompting Vil to clutch frantically at her waist. "Hold on," she remembered to caution tardily.

"Look down there," she asked, pointing toward a small clearing as they leveled out once more. "What's that?"

Vil strained, his eyes tearing against the cold, until he made out what had caught her attention. It was a thin stream of smoke rising from the edge of the clearing. As they swooped closer, he made out a cluster of long narrow huts in the shadow of the trees.

"Gnolls—this is their valley. They are the reason the Vani would not come here."

"The gnomes were afraid?" There was no mockery in Martine's question.

"Each respects the other's valley. Usually there is no trouble. Besides, it is best not to rouse the hornet's nest." As he spoke, three figures darted from the huts for the dark shelter of the woods. "Best to fly high. They are skilled with the bow."

Were she alone, Martine would have swept as low as she dared for a better view. Instead, she heeded Vil's warning and pulled Astriphie back up.

"Are there many of them?"

"The gnolls? It's not a large tribe, but more than the Vani . . . enough to be a threat."

Vil's answer sounded ominous. Although there were more questions she could have raised about the skills of the gnolls, their hunting patterns, and even their totems, Martine lapsed into silence, the cold and the shouting getting the better of her throat. There was a great deal you could learn about such creatures from things like totems, she thought idly. Take a bear totem—it meant the tribe respected strength and solidity, a good sign all in all, even in savage creatures like gnolls. On the other hand, if the totem were, say, an ice worm, that wasn't a good sign. Tribes that chose totems like that were too often cruel and ravenous like their god.

Given the proximity of the glacier, she wouldn't be surprised if this group had chosen the latter. The closeness of the ice probably made for sudden death. Hard lives bred hard gods.

A tug at her coat reminded Martine of her duty. "There!" Vil shouted at her ear to be heard over the wind. "Over there!" Tentatively easing his grip, he pointed to a swirling plume of ice, a jet of frozen crystals, that heaved and spurted like the irregular storms of the sea against the crested shore. The icy column rose up until it expanded like some swollen vegetable—a cauliflower instantly came to Martine's mind.

"See it? Is that it?" Vil shouted again, uncertain if she had heard him.

"It must be. It's certainly unusual," she howled back. Martine had no doubt it must be her goal. What else but a geyser of hoarfrost would mark a rift such as Jazrac had explained? She understood now why the wizard hadn't bothered to describe it. With a rekindled confidence that she could end this quickly, Martine leaned the hippogriff in a broad arc that would carry them toward the plume.

When they had less than a mile to go, the air around them changed, the temperature plummeting with ferocious suddenness. Bone-gnawing cold attacked every inch of exposed skin, even penetrating through the layers of fur that had managed to keep them warm till now. Astriphie rocked and struggled mightily against the increasing buffets of the frenzied gale.

The trio were close enough now to make out vaguely,

through the swirling gaps of wind-burning ice, the star-shaped fissure, crudely heaved upward in cracked blocks. The main ice jet, for now it was apparent there was a small group of lesser fumaroles, pulsed with the otherworldly tide that forced its icy discharge up from the center of the fissure and sent it flowing down one of the jagged arms. The tighter the gap became, the higher the plume shot as the pressure increased until it hit the end. Lightning couldn't have raised greater thunder as the geyser broke over the splintered end, blowing out chunks of glacial ice visible even at a distance.

Vil shouted something, but most of it was lost: "—so close!"

Martine shook her head furiously at what she guessed he had said. "Closer. The less time on the ground, the better." She hoarsely shouted her explanation, although it was unlikely Vil could hear any better than she. With a firm command, she pushed the hippogriff, its normally keen eyes now flashing with fire, closer and closer. "We'll move in quick and—"

The concussive boom of the roaring flux devoured the rest of her words. Astriphie's wingbeats faltered, momentarily pitching the group into an unplanned dive. Behind her, Vil's weight shifted, threatening to overbalance the hippogriff. Dropping the reins from one hand, Martine thrust her arm back and levered the slipping woodsman back into his seat. The effort burned her throat in frozen gasps and triggered a fit of wracking coughs. The fire of ice scorched her lungs, left her mouth filled with pasty spit.

The shuddering gasps left her unable to steer, and by the time Martine recovered, it was too late. Astriphie, uncontrolled, had panicked and plunged iceward while attempting to wheel away from the fissure, the source of the beast's terror. Just as the hippogriff slipped into a steep-banked turn, the geyser spewed forth another shuddering blast.

The great pinioned wings were spread almost full against the outrushing force of the wind, catching it like the swollen sails of a yacht leaping before the ocean breeze. Frantically sensing the danger, Martine pitched her slight body hard into the rushing wind the way a sailor on that same yacht would lean himself as a counterbalance against the tipping hull. Understanding the need for her move, Vil leaned with her. For a perilous moment, they held the balance, the arc of a perfect parabola suspended between the shattered white ground and the roiling sky. We can make it, Martine exulted.

And then it was over. Astriphie's voice, a whinnying screech of pain, sundered all hope. The hoarse cry barely drowned out the sickening popping noise as the hippogriff's uppermost wing crumpled, flexing back over Martine and Vil to angle in directions it was never meant to point. The imaginary parabola collapsed as the rushing wind seemed to roll the crippled hippogriff completely over.

Suspended time was replaced by a whirling blur of snow and sky as the hippogriff tumbled from the heavens. The beast frantically beat at the air with its remaining wing, the other flopping uselessly with each roll, feathers raking the Harper's face as she struggled to guide her frenzied mount down. Behind her, Vil could do no more than cling to whatever purchase he could gain, more than once finding himself suspended helplessly by the single safety rope around his waist.

Loosing the now useless reins, Martine lunged to the side, flattening against the hippogriff's unsocketed wing as the fall righted the creature. The agonized screech from the pain she caused echoed in the woman's ears, but the great wing responded and struggled to spread itself full once more. It was barely enough time, for the ground, all icy barbs and jagged ridges, was speeding up toward them. There was no hope of slowing their furious glide, indeed

barely any chance of remaining righted. As the glacial landing field swelled closer, Martine knew it meant the death of
her brave steed and almost surely its riders.

"Cut free!" she screamed, one thick gloved hand fumbling for her knife. "Cut yourself free and jump!" With the
jagged ice splinters that lay below, it wasn't much of a
chance, but it was their only one.

Martine heard a sharp twanging sound behind her, and
the plummeting hippogriff lurched as its load suddenly
shifted. The Harper thought she heard a human howl, and
then it was lost in the sweeping gale.

The ranger's mittened hand closed on the handle of
something she could only hope was her knife, and with a
blind slash, she hacked at the saddle's restraining belts.
Half her body, suddenly freed of its bonds, swung upward
as if it had lost all weight. Instantly she lost her position,
and the hippogriff's wing folded, slamming against her with
a force that almost knocked the blade from her grasp. Beating back the feathers with one hand, Martine slashed furiously at the last strap. As she was still sawing at the leather,
she tumbled away from the doomed mount, and at the
same instant, the last strap gave way. She flew off the rump
of the hippogriff, her feet flying over her heels just as Astriphie's wings cracked into an upthrust sheet of ice. The roar
that filled the glacier was superseded by the squealing, popping, pulpy grind as the hippogriff gouged a bloody track
across the dirty white snow.

Martine saw none of this, however, for in the instant Astriphie hit, she was twisting futilely in midair in an attempt
to land on her feet. Then all at once the white was upon
her—tearing, ripping, and beating as she smashed through
the frozen crust and sank into the needlelike snow beneath
it.

Three

Martine's next recollection was of darkness—a blessed darkness that numbed the raging fire coming from somewhere inside her body. She floated back in the light cocoon where she had been hurled and tried to pinpoint the source of the pain that dreamily eluded her understanding. Even so, the fire became steadily stronger, and with it came awareness. The pain settled over her the way autumn leaves accumulated on the ground, slowly spreading throughout her body but primarily in the legs, a frightening combination of raw, shredded nerves and cold, soothing numbness. The here and now struggled through the agonizing haze, bringing a view of a queer, phantasmagoric world, exaggerated and tilted. Shades of white, lathered red, and pink resolved themselves into angles of ivory all splattered with blood and gore.

Not ivory, Martine corrected herself. Ice . . . I'm half buried in ice tinged with blood. The crimson stains captured her attention, a clarion call to warn her of the danger of her condition—the steady glaciation of her limbs if she didn't get moving, and soon. Floundering in the broken snow, Martine twisted about to view her own body, make sure it was intact, only to have the constant fire give way to stabbing pain. The darkness swirled back, threatening to overwhelm the dim light of her world. Martine held it at bay by focusing on her self, on her mission.

Using the strange clarity that torment brought, Martine drove herself further, seeking to learn what had happened to her body. From the way her side hurt, one or more ribs were probably cracked. She had felt that pain once before, and the woman knew she could survive that. Elsewhere were more cuts than she could guess. Blood trickled down the ice crystals on her brow and clouded the vision in one eye. Reaching up to wipe the warm smear away, the Harper discovered that her arm throbbed fiercely. She remembered with absolute clarity hitting the snow with her shoulder.

After that pain, Martine gingerly put the rest of her body through a mental inventory. Although every move caused pain like fire to play along her bones, nothing seemed to be broken, other than perhaps her ribs. Ice-clotted, black-red scratches scored her once sturdy winter gear, but overall the woman was pleased she had no great gashes or dangerous wounds, at least so far as she could tell. Frantically she remembered Jazrac's stones as if they, too, were part of her body. A quick pat assured her that these had also survived unbroken.

Satisfied that she was bloodied but in working order, Martine stiffly floundered out of the trench her body had dug. She had to find Astriphie and Vilheim. To her relief, she found that at the glacier's surface, the howling wind had eased considerably, although the thundering booms from the fissure still shook the crystalline ground. It seemed that for every four steps she took, the ground would suddenly heave and tremble in response to the rift's violent shifting.

Finding Astriphie was no problem. The hippogriff's body was splayed across the glacier, smears of its blood trailing, sledgelike, in the beast's wake. Astriphie had struck the top of an ice cap, shearing that away in a neat gouge. Pinion feathers decorated the bloody grooves where the animal had slid, and Martine could see clearly the long scratches where the beast had clawed the ice in its death slide. At the base of another mound lay the hippogriff, its mighty wings ripped and pierced by jagged splinters of ice. The beast's eaglelike head was twisted around at an impossible angle. Below the neck, the left half of the mount's feathered rib cage was caved in; white angles of bone and tissue showed through the remains of the downy hide. Steam rose from the blood and viscera spilled onto the snow, partially held in by the tangled straps of the Harper's saddle.

Martine suddenly felt the intense cold penetrating deep through her body. She collapsed to the ice, seized by violent trembling, and tears mixed with blood in her eyes. Breathing was possible only in lancing heaves that sucked in swirls of icy air. Her throat burned with each spasmodic gasp.

Even after the fit passed, Martine could not move for a long time. The cold ground, smooth-slick and red, sapped her energy, making it harder than before to rouse herself. It would be nice just to sleep here with Astriphie. . . . The thought whispered insidiously in her mind. Surely she could just lie here and rest a bit before doing anything else. . . .

Martine swore as she realized what was happening. It was a decidedly creative oath, laced with a sea dog's salt and bitter references to geysers. The thought of what Jazrac might think of her less than ladylike tongue made Martine appreciate her cursing all the more. It helped immensely. Before she realized it, she was up on her feet, wavering unsteadily as she surveyed the crash site, looking for Vil.

Unsupported by snowshoes, her feet sometimes broke through the snow crust in places where the surface was a deceptive sheet of old snow. Every time it happened, the glacier seemed to try to swallow her whole. As she labored her way out of another snowy morass, she sardonically thought how fortunate she was to be on the smooth ice field here and not in the tangle of crevasses they had seen from the air.

The Harper found Vil about a hundred yards from the hippogriff's corpse. Luck had favored Vil more than Martine, providing him with a soft landing in the lee slope of a powder-crusted hummock. From the tumbled track through the snow, it appeared that the woodsman had hit near the top of the hummock and then slid to a rest near the bottom. There he lay, still sprawled out and unmoving. Hurrying to him as best she could, Martine was relieved to hear a choking gasp as she rolled his body over.

"Are you okay?" she demanded as she began examining him for broken bones.

"I'm—" Vil winced as her hands prodded his hip. "I'm all right." He heaved himself to his feet stiffly. "How about you?"

Martine shrugged stoically. "I'm walking."

"Good. And the hippogriff?"

"Dead." The wind swept away the pain in her words.

Vil didn't offer any condolences. "We've got to gather our supplies and move on," he said brusquely as he started plodding across the snow.

"I've got to finish my mission."

The man wheeled on Martine, wind whipping his crinkled face. "Your mission? Just what the Nine Hells is this about?" His voice wavered furiously. "When you needed a guide, I trusted you, and now, after damn near killing me, you want to go on. You've already killed your horse. Isn't that enough?"

"I didn't—"

"Then why in the hell did you fly so close?"

"I—I took a chance, okay? And it wasn't a horse, it was Astriphie, my hippogriff. Astriphie's dead, and I didn't want that!" Martine shouted back, shivering with cold and fury. The wind caught the tears as they welled in her eyes and blew them across her cheeks. Biting back her words, Martine blindly stumbled past the man. "Go home if you want to. I'm staying here."

The Harper cursed Vil, cursed the ice, cursed herself. The man was right, of course. She should not have pushed Astriphie so close to the rift. Her eagerness to finish the mission quickly meant everything was in ruins. All she could do was try to continue, even if that meant risking her own life. Pulling up the hood of her parka, she hid her face against the cold.

The snow crackled with Vil's steady pursuit. "I'm sorry I lost my temper," he shouted over the gusts.

The Harper nodded a bitter acceptance.

"We cannot stay."

"I must." She did not break her short, struggling strides.

"Is your mission that important?"

"It is to me."

"You could die out here."

"I won't." Words of false confidence, she thought bitterly.

"What are you doing here, anyway?" The man would not relent. "What are you hiding?"

"Nothing! My business is my own, that's all." Martine stepped back warily from the man as his tone became increasingly demanding.

The woodsman stopped her with a mittened hand on her sleeve. A swordsman's suspicion filled his face. "Who are you? Someone I should fear?" The honed words sliced through the defenses of polite trust between the two. The tenseness of his body and the hand hovering close to the sword were signs of his nervous state.

"You think I'm evil?" Her own body slipped into fighting tension to match his, a dog and a cat sizing each other up.

"I don't know. Tell me otherwise."

With the pair of them alone in a world of arctic white, Martine knew the truth was her only defense.

"I'm a Harper," she stated in flat, cold tones that matched their surroundings. "Sort of, anyway. I've come up here to close that fissure." She slowly pointed toward the turmoil overhead.

"A Harper?" Vil echoed doubtfully, though his body eased somewhat.

"Yes. You know, agents of good and—"

"I know what Harpers are. I just didn't expect to find one here."

Martine was growing increasingly testy, having bared her secret only to be met by doubt. "I didn't choose to come here. I was sent." She beat her arms together for warmth. "I'm supposed to close that—that *thing*—before something unpleasant happens."

Vil looked away. "Torm's eyes," he swore softly, "a Harper." Dropping his hands away from his weapons, he turned back to face her. "Why didn't you say something? I was ready to kill you."

"Don't worry. I wouldn't have let you," she said as she started toward Astriphie. "Harpers are supposed to keep their activities secret. That's why I didn't tell you. Now that you know, will you help me?"

Vil fell in beside her, his suspicions gone, and the two trudged back to the hippogriff's corpse, quietly listening to the sounds of the glacier as it cracked and rumbled beneath their feet. Already the hippogriff's body was cool, and the bloody carcass had begun to freeze over. Ice and feathers cracked as the two humans set to the grim business of recovering their supplies.

What they recovered wasn't promising—several blankets iced up with blood and a little food that hadn't been scattered in the crash. "It's not enough," Vil announced. "We need more food." He drew his thick-bladed skinning knife and gestured toward Astriphie's carcass. "It must be done. You can keep watch."

Up here there was nothing to watch for but stinging snow, yet Martine gratefully accepted Vil's excuse not to help as the woodsman, with the cold practicality that matched the terrain, sliced strips from Astriphie's haunch. Bloody meat plopped onto the snow as he sawed at the carcass. Finally, the work finished, Vil skewered the meat on arrows and jabbed them into the snow, leaving the meat to dry in the breeze.

"Still not enough," he muttered as he turned away from the bloody task.

"How so?" breathed Martine from where she crouched close to the ground, as if the ice held warmth.

"We cannot both live on the food we have. Not up here, at least. One of us could, but there isn't enough for two. One of us must go back for supplies."

The Harper cast a shivering glance at the meat-weighted stakes. "And?"

The woodsman was already loading one of the salvaged saddlebags with supplies. "Since you will not leave, I must. I'll take a little food and hunt for whatever else I need on the way."

The glacier rocked under their feet as the geyser shot up another of its massive plumes. Martine looked to the sky, knowing that soon they would be showered with a flurry of ice crystals too large to be snow, yet too small to be hail. She pulled one of the stiff blankets closer about her shoulders and began chipping at the frozen ground with her dagger.

Now it was Martine's turn to be suspicious as she looked up at the woodsman. "And why should I trust *you* to come back?"

Vilheim snorted, amused by something Martine did not understand. The Harper couldn't judge his reaction at all. His mouth was drawn tight, and his eyes were lost in the distance. At last he spoke in an almost perfect monotone, unconsciously beating mittened fist to mittened palm. He had all the air of a man giving testimony at an inquest.

"I am . . . was . . . a paladin of Torm."

Martine blinked, so stupefied by the admission that it overcame her thoughts even of the cold, then waited for Vilheim to continue. He waited, perhaps expecting more of a reaction, and the two stared at each while the wind whistled across the icy plain.

"You *were* a paladin of Torm?" Martine finally echoed, thrusting her dagger deep into the ice.

His reply was fierce, filled with passion that she should doubt his word. "Yes . . . Torm the True, Torm the Brave, Torm the Binder of Oaths. . . . We . . . they . . . hold his faith in trust."

Martine quickly thought back to everything she knew about paladins, which was mostly hearsay and opinion. The few she had met were stiff-necked, self-righteous, and unlikable swordsmen who were supposed to be austerely virtuous, lightened only by the glory of their god.

"A paladin? All that business about honor, truth, goodness, purging wickedness?"

Vil broke into a genuine smile, amused by the description. "Something like that. We were taught to keep our word. But it does not matter anymore. I am no longer a paladin."

The words stirred sudden concern in Martine. What had prompted Vilheim's fall from grace? She caught her breath as she waited for some sinister revelation to follow, her gaze flicking from the bloody knife Vilheim held to Astriphie's ice-whitened remains. "So I'm supposed to trust you because you aren't a paladin anymore?" she breathed, the words forming ice crystals in the air.

"I woke up one day and my god was gone. I did not sin, if that is what you are thinking." The man carefully cleaned his knife and slipped it back in its sheath, defensively aware of her unwavering gaze. "It was during the Time of Troubles. One morning I woke up and Torm was no longer there. Before that day, I could always sense Torm's purpose in everything. That day the feeling was gone. Torm had disappeared, as a good many of the gods did."

Martine only remembered the Time of Troubles somewhat vaguely. She had been young and had not yet taken up the adventuring life. For her, the gods and their turmoils had seemed distant compared to Giles, the prefect's son, who lived just down the lane.

"Torm came back, though. You could still be a paladin."

Vil spoke softly but resonantly, his voice carrying force across the frozen gap. "Life is never simple. When Torm left me, I was suddenly on my own for the first time in my life, and—and I liked it. You could not know the freedom I felt."

And now you want me to trust you? Martine thought.

Perhaps it was a raised eyebrow or a quirk in her face that prompted Vil to speak. "I give you my word I will return. I am still an honest man, Martine of Sembia. A lifetime of training does not evaporate into thin air overnight." The man rose with firm resolution, shouldering the saddlebag to go. "Besides, there is no choice. You will not leave, and two cannot stay. I will find you here in four days. Take care, and good fortune in your mission, Harper."

Martine knew she could protest. She could stand out on this glacier arguing until they both froze, but their time spent trading secrets had already chilled her to the bone,

and she knew the ex-paladin was right. There was no
choice. "Travel safely," she offered. "In four days, you'll find
me here."

The words practically vanished in the wind, and the former paladin bent forward as he turned into the gale to
begin his journey. The Harper didn't waste any time watching him leave, but instead busied herself gathering up the
supplies, the bulk of which he'd left behind. As she worked,
the ice heaved again, this time hurling her to the ground
with its violence. Three more tremors, each almost as
fierce, struck before Martine started toward the edge of
the rift.

The hike was no more than a mile, and the woman made
good time with the snowshoes that had survived the crash,
a miracle for which Martine thanked Tymora, the mistress
of luck. The snow was deeper and softer here, much of it
fresh powder from the seething fountain that created its
own massive cloud overhead. Through the cloud, light
from the the noontime sun was deflected into a million
sparkling motes of swirling silver frost. She found that looking at it directly burned her eyes, but at least it distracted
her from the ground glare that might otherwise blind her.

As she drew near the fissure, the tremors and the roaring swelled like some fulsome giant struggling to break its
frozen chains. The rift had pushed the glacier's crust
upward and outward to form a ridgelike cone. Not knowing
how close she needed to be for the seals to work, the
Harper elected to climb to the rim, in order to be certain of
success. Besides, coming this far, she had to satisfy her
curiosity. No doubt, she rationalized, Jazrac would appreciate an eyewitness description of the rupture.

The base of the slope was a jagged mass of icy scree.
Closer now, Martine watched how with each surge, great
ice blocks hove over the crack's broken edge, some to fall
back inside while others tumbled down the slope. Bound-

ing and crashing, these arctic boulders smashed into others below with sharp cracks that sometimes triggered other shifts and slides in the unstable mass. Wary of the risks, the Harper took extra caution as she picked her way through the frozen scree, mindful that an avalanche could cascade down upon her at any moment. The whistle of the numbing wind was drowned out by the grinding crashes that emanated from beyond the rim and repeated themselves all down the slope.

Finally above the scree, the woman continued her climb, using the dagger to help now, for here the ground was nothing but smooth, windswept ice. Slowly she chopped footholds in the angled slope, all the time watching for danger ahead. The work raised a sweat while her fingers went numb even through her leather gloves and thick mittens. Wedged into grips of ice, her toes felt almost as chilly. Her side throbbed, and her shoulder protested with every twist, until she doubted the wisdom of the whole mission. I can't give up, she fiercely charged herself. Not this close to my destination.

The jagged surface of the top finally came into view, and Martine dragged herself up on it with gasping relief. Every inch of her burned, inside and outside. Her throat was scorched with bitter cold, her muscles ached as if aflame, and her fingers curled with the peculiar fire that near-frostbite brings. Then the roar and tremble struck again, heightened by the crash of ice nearby, all of which urged the spent woman to her feet.

Three steps and Martine reached the inner rim. There she halted, dumbfounded by the grotesque landscape below her. From the air, she had only seen how the rift spread like a starlike crack a half-mile or so in length, but now, close up, she could see the canyon bottom. The canyon floor flowed impossibly, like water—no, she decided, more like gelatin or unset custard. The surface rippled in smooth waves that still glistened with the shining hardness of ice. Where the waves broke like water against the canyon walls, the spray turned instantly rigid, hurling hail and frost into the air. The water-ice bubbled and roiled, its feathery spouts frosting the walls of the rift, small at first but gradually increasing in speed and height.

Martine suspected another jet was forming and hurriedly dug from her pouch the first of the stones Jazrac had given her. Remembering her brief instructions, she panned it about until the internal fires lit and then buried it in the snow safely back from the edge. It wouldn't do to have the stone fall into the pit, she decided.

In another painful hour of trudging, Martine was at her second position. Stone in hand, she moved along the crest slowly until the rock began to glow in her hand. She planted it quickly. At this pace, she guessed there was barely enough daylight left to finish the task.

En route to the third point, Martine spied a movement among the ice blocks of the talus slope below. At first she dismissed it as merely a shifting in the loose boulders, until she saw another flash. She barely saw it, a blue-white form against the ice. It was small and incredibly fast, for before she could even take a step closer, it had disappeared once more. The huntress swore it had arms and legs, like some kind of little creature. Caution and curiosity warranted she track it down, but the Harper rejected the idea, since it would delay her mission. All she dared spare was a brief pause, but after a few minutes of inaction, the Harper pressed on before she froze on the spot.

It was only a piece of ice or a wayward snow eagle battered down by the wind, Martine decided as she passed the sighting point. She was too tired to ascribe it to anything else. Nonetheless, she remained watchful all the way to the next point of the seal, so much so that she almost ignored the stone when it started to glow in her hand.

With the third stone was buried at the highest tip of the fissure, the Harper began the descent along the opposite edge of the bubbling rift, swinging wide to work around the crevasse that formed the next point of the star. Eventually the crumbled crack tapered to almost nothing. After leaping the dwindling gap, the Harper blindly crisscrossed the plain, stone in hand, searching out the juncture that would make it glow. With each stone, she despaired, it took longer to find the point where all the forces balanced. Just as she was beginning to wonder if she'd missed the mark, the glittering opal lit with its internal fire. Collapsing thankfully to her knees, the Harper buried the stone. Inside, her cracked rib throbbed as fiercely as ever, but her mind was now too dulled to the pain to even notice.

The glittering orange winter sun, hanging barely over the mountain peaks on the opposite side of the glacier, reminded Martine of the need for haste. Darkness would come quickly as soon as the sun slid behind the peaks, and Martine still had one stone to place and camp to make. There was no hope of getting off the glacier today, so the Harper wanted to dig herself a shelter before darkness fell.

Her chest heaving from the long sprint, Martine reached her last goal, the southernmost tip of the fissure, only a few hundred yards from the glacier's edge. Sweat seeped out from under her parka hood to form ridges of sour frost in her eyebrows. The cloth mask that covered most of her cheeks and mouth was heavy with ice that grew thicker with each passing minute. Cold, fumbling hands shook the last stone from the pouch. The heart of the opal sparkled weakly in the setting sun. Holding it in her cupped hands like a precious child, Martine shuffled zombielike in questing arcs, searching for the stone's resting place. She mumbled curses against the coming nightfall, but the rising evening wind tore away every breath that escaped her lips so that she couldn't hear her own voice.

The last of the passing sunlight disappeared before the advancing mountain shadows, taking with it any pretense of warmth the light had promised. The deep-throated roars of the geysers sounded like thunder in the chilling air. High overhead, the soaring spume sparkled in the receding sunlight till the glittering cystals looked like descending stars in the darkness. The wind-whipped frost flew thicker, each flake biting with more sting.

After how much distance she did not know, the stone suddenly swelled with light. Exhausted and cold, the Harper stood dumbly watching it at first, not comprehending the meaning of the blue-white fire she cupped in her hands. Only slowly did it dawn on her that this was it, the end of her task. In moments, she would set the seal and fulfill Jazrac's trust in her. She was sure the wizard was watching—no, sensing—for some ripple in the cosmic sea that marked the healing of this great wound in the earth.

"Thank the gods!" she croaked through cracked lips as she knelt and scooped out a nest for the stone with excessive care. With both her thick mittened hands, she gingerly lowered the stone onto its bed. For a moment, she paused to admire how the stone glowed and throbbed in its cradle.

"The cinder," she muttered suddenly. "I must touch it with the cinder!" In her relief and admiration of the stone, she had almost forgotten the last step. Her fingers too rigid to work the strings on the little pouch, she tugged at the cords with her teeth until the neck was wide enough to shake the stone free. To Martine's terror, the cinderlike stone plopped into her palm, hung there precariously, and then fell to smack against the glowing opal with a resounding crack so sharp she was convinced both had shattered. Frantically the Harper tore off her mittens and scooped at the snow to retrieve the fallen key.

Just as she wrapped her fingers about it, the glowing opal swelled with brilliant white fire. Clutching the key, Martine flung herself away from the flare, her sight dazzled. The blaze from the stone expanded outward like an immense, unshuttered lantern until the Harper, still sprawled in the snow, wrapped an arm over her eyes, but still she could not block out the glare.

Then the shape of the light changed, though not its intensity. The diffuse brightness that burned out all the shadows on the snow drew in on itself, tightening and crimping into a brilliant ice-blue tendril. As if leaning against the wind, it stretched and strained in an arc that yearned toward the rift—and then, with a sizzling roar, the beam lanced like some wizard's fiery missile in an arc that carried it straight for the rift's heart. The crackle echoed—no, *was echoed*, Martine realized—by four other reports. Blue-white streaks like shooting stars returning skyward rose from four other points, each rocketing to a single rendezvous point in the sky. The five radiant arcs clashed over the center of the canyon in a brilliant display of sparks. Martine squawked and rose to run, only to stumble backward, tripping over her booted feet to land sprawled in the snow.

"Damn it, Jazrac, you could have warned me!" the Harper shouted in awe.

Flopping around, she blinked away the dazzling lights that hung on the inside of her eyelids and looked at the canopy strung over the canyon—five burning blue beams that glowed as they hung suspended in the air. Pulsing waves of light rippled from the intensely glowing shafts, only to break like waves over the rift. The evening darkness rose and fell with each pulse, and at the moment of brightest glare, Martine could see the canyon center, only minutes before a seething pit, erupt into ever-widening waves. The rounded, hardening forms of the frozen waves reminded her of the iron drops that fell in gelatinous puddles from her father's forge when she was young. She lay there absorbing the light, feeling the magical wonder of it all.

What had Jazrac done to make those five stones, she wondered as the world crackled with the solidifying roar.

As the pulses grew longer, a grinding bass note sundered
the calm, and lightning-lit air tingled with the ozone scent
of disaster. Fresh tremors, stronger than those Martine had
grown accustomed to, quavered through the ice, letting
loose a rolling wave of ice-rending shrieks. It was as if in
that moment all the ghosts and all the lost souls ever
devoured by the frozen waste howled out their torment.
The cacophony was accompanied by deep thunder that
shook the woman down to her toes. From the rim, fractures
fingered across the snow like streaks of lightning, zig-
zagging little puffs of powder tracing their manic paths.

"Damn you, Jazrac!" Martine howled, no longer amused.
With a crack, the rim suddenly broke off and slid into the
canyon, throwing up a wall of snow as the air rushed forward to fill the gap caused by the collapse. The fingering
fissures raced closer toward Martine, and the ranger didn't
wait to see what danger she was in but struggled to her feet
and ran.

Behind her, the snapping, ripping cracks fanned out
rapidly, lunging closer, as if trying to catch her heels in
their frozen jaws. Once, twice, Martine faltered as the
fierce pain in her ribs, almost forgotten since the morning,
spasmed and locked her muscles and nerves in pain. Her
throat no longer burned because it was too parched to
breathe, too parched to spit. Fear drove her forward toward
the safety of the glacier's edge, where her only plan was to
plummet blindly into the dark void beyond.

With no more than a third of the distance crossed, the
nipping fissures caught her. The fractures shot between
her legs and raced ahead of her, reaching for the glacier
wall. The hard ice field became a mosaic that abruptly
began to shatter, each fragment tilting, reacting to the glacier's mad rush to reclaim what the rift had stolen. The

tremors that Martine vainly fled punched the ground out from under the Harper, throwing up shards around her.

"No, by Tymora, not again!" Martine wailed as the ground slipped backward beneath her feet. Like a sailor washed overboard, she helplessly slid into the seething ice sea and rode down into its rough darkness. "Not twice in one day! It isn't fair!"

And then there was the cold and the darkness.

Four

Scrabbling noises like fingernails grating on rock, teeth crunching bones, ice freezing in my veins—I hear scrabbling noises, the woman dreamed. It's the sound of fresh earth being thrown on my grave, thumping with each shovelful. I have to scream. I have to yell and let them know I'm still alive.

But that's so much effort.

"Dig, dig, dig," said a little voice in singsong.

It's not coming from my throat, the woman concluded dreamily. It's too dry . . . my throat's too dry.

"Dig, dig, dig," said the voice again. It sounded like a peevish child. "Just because *he* says so. Does he dig? No-o-o. That's why he brought me along—so he could make me dig. He gets to sulk, while I, Icy-White the Clever, I get to dig."

"Ow!" A sharp jab pierced Martine's numbness.

"Ow?"

The pain brought things into focus. Martine was on her

side, pressed beneath a mass of ice and snow. She could vaguely see a tumbled field of ice, perhaps the base of a slide, that stood out in stark shadow from the fading blue glow that lit the night, the last light of Jazrac's magic. The slide apparently ended in the rift floor, now hard and still. The canyon walls had fallen inward, leaving a broad bowl where the rift's jagged scar had been. Distant crashing rumbles still echoed across the snow, warning that all was not yet still.

The jab repeated, not as sharp this time but still painful. "Get . . . me . . . out of here." The words were a great struggle. A layer of frost settled on her cheeks cracked as she spoke.

"Ice talks!" squeaked the voice. The scrabbling renewed, faster and closer. Suddenly sharp claws raked the Harper's cheek and harshly brushed away the snow that coated her. The sting cracked the lethargy the ice was sealing about her. The Harper struggled against the enclosing tomb of ice and heaved upright, the motion accompanied by the grinding sound of cracking snow.

"Awwwk!"

"What the—" The cry escaped Martine unwillingly as she found herself faced by a creature of ice. It couldn't have stood any taller than her thighs, though it loomed over her now as it stood on a block of ice pinning her legs. Its skin was pearly and smooth with blue-white translucence, yet cut in hard angles and sharp edges like shattered ice. The head was broad and flat, eyes gleaming under razor-edged brows.

The creature hopped back, momentarily as startled as she. "Not ice! No, no, no. This is not ice."

The Harper tested her legs, trying to shift free. The block that pinned her legs was loose, but at the first tremor, the creature lunged forward, seizing her neck with one clawed hand. Its grip was cold and strong, its fingers clicking bonily against each other as it squeezed her throat.

"No, no! You belong to Icy-White now. My prize—mine and mine only," the creature babbled, its mirror-sharp face fractured with glee. An iciclelike claw waggled through the steam of her exhalations. Abruptly the creature gave a startled squeal and snatched its hand away. "You burn, you steam!" it chirped in wonderment while licking furiously at the finger Martine had just breathed on. "I'll show you to Vreesar when he comes," it continued craftily. "Then he'll let me stop digging."

Scampering like a monkey, the creature seized the Harper's shoulder in its cold claws and dragged her from the icy debris, all the while taking care to avoid the steam of her breath. Its talons dug through her furs and drew blood beneath them, but Martine was too tired to fight back. It was all she could do to feebly kick free of the last bits of crust.

"Now, no fight from you, hot one, or Icy-White kill you and feast on your cold meat," the creature cackled near her ear before it released her. Its breath was chilling, without a hint of warmth either in spirit or body.

The ranger didn't answer, nor did the creature care. In springing hops, it leaped from block to block, bounding across the slide, but never far from where the Harper lay. Martine remained still, watching and gathering her strength. I'm too weak to get away yet, Martine calculated after noting the creature's nimble speed as it crossed the treacherous tangle of the slide. She felt wary but not fearful, since the thing didn't seem immediately intent upon killing her.

Indeed, for the moment, it seemed to have forgotten her as it scrambled over the slide, poking here, sniffing there, all the time muttering to itself. Eyeing her weird captor, the ranger tried to match the creature to all the fiends she'd ever seen or heard of. With its stunted size and shimmering skin, it looked like a malevolent sprite sculpted from ice. Its form lacked gentle curves, each joint capped by glittering little spurs. Nothing about it matched her experiences nor any of the tales she'd heard. Glacier lore was not her strong suit.

While the strange creature capered in the ghastly light of fading magic, Martine discreetly probed the snow for her gear, a search that turned up her sword and pouch but little more. Jazrac's cinder was still there, she noted with relief, along with his dagger. She thought of staking it in the snow in hope Jazrac might be at his crystal ball at that very moment, but she couldn't. Calling for his help now was admitting her own failure—and she still had hopes of succeeding. All she needed was a little time to get away.

"Who are you?" she called to the impish thing. The question was partially a stall and partially curiosity.

"You talk—you talk again!" Sliding and bounding, the ice sprite careened down the slope to land not far from her feet. A stream of dislodged ice and snow clattered down after it.

"Who are you?" she repeated.

"Me? Me?" The thing sprang about in glee, all the while grinning in cold, false modesty. "Hot Breath, you were captured by Icy-White the Clever, Icy-White the Quick—"

"The greatest of the . . ." It was a thin trick, but Martine was banking on the thing's simpleminded vanity to finish the phrase.

"Yes, yes. The greatest of Auril's children, the greatest of the mephits. Clever warrior I am to capture you. Vreesar will be much impressed with me."

Auril, mephit, Vreesar . . . Martine seized on the three clues, even as she nodded in false awe. Auril was the Frost Maiden, goddess of cold, and supposedly worshiped by the people of the far north, not that the Harper had ever seen one of these so-called ice priests. Mephits she knew even less about—some type of elemental imp or fiend. Still, it was enough to confirm her suspicion. Shifting closer to her sword, she asked anyway.

"This isn't your home, is it?"

The mephit stopped and looked all about, head snapping to and fro in nervous tics. "Home? Oh, no. Oh, no. This place is too warm. But Vreesar found the path and wanted to explore. Dragged me with him, he did. Made me come."

Her guess was right; something had passed through the rift. But how many, and how dangerous were they? She needed to know if all her work to seal the rift was too late.

"Vreesar?"

"Vreesar's mean, bosses me around, thinks he can tell Icy-White what to do, but now look who caught Hot Breath. Now Vreesar's just—" The mephit's gaze strayed upward, looking at something behind Martine, and as it did, the bold words in its throat choked off in a stunted gurgle. "Vreesar is very clever—and quiet," Icy-White concluded in a squeaked whisper.

The mephit had barely spoken before Martine, her fighting senses coming back to her, scooted around to the side so she could see both the mephit and where it gazed, pressing her back against an upturned ice block.

Towering over both of them, a good two feet taller than Martine's five-foot frame, was an overgrown version of the mephit that had captured her. The beast had the same armor-sheened skin, smoothly flowing over its body to taper off into sharp-edged flares. The icelike carapace rendered the creature insectoid, even though it stood like a man. The look was further enhanced by the fact that its frame was overly thin and elongated, yet that same thinness made menacingly powerful the hard bands of muscle that swelled like cables across its body. It was the effect one might have gotten, Martine imagined, if you pared all the soft parts away from a normal creature, leaving nothing but the hard masses behind.

The creature's head was triangular, tapering at the chin into a beard of icicles that grew out of its flesh. The barbed ridge of its brow was crusted with more of the same, veiling the deep pits of its eyes. A mouth, small and precise, set below two narrow slots that were its nose, gaped eagerly, revealing a formidable line of spinelike teeth.

"What iz thiz?" the creature buzzed in one rapid breath. It stared at Martine, pivoting its head on a virtually nonexistent neck. "What have you found?"

"Vreesar, I captured it," the mephit boasted with a prattling squeal. The ice-bred imp sprang forward to show off its conquest, staying just out of Martine's reach. "It breathes smoke and steam, hot enough to burn me, but I captured it." With those words, the mephit danced about in triumph, waggling its long claws overhead. "I captured the Hot Breath! Me!"

"Simpleton! It iz a human!" The creature's buzzing snarl rang through the cold air like the scrape of a cutler's grindstone. With a fluid stretch that defied its angular legs, the creature stepped off the slope to place itself before the Harper, twisting its head this way and that as it eyed her. "The little one found you?"

Martine nodded slowly, doing her best to meet the creature's gaze. Her previous confidence was fading fast. It was one thing to be the bold prisoner of a small, silly mephit, but the smooth power—and evil—of this creature raised the stakes dangerously. *You should have tried to contact Jazrac,* a small part of her whispered. Martine doubted her strength or speed could ever hope to match this creature's.

"Did you do thiz, human?" The creature leered straight at her with its frosty face till its icy breath, colder than the glacial winds, burned her skin.

Martine bit the inside of her lip. Silence was her only plan, even though she had no idea how the creature might react.

Perhaps it found the answer in her eyes, or perhaps it saw her determination, for the fiend drew back. "Do you see what haz happened, human?" The creature turned its gaze to the tangled floor of the rift, shifting and wavering in the last light of enchantment. The sapphire-colored fire was gone from the sky, although it still seemed to tinge the color of the stars as they washed the glacier in weak light.

"You have trapped me!" the beast shrieked, its voice ringing from the sides of the bowl. A hundred fiends seemed to stand among the distant ruins, echoing back its words. "You have closed my door!"

In a blur, it sprang over Martine, straddling her. Clawed hands pressed against her parka. Its hoary face hung over her, thin lips pulled back in the menace of a smile. "What did you do?"

"Nothing." It was a desperate surge of bravado. She tensed her body for the strike.

"Liez," it hummed, pressing its claws against her harder. "You and your friendz did it. You will tell me how to reopen the path."

Friends? she wondered.

"No." It was only her determination not to fail in her mission that gave her defiance voice.

"No?" the beast shrieked. "You defy Vreesar, one of the great elementalz? My brotherz waiting to come will not be halted by your little trickz. I will learn how to reopen the gate." In its rage, the creature raised up one taloned hand to strike. Martine, ready for her last desperate act, closed a hand around the hilt of her sword. I will not die easily, she told herself fiercely.

"Vreesar, the Hot Breath is my prisoner! Mine!" screeched the mephit from its perch up the slope. "You cannot kill it!" In frustrated rage, the imp pelted the larger creature with fistfuls of ice.

"Cursed mephit!" the fiend roared, batting away the

missiles. With its claws finally removed from her ribs, Martine took advantage of the distraction to jerk loose her ice-encased sword. Before she'd gotten the blade free, the shadow-cloaked elemental seized his little tormentor and whirled back on the Harper, swinging the mephit about by its scrawny neck. The dark fiend, lit by the last flashes of blue, trembled and twitched as its vile passions warred within it. The mephit writhed helplessly in the great creature's strangling grasp.

The monster's head tipped left, then right. Finally stopping, the gaunt monster looked curiously at the mephit, now nearly limp. Evil light glistened in the ice-bearded eyes, and with a callous gesture, the gelugon hurled the mephit at Martine's feet.

The little ice imp flopped feebly on the ground, gasping for air, and Martine seized the opportunity to scramble backward, putting more distance between her and her captors.

"Icy-White, I forgot your great might to have captured so powerful a human," Vreesar mocked as it crouched down spiderlike before the mephit, looking beyond it to Martine. "Waz foolish, yez, to think thiz human waz strong enough to close the gap. There must be otherz who did thiz—and I will find them. Keep your prize, Mephit. Make it tell you of the otherz."

"I will do this, Vreesar." Long claws scissored the air as the creature sidled over to Martine until it could reach out and chuck its taloned tips under her chin. "The Hot Blood will talk. It will tell me everything."

Martine's boot lashed out, but it was a little too stiff and slow to catch the agile creature, which scooted aside.

"See, Vreesar, it fears me already," it chuckled gleefully. It skipped back close, watching Martine carefully. "It knows I will make it talk."

"Then do so, pest! I hunt!"

With a sinuous leap, the elemental departed into the night as suddenly as it had arrived. The clatter of loosened ice tumbling from upslope echoed its retreat.

Martine tensed as she waited for the last sounds to fade away. The howling wind and distant rumbles from the rift quickly separated them from the world. Human and mephit faced each other at the bottom of the snowy world.

"How will I begin?" the thing across from her chortled, almost forgetful of her presence. "A finger? A nose? A cut here . . . or there?" With each question, it mapped out its intentions in the snow.

Preparing to spring, Martine drew in a great breath, a breath the mephit mistook for fear. It was time to strike, she knew. Her fingers dug into the snow until they squeezed tightly on her sword hilt once more.

"How—"

The question was cut clean by Martine's charging scream, bellowed out as if to waken her rigid muscles. Snow burst outward as she jerked the sword free in a wild, slashing arc. Her legs were too stiff, her arms too weak as she lurched to her feet and lunged wildly toward the mephit.

If only she'd been faster, unfrozen and unspent, the ranger knew she could have caught the creature in that transitory moment when it froze in surprise. But her legs sagged under the need to move, her arm pulled the arc of the sword just a little too slow. With the blade still in midswing, the mephit lashed out a clawed hand. Martine heard the tear of leather and skin as the talons swept across the shoulder of her sword arm. Fire and ice mingled as blood rushed from the gashes and over her exposed skin. Pain charged her cries now.

The mephit didn't wait for the sword to complete its crippled arc but lunged forward to meet her charge. Its barbed arms sliced viciously at her legs and left her sprawled in the snow. Springing onto her back, the imp wrapped its hard arms around her like a wrestler. With one arm, it wrenched her bleeding shoulder, triggering fits of pain, while the other wrapped around her neck and pulled at her hood to expose the soft flesh. She could feel its bitter breath, hear its teeth snap as it struggled to tear her throat.

Martine writhed and thrashed, desperately trying to reach the sword that had skittered once more beyond reach. Like a wild mare, she bucked and rolled, slamming the little imp on her back against the jagged ice.

"Let go, damn it!" she raged, but the imp clung with stubborn determination. Each rolling smash brought the Harper more numbing pain, at best preventing the little monster from biting home. But it seemed each lunge brought her sword no closer.

I'm not unarmed, she suddenly realized. Twisting, she gazed directly into the imp's face. Its tiny jaws snapped, crystal teeth shining fiercely. Gulping for air, the Harper blew as warmly as she could into the mephit's ice-ridged eyes.

"Burns!" squealed the imp. Its death lock grip loosened as it clutched at its scalded face, and in a flash, Martine clenched Jazrac's knife.

"Burn, Hot Blood! You burn!" the creature squealed in her ear.

Martine wrenched her bloodied arm free and reached up to seize the creature's forehead. The stretch of muscles triggered fires of pain that she forced herself to ignore. Somewhere she'd lost a mitten, and now the mephit's icy ridges tore at her hand. With a panting effort, she bucked once more, twisting the imp's head back as she did. Blindly she jabbed the dagger over her shoulder. It hit something solid, held, and then dug in farther. The mephit shrieked in her ear, proof enough she'd hit home. With all the strength she could muster, Martine shoved the blade outward, feeling it slide in jerky pops as it cut through something. All at once the blade broke free, and her arm shot out like a punch-drunk fighter's.

The shriek still rang in her ears, almost blocking out the choking gurgle that replaced it. Clear blood, colder than ice water, washed down her shoulder as the arms of the imp broke loose in wild flails. Martine flung the creature off her and spun around to deliver the *coup de grace*. The killing stroke was unnecessary, for the mephit already lay on the ground, its head lolling as the body heaved in reflexive jerks. Her thrust had caught it just below what looked like its ear and sliced down the length of its neck, releasing a flood of silver-white blood.

Martine didn't wait for the creature to die. Already she felt unsteady on her feet, and her wounds were icing up with blood-soaked frost. Concentrating dully, she gutted her pouch, first taking care to pocket Jazrac's keystone, then plastered the leather over her shredded shoulder. A quick inspection gave her no relief, for her wounds were both bloody and deep. She recovered her mitten and gingerly slipped it over her scraped hand.

"I can't wait here. Vreesar might be back." Talking kept her focused. She looked up into the darkness at the jumble of the slide. Somewhere up there was the glacier wall and the valley beyond. Gathering her sword and her few recovered possessions, the woman began to climb.

Two steps up, one back; two steps up, one back . . . So it seemed through the long ascent. Boulders tauntingly gave beneath her feet, triggering slides that threatened to drag her back down to the bottom of the slide. Ice made her footing treacherous. Wind froze her hands into claws. She stabbed into the ice with her sword like an ice axe, chipping footholds with the point, driving the blade in as deep as possible. The blue light of magic was gone, leaving only the feeble starlight to suggest the way. More than once she almost plunged into darkened hollows, thinking they were solid ground.

How long it took her to reach the top or how she reached it, Martine could not say. After a point there was no memory of the climb's details, only the need to climb and keep moving. The exhausted ranger wasn't even aware she'd cleared the worst of it until she found herself staggering across the cracked ice plain of the surface. Up here, with all the stars of the night to guide her, Martine could just see the subtle change where the frozen wall sagged to the valley floor, a descending road to safety. She made for it.

At least I can die in the forest, she thought morbidly.

At the edge of the great ramp, Martine heard voices. Dumbly, she froze where she stood, unable to think of cover or safety. She concentrated on the voices. They were guttural and sharp, not like Vreesar's hissing buzz. There were several of them, too—a group, though she couldn't tell how many. Numbly she moved slowly closer to the source.

Then she saw them, no more than twenty feet below her. There were six, perhaps seven gnolls, working their way up the slope, well armed and thickly furred. They were still too far away to understand their words, but Martine could only presume the night's events had drawn them here. Vreesar wasn't with them, and she doubted they even knew of him.

Perhaps it was blind exhaustion that gave her the idea, or perhaps it was the need to survive. Although the Harper knew she could hide and let them pass by, instead she stepped boldly into the path—or as boldly as her wavering muscles could support her—and raised her arms above her head in the universal sign of surrender.

Five

For a moment, the gnolls stood gaping at the apparition over them, their weapons dangling at their sides. The leader tore back its parka hood and sniffed the air in suspicion, its glistening muzzle quivering to catch the scents of the night. Its black lips curled back from yellowed fangs as it barked orders to the others. In a concerted rush of flapping furs and clanking weapons, they fell upon their prisoner with astonishing haste.

The five dog-men acted quickly to take control of their prize. Martine was so weak and consumed with fatigue that she practically fell into their arms. She knew surrendering was a risk, but if it worked, it would at least get her off the ice. She denied to herself the other possibility—that they just might kill her.

Under the leader's command, the group stripped her of weapons with brutal efficiency, even finding Jazrac's pretty little knife, before lashing her wrists with a spare bowstring. Her torn shoulder hurt terribly, but at least they hadn't killed her outright.

"What do we with it?" the smallest gnoll in the group yipped finally. The fur of its hide was still raw beige and downy. It was barely more than a cub, Martine guessed.

"Kill it." The snarl came from a stocky male, the long jut of its muzzle barely visible under the cowl of its hood.

The leader of the pack, its hood pulled back as it surveyed the glacier, flicked a loose ear in irritation. "No killing now," it barked in gravelly whisper. "Later—back in camp. We will share meat with our females." A sharp finger prodded the Harper's side, as if testing the thickness of her fat. "Or maybe we eat it all ourselves." The group broke into a coughing laugh, stomping their snowy feet with approval.

It was clear her captors didn't realize their prisoner understood every word of their guttural language, knowledge gained from her years as a huntress. Nor was she about to tell them. It might be the only advantage she would get, so it was best to keep her knowledge concealed for now. Doing her best to play dumb, Martine waited for the last of their chuckles to die.

"And the lights on the tall ice?" the runt asked with a nod toward the crest of the plain. "Do we go closer?"

The bareheaded one, its thin white fur wisping in the breeze, shook its head from side to side. "We came to hunt, not to look at colored lights. Now we have good game. We go." There was no debate against the old gnoll's decision, and Martine could tell it expected none.

The group made a quick descent, their keen night sight allowing them to move easily through the darkness. Martine, her bound hands hampering her balance, unable to see the path in the blackness, stumbled along trying to keep up. None of the hyenalike men ever once slowed its pace or suggested concern for the struggling human. Each slip and fall was rewarded with a savage jerk or shove to set her back on course, the fire in her shoulder renewed.

Even at their breakneck pace through the starlit night, Martine tried to note their passage. It was an attention to detail born of habit. The curl of a drift, the switchbacks of their trail, even the grating shifts of crumbling snow beneath her feet were like islands of reality in a nightmarish sea of ice. The slide they were on was not fresh. She could tell by the way the wind had sculpted the snowy blocks and by the stiff-crusted drifts that nestled in the hollows. Near the base, where the slope tapered off, the path crossed a ribbon of ice that left the ranger confused. Even in the starlight, it glinted with clear purity, reflecting the night back in the smooth ripples of its surface. It should have been jagged and cracked, the way ice gets when it warms and freezes, but she could only imagine it as a flowing river.

She noticed, too, that there was something about the ice that spooked the gnolls. Their rapid pace broke as they neared its edge, and they crossed almost gingerly. The eyes of those closest to her were filled with fear, constantly straying to one another as if waiting for some hidden peril. Once they were off the ice, the tension faded as quickly as it had risen.

At the leader's barked call, the pack plunged across the snowy moraine at the glacier's base. They followed the winding moraine straight into the woods, moving along a well-packed track that cut through the waist-deep snow.

In the darkness of the screening branches, Martine had no opportunity to take sightings and therefore had no clear idea where they were when the pack finally rounded a dense thicket and broke into a shimmering clearing. Five dark arches of primitive longhouses were nestled at the forest's edge. The tang of pine smoke and burnt meat filled the air.

"Harrrooo!" the pack's leader howled before stepping

into the clearing. A deep-throated howl blended with the echo. Satisfied, the pack hurried across the trampled snow, past cold fire pits and snow-buried mounds of wood to the largest of the longhouses, an arch of bent wood clad in birch and leather that flapped in the breeze, as if welcoming the hunters with ghostly applause.

The leader threw open the thick hide doorway and barked at Martine to go inside. She stumbled at the sill, and a gnoll shoved her through, mistaking the near fall for hesitation. The inner curtain was pulled aside, unleashing a thick rush of humid odors, a mixture of leather, blood, smoke, flesh, birch, and sweat. A mumbled snarl rising from a horde of throats greeted her entrance.

The lodge was filled with warm yellow flickers of fire that made Martine blink. The long hall was draped with furs and hides. The work was sloppily done. The coverings didn't always match up, leaving the frame of woven saplings that formed the longhouse's arch exposed. Elk skulls and antlers hung from the arch as macabre decorations, along-side soot-black strips of jerky. The general impression was that of a moldering cellar. The ranger could guess the rest of the lodge's construction—a layer of pine boughs for insulation, capped by the outside shell she'd already seen.

This place is a tinderbox waiting for a spark. The thought came nervously to the Harper's tired mind. Perhaps it was prompted by the source of the glow, a long fire trench dug at the far end of the hut, filled to the edges and beyond with glowing coals.

The fire illuminated a tangle of furry bodies that covered the floor, a carpet that drew back before the blast of winter air that accompanied her entrance. Tawny, spotted arms stretched curiously while muzzles raised to sniff the new scent that had suddenly intruded upon them. Ears twitched; fleshy lips curled back from needle-sharp fangs.

Just beyond the sprawled mass, at the far end of the

lodge, stood a high bench, the only recognizable piece of furniture in the place. The wooden benchtop was heaped with elk robes and mantles stitched together from the pelts of innumerable sables. Planted deep in its center was a burly gnoll. He dozed upright, robes pulled around him till they fell away from his shoulders like the talus slope of a mountain. Even asleep, his immense size and his passive dominance over the rest of the pack left no doubt that he was the chieftain.

"Forward," grunted her guard. The command prompted another of her guards to step forward and force a path through the pack, which reminded Martine of dogs or wolves sleeping in huddled mounds to generate warmth as she gingerly stepped through the narrow passage.

Unlike the party that had found her, most of the gnolls in the hall were nearly naked, their winter gear hung from the arches near the entrance. Propriety was served only by simple loincloths and ornaments of bone, wood, and feathers. Each was covered with tarnished white fur, dappled with spots that ranged from red to black.

"What is it?" The chorus of whispered voices slithered through the cramped lodge.

"Human."

"Trouble."

"We kill it?"

"And eat it."

"Too stringy."

"What is this you bring me?" rose one voice above all the others, speaking with presumptive authority. The whispers stilled only slightly.

"Tonight we found new game, Hakk," the old gnoll boasted, shoving Martine forward roughly. Pain shot through the Harper's wounded shoulder, penetrating through her freezing numbness. With a strangled moan, the woman lost balance and sprawled onto the dirt floor just before the fire pit. The landing caused another searing stab of pain, which left her sweating, almost writhing before the coals.

"We trapped it on the tall ice, Hakk," the old one continued. "It was doing terrible magic, but me and my pack mates caught it." He proceeded to tell a tale of their great victory, more fanciful than real. In it, Martine became a powerful fiend, able to make the whole glacier tremble. The gnoll's lies were palpably obvious as it strutted about, miming out the tale. Martine was astonished to note the rapt acceptance of the huddled pack. Martine was in no position or condition to object. As the pain finally eased, she struggled to a kneeling position, no small accomplishment with her hands still bound.

Just as the mighty sorceress of the tale was about to fall for the final time in the leader's spirited retelling, the one called Hakk cut in. "Enough! You are a brave pack leader, Brokka. You will have the choice meat." With a thick-necked shrug, Hakk stood, letting the robes fall to the floor. Golden fur with fat rubbed into it was plastered smooth against the gnoll's hard muscles. With a casual move, the chieftain sprang across the fire pit, landing in a squat just before the Harper.

Hakk is not without his share of vanity, Martine noted. That might be useful.

"It might need fattening up." The chieftain prodded at Martine, reigniting the shuddering pain in her shoulder. Instinctively she reeled back, only to be shoved forward again by strong hands behind her.

"Kill me and you won't know the danger of the tall ice," Martine sputtered out in a mixture of gnoll and trade common.

The chieftain's eyes flared, and a deep snarl forewarned her of the savage backhand that followed. Martine barely had time to pull back and roll with the blow, but the gnoll's

fist still glanced viciously off her temple. Her vision blurred
in one eye, and it took more willpower than she thought
she possessed to face the chieftain once more. She dare not
show weakness now. She had to play it out all the way.

"There is someone else on the ice." The words came
hard as she blinked, half-blind and shivering.

"You speak only when I say!" the chief raged, but his face
gave away his curiosity.

The Harper took a deep breath and then daubed with her
bound hands at a trickle of blood seeping into the corner of
her eye.

"What other? Speak, human, or I kill you." The gnoll's
hot, greasy breath steamed against her skin.

"If you kill me, you'll never know," she whispered. She
heard him snarl, heard the clawed arm draw back. She
tried to swallow, but her mouth had gone bone dry.

"Consider the human's words before you strike her
again, Hakk." The voice came from the very back of the
lodge, from deep behind the antlers, the skeletons, and the
furs. It was clear and authoritative without being loud.

The chief's arm remained poised. "I asked for no advice,
Word-Maker."

The darkness rustled, and from its perimeter emerged
the speaker. As the creature neared, his features resolved
themselves out of the gloom. Martine's first impression
was of a skeletal mockery of a living thing, even of its own
kind. He appeared emaciated, with a sunken muzzle and
bony pits for eyes. Mustard-brown skin was drawn tight
over hard ridges, while patches of fur hung in stringy
clumps from his long jaw. Unlike the others in the lodge,
the stranger was dressed for warmth. Ragged ears jutted
through gaps in a dirty scarf wrapped around his head.
Bandagelike wrappings covered his arms, twining all the
way down to his clawed fingertips. Leather straps, gleaming red in the firelight, crossed and wound over themselves

to hold the rags in place. Where the straps crossed the
backs of the gnoll's hands, they glittered with spiked silver.
Broad crossbelts of dark brown banded his skeletal chest.
Each was decorated with metal studs and beadwork worked
into crude designs of birds, wolves, and other symbols the
Harper could not identify. They rippled in the lodge's
wavering light like things alive. A grimy bearskin cloak was
draped over his gaunt shoulders. The incongruity of his
dress made him stand out from the bestial crowd.

The gnoll came forward almost hesitantly into the light.
As it had for Martine, the pack parted before the new
arrival's advance, shrinking back with his every step forward.

At the edge of the fire pit, just short of where Hakk
stood, the challenger stopped. His black lips pulled back
from his long muzzle in a brutal smile. From this distance,
the Harper could see that fully half his taut face was etched
with tattooing. Two purple-black scars radiated from one
eye, the first cutting a wedge from his matted hairline, the
other running down the length of his muzzle.

With the sweep of one long arm, the new arrival threw
his heavy bearskin cloak off. It landed with a dull thud on
the ground behind him.

"You may not wish to hear my advice, but a corpse tells
neither truth nor lies."

"It lies about another creature on the ice, mighty chief!
We told you the truth about what happened. Nothing else is
on the ice." Brokka stepped closer to Hakk, leaning over
the chieftain's shoulder to hiss the words.

The chieftain took it as a cue. "You question Brokka's
word, Word-Maker?"

"I am sure Brokka saw what he saw."

Clever, thought Martine. His answer ducked the chieftain's challenge. Better still, it was beginning to appear as if
Word-Maker wanted her alive. Tymora's wheel seemed to

be turning back in her favor.

"Then she knows nothing and is of no use to us. We will kill her for the meat."

The Harper could see her chances doing an about-face again and refused to remain silent about her own fate. "Brokka did not see the death creature . . . the fiend. The fiend hunts us all."

Barely had she finished the words before the chieftain threw his head back and burst into a chorus of baying yelps that sounded like laughter. The pack held silent for only a moment before the young curs began to yip derisively. The joke grew as they drummed the earthen floor with savage delight.

"This is our valley. No one comes here who does not fear the Burnt Fur. Let this fiend come if he does not fear our might." Hakk's boast triggered scattered howls of approval as the drumming faded in the hall. Then he turned once more to face Martine. "As for you, you will be meat in our stewpots." The chieftain drew a knife of curved bone from its sheath.

"It is a shame to kill such a prize, Hakk Elk-Slayer," the one called Word-Maker said, nodding toward the woman. Already tensed for the deathblow, Martine grew tenser still as she wondered what the gnoll was up to.

"I do not fear a shortage of meat for the tribe," the Word-Maker continued, so softly he was almost whispering. "You are a great hunter and will lead us to game. You do not need to kill this scrawny human for our pots. Let her live, and we will steal the humans' secrets from her."

Hakk shook his head. "Humans are weak. They teach us nothing. She will merely be another mouth to feed."

"But think of the fame you would gain with a human captive in your lodge. In all the tribes, the packs would repeat your name with respect around their fires."

The chieftain paused and gave a sly glance toward the

one called Word-Maker. By now the lodge had quieted as their audience slowly realized something was afoot.

"What other chief could rival you?" Word-Maker pressed on. "The human is a good omen. Brokka said the ice stopped moving when he found her. She might have great powers." His long tongue licked greedily as the chieftain prowled before the fire pit, considering the Word-Maker's words.

The scene swirled before her as Martine awaited the outcome. Blood loss, fatigue, and the raw grate of overtaxed nerves were overcoming the Harper. Only fear kept her conscious. The scene around her blurred until she saw only Elk-Slayer and Word-Maker standing before the glowing pit.

The chieftain stopped pacing and reclaimed his position on the wooden platform. Martine snapped back to full consciousness. "I have chosen!" Hakk barked loudly to the pack. Ears eagerly perked to listen, the gnolls ceased their murmured barking and focused their attention on the platform.

"Brokka, you are a brave hunter. You bring the tribe much meat." At these words, the old gnoll smiled toothily at the rest of the pack. Praise from the chieftain probably translated into improved status—better meat, better females, Martine guessed.

The chieftain wasn't done speaking, however. The ranger tensed again, fully expecting him to pronounce a grim judgment for her. "Let the tribe know I offer three fine robes and the first meat of our next kill for the human. Does my hunt-brother agree?"

Martine hadn't enough skill to read Brokka's emotions accurately and could only guess that the gnoll was surprised. Still, considering the honor just accorded, the gnoll was not in a position to refuse. "Elk-Slayer is kind. He gives me more robes than the human is worth." Apparently the old gnoll knew how to play the game.

"It is good," the chieftain said. The pronouncement ended what little bargaining there was. With cold yellow eyes, he sized up his new possession, still sprawled on the floor. "Word-Maker!" he roared.

"I am here, Elk-Slayer."

"I claim the female for my harem. I will not eat the human unless she displeases me. Will this bring me honor?"

"A human female among your wives—every lodge will speak of it."

Wives! Weak or not, the word electrified Martine. She was to be one of this brute gnoll's wives? She was about to lurch to her feet to protest this arrangement when a cold glare from Word-Maker stopped her. The look was clear; it carried in it neither lust nor kindness, but rather a cautionary warning to stay out of something she did not understand. The Harper sagged back to the ground, quaking with anger that quickly turned to violent shivering as her weakened body finally surrendered control.

"Krote Word-Maker, say the words to finalize my claim." The chieftain's voice rang deeply through the lodge, triggering an excited buzz from the assembled tribe.

The gaunt Word-Maker nodded sharply and turned to the pack. "Hear the words of the servant of Gorellik. Hakk Elk-Slayer has claimed the human female. To take her is to challenge him. To injure her is cause for blood feud. This female is claimed. Gorellik approves this." The words were recited as an old formula, familiar and easy in their utterance.

At first the tribe's response sounded like a low grumble of snarled voices laden with discontent. The Harper's ears proved wrong, however, as the growl quickly resolved itself into a rhythmic chant. The drumming of paws slapping against the earth rose higher and higher. Though the accompanying words were garbled by the clustered voices and unfamiliar phrases, Martine caught the unmistakable strains of a mating chant.

I've just been married! she realized suddenly.

The realization left her stunned, both by the deed itself and by the haste at which it had been accomplished. Married to a gnoll! Fortunately weakness and fear blotted out any thoughts of what her new duties might be, leaving only the vague realization of the hopelessness of her situation. Blackness swirled into her vision, leaving only the two, chieftain and shaman, before her in the firelight.

"Word-Maker!" her new husband barked over the rising chorus. "The female must not die. Heal her or suffer the consequences."

The other gnoll bristled instinctively at the command, lips curling slightly to expose yellow fangs. Then, just as quickly, the Word-Maker recovered his composure. "I will do it," he grunted with a nod toward the chieftain. "Take her to the spirit lodge."

Someone seized Martine under the arms, tearing open the half-frozen bandage on her shoulder. Fresh blood oozed out through the crystals. Martine tried to stand, but her legs gave out beneath her as a new wave of pain assaulted her body. She could barely feel the ground as she staggered along, half-dragged by her captors.

Even the bitter cold outside did little to revive the Harper. Packed snow crackled as her captors led her across the clearing, jerking her upright each time she stumbled over the gnarled ground. In the dim light of the late-rising moon, they reached a little leather and birch hut, a round gray shape against the darker border of the trees. In a moment she was inside its steamy warmth. With ungentle grace, her captors dropped her onto a mass of greasy furs. To Martine, the flea-bitten pelts felt like down.

"Leave now," a voice, the shaman's, barked. There was a rustle of closing curtains, and the last of the cold blasts ended with it.

The ranger was already sliding into darkness and relief when cruel pain jerked her back to wakefulness. Eyes bolting open, she stared into the animalistic face of the Word-Maker as he squatted over her. In one clawed hand, he held a knife; in the other, he held bloody strips of clothing. There was a sharp tearing sound and more pain as he sliced away the frozen shreds of her parka.

In a matter of moments, her hands, shoulder, and toes burned like fire as the lodge's heat penetrated her frostbitten skin. Martine's muscles trembled uncontrollably. The gnoll pressed a bony knee into her stomach and snarled, "Lie still, human. I will not let you die." The words were more threat than promise.

Finally the shaman finished cutting his patient free from her garments, leaving her gashed shoulder exposed. With a sharp claw, he scraped away the frozen blood and dirt in each gouge, releasing new welling streams that flowed down over her skin. With each scrape, the ranger felt hot jets of pain. Finally the shaman sat on her torso to pin her down. Martine ground her teeth in a futile effort to keep from screaming. Nothing remained of the real world but the gnoll's grinning face and her own agony, until finally the pain was so intense it no longer mattered.

At last the gnoll stopped, and the spasms subsided. Dimly the ranger could see him holding an unfamiliar charm, circling it over her wounds. "Bones knit. Skin seal." The shaman chanted his droning prayer over and over as he rubbed one hand over her injured shoulder.

Almost immediately the pain in Martine's wounds took on a new dimension. The dullness of overstressed nerves transformed as new pains jangled alarms. Tendons and muscles shifted under the tingling fire emanating from the gnoll's palm. Her whole arm jerked spasmodically as strange signals aroused her dormant muscles. Without stopping his prayer, the shaman slid his hand across the woman's body, letting the power of his spell penetrate. Deep in her chest, Martine felt her ribs clutch and seize, then settle into a soothing numbness. The frostbitten fire surged in her extremities.

Then suddenly the pain, all of it, old and new, abruptly ended. The absence of any feeling was almost as excruciating as the pain itself. Dimly Martine realized she lay soaked in sweat, her jaw clenched so tight she thought it was locked.

It was done. Word-Maker took his hand away and ended his prayer with a final harsh benediction, then prodded and poked at Martine, examining his handiwork. "Gorellik has favored me, outsider," the shaman remarked as he packed away his charm. "He has shown his blessing to a human and let us both live. Your wounds are healed."

Martine barely heard the gnoll, so overwhelmed was she by the emptiness that replaced her pain. *Thank him,* a small voice within her said.

"Thank—thank you," the Harper stammered brokenly. In a language she seldom used, her words were stiffly formed. The cold, the battles, and the healing had left her drained, until even speech was a prodigious effort. She tried to raise a hand, but her muscles were limp and helpless after her ordeal.

Word-Maker noted her effort and snorted as he stood, wrapping his dirty robes over his sharp shoulders. "I go tell Elk-Slayer of my success. I leave you here—unbound. If you try to escape, you will only freeze in the snow." Saying no more he slipped past the door flaps and out into the night.

It's an accurate prediction, even if I could get outside, the Harper thought, *but I'm not helpless. If only I can get a message to Jazrac . . . a letter. He might scry and see it, even without the dagger.*

That thin hope kept Martine from collapse as she slowly

gathered the simple materials for the task. A half-burnt stick, scraped from the lodge's small fire, became a pen, a curl of birchbark her paper.

Poised to write, Martine paused. I'm overreacting. I've made it through the worst, she chided herself. If I call for help now, that'll be a sign of weakness. I've got to prove to Jazrac I can be a Harper. I can make it. I know I can.

Taking a deep breath to steady her hand, the ranger slowly scratched block letters on the inside of the bark.

J—

Hole sealed. Guest of gnolls. Will escape. Don't worry. Not hurt.

M.

Finished, the ranger looked at the message with the addled confidence of exhaustion. I *can* do this. All I need is Jazrac's knife, she told herself as she carefully rolled the bark into a tube and tucked it away out of sight.

Disregarding the fleas and lice, Martine pulled the furs around her and lay back, waiting for sleep to overtake her. Overhead, the whistling blasts of the wind shook the wicker frame of the hut till the necklaces hanging from its spars began to vibrate softly, chattering their tales. Just as she was about to drift into sleep, she heard a hissing wail from somewhere in the frigid night. It was a cold voice that scoured the sky with its fiendish rage, and Martine knew the thing on the glacier was hunting.

Comforting sleep never came.

Six

 Martine was awake again when daylight seeped through the cracks around the hut's doors. The woman felt none of the relief rest would normally bring, only a blurry haze of fear and confusion. She couldn't even remember sleeping. Perhaps she had, only to suffer dreams no different from her waking fears.

With the magical healing and what little rest she might have stolen, the ranger did feel somewhat stronger, although not fully herself yet. Martine gingerly touched the still unclosed wounds on her shoulder. The imp's slash marks were smaller, crusted over, and free of infection, but the skin was still stiff, and each move risked pulling the gashes open. Clearly the damage had been more than the gnoll's single spell could mend.

No fighting for me yet, she decided, not for a few days at least. She smiled ruefully. It was unlikely there would be any need to, at any rate. Weaponless and opposed by an entire tribe, her chances of escaping seemed dim indeed.

The ranger's thoughts were interrupted by the stiff rustling of the door curtain. Bright sunshine illuminated the hut as the gaunt Word-Maker stooped to pass through the doorway. The wind swirled ashes from the ebbing fire, adding to the thickness of the air.

The gnoll held the door flap open with one lanky arm, draining the scant heat from the small lodge. He was still dressed as the woman vaguely remembered him from last night. The bindings wound round his arms and legs were not bandages as she thought then, but wrappings made from scraps of cloth and leather layered over buckskin. Thongs bound the windings like cross-gartered hose, reminding Martine of an impoverished courtier she'd once met in Selgaunt. Bits of fur and fabric hung in loose bits beneath the straps. In the light, Martine could see that the straps were spiked where they crossed the backs of the gnoll's hands and wound through his fingers. It was ornamentation heightened to barbaric fashion, for the nails, gleaming silver, seemed incredibly sharp. She remembered his bare chest from last night; today it was covered by a dyed leather shirt, printed in block patterns that duplicated the shining nailwork of his cross-belts. The bearskin cloak of last night hung loosely from one shoulder.

"Good. You are awake, human," grunted the gnoll.

Martine was too dazed to do anything more than stare wildly at him.

"Get up. Hakk wants you."

The command jolted her back to the present. "To kill me?" the Harper asked warily. In all her years on various frontiers, Martine had never heard of gnolls taking prisoners.

"No," the gnoll answered sharply, glaring at her with his deep-sunken eyes. "I have questions. If you are dead, it is difficult to get answers."

But not impossible, Martine mentally added upon noting

the unmistakable threat in the shaman's tone. Perhaps she couldn't tell when a gnoll was happy or distrustful, but threats were clear enough.

"Now get up, human. Hakk awaits."

"I have a name, gnoll. It's Martine . . . Martine of Sembia." The fact that the gnoll preferred her alive gave the ranger heart, at least enough to put on a show of pride.

"Margh-tin." The gnoll mangled the foreign-sounding syllables of her name. "Easier to call you human. I am Krote . . . Krote Word-Maker. Do what I say and you may live."

"Yes . . . Word-Maker. The name means you're a . . ." The Harper searched for the right word. Her grasp of the harsh gnoll tongue was rusty and far from fluent.

"The speaker for Gorellik," Krote completed impatiently. In case the human didn't understand, he plucked an amulet from the latticework and dangled it in front of Martine. It was a crudely carved animal head, similar to a hyena the ranger had once seen on the plains south of the Innersea. Fetishes of feather and bone dangled from it, leaving no doubt Gorellik was a gnoll god.

"Now, go," the gnoll demanded as he tucked the icon way.

Martine lurched to her feet, wrapping the fur robe she'd slept in tight around her shredded parka. The thin winter sunlight did little to warm the air, and she had no desire to expose her healing wounds to frostbite once more.

The shaman moved aside warily as Martine stepped outside. Blinking against the ice-reflected sunlight, she surveyed the gnoll village. It was a meager collection of vulgar huts spaced in a wide circle around the edge of a roughly circular clearing. There were five huts all told. The nearest was typical of them all, built from old, stiff skins and strips of papery white bark lashed to a simple curved frame. Snow was mounded against the long sides in an attempt to provide some insulation. Smoke curled from a hole in the

roof. By some trick of the air, the smoke rose into the
sparse branches of the birches and massed there, a greasy
pall that transformed the gleaming blue of the sky into a flat
haze.

Yipping cries drew Martine's gaze away from the lodge.
A small figure darted around the edge of another hut and
then stopped short at seeing her. Immediately on its heels
came another. The second sprang upon the first from
behind, and they fell tumbling across the churned snow.
They were young gnolls—Martine wasn't sure whether to
call them kits or cubs—and were playing like children
everywhere, though much rougher. Furry muzzles bit at
each other in mock battle; then the one on the bottom
grabbed a chunk of ice and smashed it against the snapping
jowl of its playmate. The gnoll cub flopped back with a
whimpering yowl, clutching its face, and the other lunged
on top of it, pinning its prey with knees clamped against its
chest. The victor barked and growled in triumph and then
bounded away.

It reminded Martine of the way her brothers used to
wrestle, though maybe without the biting. The thought
came so naturally to mind that the Harper had to force herself to remember that they were not the same. These were
her captors, and not even human.

Krote pushed her toward the largest of the lodges. The
chief's lodge looked no different from the others, only
slightly higher and longer. The main distinctive feature was
an arch of painted skulls that hung over the entrance. Invisible by night, the gaudily striped and spotted faces stared
down at Martine now. They comprised all manner of creatures. Some, like the elk, bear, and griffon, she could identify. Others were mysteries, although the ranger guessed
that at least two small skulls were those of gnomes.

Inside, the lodge was lit by the fire pit, whose dull glow
made the hanging bones flicker and dance. The massed

gnolls that had filled the hall the night before were gone, no doubt at the day's work. Krote pushed Martine across the cool earthen floor until she stood once more before the chieftain's platform.

Meticulously laid out on the far side of the fire in the brief space between the rock-ringed pit and the wooden dais was Martine's gear. Her long sword, leather backpack, and a few sausages from Shadowdale were testimony to what little she had been able to salvage from the glacier. Ignoring the chieftain, who glared at her from his crude throne, the ranger eagerly scanned the gear until she spotted the ivory gleam of Jazrac's dagger. Right next to it rested the dull black rock that was the seal's keystone. The Harper's spirits leapt with both relief and dread. The sudden panic that she might have lost the keystone was replaced by the realization that it was now part of Hakk's booty.

"Wife, is this all your *kaamak?*" Hakk's lips curled in a snarl as he spoke. There was no affection in his words.

"*Kaamak?*" It was a term the ranger had never heard.

"*Kaamak!*" Hakk repeated loudly as he jabbed a sharp finger at her goods before him.

Gear? Magic? Possessions? Martine thought desperately as she tried to fathom the gnoll's words. She warily shook her head in incomprehension, trying not to provoke another outburst.

Krote interceded, his voice rasping softly behind her. "*Kaamak* . . . wife's payment . . . gifts to the mate."

"Dowry?" Martine blurted in Sembian, startled at the suggestion the marriage had anything to do with her wishes.

"Yes, dow-ry," Krote responded with satisfaction, once more having difficulty with the foreign shapes of the Sembian tongue.

Martine goggled at him, too amazed to attempt any reply. The chieftain was acting as if she had agreed to this wedding, as if she weren't a prisoner! I hope he doesn't expect me to have any goats, she thought.

"Is this your *kaamak?*" Hakk bellowed, now infuriated with her impudence.

"Answer, female," Krote hissed. "Be respectful to your mate."

"Yes, those are my things," she answered dazedly.

Hakk smiled with satisfaction and ignored her. He picked up the long sword she'd won from a captain of the Pirate Isles and jabbed it into the ground to test its blade. "The sword is good. I will keep it."

Martine bristled. Winning that sword had cost her an ugly scar across her back. Perhaps noticing her reaction, Krote gave her a cautionary jab to remain silent.

Flourishing the sword, Hakk bit into one of Jhaele's sausages, only to immediately spit it into the fire with a retching growl. "This meat is spoiled!" he pronounced, kicking the rest of the links into the fire. The coals hissed and spattered as the grease oozed from the casings.

"Those were good sausages, smoked and spiced, you fly-specked idiot," Martine muttered under her breath, unable to repress her anger. This time the jab from Krote was considerably harder.

"Krote, I give you the dagger," Hakk offered expansively after examining Jazrac's knife. With an easy flip, the chieftain tossed it across the fire to land point-first in the dirt.

"Elk-Slayer is generous," Word-Maker said. "I will speak of your generosity to Gorellik."

While Krote was busy with formalities, the ranger eyed the dagger eagerly without trying to show too much interest. The dagger was her primary hope. If she could only place it with her scrawled plea for help, then Jazrac might learn of her plight through his crystal ball. True, he might be scrying the dagger right now, but if he didn't find a letter from her, the wizard would probably give up.

"What is this?" Hakk demanded in brutal tones. In his clenched fingers, he held the pitted keystone of the rift's magical seal.

"It's—it's nothing. Just a rock." Preoccupied with the knife, Martine was caught off guard. She flinched inwardly at her halting reply, which sounded unconvincing even to her. She could only hope gnolls were no better at judging her emotions than she was at judging theirs.

Toss it aside, she mentally urged the gnoll. Just forget about it.

Hakk glared with curled lips at the simple rock, and for a moment, Martine held hopes she was right.

"Krote, why does the human come here to gather rocks?"

The shaman behind her sucked the air in between his fangs, clearly without an answer. Finally, he said, "Maybe she is like the little ones, the dwarves. They put much value on stones dug out of the earth."

"Since the human came here to get this rock, what you say must be true. I will keep it." With those words Hakk tossed the stone among the furs of his dais.

Martine winced. Krote had clearly guessed wrong, but too well nonetheless.

"It's just a—a souvenir," Martine stumbled over the term and at last resorted to Sembian. "I mean, something to remember things by, Chieftain Elk-Slayer. The rock is worthless. I mean, do I look like a miner?" Stepping forward with mock helplessness, the ranger hoped, perhaps futilely, that she might persuade the chieftain by playing up her own ignorance. In the dogman's eyes, after all, she was only a human—and a female at that.

Hakk had let one ear loll as he cocked his head to listen. Before the gnoll could say a word, however, Krote spoke in suspicious tones.

"Brokka said the human had great magical powers, Hakk . . . that she shattered the tall ice."

Across the fire pit, the chieftain grunted understanding as he eyed Martine sharply. "I keep this rock."

Crestfallen, Martine realized she'd overplayed her hand and underestimated the gnolls, Krote in particular. The gaunt shaman didn't know why the Harper wanted the stone, but he had correctly read her desire to keep it. Don't show disappointment, she chided herself. Don't let on they're right.

"My power has no need for stones, Word-Maker." Her words were a softly spoken boast, but one which she voiced with confidence, for it was the truth. All she really needed was her sword, and then Krote and Hakk would discover just how fierce an opponent she was.

Krote's hard stare told her the gnoll had heard and understood her words. She noticed he kept one paw close to the dagger at his belt. She smiled slightly, just enough to show her pleasure at unnerving him.

"Take my mate out, Word-Maker. She has no more *kaa-mak*. Take her back to your lodge and learn her secrets," Hakk grunted from across the fire pit where he had remained oblivious to the exchange. Stifling a bored yawn, the chieftain scratched at the fleas that infested his golden-furred hide and clambered lazily back onto his platform.

Prodding her in the back, Krote hustled Martine back into the cold daylight. A pair of female gnolls butchering a rabbit in the bloodstained snow eyed Martine eagerly, their knives flashing too suggestively for her taste.

"What is the significance of the stone?" the shaman demanded as he pushed the woman past the smoldering remains of a fire.

"It's just a souvenir." Martine gamely tried to stick to her story. The shaman wanted answers, and she wasn't about to supply them. So long as that remained true, he would keep her alive, Martine figured.

"That's a lie."

"It's my good-luck charm," she said with cheerful defiance.

"Another lie," the shaman shot back in a tone that showed no glimmer of humor.

"True enough," she countered wearily. "If it had been lucky, I wouldn't be here."

"What is the rock?" This time the question was more a snarl, and Martine knew she'd better sound convincing. The only problem was she was too tired and afraid to think of something clever.

"I don't know," she lied again. "I was paid to deliver it."

Krote furrowed his bony brow as he considered her claim. "Still another lie," he finally said accusingly. "The Burnt Fur are the only people around here. You did not come to trade with us. The rock and Brokka's story about lights on the tall ice—these two are connected."

Martine didn't bother trying to deny his conclusion. From the way the Word-Maker had countered every tale, it was clear she was too shaken by exhaustion to lie convincingly. In desperation, the ranger chose to remain silent and let herself be led across the clearing.

Krote asked no more questions, and for a moment, Martine hoped that he had relented. Then, just as they reached the small lodge that was her cell, the shaman stopped abruptly. With a swift move, he wrapped his rough fingers around Martine's neck. She floundered in his strong grasp, suddenly choking.

"Human woman," the gnoll snarled in methodically grim words, "if you do not speak the truth by tonight, I will stake you outside naked. Then you will talk—or freeze."

Twisting in his grasp, the ranger finally sucked in a breath of frigid air. "You would heal me, then kill me?" she challenged. "No, Krote. You want me alive. I'm no good to you dead."

Krote dropped his hand with a laugh. "I like you, human.

You have much—umm—anger, strong feeling, for a female. That is good. In our tribe, females must be ready to fight to claim mates. The kits you bear Hakk will be strong and clever." Laughter mingled with wheezing chuckles accompanied his claim. The tall shaman stooped to pull open the lodge's door curtain.

Martine paled. Unschooled in gnoll ways, she still couldn't miss the irony in Krote's thin voice. The thought of bearing the spawn of a monster like Hakk shook her body to the core.

Still chuckling, Krote shoved her through the doorway of the lodge. Stumbling into the darkness, she let herself collapse weakly on the furs. Faintly she could hear the birch scroll, her letter to Jazrac, crackle beneath the layers of her fur bed and remembered the knife Hakk had given to Krote. Rolling over, she saw the gleam of the ivory handle jutting from the edge of Krote's crossbelts.

Desperate plans raced through her mind. The thin shaman was clearly not a fighter, but right now the ranger doubted she had the strength to best a kitten. Guile was her only chance, if she could just think clearly.

"Who are you?" Krote demanded, interrupting her thoughts.

"I told you—Martine of Sembia."

The shaman thrust a stick into the fire's coals, just enough to make the end smolder, and Martine sensed the interrogation was about to begin in earnest.

"Why are you here?" The gnoll jabbed at the coals.

The truth, to a point, seemed her best response. "I crashed nearby."

Krote raised one ear, though whether in interest or skepticism, Martine did not know. "Tell Krote about it."

"A storm brought down my hippogriff." Once again she had to resort to Sembian, not knowing the gnoll term for hippogriff.

"The storm on the tall ice?"

Martine guessed he meant the rift's geyser, which from the base of the glacier must have looked like a roiling thunderhead. She nodded.

Krote pulled the stick from the fire and blew on the ember at its end until it glowed orange-red. "You are a spy for the little ones, right?"

"Little ones?" Martine slid back, trying to keep as much distance between herself and the gnoll as possible.

Krote smiled, his black lips pulled back to show yellow, cracked fangs and pinkish gums. "The little people in the south valley. They sent you here to spy on us."

"No," she said, emphasizing it with a shake of her head. "I didn't even know you lived here!"

With a snort, the gnoll thrust the stick back into the fire, making Martine wonder just how sincere his threat had been. "My people have lived here since Arka, the chieftain before Hakk Elk-Slayer. Now the little people steal our hunting grounds."

The shaman's claim made no sense. Judging by what she'd seen of the Vani warren, the gnomes had been there a century or more, building and tending to their home. No gnoll chieftain, she guessed, could have that kind of lifespan.

"What do you mean, they stole your hunting grounds? Surely they were there first." The Harper part of her, the part that always hungered for information, was speaking now.

"It is our right because we need it," was the shaman's sharp answer.

"Because you need it, the valley belongs to you?"

Krote's long tongue licked his lips. "It is right of—*rrachk-kiah.*"

"*Rrachk-kiah?*"

The gnoll groped for an explanation as he unexpectedly

warmed to her interest. It seemed as if he wanted to explain, to justify the ways of his tribe. Perhaps she had triggered a passion within him, part of what earned him the title Word-Maker.

"What is seen is owned," the shaman continued. "The gods gave my people everything in the world. Everything we can see belongs to the gnolls. So the little ones steal our hunting grounds."

"That's . . . quite a claim." Martine picked her words carefully, trying not to let any sarcasm creep in, despite the arrogant egotism of the gnoll's beliefs.

"It is right. Why else would the gods make the world?" Word-Maker proclaimed.

A series of shouts from outside interrupted any need to reply. Krote's ears twitched as he stepped to the door flap and peered outside. The woman braced herself to spring at him while he was distracted, but before she could act, the shaman whipped out a knife. Involuntarily a savage growl welled up in his throat.

The chorus of barking yelps from outside intensified. The dog-man suddenly whirled, pointed the knife in her direction, and barked, "Stay!" before disappearing through the door flap. It wasn't the ranger but something outside that had triggered Krote's reaction.

Martine sat dumbfounded for a moment, but only for a moment. Scrambling to her feet, she hastily gathered whatever she could find that might be of use in her escape—furs, a pouch, a sharp stick, even a few trinkets from the walls. Wrapping them into a tight bundle, she paused at the lodge's flap to listen before venturing outside.

Whatever was happening, it was important, judging by the noise. From the mingled chorus of barking shouts, Martine imagined the entire tribe had turned out. The words were unclear, but the excitement was obvious.

This is my chance, the Harper thought as she crouched

low by the entrance. With luck I can make it into the forest unnoticed.

Pulling back the door flap slightly, Martine was greeted with a view of an assembled throng, their backs facing her. The massed gnolls, some robed, others bare-skinned in the cold, were gathered in the center of the clearing, their attention transfixed by something the Harper could not see. The gathering piqued her curiosity, but not nearly as much as the chance of escape. Grabbing her bundle, she slipped through the opening and edged her way along the front of the lodge, moving quietly in hope of avoiding attention. Her breath steamed out in tense bursts, and each crunching footstep made her wince even though there was little chance of being heard over the racket made by the gnolls, which sounded like battle cries and war alarms. Had Vilheim returned with the gnomes? Or was it Jazrac? Martine paused, hope rising that someone might be coming to rescue her.

Even as she stood eagerly waiting, the fierce war cries of the gnolls gave way to howls of panic, and the tightly knit mass of bodies abruptly exploded as the gnolls turned and bolted, those at the back thrust aside by others from the front lines. Females scooped up their kits and ran for the shelter of the lodges. Latecomers scrambled for weapons stacked near the lodge doors. Through a brief gap in the crowd, Martine saw Elk-Slayer, muscular and nearly naked, berating his warriors to form a wavering arc of spears against whatever approached.

Then Martine saw the intruder and understood the cause of the gnolls' panic. It was her tormentor, the creature from the rift, icy bone-white, moving with clicking stiffness as it stalked into the center of the village. Its head snapped from side to side, its icicled brow hiding eyes that swept over the gnolls. The small, rasping mouth clicked together in threatening snaps, while its long arms swung to and fro, thin claws cutting gouges in the hard snow.

Seeing the fiend, Martine paled and promptly forgot about caution. Relying on the confusion the creature's arrival was creating, she clutched her bundle tightly and sprinted from the shelter of the lodge into the gap that separated it from the gloom of the forest. A gnoll charged past, forcing the ranger to veer madly, but the creature seemed to pay her no mind.

I've made it! she started to think as the trees drew nearer.

The second she entertained the thought, the woman knew it was precipitous. Before she had completed another two steps, a rough hand seized her. "Hah!" snarled a harsh voice as clawed fingers gouged into her tender shoulder. Her arm jerked in a spasm of pain and her bundle spilled from her grasp. Kicking and struggling, she tried to break free from the gnoll, but his grip did not loosen. With a fierce twist, she was pulled about to face her captor.

"I thought you might try to escape," Krote grunted as he held her fast, his amulets jingling as she squirmed about.

"Cyric take you!" Martine tried to kick him, a move the gnoll easily avoided.

"Varka, bring the human," the shaman barked to a warrior hurrying by with sword and shield in hand. Varka, a short, mangy creature, grinned wolfishly, and with a sharp poke of his sword, urged Martine into obedience. Realizing her chance to escape was lost, she sullenly pretended surrender, all the while still hoping for a chance to break free once more.

"Female, what is that creature?" Krote rasped as they hurried to where Hakk's warriors uneasily faced off against the intruder. So far, neither the gnolls nor the fiend had done more than glower at each other.

"I don't know. It's the same creature that captured me on the glacier." Her near escape and failure had crumbled the

Harper's resistance.

Krote started to say something else, but his words were silenced by a warm buzzing as the fiend spoke.

"Warm thingz," the newcomer droned slowly as it surveyed them all, talking as if they did not matter. "Many warm thingz. Good. You will be my slavez. I am your master."

To Martine's ears, the claim would have been preposterous were it not for the monotonous confidence with which the creature spoke. It was not a thing of this world, and there was no sure way to say what it was capable of doing. Beside her, Krote sucked in the cold air with a snarling hiss.

An eerie silence fell upon the tribe. Martine had expected outrage, or at least more of the wild tumult that had heralded the fiend's arrival, but instead the gnolls seemed to go dumb. The warriors in the half-circle around the fiend wavered. Martine assumed it was cowardice until she realized they were waiting. The eyes of the warriors, indeed of all the crowd, turned to their chieftain, Hakk Elk-Slayer.

"What are you waiting for? Your tribe can kill it," the Harper found herself urging the Word-Maker. Though still a gnoll prisoner, she feared the fiend more.

"Quiet," Krote whispered. "The creature challenges Elk-Slayer. He must fight to remain chieftain."

"What? Against that thing? What kind of a challenge is that?" Unable to contain her disbelief, Martine nodded toward the elemental.

"Quiet! It is the way things are done."

It seemed to Martine that the fiend was as confused as she was by the sudden silence of the gnolls, for it swayed from side to side, glaring this way and that as it waited for an attack. The droning buzz of its voice went higher, perhaps in amusement, as it spoke again. "No fight? Good slavez . . ."

"The Burnt Fur are not slaves," Hakk finally roared out. Even before the first faint echo rebounded from the dense woods, the chieftain sprang forward, using two hands to whirl a gnarled club over his head.

Crack! The resounding crash of wood striking bone broke the spell over the crowd. The elemental reeled from the blow, pinkish-clear blood seeping from a crack in the smooth carapace of its leg. The tribe roared in approval of Hakk's assault, and the chieftain launched another blow while the creature was still reeling. The gnoll ran straight at the fiend, his club pointed toward its skeletal chest like a battering ram driven against a city's gate.

Just before the wooden club drove home, the fiend twisted sideways and let the chieftain charge past. Long, icicle-like claws flashed, and suddenly the dirty white snow was splattered with red. Hakk wobbled and then dropped to his knees, his fingers clutching at his side in a futile attempt to stanch the flow of blood. The gnoll's massive chest rose and fell in desperate pants. He dropped his club and doggedly lurched to his feet, sword in hand.

The fiend seemed to be in no hurry. Mockingly it waggled its bloodstained claws, flicking little drops of blood over the onlookers. The gnolls shifted and wavered with uneasiness, but none made a move to intercede. Krote's hand, firm on Martine's shoulder, restrained her from fleeing.

"I'll kill you," Hakk croaked as he advanced, more cautiously now, having gained a new respect for his foe.

The naturally armored fiend responded with a trilling buzz that Martine imagined was laughter. It was a morbid and heartless humor that the fiend punctuated by clacking snaps of its gleaming jaw. "Come, then, and kill me," it intoned.

Hakk was not to be goaded so easily, and the two circled round each other. The tribe formed a ring surrounding the

duelists, the warriors at the front with their spears and
swords held in readiness. Krote pushed Martine, whom he
still held firmly, into the forefront. There the shaman fingered his charms and amulets, his lips moving silently.
Martine wondered if it was a prayer and, if so, what the shaman was praying for.

All at once the fiend staggered as its wounded leg
wobbled beneath it. One clawed hand dropped to the snow
as it recovered its balance, and in that brief instant, Hakk
sprang forward with a wild, howling rush.

In a blur of movement, the fiend struck, and Martine saw
instantly that its apparent weakness had been a trap. As the
chieftain's golden-furred body lunged beneath the fiend's
intentionally clumsy sweep, Hakk overconfidently left his
side exposed. Even as Hakk's sword flashed upward for the
kill, the fiend's head lashed downward, striking faster than
Martine could imagine. Hakk's strangled shriek mingled
with a pulping crunch as the fiend's razorlike teeth clamped
on the gnoll's neck. Elk-Slayer's thrust was never completed, with the nerves that linked thought to action severed. The pair plunged to the ground, and the air filled with
a buzzing roar as the fiend tore at the spasmodically flailing
gnoll like a terrier with a rat. Blood splattered the snow.
The gnolls recoiled from the gruesome scene, widening the
circle around the carnage.

The end came with painful slowness. Even though the
jerking convulsions had long since stopped, the creature
still huddled over the body, savagely gnawing at the gnoll's
neck. The tribe was held frozen in shocked surprise, the
first yips of fear radiating from the edges of the throng.
Martine could only gaze helplessly in disbelief, suddenly
terrified at how easy it would be to pick her out of the
crowd. Warily she tried to edge backward, to put bodies
between her and the fiend. The shaman noted her movement and seemed to nod conspiratorially. In any case,

although he didn't let her slip free, the gnoll pulled her back a step into the crowd.

As if on a signal, howls rose from the foremost gnolls. The pain and fear behind their voices was unmistakable. At the dueling ground's center, amid the crimson-soaked snow, the fiend rose to its full height. Red streaked the ivory armor of its body, and blood glistened from its quivering, sharp chin. One bonelike arm reached over its head, and clutched in those claws was the severed head of Hakk Elk-Slayer, his dead eyes seeming to gaze out upon his tribe.

"Warm thingz!" the creature shrilled to the stunned gnolls, whirling about to face them all. "I am your leader now. You are my slavez!"

The gnolls wavered, caught between fear and their own traditions. Those closest to the shaman looked to him for guidance, but the Word-Maker had no answer.

As they hesitated, the fiend hurled the still-warm head at the assembled warriors and sprang in a bounding hop upon the nearest gnoll. Seizing the terrified tribesman in its long claws, the fiend shrilled, "I am your master! Vreesar is your master!" Each claim was punctuated by a brutal shake.

"Y-Y-You . . . are . . . chieftain," the gnoll stammered. Gradually the chant was taken up by those nearby until it grew into a fear-stricken chorus of confirmation.

Vreesar flung the quivering gnoll aside with an easy toss and triumphantly turned to survey its new subjects. All at once it stopped and pushed its way through the rapidly parting sea of gnolls.

Martine suddenly felt the burning gaze of the fiend's eyes. Its foul voiced buzzed in her ears.

"Human, you are here! You must come to my new throne!"

Seven

A biting wind deadened Martine's limbs as she stood before the dais of the great Vreesar, new chieftain of the Burnt Fur. With its conquest, the fiend had taken possession of Elk-Slayer's lodge and quickly found the accomodations not to its liking. Heaping a miscellany of wood and baskets at the entrance, Vreesar sat poised on a throne made from a cradleboard laid between two stools. This crude dais was much more to the fiend's liking, since it was safely away from the scorching fire pit at the far end of the lodge. Elk-Slayer's furs and robes were banished, eagerly snapped up by the tribe members determined to gain something from the chaos. Instead of rich bearskins, the platform was coated with a heap of caked, dirty snow dug from the clearing. The door flap, formerly sealed with care against the hostile outdoors, was now pulled wide open to let the bitter breeze blow through.

No gnolls lounged half-naked in the steaming heat, as they had the night before. Those tribe members in the lodge huddled tightly together as far back from the entrance as they could, trying to capture the precious warmth of the smoldering fire pit.

It was a warmth the ranger did not feel from where she stood in the bare earth between Vreesar's throne and the clustered gnolls. Since the occupation of the lodge, Vreesar had kept her near its crude throne. No more than three paces behind her, Krote squatted, waiting for the new chieftain's words.

Atop the ice-encrusted dais, Vreesar gave no heed to the suffering of its subjects. The fiend was in no discomfort, clearly relishing the frozen winds that blasted through the open doorway. Martine suspected that it enjoyed more than just the cold, for it seemed to deliberately prolong every action as a means to torment all those assembled with the freezing cold.

"Where iz my tribute? Did your chieftain have nothing? You!" Vreesar hummed as it jabbed a finger at Krote. "You wait and wait like an *ennchi* waiting to tear the hope out of a carrioned soul."

Martine shivered in cold fear. She did not know what an *ennchi* was, or a carrioned soul, but together they did not sound good.

Krote must have thought so, too, for his answer was long in coming. "This is Hakk's longhouse. What he owned is here." The shaman guestured to the spread of goods on the dirt floor in front of Vreesar. Standing just behind the array of items, Martine felt as if she were being presented as property, too.

The Harper held her breath as Vreesar languidly drifted one clawed foot over the line of Hakk's goods, pausing to touch a peculiar stone that rested among the dented breastplates, bone necklaces, and wooden carvings. Martine worried about what one sharp tap of the fiend's toe might do to Jazrac's seal. The wizard had warned her, after all, that the

stone was breakable. One hard rap, and all her efforts to
close the rift could end in failure.

The fiend kicked a carving with one taloned toe. "Fah!" it
hissed contemptuously. "These are mere toyz. No strength
in toyz."

Martine trembled with relief. Thank Tymora for some
small luck, she silently praised.

"Human, I meet you again," Vreesar droned in chilling
tones. The elemental leaned toward her, never leaving its
seat.

Like a small child expecting a thrashing, Martine barely
nodded her head up and down. In truth, the woman held
herself in rigid control to prevent her body from collapsing
in a spasm of nerves. There was no point in denying anything so obvious. This creature was clever and perceptive,
not like the little one she had slain. There was no hope of
fooling it into believing she had not been on the glacier.

"You killed Icy-White?"

How should I answer? This thing knows I did. What will
it do if I tell the truth? Or is it trying to trick me into a lie?
Martine felt her blood surge with panic. With a deep
breath, she forced her body, but not her mind, to be calm.

"It wanted to play rough." The Harper hoped her words
sounded as tough and cynical as she thought they did.
Barely suppressed fear made it impossible for her to accurately judge the tone of her own words.

The lodge filled with the fiend's quavering buzz.

Oh, gods, I hope that's laughter, or else I'm dead. The
Harper could feel her nerves making her begin to tremble.
The strain of the last few days made them diabolically hard
to control.

Behind her, the gnolls milled in consternation, no more
able to fathom the fiend's mood than she was.

At last the buzzing subsided. The fiend swiveled its glittering eyes, sparkling beneath its shadowed brow, on her.

"You close my gate?"

Despite her dry throat, Martine tried to swallow before she answered. "No. What gate?"

"Again you lie!" it thrummed, springing down from the dais. With a kick, it sent Hakk's possessions flying. Martine bit her lip and tried not to let her eyes betray her interest as Jazrac's stone tumbled across the floor and came to a stop against the lodge wall.

With jerking, angular steps, the creature stalked around her, each stride drawing it closer to her until Martine felt the crystals of icy breath on her neck. "I want gate open," Vreesar whispered, constantly circling her. "It iz cold and empty here—nice. Open the gate and I will make you my general. Open the gate and I will give you armiez of Icy-Whitez. You will rule the warm landz for me. I will make you powerful, human."

Vreesar stopped behind her. Cold claws gently wrapped over the Harper's shoulders, the sharp click of its fangs sounding next to her ear. "How do I open the gate?"

I'm a Harper. I can't betray that trust. I *must not* betray that trust. Martine seized on these thoughts, focusing her mind on her duty as she steeled her body for her death. It would surely follow, the minute she refused Vreesar. All she had to do was say, "You can't," and the fiend would fly into a rage, and she would be dead. She knew it instinctively. A few quick words, some pain, and then freedom from this terror. It would be a true Harper's death.

"I—I don't know." They were the wrong words, said before she even realized what she was saying. She wanted to refuse Vreesar, to deny the fiend all hope, but fear overpowered her. Her own death was too close for her to be brave.

"It can be opened again! It must!" The fiendish creature hissed in frustration. "How?" Its claw tips pressed into her shoulders.

"I don't know," Martine gasped, her knees starting to buckle as the pain of unhealed wounds flared beneath the creature's talons.

With the flick of a clawed finger, Vreesar sliced a ribbon of red across her cheek. "Tell me or I cut more."

The cut's burning sting made bitter tears well in her eyes. Were she uninjured, it would have been a small matter, but now the cut added far more than it should have to her ledger of pain. "I was never told." The ranger could barely gasp the words out.

"Uselezz!" Vreesar flung the shaken woman to the ground like a rag doll. Martine clutched the cold earth, relieved to still be alive, her body weak from the questioning.

Vreesar angrily turned to Krote. The shaman was still crouched at the very forefront of his people, intently watching the interrogation. His eyes took in every detail as his mind calculated the strengths and weaknesses of the tribe's new chieftain.

"Did she have anything when you found her, shaman?"

"Only that"—Krote pointed to Martine's leather backpack in the dirt—"and a sword. It was of no value."

The hells it was, Martine thought in the midst of her fog of pain. Her sword was made of good magical steel. She had had to fight a pirate lord for it. From where she lay, the Harper waited for the Word-Maker to point out the stone, but he never did. Perhaps he's forgotten about the rock, she thought hopefully. I can still get it back. Get the stone, escape, and get back to Jazrac—that's all I have to do.

The fiend snatched up her backpack and shook it. When nothing fell out, it tore at the leather bag with its claws and teeth, all the while growling with inarticulate rage. Bits of shredded leather rained on the bare ground. Metal buckles jangled as Vreesar hurled them across the lodge.

"There iz no key here. Where are her other thingz?" The

barbed fiend strode back toward Krote, claws flexing convulsively. Seeing the icy body with the needlelike teeth advance toward them, the gnolls scrambled backward.

"What about the little ones? Maybe they have it," a trembling voice deep in the throng barked out. The suggestion was quickly taken up by other gnolls in the lodge. Belief or truth had little to do with their agreement; all that mattered was diverting the fiend.

"Little onez? Explain, shaman."

"The gnomes, great chieftain. They live to the south, beyond our lands."

"Iz their land warm or cold?"

The question flabbergasted the gnoll. "It's snowy, the same as here, but their valley does not have the tall ice."

"Warm, then," Vreesar calculated, its icy brows tinkling as they knitted. "And they helped the human?"

"Perhaps." Without better knowledge, the Word-Maker wasn't going to commit himself one way or the other.

Martine didn't like the sound of these questions and cursed herself for being helpless.

"Are these gnomes powerful?"

Krote shrugged in puzzlement at Vreesar's question. "I do not know. They are little people and do not raid our land. Some think they are grass-growers and do not know how to hunt."

"Then they are weak."

Krote shook his head firmly. "The stories of the Burnt Fur say the little people are strong in magic. If the stories are true, then they are powerful."

Vreesar cackled, its laugh like shattering icicles. "I am magic. I am powerful. The little snow people are nothing, like mephitz, like Icy-White. If that iz all they have, they will be easy to destroy. We will attack them." The fiend glared at the gnolls huddled near the fire pit, waiting for any to speak out against the plan. The frigid creature's gaze was a fierce challenge none of the dog-men dared accept, and their silence signaled their acceptance.

It's only a boast, Martine hoped as she heard Vreesar's proclamation. It was bad to have let the fiend escape the rift. The attack on the Vani would be yet another black mark against her in the eyes of the Harpers. If a single one of these creatures could create such chaos, Martine knew she could never allow hordes of Vreesar's kin to enter into the world. While the fiend ranted its threats and schemes, the Harper slid stealthily across the floor, moving in tiny increments toward Jazrac's precious stone.

Krote's ears flared at Vreesar's declaration, his eyes suddenly darkening. Standing up to his full height until he almost looked the fiend eye-to-eye, the shaman alone rose to the challenge of Vreesar's words. "Chieftain, we are one tribe. If we fight the people of the snow, many of our warriors will die, even with you to lead us. The little people have strong homes, dug into the dirt like the dens of foxex. The old songs called them fierce like the badger."

"What iz badger?" The shaman's point was lost on the otherworldly creature.

"A demon of the forest," Krote explained. "The badger is small but fears no one, not even bears. The gnomes to the south are said to have badger blood in their veins."

"No creature fightz more fiercely than Vreesar," the fiend hissed.

Krote still wasn't ready to relent. "And if Brokka is killed, who will take his mates and find game for his kits? Or Varka? Or Split-Ear? Attack the little people and many mates will howl for their dead warriors."

"That iz the way of femalez," the fiend droned unconcernedly.

Martine froze as the elemental turned to resume its place on the dais. She could only silently pray that it hadn't noticed that she had crept halfway to the wall, or if it did, that it thought nothing of it.

"Great chieftain, it will take our warriors much time to attack the people of the snow," Word-Maker hastily pressed as he tried yet another tack to dissuade the fiend from its plan. Martine almost believed the gnoll was trying to distract the fiend's attention. If that was so, he was succeeding admirably, for the elemental wheeled about, its icy joints clicking as it moved.

Krote stepped forward to face the fiend. Though the gnoll was gaunt and tall, the fiend was even taller and thinner. The bones and antlers that hung from the arches tangled with the hairlike barbs on its head.

"The winter is hard," Krote insisted. "There is little food in the lodges. Our warriors must hunt to feed our kits, or they will starve. We must wait for the snows to melt."

Vreesar turned upon the shaman and hissed, "Wait? No . . . the ice makez the warriorz strong. They will attack now."

"But what about the females?"

"They will fight, too, or starve. Femalez fight! Young onez fight. All of them!" the fiend buzzed furiously through clenched, needlelike teeth. "Give the femalez swordz and the young onez knivez. Everybody fightz. All of the Burnt Fur must fight!"

A murmur rippled through the assembled gnolls. Voices raised in both eagerness and fear. Though loath to concede it, Martine was impressed that the shaman stood his ground, refusing to give in to the fiend. They were still distracted, and she inched forward.

"You will kill the tribe," Krote predicted. He clutched the icon that hung from his neck. "This is not the will—"

Krote's words ended in the snap of his jaw as the elemental swung one lanky arm in a lashing backhand. The shaman's head whiplashed to the side as he reeled backward for three steps before his legs half-buckled and he dropped to one knee.

The creature didn't press its attack but stood watching the gnoll. "I am the chieftain and not an imp of the godz, like you, shaman. Do you challenge me?"

Krote's lips rolled back to bare his fighting fangs, and the shaman tensed for the attack. Like all the others in the lodge, Martine was certain bloodshed was imminent. Word-Maker's's flattened ears twitched eagerly. A low growl rumbled in his throat as the hackles on his neck rose.

The lodge came alive with an undulating buzz. "Attack me," the fiend taunted in soft whispers. Even as it spoke, the creature gouged long furrows in the dirt floor.

Then the moment passed, and Krote slowly lowered his head in submission.

"Good," Vreesar breathed, making no effort to conceal its disappointment. "No more challengez." It turned away from the gnoll and stood over the sprawled Harper. "No escaping either," it said, noting her movements, then kicked her in the side to emphasize the point. Her body collapsed into the dirt, leaving Martine clutching at her ribs while her breath came in sharp bursts.

"Hot Breath, you have friendz in thiz valley of little people? Family? Are you ready to see them die?" The fiend squatted beside her, tilting its head owlishly to meet her tear-filled gaze.

"I know no one there," Martine gasped.

The fiend grinned brittlely as it knelt close to her. "Perhapz you lie again. Tell me where the key iz, or I will lead my people there and kill them all."

"There is no key."

"There iz alwayz a key. Every door haz a key," the fiend insisted, "and you know where it iz. Tell me. Think of your friendz, the gnomes. I will kill them unless you tell me."

"I don't have the key." That, at least, wasn't a lie.

"So there iz a key! Where iz it?"

Martine winced at her blunder. She had just removed

one uncertainty for the fiend. If she told Vreesar the truth
—which she could not—the creature would kill her. If she
resisted, it could just as easily kill her in a rage.

"I'll never tell you," she swore bitterly. She braced herself
for another onslaught.

"Oh, yez, you will, human," Vreesar droned soothingly. It
seemed as if the fiend had suddenly lost interest in her.
"Shaman, take my human away."

As she was taken from the lodge, the Harper couldn't
resist a wistful glance at the stone. The ranger stopped the
instant she noticed Krote watching, but by that time it was
too late. The shaman had already taken note. If he didn't
know now, the ranger was certain Krote would quickly figure it out.

Outside, Word-Maker shoved her toward the small
lodge. Martine was so exhausted she barely noticed when
they arrived at her crude prison. Once inside, the woman
collapsed onto the furs, ready to surrender to sleep. Krote
had other ideas, though. With a firm touch, he pressed his
thick-padded hand against her side, seeking out the broken
rib.

"What are you doing?" Her words were groggy, confused.

"Healing you." The shaman waved a primitive icon over
her side. "You must not die when the thing questions you."

Now the Harper was truly confused. Was this an act of
kindness, or was it a cruel desire to prolong her suffering?
"Why?"

Without pausing, the gnoll explained. "You are from the
warm lands, where humans live, and know many things
about them. You must not die before teaching me these
things. Remain still." Krote didn't wait for her to respond,
but began chanting the words to his spell, the same one he
had used before on her wounded shoulder. Once again a
warmth pervaded her from his hands, flowing into her

body. Deep inside, her body twitched in response. Suddenly intense pain shot through her ribs. She writhed in agony, but the gnoll fiercely pressed her down. Martine bit her lip, determined not to scream.

Almost as swiftly as it came upon her, the pain washed away, leaving her feeling stronger and more vigorous than before. The exhaustion that had afflicted her had disappeared, as if she'd had a full day or more of rest.

Krote carefully hung the icon back around his neck. "Now teach me, human," he insisted as he sat crosslegged on the opposite side of the hut.

"Teach you what?" Martine sat up, wary of the gnoll and perplexed at the same time.

From a leather pouch, the gnoll dug out a roll of birchbark. "Teach me the symbols," he demanded as he tossed the scroll over to her. "You made it. What does it mean?"

Martine recognized what it was as soon as Krote produced it. It was the letter she'd written in desperation to Jazrac. There could be no doubt now that it had gone unread.

"What is it?" the Word-Maker demanded.

"It's called writing," Martine explained. In nearly any other circumstances, Martine would have been incredulous to discover someone completely ignorant of writing. Many folks throughout the Realms couldn't read, but at least they were aware of letters and words. The shaman apparently didn't even comprehend what they were.

"It's like speaking on paper," she continued. Her explanation couldn't compromise her mission, nor could she believe that teaching the gnoll writing would threaten anyone, either herself or the gnomes of Samek. But it *could* gain her an ally in the tribe, an ally who might prove useful later. Furthermore, she saw an opportunity that she might be able to get a message off to Jazrac after all. All she needed to do was trick Krote into using the bone-handled knife.

Unrolling the brittle sheet of bark, she began the lesson. Slowly and carefully she played the role of tutor, a part she wasn't particularly suited for. It took more verbal skill and patience than she had to explain the mysteries of writing.

Fortunately for her, the title Word-Maker was no misnomer for Krote. She was impressed by the gnoll's quick mind and prodigious memory. He could watch her make the strokes of a letter with a piece of charcoal and repeat them perfectly.

Martine decided to take a chance. Pushing a smooth split log in front of the gnoll, she said, "Carve what I show you. Then you can practice on your own."

Martine knew it was a gamble and tried not to show her eagerness. Her heart leaped as Krote drew Jazrac's knife and held it ready to carve.

"All right. Copy this," Martine instructed as she smoothed out a piece of leather. Carefully she drew the symbols in a neat row for Krote to copy. "These are all different letters you can practice later. Just do them in this order when you do."

With a generous smile, she slid the leather to Krote. In neat block letters, it said, "CAPTURED BY GNOLS. M."

"You must teach me more," the shaman insisted, not ready to stop.

Martine shook her head. "You must practice—like a young cub learning to shoot a bow. Then I will teach you more." The whole success of her plan hinged on the shaman carving the message for her. And while he was doing that, she could plan her escape.

"I will practice," the shaman said with reluctance as he rolled up the leather. "Remember, you must not die when our new chieftain questions you." Martine was sure she heard a note of distaste in the shaman's words when he said "new chieftain."

"I have no intention of dying, Word-Maker," she assured

him as the gnoll left the hut.

Martine flopped back onto the flea-infested furs as all the tension drained out of her body. "Tymora be praised!" she sighed. She'd done it. She'd tricked the Word-Maker into sending her message. It hadn't been easy. Now she could only hope that Jazrac looked into his crystal ball at the right time and understood what he saw. Too much still hinged on luck for her to feel secure.

I have to escape soon or I'll be dead, she thought frankly.

Eight

Martine was grateful for the wakefulness Krote's spell provided. It was the first time her head had felt clear since the one called Brokka had brought her down from the glacier. She needed a clear head if she was going to escape.

Carefully the ranger peered through a crack in the door curtain and looked out onto the white clearing beyond. Immediately alongside the entrance was the thick-furred leg of a guard. The leg was at an odd angle, and the ranger guessed the gnoll was bored and leaning on his spear. She slid away from the entrance, trying not to reveal that she'd been spying. The guard would be a problem, though the fact that he was probably bored might help.

The first thing is to get together a survival kit . . . anything that can help me stay alive once I get away, she thought. Unless I can survive in the snow, there's no point in even trying to escape. Whatever I can scrape together in this lodge will have to do.

The Harper fell to searching the birch-bark hut as quietly as she could. She set aside anything potentially useful, whenever possible hiding it under the furs of her mattress. There was precious little, but it was still better than nothing at all. By the time she was done, her hoard consisted of several sharp pieces of bone, a long fire-hardened stick that she could sharpen to a point, a leather pouch stuffed with tinder, a gourd dipper she could rig up as a firepot, and the flea-infested but warm furs she was sitting on. Working carefully so as not to bring the lodge down upon her, the ranger undid some of the bindings that lashed the frame of the hut together. The cords were made of strong sinew. Stretched between her hands, it would make a crude but effective garrote.

Martine meticulously rolled and tied the items into a bundle, pleased with her luck. Her finds provided more than she expected—crude weapons, fire, and shelter. What remained were food and a better weapon, but as a prisoner, the woman doubted she'd be able to get her hands on these.

There was still the matter of the guard outside, and once she was past him, the rest of the tribe. If she had a knife, she reasoned, then she could cut her way out the back of the lodge, but a few experiments showed the wall was too firmly built for her to cut through with her crude bone tools. If she was going to get out, it would have to be through the front door.

With her sharp stick in hand and escape kit within reach, there was nothing for Martine to do but huddle by the door and wait. She waited as her fire, lacking more wood, died away to a ruddy bed of coals that warmed the hut but provided little light. She waited as the sun traveled across the sky till it slowly gave way to the mountain shadows that preceded night. She waited as the magical vigor faded from her nerves and her stomach started to knot with hunger.

Finally she allowed herself to doze, trusting her senses to wake her should any opportunity arise.

Perhaps her instincts failed her, or perhaps nothing happened, for the next thing she knew, the thin light of morning was seeping through the gap around the curtain. She heard voices shouting outside. Her legs were knotted from sitting all night, she discovered when she unwound herself to peer through the crack.

Across the clearing, the main lodge was the heart of pandemonium. Gnolls tumbled from the longhouse, shouldering each other aside in a savage rush to escape from something inside. Their shouts, barks, and howls quickly alerted the rest of the village. From every hut, close and distant, warriors snatched up spears and sprinted toward the commotion. The guard outside her hut wavered, torn between the conflicting courses of duty as guard and warrior. The beast's hesitant steps toward the fray gave Martine hope, and she quietly tucked her bundle under her arm in preparation to make a dash for freedom.

Before the guard could reach a decision, a furry figure hurtled through the great lodge's doorway and crashed against the backs of the slowest sprinters. Thundering after it came Vreesar, barely able to squeeze through the narrow doorway. Its chest was mottled with a ghastly pinkish stain, livid on its silvery whiteness like a fresh scar.

"Where iz the whelp who burned me?" With long, cold arms, Vreesar sifted through the terrified gnolls, seizing those closest to it, only to cast them aside once it was satisfied they were not its prey. Even at the distance between the two lodges, Martine could see the fiend's ice-spined brow tremble and twitch with fury. Abruptly it lunged forward and caught something with a triumphant cry. "Ahhh! You would try to kill me? Who told you to do thiz?"

The elemental hoisted aloft a squirming gnoll, not much older than a kit, judging by its size. Vreesar's chilling claws encircled the gnoll's neck tightly, but the fiend took sadistic care not to squeeze its prize so tightly that its struggling ceased.

"You burned me. Now you will freeze. That iz your punish—"

"Lord of the Burnt Fur, it is our custom that a chieftain does not kill warriors," Krote Word-Maker interrupted boldly, almost shouting to be heard over the din. Standing in the dark doorway of the main lodge, the shaman had only just appeared on the scene. Like one accustomed to enforcing the burden of tribal memory, the Word-Maker spoke with the absolute certainty of tradition. His words silenced the gathered warriors as they expectantly awaited the outcome.

Vreesar peered back over its shoulder and stabbed the shaman with an incensed glare. "What do I care for your customz?" it crackled.

The gnoll snapped his fangs in surprise that anyone, even a thing as alien as the elemental, should ask such a question. "That is what makes us the Burnt Fur," he replied, his tone one of horrified amazement. "Great chieftain, without the laws, the right ways of doing things, we would be no more than—than the wolves of the forest. The old ways made you chieftain. If custom is not followed, then you will not be our chieftain."

"Fear makez me chief," Vreesar snarled evilly. The prisoner's kicks grew weaker and weaker. "What do I care for thiz weak tribe'z customz? You are my slavez. Thiz pathetic creature tried to kill me, and az hiz master, I can kill him if I choose."

Whether from bravery or foolishness, Krote stepped forward to stand directly in front of the chieftain. "Only if there is a duel. That is the correct way." He spoke in a soft voice that the wind barely carried to Martine. "It was an accident. The kit did not mean to spill his soup on you. Spare his life, and the kit will die willingly for you in battle."

The fiend paused as if considering Krote's words, although at her distance Martine could not read any expression into the creature's face. The Word-Maker stepped back a pace, trying to ease the tension of the scene.

"You are right, Word-Maker. The kit will die—but not willingly." The elemental clenched its hand more tightly. The young gnoll convulsed in a single twitching spasm as its larynx and vertebrae were crushed with a series of thick, meaty popping sounds that echoed over the silent clearing. Martine had heard that sound before, many years ago in the port city of Westgate, when a mob had hanged a pair of suspected thieves. Like those hanged men, the gnoll's jerky struggles lasted longer than its life, the muscles flailing long after the mind had ceased to control them.

As if the dead body were no more than a soiled rag, Vreesar let the corpse drop. "My slavez will not be clumsy," it hummed. Of all the warriors, females, and kits gathered before the longhouse, the elemental ignored them all save one—Krote, who still stood directly facing the creature. The Word-Maker was rigid with outrage.

Martine could read in the gnoll's flattened ears and curled lips the warnings of a dog about to fight. So intent had she been on the confrontation that it came as a surprise when she suddenly noticed that she was alone. Her guard had vanished, apparently joining the onlookers who circled the pair. The ranger needed no more prompting. Grabbing up her bundle, she wriggled through the door and immediately sprinted for the woods. Having already failed once because she had been too cautious, she decided now to act boldly and trust Tymora's wheel. By its spin, she'd either make it or be captured once more.

"Word-Maker!" The elemental's shrill cry made the Harper's heart drop, for in that moment, she was certain her flight had been discovered. Panic forced her to increase her speed.

I've got to reach the woods before them. I'll be safe there. Martine knew her skills as a ranger would serve her well in the forest. The forest would become an ally. She knew how to travel without leaving a clear trail, how to conceal herself in the shadowed spaces between the trees.

"Word-Maker!" Vreesar shrilled again, its buzz keening like a furiously spun grindstone. "Do not defy me!"

Even as she sprinted across the last bit of open ground, Martine breathed a sigh of relief, for behind her the drama had not played out as she had feared. The onlookers would still be watching, her guard still away from his post, and her escape might yet go unnoticed.

There was a jumble of voices behind her, none of which Martine could hear clearly, and then Vreesar's stinging drone once more pierced the clamor. "I do not care for your advice or your customz, Word-Maker. Get out of my sight before I kill you, too. Hide in your hut, weak one. Do not come into thiz hall again!"

The elemental's orders gave Martine very little time. If Krote went to the hut, he was sure to discover her escape. Nonetheless, at the very edge of the clearing, the Harper deliberately veered from her course. The shelter of the thickets beckoned to her, but the woman resisted plunging through the unbroken snow. Just ahead was what she sought, a well-used trail that wound through the woods. Her plan, quickly formed, was to follow it until she was well away from the village and then strike out on her own. With luck, she'd hide her own escape route among the footprints of her captors.

At the entrance to the pine forest, she paused to scan for pursuers. Success hinged on secrecy, and if she had been discovered, the ranger wanted to know now. There were no gnolls in sight. She didn't wait for the cry of pursuit. Turn-

ing onto the path, she plunged into the welcome gloom of
the winter forest. The trail almost instantly twisted out of
sight of the camp, bending past tall pines, birch thickets,
and the bare canes of last summer's berry bushes.

The temperature was frigid, whipped colder by the
strong winds that swirled through the trees. She welcomed
the wind, though, for the fine powder it swept along with it
would quickly drift over the trail, making it harder to distinguish her tracks from all the others. Without weapons,
food, or proper gear, Martine needed every advantage possible. Even though the snow was fairly well packed, following the trail was arduous without skis or snowshoes. It
didn't take long before the cold was forgotten. Sweat
worked into the thick weave of her clothes, where it froze,
making her legs and arms crackle with each step.

A half-mile along the trail, perhaps more, the ranger
heard the first sounds of alarm. A series of baying howls,
like jackals calling together the pack for a hunt, drifted
through the woods. In the silence of the forest, the voices
of the gnolls were unmistakable from the hoots of the owls
or even the occasional call of a lone wolf.

Maybe they won't find the trail right away, Martine
thought as she ran. No, wishful thinking like that gets
people killed, her warrior instincts reminded her. They'll
find my path soon enough. It's time to get off the trail.

With that in mind, Martine stayed on the path until it
skirted a granite upthrust, one of many that marked the
lower slopes of the surrounding mountains. The weathered
stones rose from the undulating snow in a series of spires,
tilted and tumbled to form irregular terraces. Few trees
grew around the base, leaving a windswept area where the
snow had thawed and frozen with each sunny day until the
snow was a hard crust of wind-rippled ice.

It was the perfect place, since she would leave no tracks
on the hard bare ice, so Martine abandoned the trail and

clambered over the rock, taking care to avoid the patches of snow that clung to the cracked stone. Slipping through a cleft in the spires, she came out on the back side of the out-cropping. There she waited, crouched in the lee of the stone, screened from the wind-driven snow, listening to the brutal squawks of the ravens answered by the titters of the chickadees. Already her fingers were cold and her feet numb inside her fur-wrapped boots, but her patience was at last rewarded when she heard the barking voices of gnolls nearby. The hunters were on the trail.

She set off into the deep snow, this time heading back toward the gnoll village. Martine knew she didn't have to leave the rocks. She knew she didn't have to go back. She could have turned her footsteps south and made for the pass to Samek. Still she slogged through the drifts that coiled around the pine trunks, always taking care to stay in the deep woods, well away from any trails.

Duty drove her back.

Jazrac's key was still in the village, against the wall in the main lodge, and she had to go back and get it. It's my duty as a Harper, she thought. That's what Jazrac or Khelben or any of the others would tell me. I'll never be a true Harper if I'm afraid to go back. I'll have failed, and they'll all know it. I have to go back.

It's all part of a plan, she convinced herself. First I lure the gnolls out of their village, then I slip behind them, get the stone, and escape. They'll never find me, because I'll be behind them. It's a brilliant plan—or is it? Martine didn't know, couldn't know, until it either succeeded or failed.

Using the sun and a few landmarks she had noted, Martine backtracked slowly. The voices of the gnolls grew louder until she was certain they were just off her left flank. The huntress took shelter in a thicket until they passed and the voices had faded farther up the trail.

When their barked commands were no more than dim

echoes, Martine angled back onto the trail. It was a risk. There might be a straggler or even a second search party, but she needed to make better speed. Breaking trail through the deep snow was exhausting her, and that was a condition she couldn't risk, especially without food. With exhaustion would come uncontrollable shivering, then frostbite, collapse, and a dreamlike death as the cold overcame her. As a precaution, she found a stout branch. Swung with two hands it would make a fair club—the crudest of weapons, but a weapon and therefore useful.

As she trudged along the trail and read the signs of her pursuers, Martine caught a flash of movement off to her left. As quickly as she could focus her vision on the spot, the shape vanished, leaving only the glimpse of a burly, stoop-shouldered shadow. A gnoll? She couldn't be sure. It could be a bear, or even a change in shadow as clouds drifted across the sun. Hefting her cudgel, the ranger slowly approached the spot where she had sighted it, silently picking her way from shadow to shadow.

Ten feet and several moments later, a gnoll suddenly stepped from behind a tree trunk, sword drawn but oblivious to her presence. With a great roundhouse swing, Martine smashed her stick against the side of the creature's head and was rewarded with the metallic twang of wood cracking against a helm. Her cudgel split with the force of her blow, and the jolt rang down through her arms. The gnoll dropped like a felled ox.

Martine sprang astraddle the body, doubting that she'd killed her foe. With numb hands, she fumbled in the snow to recover the dropped sword. Stepping clear, she pressed the blade to the gnoll's throat just as the creature began to stir.

"What . . . what happened?" the gnoll groaned, and the Harper instantly recognized the voice. By some capricious whim of Lady Tymora, it was the Word-Maker who lay sprawled before her. A trickle of blood soaked the fur that stuck out from beneath his helm, but the wound didn't appear to be serious.

"Lie on your back, arms up, hands together," Martine ordered, all the while smiling in grim amusement at this sudden reversal of their situations. The shaman groggily complied, and she quickly bound his wrists with some of the sinew she had salvaged from the hut. "Not one sound," she ordered next, sword still held at his throat.

Krote obeyed, clearheaded enough to recognize the peril of his situation. She began searching him for other weapons.

"Why are you here?" the shaman asked in a whisper. With the blade held close to his jugular, he took care not to alarm his captor.

"The rock . . . the one in my gear. I need it. Is it still in the lodge?"

His answer was a choked laugh. Before she could demand what was so funny, her hands patted a hard lump in one of the shaman's pouches. Quickly she opened it and pulled out the familiar reddish cinder that was Jazrac's stone. In the same pouch, she discovered the wizard's bone-handled knife.

"I knew you wanted it, so I took it," Krote explained, grinning. "Am I right? Is the rock why you came back? It is the thing Vreesar seeks, true? The way back to his home?"

"Get up," she ordered abruptly, ignoring his questions. The discovery of the rock and the knife eliminated the need for several steps in her plan, but now it left her with a new problem. She couldn't leave the Word-Maker behind. Already the shaman had correctly guessed too much. Vreesar would almost certainly learn the truth from the gnoll. Nor could Martine bring herself to kill the shaman now that she'd caught him. The practical solution was too cold-blooded for her to stomach.

Like it or not, I've got myself a prisoner, she thought ruefully.

"Move," the ranger snapped, furious with the situation, herself, and her ever-present sense of right and wrong. Once more she doubled back, this time turning in the direction of Samek. Dragging along Krote as a prisoner didn't improve her chances of reaching the gnomes safely. She doubted he'd be of much value as a hostage, and there was every chance the gnoll would betray her at the first opportunity.

With the shaman in the lead, the pair followed the gnoll trail once more, traveling the same direction as she had before. It was a good plan. Certainly any tracker would be confused, although there was considerable risk that they might run into the returning gnolls. Knowing these things did nothing to lessen her nerves, which were as jittery as a rabbit's.

They reached the granite outcropping that marked the place where she had begun to backtrack. Kneeling, Martine examined the trail she had not taken. It was with some relief that she noted the tracks of the hunting party continued on. They missed my backtrack, she thought, pleased with herself even though she knew they might return at any time.

Leaving the trail once more, the Harper guided her prisoner over the ice and rocks, rousing the dark ravens from their roosts. As before, she used the hard surfaces of granite and ice to make their trail disappear, although this time she did not backtrack toward the village but instead headed south toward the dark saddleback ridge that was the pass to Samek.

Descending from the rocky ledges, Martine plunged into the darkest heart of the woods. At sword point, she forced Krote to plow through drifts that sometimes reached well beyond his knees. There was no hiding their trail now, should her pursuers somehow find it. Speed was all-important, and the race was against cold and exhaustion as much as those who hunted for her.

The forest here was virgin pine, the kind cut elsewhere for their long, straight logs. The Harper doubted that any axe had ever touched most of this wood, for the trees were incredibly tall and barren except for bursts of needled boughs near the top. The drab green canopy was laden with snow, casting the forest floor into a perpetual quasi-twilight.

Their journey wasn't easy. The snow ranged from shallow to deep as it drifted around the tree trunks. Frequently brambles conspired to block the way, and steep ravines stood in their path at several points. Massive deadfalls, where several trees had fallen in a single storm, created impassable snarls that could only be bypassed. All around these falls, uprooted pines leaned perilously on their neighbors. The woods softly resounded to the creaking trunks and the dismal hiss of the wind. Ravens spoke of their passage, the birds' harsh voices ringing far through the mute woods.

Although Martine was born to the outdoors and knew it well, this forest was different from others she was familiar with. The endless tracts of pine were not like the woods of oak and elm in Sembia and the Dalelands. The forest here was tall, muffled, and cold.

A feeling of dark watchfulness tingled at the back of Martine's neck, and she knew it was the spirit of the forest. Others, townsfolk and farmers, never felt it. That sense was knowledge only true woodsmen knew by the way the wind rustled the leaves, the direction the water flowed, or even how a rabbit left its tracks. This forest's spirit was ungenerous and unforgiving, barely tolerant of intruders. Martine didn't feel any warmth in these woods like those of her homeland.

Exhausted, the Harper finally called a stop as she leaned,

perspiring in the chill, against the trunk of a tree. Krote squatted, his jaw slack and tongue hanging as he panted clouds of frost, almost as spent as she and glad for the rest.

"You do not need to threaten me with the sword. I will not escape," the shaman finally growled as he brushed snow from his dirty bindings.

Martine thought she heard an edge of bitter irritation in his voice. "Why not?" she asked doubtfully.

"I cannot go back."

"Why not?" It seemed all she could manage to say.

Krote's lips curled in a snarl. "Vreesar banished me. If I go back, I die."

"I heard him bar you from his lodge. That's not banishment." Martine poked her sword at the snowbank, carving little holes near the gnoll.

"Lodge and tribe are one."

"How come he didn't kill you? He killed Hakk and that other gnoll."

Krote waggled an ear at her words. "You saw that, human? I live because even Vreesar fears the gods." Krote jangled the charm that hung around his neck. "Kill me and you anger Gorellik, the god of my people."

That was enough talk for Martine. She didn't like the implied threat in the shaman's words, and so with a rough shove of her foot, she got the gnoll back on his feet.

For the next hour, the woman plodded in silence. It took all her effort just to keep her attention on the trek, and she had no desire to talk through her cold-burnt throat. The path became even harder to follow as dusk fell, the thick shadows hiding jarring bumps and holes. Her leg muscles were beyond aching, numb with incessant pain. Sweat weighted her clothes. Even with the growing cold of nightfall, she drove them on by moonlight. Moonlight was almost a euphemism, silver Selune not yet even half full and barely penetrating through the black-needled boughs. Silver rivers ran through the trees, broken by black rapids of bare rock and exposed moss.

Martine had no idea how many hours or days it had been since starting when she finally called their march to a halt. Krote, exhausted as well, stood still among the dimly lit trees. "If we stop, we freeze," he warned grimly.

Freezing almost seemed appealing to Martine, but the gnoll was right. They needed protection from the night cold.

"We'll dig a shelter," she said, pointing to a large snow-bank at the base of a bluff. She began to scoop away handfuls of snow. Krote did not resist or argue but mutely held up his bound hands for her to cut them free.

In a short time, the two had tunneled out a chamber—a tomb fit for an ice queen, Martine felt—barely big enough for them to lie down in. "This is where we sleep," the woman explained as she re-bound the gnoll's wrists. She didn't have enough cord to tie his ankles, so she could only rely on common sense and trust. "If you run away, you'll freeze in the cold. If you kill me, you'll freeze here. Understand?"

The Word-Maker nodded. "And if you kill me, human, you freeze. This night we need each other."

Martine nodded, her sore shoulders screaming at even that slight turn of the head. With tinder and Jazrac's knife, Martine kindled a tiny fire in the entrance that barely warmed them.

Dinner consisted of moss and tender bark, the best the ranger could gather in the snow. Normally she wouldn't have bothered, but her captivity had left her starving. Krote was not that desperate and so only watched her eat.

"Inside," Martine said after the unappetizing repast. As the gnoll squeezed in through the entrance, Martine gave one last look skyward. Selûne's Tears, a waft of star motes that hung off the crescent hook of the butterfat moon, weaved through the sparse branches of the wind-blasted pines along the cliff face. The sky was clear and bitter. Night birds lurking in the icebound woods called to any listening ear, speaking to each other of their might and wisdom. Something, a breeze or a small beast, snuffled beyond the rim of light. The night forest excited her; even here, it was a world she understood and loved, more so than the timid towns and villages she had sworn to defend as a Harper.

A grunt from Krote broke the mood. Drawn back from her reverie, the Harper numbly crawled inside, taking care to keep her sword ready. Now came the time when she had no choice but to trust the shaman. Trust out of necessity did not come easy.

In the near darkness, the Word-Maker had twisted and squirmed his rude bed closer to the ice-sheened wall, distancing himself from Martine's space. Even so, the two, woman and gnoll, were still pressed tight to each other. Martine placed her drawn sword along the wall, just in case. Only exhaustion would grant her any rest tonight.

As she lay in the darkness, the ground chill insinuated its way through the layers of her leather parka, into its sweat-matted fur lining, through torn and stained clothes, past skin, until it reached muscle and bone. Martine could feel it creep through her body. The cold wanted to kill her, to stalk down the warmth within her and leech it into the snow until she was left an ice-filled husk. In the near darkness, these thoughts obsessed the woman. She had camped in the woods as much as she had lived indoors, but never could she remember a night so hostile.

"Gods, I'm freezing," she chattered softly.

"So am I," her companion answered unexpectedly from the darkness.

Tentatively the pair inched closer to each other. Neither wanted to get close to the other, but they needed each other's warmth. Finally their bodies huddled together. The gnoll stank, and where his fur poked through, it scratched her, but the contact kept the cold at bay. Finally the Harper drifted into a dim semblance of sleep.

When the cave walls began to glow autumnal gold, Martine at first dismissed it as another waking dream. The light persisted, until she finally realized it was no fantasy. Wriggling through the narrow entrance, she gratefully drew in a lungful of clear morning air. Accustomed to the den, she had forgotten just how thick, rank, and humid the snow cave was until she was outside of it.

It was incredibly bright outside, the kind of brightness that comes when all the moisture has been frozen out of the air, allowing the sun's rays to burn unhampered onto the ice-sheeted ground, where the sunlight reflects back up and for a brief moment crosses itself to intensify the glare. On such mornings, it seems as though the whole world has risen up from an ocean of light.

Retrieving her sword, the Harper tugged on the Word-Maker's boot until the gnoll finally woke. She had expected the shaman to wake quick and alert, as matched the feral reputation of gnolls, but Krote, it seemed, was a terrible sluggard. Only after a fair amount of growling was she able to get the gnoll outdoors.

"Why get up? It was warm in the cave," the shaman grumbled as he suppressed a yawn.

"I want to cross the pass before noon. Once we're in Samek, we should be able to find a farm or something." Martine was already stowing her bundle for the journey.

"What will happen to me? The little people are not friendly." As he spoke, Krote held his wrists up, asking to be unbound. Catching the suspicious look in her eye, he added with an angry snarl, "Wrists hurt. I could have killed you in the cave."

Martine drew the bone-handled knife and absentmindedly stroked the blade as she considered the gnoll's request. "Your oath, shaman. I cut you loose and you come with me. No tricks."

"So you give me to the little people?" he snorted.

"You're my prisoner. The Vani won't hurt you."

"Your oath, human?"

"By the blood of my family."

"That is good. I give you my oath, human—but only until we reach your valley."

"Only if you swear by Gorellik, your god." Martine bit her lip.

Krote scowled. Martine was getting better at reading the gnoll's expressions. "Gorellik sees all and knows Krote gives his word. We will travel in peace, Martine of Sembia."

"Praise to Mielikki," Martine added, beseeching in her heart the blessing of the Lady of the Forest. It might mean everything or it might mean nothing, but Martine instinctively believed the Word-Maker's oath to be valuable. Now that she had it, the Harper cut the bonds with some sense of confidence.

The pair started the day's march without delay. To an untrained eye, it would have seemed as if they were traveling through more of the same as yesterday—the same gray pines, the same dazzling whiteness, the same rocks, the same streams—but to Martine's practiced eye, there were important differences. Gradually the pines no longer grew as high and the brooks gurgled with less water, both clear signs that they had begun the climb up the pass. The snow was deeper, too. Krote waded on through drifts up to his waist, drifts whose smooth tops came as high as the smaller ranger's chest. Woodpecker drills echoed through the woods while the squawks of the ravens grew less frequent. Overhead, an eagle circled a nearby meadow, patiently waiting for a marmot or a field mouse.

By midmorning, Martine's hope was revived. There was

no doubt they would clear the ridge today. At worst, it would be one, perhaps two more days before they reached the Vani warren. The prospect of rest and hot food renewed her flagging energy.

The huntress was waiting, feet stomping impatiently, as Krote crossed a fallen tree spanning a frozen stream. Just when the gnoll was halfway across, six small shadows stepped from the thickets that lined the far bank. Their spears were ready, their bows drawn. Unarmed and exposed, Krote froze on the log bridge as his muzzle flared and his ears stiffened straight back, ready for a fight.

The six small shadows were short and stocky—Vani gnomes. The grins of their successful ambush played across their faces.

"Don't hurt him!" Martine yelled as they sprang onto the slick log. "He's my prisoner!"

Nine

"Hold! Don't harm him!" rang Vil's bass voice from the woods.

Martine wavered with uncertain relief. Am I saved? Can I stop struggling and sleep? Her exhausted mind was too befuddled to do more than vaguely imagine the reality before her. She fought back the sudden flood of exhaustion that came with trying to comprehend.

Dumbly the Harper scanned her rescuers, staring at them like mirages. She thought she identified Jouka Tunkelo's belligerent scowl, although it was hard for her to see clearly enough. Ice crusted around her eyes, and her pupils burned from hours in the brilliant snow. The blurry faces of the gnomes were little more than thick stockings, black bristling beards, and slitted wooden goggles that shut out the glare of the snow.

"Four days . . . I told you, Martine." The thicket rustled and cracked as Vil stepped through the center of the Vani line. Seeing her, he stopped abruptly. "By Torm, what happened?"

"Avalanche . . . Vreesar . . . gnolls . . . cold." The jerky words were clear to her, her memories filling the gaps between each. The sight of her rescuers drained her of the instinctive fear that had kept her going for the last several days. Suddenly, after days of ordeal, the woman was tired, raw, wet, freezing, thirsty, hungry, and more things than her numb mind could comprehend. "I'm . . . alive," she croaked even as she wavered.

"Don't hurt Krote. I gave my word." As if her will had kept her standing long enough to say that, the ranger's legs gave out from under her and consciousness slid away into a dream.

There was a faint feeling, deep in the core of Martine's body, that she was flying—perhaps ascending to the planes of her ancestors, she thought bemusedly. It ended abruptly in a thump. The landing launched a dull wave of pain that spread throughout her body, transforming the gray haze into turbid and unrestful darkness.

It was warm, wet liquor, strong on caraway and heady alcohol, that revived her. Vilheim Baltson, four days unshaven, knelt over her, carefully forcing a thimbleful of spirits through her lips. The curious faces of gnomes clustered behind him, but Krote was nowhere in sight. She tried to rise to find the gnoll, but the man's firm hand pressed her down.

"Drink," he advised, tipping the small cup to her lips.

Martine sputtered and then let the warmth trickle down her cold-scorched throat. Another thimbleful followed the first. The alcoholic warmth numbed the pain she felt.

"Where's the Word-Maker?" she whispered.

"The gnoll? He's unharmed. Take my word for it. Don't worry."

Martine didn't worry. She knew Vil was good for his word.

"Vreesar's hunting for me." Martine surprised herself,

remembering to warn them about her pursuers.

Vil nodded. "Then we should get going. Drink some more." He pushed the cup into her trembling fingers and then turned to the gnomes behind him. "Master Jouka, the woman cannot ski. Can you build a drag for her? She says there are more gnolls coming."

Martine wanted to correct Vil's error, to tell him that Vreesar wasn't a gnoll, but the words wouldn't form. Soon the forest rang with the bite of axes against wood.

Once the drag was built, Vil helped Martine onto the frame and bundled her in dry blankets, all the time fussing over her wounds. I must be a sight, Martine decided, judging from Vil's concern.

As she was settling into her bed, Krote was dragged into her view. A burly, thick-browed gnome, Ojakangas by name, pulled the shaman along by a rope that bound his wrists. The Vani had given Krote a pair of snowshoes, but other than that, they showed him none of the kindness she had received.

"Move, dog-man," the guard rumbled, jerking the weary gnoll onto the trail. The gnome acted without cruelty or kindness, only a matter-of-fact coldheartedness. The Word-Maker staggered a bit as he followed, but held himself stiff. His pride was fierce and far from broken.

"Treat him well, Vani," Martine croaked fiercely as the gnome and prisoner passed by. "He saved my life."

The gnome started to glare at the human disdainfully, but the passion in her eyes put him off. Chastised, he motioned the gnoll forward and the pair passed out of sight.

Shortly after that, Martine felt the drag lurch from the ground, towed by Vil and a pair of gnomes. Bundled and lashed in, she could only let herself be jounced along as the party began the journey home.

At some other time, the trip would have been too rough

and uncomfortable to sleep, but now was not such a time. The rhythmic swish of skis over snow, the chill in her limbs, and the monotonous parade of green pine branches overhead lulled the Harper to sleep. She had memories of waking several times, though each was barely enough to lift the veil that lay over her consciousness. There was little notable about these brief moments of lucidity—the rattle of a woodpecker as it drilled into a pine, the burn of painful sunlight as they crossed a frozen meadow. There was a brief moment of interest as they passed a Vani farmstead. In her present state, Martine would never have even noticed it had not a pair of their party taken their leave here. The farm was a miniature warren, hidden in a hillock. Its only outward sign was a small door into the mound, hidden within a clump of birches. After brief good-byes and a round of drinks, the trek began once more.

Only a final jolting stop broke her dreamless haze after that. Groggily she became aware of the barely familiar surroundings of Vil's cabin—the hewn log walls, the scent of woodsmoke, and the outline of a tree that arched over the cabin's roof. Bound into the drag, the Harper could only wait impatiently as Vil undid the lacings. Krote was still with them, bound but unhurt, and although the gnoll's pride was certainly wounded, Martine doubted the gnoll had expected any more.

"Vil, is there someplace he can be kept?" Martine wasn't sure it was necessary to treat the shaman as a prisoner, but she also wasn't quite ready to take the chance. Last night in the snow cave had been a matter of survival; now the situation was slightly different.

The former paladin scowled as he undid the last lacing, thinking. "Someplace, yes, but not in my house. The Vani will have to take him."

Now it was Martine's turn to scowl as she considered the wisdom in handing her prisoner over to the gnomes. "How do you know he'll be safe?" she asked softly.

"They're not beasts, woman," Vil rumbled. "If he doesn't provoke them, the Vani won't harm him. You'll have to trust them on this."

The Harper wasn't quite so sure about the gnomes, but she knew she was in no condition to be responsible for a prisoner. "All right, it'll have to do," she said with a nod before turning to the others. "Master Ojakangas, will your people take this prisoner and guard him? You can see that I am in no shape to do so."

The broad gnome nodded. "This was expected," came his taciturn reply.

"You said I would be treated well, human," Krote hissed, furious at being turned over to his enemies. Ojakangas jerked the rope around Krote's wrists, warning him to be silent.

"I said you wouldn't be harmed. You're still my prisoner, Word-Maker." The Harper was too tired to argue the point. Krote would just have to accept whatever happened. "Thank you, Master Ojakangas. Guard him well."

Prevented from killing their enemy, the gnomes, Jouka in particular, set to the task of binding Krote with such relish that Martine worried about their intentions. Still, there seemed to be no effort to seriously mistreat the prisoner, and she said nothing more as she watched the gnomes leave.

Once the Vani were gone, Martine turned and went into the cabin. Her body throbbed; her fingers and face burned as the warmth of the cabin penetrated her frost-kissed skin. Her feet felt leaden and numb, sure signs of encroaching frostbite. Barely four steps inside the cabin, she collapsed in front of the fire and ungracefully fumbled at her boots. When they were both finally off, she thrust her feet as close to the banked coals as she dared. Heels propped up, she shed her improvised cape and pawed at the remains of her parka, peeling away the sweat-stiffened clothes.

"Thank gods we're back!" the ranger said as Vil stomped through the door.

"Thank Torm indeed," Vil wearily agreed. He selected tinder for the coals and quickly had a small, welcome blaze coaxed from the embers. When the fire was lit, he sat on the sooty stone hearth, where he carefully eased off his boots.

"Heat . . . I never thought I'd feel it again," Martine moaned as she lay with icy feet almost in the fire. Tiny curls of steam began to rise from her damp woolen socks. Already her soles were starting to itch and burn as the frostbite was slowly driven out of her toes. Even that pain couldn't keep her awake, though.

An untold time later, the woman surfaced from oblivion surrounded by the startling warmth of a thick comforter. After the comforter, the glimmer of firelight and the gnawing pain of hunger were the things she was most keenly aware of.

I'm dreaming, she thought, staring at the scarred rafters over the bed. It took several minutes to realize she was once more lying in Vil's bed, buried deep in blankets and a faded goose-down comforter. Her host sat at his rickety table whittling curls from a block of wood. "Oh, gods," she gasped as the dull ache of consciousness moved through every muscle in her body. "How long have I been sleeping?"

"All night and the better part of a day," the big man said as he set down his work.

Martine sank back into the featherbed.

"Hungry?"

"Yes!" she blurted. She was famished.

Vil fetched a big bowl of broth and set it carefully in her lap, then remained hovering over her to see if she needed some help eating. Although the spoon was unsteady in her

hand, Martine slowly and deliberately scooped up a few
drops of the broth and greedily slurped it down, determined not to be fed like a child. The soup was fatty and
over-salted but rich nonetheless with the pervading taste of
smoked venison. Chunks of meat and fat and bits of ash
swirled through the murky liquid, and it all tasted wonderful.

Only later, after she'd bathed and changed, did Martine
finally start to feel human again. The gear she'd stored at
Vil's cabin provided clean clothes, and after a quick inspection of her ragged parka, she decided the best course was
to burn it. The tears in the leather were impossible to
patch, and she saw black specks moving in the fur trim—
fleas, no doubt. The former paladin rummaged up a coat to
replace hers. It was more than a little large, but serviceable
with some alterations.

With a sheet of foolscap and her writing kit, the Harper
sat at the table. Finally, after so many days, she could com-
pose a proper letter to Jazrac. So much had happened and
there was so much to explain that the woman didn't know
where to begin—nor did she know just what she should
say. The crash . . . the elemental . . . her capture by the
gnolls . . . For what was supposed to be a simple job, I certainly made a hash of it, she thought ruefully.

Martine decided to use discretion.

Jazrac:

> *Your seals worked fine, and I have the keystone. The
> rift is closed.*
> *I had a run-in with some gnolls, and I'm sad to
> report that Astriphie is dead. If you received any of my
> earlier messages, please don't worry, because now I am
> safe. I'm in the valley of Samek. There's a woodsman
> here who has taken me in. I will be back in Shadowdale*

as soon as the passes are clear.

Again, do not worry about me. I'm fine. Looking forward to seeing you again. Tell Jhaele I miss her ale.

Martine

That should do it, the ranger thought as she gently blew the ink dry. Taking the bone-handled knife, she set it upon a corner of the page. She wasn't quite sure how long to leave the letter sitting out—at least a day, she guessed. "Is it all right to leave this out on the table?" she asked her host.

The big man shrugged. "That's fine. We won't be around anyway."

"What?"

Vil clapped a hand to his forehead. "Sorry. I forgot. The gnomes are celebrating the safe return of the search party tonight."

"And they invited us?" Martine asked dubiously. "We were the cause of all their trouble, after all. Besides, I thought they didn't like outsiders." She was still tired, and the thought of several hours of socializing with the gnomes was already giving her the beginnings of a headache.

"I told you they were good neighbors," Vil said, grinning. "Besides, they like parties. They use whatever excuse they can to have one."

Martine looked at the rough outdoor gear she was wearing. "I didn't bring clothes for something like that."

"Everybody will understand, I'm sure," Vil countered. "Besides, they brew a very tasty hard cider. You could probably use a few drinks after your ordeal."

That, Martine had to admit, was a point she could not dispute, and so, feeling bemused by the unexpected invitation, the woman finally consented to go.

Two hours later, Martine found herself in the entrance

hall of the warren, the sounds of revelry all about her. The whiny music of *hardrangers*, curious fiddles with extra strings that droned like bagpipes, and a hurdy-gurdy echoed from the smooth wooden walls. Gnomes laughed and giggled as they hurried to the council chamber, adapted as a dance hall. Their fat round faces seemed festive enough, but to the Harper, it seemed their merriment was forced.

The din reached its peak at the doorway to the council hall, which was already jammed. White-bearded musicians scraped and bowed from atop a rough table made from several hogsheads and boards. Bungs hammered into the barrels beneath them flowed freely with strong cider. Courting couples danced a furious reel across the floor while the uncommitted lasses giggled and whispered as they watched the young swains from the shadows of the arches. The quadricentenarians of the colony sat on the foremost benches, nodding numbly to the drone of the *hardrangers'* strings, their liver-spotted fingers rippling to the runs of the tune. Married men sat clustered around the taps, the air over their heads thick with pipe smoke. Behind them, in the higher seats, their squat wives looked out on the dancers, dreaming of times when they once whirled on the floor.

Only the martial figures lurking near the back walls belied the cause of the celebration. Jouka was there, still stiff and grim, even off duty. Gathered around him were a few other members of the rescue party, young warriors who savored the heroic image of their elders. Martine noted that shy Turi had distanced himself from his brother. The quiet one sat in a corner, hands fidgeting with the hem of his robe.

Before she could move any farther into the chamber, the woman was whisked aside by a cluster of gnome maidens. The little damsels cooed and fussed around her, the festive

spirit of the hall giving them the courage to overcome their
innate bashfulness. Martine found herself subjected to a
flurry of questions. Did all human women dress like her?
Did they dance? Did they all carry swords and curse like
farmhands? What were the men like? On and on it went, till
the ranger felt positively dizzy.

The Harper was relieved to see Vil, holding a broad-
mouthed mug in one hand, rising a good two feet above the
throng of smoking Vani. Breaking through her inquisitors
to make her way to Vil's side, Martine ignored the glares of
the Vani men as she intruded into their clique.

"Ah, there you are, Martine," the man cheerfully commented. "Drink?"

"Absolutely," Martine said with relief. "If I have to answer
any more questions, I won't have any secrets left."

Vil held up his mug and grinned. "I saw you trapped over
there."

The old men around them scowled at the Harper, though
they said nothing since she wasn't used to their ways.

Martine noticed their reactions. After a quick sip, she
raised her mug. "You Vani make a fine cider," she said.
"This is the best I've had anywhere." The words weren't far
from the truth, for the cider was crisply sweet, yet just sour
enough not to linger thickly in her mouth. Already she
could feel the strong kick it carried.

The gnomes near her nodded in polite acknowledgment.
Apparently placated by her compliment, they returned to
the serious business of socializing. Martine listened in
silence for several minutes, then gradually began to ask
brief questions of her own. Seeing that she had gained
acceptance among the circle of elders, Vil went out to circu-
late among the feasters.

Martine's conversation was limited by the growing intensity of the fiddlers' tunes. The musicians segued easily from
waltzes to polkas, with a liberal sprinkling of schottisches,

hornpipes, reels, and furious jigs. With each round, the pace quickened, till finally the floorboards trembled with the thundering capers of the dancers. Martine gave up trying to shout over the din and savored her cider, letting the warmth of the drink blank out the pains, concerns, and tensions of the day. Spotting Vil nursing his tankard, the Harper topped off her own mug from the free-flowing tap and rejoined him, reeling only slightly as she strode across the floor.

"Want to dance?" she asked.

"What?" Vil's beard bounced as his jaw dropped in surprise.

"I said, do you want to dance?" Martine repeated, more loudly this time.

"Me?"

"Of course you! The others are a little short, even for me." Feeling the exuberance of the drink, the Harper grinned and tugged the man to his feet.

"I'm not much of a dancer," Vil protested lamely.

"Oh, come on. Don't be a spoilsport. I don't care if you're one of those one-legged *fachans* that haunt the forest. Drink up," she ordered as she tossed back the last of her cider. The fiddlers launched into a reel.

"I'll never keep up with this!"

She hauled him onto the floor, ignoring his pleas. The gnome dancers cheerfully opened a space for the giant couple. "Just watch them."

Before he could begin to absorb her advice, she seized his hands and swirled them into the high-stepping reel. Gamely Vil struggled to keep pace, his face an agony of concentration as he watched her feet and tried to match the whirling steps. As a consequence, he was always at least a half a step late, and forever doing higgledy steps to regain the rhythm.

They spun and crashed into the small couples around

them like a tavern skittle caroming from pin to pin. Martine's obvious enjoyment and Vil's flustered apologies only added to the entertainment of the other dancers.

The song ended, but for Martine, it had been too long since she had released herself to such simple pleasures. The fiddlers, perhaps sensing her mood, launched into a rousing polka that swept the pair around the dance floor once again. Despite himself, Vil was managing to gain enough confidence in his simple steps to look up from her feet and smile occasionally, although his head still counted out the musicians' beat.

With heels flashing, they circled the floor dizzily, Martine leading Vil through the capering steps. With its under-size furnishings and people to match, the warren became a child's dollhouse. They whirled past wizened toadstools posing as solemn ancients, past dames dressed like dried pippin dolls, past warriors lining the walls like martial puppets, past courting lovers who teased each other like children. For an instant, all Martine's cares evaporated with the soaring music. The fiddle bows flew faster as she shed her mantle of formal reserve.

When the polka came to a sudden halt, the Harper collapsed, panting, against her partner. His chest rose and fell strongly, slightly winded by their turns. She let herself savor the sharp tang of his sweat and feel the rough muscles of his chest.

Atop his barrel, the lead fiddler uncricked his neck, then threw his long white beard over one shoulder and placed the fiddle in the crook of his arm. While the other fiddlers rested, the old gnome coaxed the first aching chords of a mournful air from his instrument. Gradually minuscule dancers—warrior husbands and their wives, hopeful lovers, and aping children—crowded into the center of the hall. Martine held Vil on the floor as the dance began, her head still pressed close against him. Gently the dancers swayed about the floor, the two humans at the center like a living maypole at a spring festival. Unconsciously, Vil's arms closed about her.

The fiddler's tune seemed to draw out the community's concerns, the droning strings of the *hardranger* ominously rumbling of some future fate. The drinkers on the benches fell silent as the musician's bow sang with the voice of the winter wind and the moonless night.

The music lingered in the air even after the last note died, and everyone held his breath, savoring the memory of the mournful tune. Finally the other dancers slowly stopped, but still no one spoke for fear of breaking the spell. Vil and Martine remained in their embrace, unaware how closely they held each other. Only slowly did the life return to the party. Then, with clear reluctance, Martine slid out of Vil's clasp and allowed herself to be led off the floor.

"Dancing certainly brings up a thirst." Vil's words were strained as he picked a path to the hogsheads.

"The little fiddler was very good," Martine said with equal awkwardness while trying to straighten out her rumpled clothes.

"That's Reko, their bard," the former paladin explained. "At three hundred and forty seven, he's had a lot of time to practice."

For a moment, Martine was taken aback, until she remembered that most gnomes lived well past three centuries or even more. The thought suddenly made her wonder how old the warren was. How long had the Vani laid claim to this valley?

Her questions were never asked, for at that moment, a pudgy youth stormed into the hall. In his rush, the gnome charged through the throng like a small boulder, startling one benchful of drinkers so that they almost spilled to the floor. The chatter in the hall suddenly ceased, though no one moved, fearing what they might hear.

"Father's dead!" the gnomish youth blurted out, his eyes wide and voice breaking with tears. "Our farm was attacked by the gnolls. Hudni . . . Father . . . everybody's dead!"

Ten

 The revelers were struck silent. The clogging stomp of the dancers lurched to a halt, and the fading drones of the fiddle strings echoed down the wooden halls. Gossips hushed their prattle. Mugs ceased to clink. Ancients strained half-deaf ears to hear the next word, uncertain of what had already been said.

"Brother Buri, what has happened?" Elder Sumalo asked softly in his thin, wheezy voice. The old priest forced his way through the stunned gnomes to reach the trembling youth. Sumalo kept his voice calm and soothing to prevent the boy's terror from spreading panic among the revelers.

"It was the gnolls," Buri blurted, his fat cheeks quivering as he gasped for self-control. "Father and I were just finishing the chores—we were going to come to the dance—and I went inside, and then Father shouted that there were gnolls coming, and then he screamed, and then they broke down the front door, and I . . . I . . ." His words floundered as the young gnome's voice broke, caught up in tears that trickled into his thin beard.

Sumalo gripped the youth's shoulders, giving comfort in strength. "And?"

"I got away through the escape hole . . . but Father didn't."

By this time, the menfolk of the Vani had clustered close to hear the tale. Those of warrior age pressed closest and listened most intently. Martine, pressed back by the swarming small warriors, spotted Jouka, Turi, and Ojakangas in the forefront.

Jouka turned the youth away from Sumalo to face him. "Buri, how many of the dog-men were there?" Though Jouka spoke softly, there was no softness in his voice. His eyes were decisive and bright.

"I don't know."

"Think. Think carefully. We must know their numbers. Think of the warren here! How many were there?"

"Ten . . . maybe more. I'm not sure! There was a great white creature with them, though. It broke down the door." The youth's rotund body quivered as if it were going to melt in Jouka's hands.

"Vreesar!" Martine choked back the name, but the warriors heard it anyway.

"Enough, Jouka," Sumalo said firmly, rescuing the boy from the woodsman's grasp. "Buri, you've had a hard time. Stay here with your cousins and sleep. Kara . . . Heikko . . . will you take the boy in?" The priest steered the youth toward a golden-bearded warrior and his stout wife. Their faces lined with concern, the couple wrapped their arms about the youth and led him away.

Satisfied the young gnome was cared for, Sumalo hurriedly turned to the Harper, his stocky body stiff with displeasure. "You know something of this?"

Martine nodded.

"Jouka, Turi . . . bring the others. We must have a council

now. Mistress Martine, you will attend." Elder Sumalo's
decision was quick and precise, and nobody, not even Martine, thought to question his authority as the white-bearded
old priest began to march to the council chamber. "Reko,
play something soothing," he advised the bard in passing.
The old fiddler nodded and set his bow to the strings. As
Martine left Vil in the dance hall, she heard the strains of a
gentle lullaby swell behind her.

The raucous dissonance of debate began even before the
knot of gnomes who preceded Martine had clambered onto
the tiers in the council hall. Worming through the specta-
tors jammed around the door, the human woman reached
the edge of the tiers at the council floor. All eyes were on
her, curious and wary, but the debaters never paused to
acknowledge her presence.

Over the buzz of excited voices, Sumalo finally made his
voice heard, pounding the floorboards with the speaker's
rod.

"Speak in the common tongue!" the priest bellowed
hoarsely to a knot of elders who spoke in a dialect so
ancient Martine could barely understand it. "The outsider
must understand our words!" A grumbled sigh ran through
the Vani, but they complied with his command.

Elder Sumalo continued quickly before the pandemonium could begin anew. "The question before the council is
what to do now about the gnolls outside. This human, Mistress Martine, has recently been their prisoner. I ask her
now to tell us what she saw."

His iron charms jingled as the priest waddled forward to
present Martine with the speaker's rod. Respectful of their
traditions, she kissed the smooth wood before beginning
her tale.

The hall was packed tight with gnomes, with the whitebeards in the lowest tiers, while the farmers and woodsmen
filled the upper benches. Martine faced them, acutely

nervous to be speaking before them.

Where do I begin? she thought, her mind reeling. Should I tell them about the rift? It was a Harper mission, and after all, Harpers and their jobs were supposed to be secret. It was a time-honored principle that the less said, the better.

The ranger decided to avoid any mention of the details of her assignment. The recounting began with the events of her capture. Martine's audience craned forward, engrossed in the details. The Harper did her best to assess the number and skill of the gnolls. She stressed the actions of the Word-Maker, pointing out that Krote's absence deprived the tribe of their medicine man.

Heads waggled when she reminded them of the prisoner. Voices thick with accents murmured darkly, but none rose to interrupt her. Sumalo listened impassively, his head nodding, while Jouka fidgeted and fingered his sword nervously. Turi, his ear cocked to catch every word, leaned forward attentively on his wooden bench.

The calm broke into storm when she described the arrival of Vreesar. Leaping to his feet, Jouka Tunkelo seized on her revelation. "A fiend—a thing of the elements? Where did this come from, human? What have you failed to tell us?" A chorus of murmuring, even from the white-bearded front tiers, supported his question.

Martine was on the spot. In situations like this, the ranger knew she had little skill to concoct a convincing lie. Holding the speaker's rod aloft in a vain attempt to maintain silence, she explained, "He came from a rift in the glacier."

"A rift? What does this mean?" queried a gap-toothed ancient in the front row.

Martine could feel the veil of secrecy slipping from her grasp. "It's a hole between the worlds—between this world and the realm of ice."

The explanation triggered debate as to whether the council had heard her correctly. The discussions flew in heated whispers as the gnomes huddled in small knots, each trying to have his say without raising his voice too loud. Only Sumalo in the center chair nodded with understanding.

"Realm of ice? How do you know this?" Jouka demanded.

Martine hoped a little more of the truth would satisfy the gnomes' curiosity. "Because that's what I was told. I was sent to close it."

"Sent?" The word rolled through her audience as they seized on its import.

"Mistress Martine, you said you were sent. Who sent you?" Now even Sumalo, quiet up to now, joined the questioning. The priest's leathery old face was wrinkled with concern.

Martine resigned herself to tell the whole truth. "The Harpers sent me. I'm a Harper."

In the few previous times when she had revealed her affiliation, people had reacted in one of two ways. The most common was one of subdued awe. Harpers were the stuff of legends, most of which painted the agents as mysterious and powerful. Martine suspected the bards of the Harpers, of which there were quite a few, spread such stories intentionally, since a good reputation was an effective tool. The other reaction, not as common, was fear—the fear of the villain. Those same tales made clear the fate of Harper foes.

The gnomes were neither awed nor afraid. Instead, the room became completely silent. The old gnomes cocked their heads quizzically, wondering if they had missed something important. Some of the younger gnomes nodded their heads dumbly in a pretense of worldliness.

"And what are Harpers, Mistress Martine?" Sumalo asked for the benefit of the entire council.

Now it was Martine's turn to be dumbfounded. It had never occurred to her that the Vani didn't know about the Harpers. In her world, everybody had at least some inkling of the Harpers and their code. A peasant might have a false impression, but at least he had heard of them. These gnomes hadn't a clue.

Martine wondered how to explain without making it sound sinister or arrogant. She had little time to ponder her answer. Taking a deep breath, she gave it her best try. "We—I mean, the Harpers—have been around for several hundred years—"

"I have been around for several hundred years, and you do not look like you've been here as long as I," interrupted one of the oldest of the group before her. Those around him chortled and snickered while the old gnome thumped his cane at his own joke.

Martine flushed. "I mean the group has been around that long, not me. We try to keep peace."

"You were sent here to rule us?" big-nosed Ojakangas asked, his voice filled with confusion.

"No . . . no, that's not it at all." The ranger threw up her hands as a gesture of her good intentions.

"You were sent to deal with the gnolls? Is that why you've come?" Jouka asked before she could continue.

"No, you misunderstand," Martine said hurriedly as she turned to face Jouka. "As I explained, I was sent here to close the rift. I didn't even know about the gnolls. The gnolls aren't a threat to peace in the land."

Once more Jouka stood from his seat, his face grim behind his black beard. "The gnolls attack us. Is that not a threat to peace?"

"Your peace, yes, but . . ." The ranger fidgeted, feeling miserably awkward before the council.

"Because your lands are not threatened, you mean, human," Jouka said sarcastically.

Oh, gods, this isn't going right, Martine moaned inwardly. Valiantly she tried once again to explain.

"It's not your lands or my lands. It's just that they're, well, gnolls. Even if they were attacking the Dalelands, it wouldn't be a Harper concern. People have to stand on their own. Harpers can't do everything for everyone. There aren't that many of us." Martine felt exposed in the center of the floor, painfully conscious of her hands as she twisted the speaker's rod. There was a reason she had chosen to be a ranger, born to the woods, and not an outgoing bard like many other Harpers.

Jouka wouldn't relent. "So now that you have stirred up the gnolls, Harper, it's not your problem," he accused, his face almost sliding into a sneer. "We did not ask you come here, Harper. The Vani do not want to be pawns in your intrigues. We choose to live here to be far from big folk like you."

A chorus of approval ran through the chamber. Jouka's words had tapped a vein of outrage that ran through the younger Vani. Seizing the moment, he turned to face his fellows.

"The Harper says it is our problem! Very well, then I say we must fight the gnolls. We must drive them out of our valley!" the woodsman insisted. His eager audience, their unwrinkled faces gleaming with eagerness to prove themselves in battle, began to clap rhythmically in agreement.

The primitive swell threatened to overwhelm any possible debate. Finally Sumalo was forced to clamber from his high seat and reclaim the speaker's rod from Martine.

"Silence! Silence, everyone!" Sumalo banged his ash rod on the wooden floor, his iron charms bouncing with each beat. *Thump-jingle, thump-jingle.* The beat repeated several times until the unruly younger gnomes in the upper tiers finally calmed down. "I hold the speaker's wand, and we are still in the council chamber," the priest chastised, his wrinkled face soured by the outburst.

"Vani, think of your wives, children, loved ones!" Sumalo boomed, his voice strong now. Rod in hand, he stalked a circuit round the council floor, his eyes fixed on the raucous upper tier. "War is not an easy thing. It is not like hunting a deer or even fighting a badger when it breaks into the warren. There are many gnolls, and they, too, are ready to fight. They will not run away simply because we kill a few."

The elder paused, stroking his white beard while scanning the council chamber. He set the speaker's rod before him like a staff, forestalling any interruptions. Finally he began again. "Our warren is strong and the winter is our friend. We should not give up our best strength. We can wait here. These dog-men will be weak and frozen before the spring comes. Let them freeze while we stay warm." Older voices echoed their approval.

The logic was sound, Martine knew. The warren was the Vani's best asset, an underground fortress the gnolls would find hard to break. Studying the faces of the council, however, it didn't look as if the priest's argument was carrying. Jouka's call for glory and action was irresistible to many. Compared to it, Sumalo's counsel of patience and cunning seemed weak and cowardly.

The debate continued, and Martine resisted every urge to leap forward with her advice even when the most outlandish claims were made. It was clear to her that the Vani were not a warrior people. Many of them, particularly the younger ones, had no concept of what a full-scale war against the gnolls would be like. Comparing the two camps, Vani and Burnt Fur, the ranger could tell the gnomes were outmatched in savagery, let alone sheer numbers. However, having already been dismissed by Jouka's faction, Martine knew her words would carry little weight.

At last the speaker's rod passed to Jouka. With its authority in his hands, the council fell silent, waiting to hear what he would say. Seated, with his head bowed, the young warrior spoke in a calm, slightly nasal voice. He framed his words with surprising coolness, not delivering the tirade

Martine expected. "Elder Sumalo, you have spoken with the conviction of your age. You have said such a war would be dangerous, and I am sure it will be. But it is more dangerous to do nothing. The dog-men have killed one of our people. It is our right to seek revenge. I say no more debate. It is time to vote."

Once again the council chamber echoed to the clapping of Jouka's faction. This time, though, Jouka held the rod and would not relinquish it, so there was no silencing the outburst.

At last the old gnome reluctantly nodded, stung by the chorus of support Jouka received from the back of the hall. "Show the human out," he instructed Turi. Slowly and stiffly, Elder Sumalo returned to his seat.

"As you wish, elder," the rotund gnome replied as he slipped off the bench with a downcast look. "Bad business, this is," he mumbled while hiking up his robes and heading for the door.

Martine was almost relieved to be escorted out of the chamber, feeling as helpless as she did during the debate. She didn't need to stay to know how the vote would turn out. Jouka's supporters were fired with the passion of war. Their voices would overwhelm the wiser arguments of those who knew better.

In the hall where the dance had been held, Martine found Vil at the center of a swarm of gnome children, still here while their mothers waited for the menfolk to end their business. With strong hands, the former paladin playfully scooped up a young gnome and hoisted him to the ceiling, an immense height for one so small. The child's squeals of delight momentarily dispelled the pall of fear that hung over the hall as others clamored for a turn. Besieged, Vil greeted Martine's return with a grin of relief.

"How about a hand with these children, Martine? Make yourself useful."

"I've been trying to, blast it!" the ranger blurted in frustration. "But it looks like your friend Jouka—"

"Quiet!" the man warned softly as he hoisted another squealing child high overhead. "Not here."

Looking about, Martine realized how frightened the gnome women looked. She had forgotten that they were wives and mothers, not warriors like her. Suddenly she felt like a mercenary who had been so long at war that she had forgotten the ways of a normal home.

Feeling as self-conscious as she had felt before the council, the huntress found a gnome-sized stool and perched upon it awkwardly. "How about a story, children?" A few came closer, but most hovered back, shy of this newcomer. Martine motioned for the women to bring their children closer.

She had just reached the point in her story where the heroine, not altogether unlike Martine, was facing off against the captain of a pirate ship when a flurry at the council doors heralded the end of the meeting. The women gathered their children against their starched skirts and waited breathlessly to hear the council's decision.

The council filed out of the chamber in solemn order. Elder Sumalo was first, followed by the older members of the assembly. After them came the younger gnomes. Martine noticed very little mingling between the cautious whitebeards and the quick-tempered younger members of the council.

Reko's fiddle music stopped, and the few remaining dancers cleared the floor as the priest entered the hall. Sumalo's face was set like stone; his color was pale, and his shoulders sagged. Finally he stood in the center of the hall and motioned the crowd to silence.

Thump, thump, thump. The priest banged his iron speaker's rod for attention. The pounding was hardly necessary, but it punctuated the solemnity of the moment.

"Brother Vani, as leader of your council and voice of the Great Crafter, hear the decision of the council. By the laws of the last high king, there will be war."

A collective gasp escaped from the throats of the women in the room. Mothers clung tightly to their children. A few crooned lullabies to soothe their infants, who sensed something was wrong in spite of their tender years. Wives sought out their husbands, and when they met, they spoke not a word. The younger women paled as they thought of their swains. Martine could see fear for their loved ones in their eyes. Old Reko brushed back his beard and struck up a mournful tune.

Martine leaned over and whispered to Vil, "I think I'd best see Krote." She didn't feel welcome enough to intrude on the Vani at the moment. The families needed time together, and she would only be in the way. She was aware, too, of neglecting the Word-Maker ever since her arrival. Against all logic, she felt she owed a good deal to Krote.

"Good idea," Vil agreed. "I'll go with you." The pair rose and, after quickly stopping to bow to Sumalo, took their leave.

Outside the council room, the halls were chilly, since all the warren's heat was kept sealed in closed chambers.

Why should I care about a gnoll? Martine asked herself as they made their way down a long hallway. She hadn't told Vil her concern about leaving Krote in the care of the Vani. A few of the young gnomes on the council had looked hot-tempered enough to decide on a lynching. With passions running high in the warren, it wouldn't take much to sway other gnomes into a dangerous mob.

If that happens, she thought, I don't know what I could do to stop it. All the same, I have to be there.

Vil guided her through passages, down staircases, and around turns, gradually leading her into the colder regions of the warren. In these distant corners were the animal pens, root cellars, and storerooms, tucked far away from the brightly lit halls of the central warren.

At last they reached the sties. The tunnels here were old and unplanked, with ceilings of dirt supported by thick beams. The air had the stagnant smell of a stable, though a chill breeze provided some ventilation. The hallway echoed with the clucking of chickens and the occasional bleat of a goat. A single magical taper, jammed into the earthen wall, gleamed steadily. The pens and their occupants cast unnaturally stark shadows, which fell away in a circle from the single pool of light.

"Word-Maker?" Martine called.

A guttural snarl came from the darkness. Removing the wooden taper, the Harper illuminated a small pen of bare earth covered with straw. Thick wooden planks made the bars of the cage, dividing her view into vertical slats of darkness.

"Word-Maker?" she called again.

"I am here, woman." Martine heard a rustle in the darkness in the depths of the cage, and then a black shape crawled forward into the thin orange light of the magical taper. Krote emerged from the gloom, stooped nearly double since the ceiling was too low for him to stand. The gnoll flashed his long canines upon seeing the Harper, but Martine couldn't guess if this was a show of rage or relief.

"You promised me safety, human," the shaman snarled. He was bare-chested, his crossed belts and arm wrappings gone. The gnomes had taken his charms, necklaces, and all the signs of his god to prevent the shaman from calling upon Gorellik. The only symbols of the shaman's office that remained were the thick-scarred tatoos around his eye.

"You're alive."

"This is an animal pen!"

"Word-Maker, I didn't promise you comfort. I don't remember you worrying about me back in your village."

Krote settled into a squat. "I healed you and saved you from Hakk's hunger."

Martine jabbed the light stick into the ground. "By marrying me to him!"

Her outburst caused Vil to perk up his head. Until now, he'd been listening with only mild interest, unconcerned with the complaints of a gnoll. "Married?" he asked in the trade tongue.

"I did this so Elk-Slayer would not kill the female."

Martine couldn't see the grin on Vil's face, but she clearly heard him speak. "By Torm, Madam Elk-Slayer— *ooof!*"

A quick elbow to his ribs put an end to his playful mood. "That will be enough from you!" she cautioned.

"Why you come here?" Krote asked.

"To close the rift. You know that," the Harper answered as she shifted her weight and tried to guess what the shaman's point was.

Krote shook his mangy head. "No, human. Why you stay here? You guarding me?"

"I came to see if you were all right. I owe you that much."

"Owe me? Why?"

It was obvious to Martine. "Because you saved my—"

"I know what I did," the shaman growled in perplexity. "How do you owe?"

"Kindness for kindness," Martine answered, equally perplexed that the shaman didn't understand this simple concept. "You—"

Further explanation was cut off by a clamor that echoed down the hall. "I'll go see what's going on," Vil volunteered. As Martine laid a hand on his arm, the former paladin added, "Don't worry. I'll try talk them out of anything rash, if that's what they're up to." He hurried down the hall, stooping under the low beams as he went.

"What is happening, human? Have the little ones come

for me?"

"No, not that." Martine hoped that was the truth, but her voice, like her heart, lacked the strength of conviction.

"You think the little ones come to kill me."

"No," the woman lied badly.

Krote rocked with a barking, staccato cough. "I am your enemy, human, but you fear the little people, too, eh?" The shaman pressed close to the slats. He leered wolfishly so that his long canine teeth glowed dully in the unflickering light. "Let me go, human, or give me a sword to fight them."

Martine moved away from the cage, shocked by the suggestion. "No!"

The shaman's fingers wrapped around the thick slats. "Why? You have honor. You know the Burnt Fur are better, more honorable, than the little people."

"Better? That's not true!"

"I would kill for freedom; little ones kill for blood. Now who is better?"

"They're not like you! They don't threaten to eat you or marry you to impress the tribe. The Vani are afraid and angry. Your people attacked them today and killed a farmer. He hadn't done anything to harm your people." The Harper found herself leaping to the defense of the gnomes, of whom only moments ago she had feared the worst.

"I just don't want them to do anything foolish," the Harper added. With one finger, she nervously scratched patterns in the dirt. "I gave my word you'd be safe."

A dry chuckle purred in the gnoll's throat. "My people, your people—all alike," Krote whispered as he slid into the darkness. After only a moment, he returned from the shadows and tossed something through the pen's slats. Martine started and scooted backward. Krote broke into a dry laugh once more. "Look at it. It does not bite. Hakk was making it."

Martine gingerly picked up the small object, which curiously felt both smooth and raspy to her touch. In the light, it flashed wheat-gold. She saw it was made from bundles of straw twisted and woven into a crude doll.

"Hakk make it for his cubs." The gnoll's voice was a gravelly whisper. "My people, your people, who is different?"

The doll was cunningly fashioned from scraps of leather and cloth. The head was decorated with two specks of color for eyes, while two tufts of fur gave it wolflike ears. The hair was a thin daub of mud. Martine could imagine Hakk carefully mixing spittle and dirt until the texture was just the right consistency. In one knotted hand, the doll held a stone flake that looked almost like a sword. A braid of straw formed a belt; another scrap of fur made a loincloth.

Looking at the crude toy, Martine remembered the dolls her own father had made for her birthday, lovingly carved from a block of wood and then dressed in little gowns sewn by her mother. In her mind, she saw the image of Hakk, writhing beneath Vreesar's blood-soaked jaws. A lump choked in her throat, and tears blurred her vision. Furious with her lack of control over her own emotions, she flung the doll away into the darkness. "No! Cyric's damnation on you! You're not the same! You're not like the gnomes, and they're not like you!"

As if to prove her words, Martine sprang to her feet, and as she hurried down the hall, she heard Krote chuckle grimly as he crawled once more into the darkness.

It took Martine little time to make her way back to the main hall, her natural sense of direction holding her in good stead. The other gnomes were gone and the hall was almost dark, but Vil remained, squatting on the floor in serious conversation with Sumalo. The pair rose as she approached and had said their good-nights before she even joined them.

"This way," Vil said as he guided her down the hall to a

door. "Sumalo's arranged for us to stay the night. I accepted for both of us. It wouldn't be a good idea to go back to the cabin tonight if the gnolls are about." He pushed the door open and waited for her to duck through the short portal before following her inside.

The room was narrow and windowless, a claustrophobic little chamber. It was furnished with a bed, table, and chairs, all gnome-sized, but these were all pushed against the back wall and stacked on each other to clear as much floor space as possible. The floor was covered with two neat mounds of thick bedding.

"The warren doesn't have many human-sized rooms," Vil explained as he edged past Martine, "and Sumalo didn't want us sleeping in the halls in case they need to be used in an emergency. Hope you don't mind."

"It's fine. Almost as nice as your cabin." Martine pulled off her boots and laid claim to one of the beds. Compared to the snow cave she had slept in several nights earlier, this was positively spacious. Besides, she couldn't help noting, the company was much better.

Suddenly there was a loud, thunderlike clap, followed by the acrid smell of ozone in the air.

Vil sprang to his feet, practically upsetting Martine as she rose, startled by the explosive report. Quickly the pair sprang for their weapons.

With their blades flickering in magelight, the pair whirled on the source of the disturbance. A cloud of sulphurous smoke billowed in the doorway. When the smoke began to clear, a thin-faced man, smartly dressed in a traveling cloak, puffed and slashed doublet, and woolen breeks, strode out of the swirl of fumes, brushing tendrils of smoke from his slender goatee. In his other hand, the stranger carried a large satchel made of well-worn leather.

"Martine, my dear," the stranger said in an easy, familiar voice, "put away your sword. You're not under attack."

"Jazrac?" the woman blurted, practically dropping her blade in the process. Vil stood alongside her, his sword wavering with uncertainty.

The wizard casually sauntered across the room, giving the small quarters a disparaging once-over. The light from the unflickering wall scones highlighted the silver and black of his hair with a theatrical glow. "Precisely, my dear Martine. It was the deuce to track you down. Now, may I put my bag here?" the tall wizard continued, hoisting his luggage. Vil let the tip of his sword sag to the floor in confused stupefaction.

"What—what do you mean, track me down?" Martine stammered. "What are you doing here, Jazrac?"

"I read your letter," the wizard replied calmly as he plopped his satchel onto the furniture-laden bed. The straps undone, the bag opened with slight hiss, like the sucking in of a breath. "And that curious bit of carving you got that gnoll to do. That was a clever bit of work on your part. But as I said, you're a hard one to track down. It took me a while to figure out just where you were."

As he spoke, Jazrac reached into the small bag until his arm disappeared all the way up to the shoulder. He removed his arm to produce a thick bundle of scrolls, neatly bound with string. That set aside, he reached back inside the bag and rummaged for something else. Confused, Vil watched the unannounced visitor shove his arm into the small satchel again.

Martine had no patience with the deliberately obtuse tack her mentor was taking. "Jazrac, I repeat, what in the hells are you doing here?"

The wizard paused in his unpacking and stared at the woman with mock injury, his arched eyebrows raised even higher. "Why, Martine, I've come to find out what kind of a mess you've made of things."

Eleven

 Oh, gods, I'm doomed! Martine thought as she sagged against one of the paneled walls. At the same time, the color drained from her face, leaving her deadly pale. The thought that Jazrac needed to check up on her inspired in her a dread awe of the wrath the Harpers.

Where do I begin? How do I explain what's happened? Martine couldn't see any simple way to tell about her misadventures that wouldn't cast doubts on her judgment. Lying was unthinkable. The woman knew there was really nothing she could do to avert Jazrac's displeasure, and trying to conceal any of her errors would only make it worse. The knowledge that there was no escaping the truth didn't help her either. The fear of her superiors was instilled too deeply to ignore.

"Excuse me," Vil said sharply as he banged the flat of his sword against the wall. The loud crack was a sure attention-getter. "What in the world is going on?" The warrior looked to Martine for an answer, all the while watching the stranger from the corner of his eye.

The color rushed back into Martine's cheeks and blossomed into a full blush as she was suddenly reminded that Vil was a spectator to her mortification. "Uh, Vilheim, this is Jazrac, Mage of Saerloon. Jazrac, this is Vilheim Baltson. He's the one I mentioned in the letter."

The wizard stopped unpacking, which was fortuitous, for the bed was almost overflowing with furniture, scrolls, bundles, shoes, even a thick pair of robes. Holding one hand to his chest, the senior Harper bowed slightly toward Vil, tilting the tip of his goatee toward the floor. "Greetings, Vilheim Baltson. Your home is extremely well built." The wizard looked down at the sword Vil still held clutched in his hand.

"Greetings to you, Jazrac, but I must explain that this is not my cabin," Vil replied, grinning at the error. "I'm not that good a carpenter. You're in a gnome warren."

"Really? I've never been inside one before." Jazrac's face brightened as he peered at the walls with renewed interest. "No wonder I was confused about the small size."

"You don't intend to stay here, do you?" Martine ventured. She pointed to the bed piled with things, a mound already twice the size of the wizard's small valise.

"I've come to talk with you," Jazrac easily replied, avoiding the question. His gray eyes were dark pits rimmed by deep creases, his sharp nose a brilliant highlight. Martine couldn't guess her mentor's thoughts behind his veiled expression, and so filled that void of knowledge with fearful imaginings.

Jazrac put her fears to naught with a shrug. "Well, I should explain for Master Baltson's sake, I suppose." With a flourish of his cape, the mage sat on the edge of the bed. The stack of scrolls behind him teetered ominously.

"I'm a Harper, and this young lady is a Harper, too." Jazrac paused, awaiting some sort of reaction.

There was only silence. No gasped breath, no protestation of disbelief.

"So she told me," Vil said calmly.

Jazrac looked crestfallen that his dramatic announcement had been spoiled. With one eye cocked toward Martine, he continued, "Well, we're normally not supposed to reveal that, but I'm the reason Martine's here. I sent her on a mission—"

"I know. To close the rift." Vil's bland interruption once again foiled the wizard's theatrics. Now Jazrac fixed both eyes on Martine, missing the former paladin's mischievous grin.

"Well, anyway," Jazrac continued coldly, "since I hadn't heard from my protege for some time, and then I get two alarming messages, I thought it best I come to see if all's well. We Harpers do that sort of thing," he added cavalierly.

"Indeed."

Jazrac made a stab at small talk as he rebalanced the scrolls behind him. "I don't imagine you know what a bother it can be, keeping tabs on each other. You seem more the independent type. You probably never had to worry about anybody else, eh?"

Martine bit her lip; she knew Vil was once a paladin. She didn't know much about paladins, but she did know their lives were committed to serving others. Vil merely smiled wryly. "Oh, I've had a few duties in my life."

"Indeed! Then you do understand how it is. I've come to see if everything is well—" here the mage hesitated significantly—"and talk Harper business with Martine." He paused broadly, spreading his hands in an obvious hint. When Vil failed to move, Jazrac cleared his throat. "Harper business. *Private* Harper business."

"I see," Vil answered with mock naivete. "You want me to leave."

Vil was mocking Jazrac, the woman knew, though she

couldn't guess just why. It probably had something to do
with the traditional rivalry between paladins and wizards.
She'd never known the two groups to get along well. Paladins were painfully noble and suspected the motives of
most sorcerers, which naturally irritated the sorcerers. If I
were a wizardress, it'd annoy me, too, she thought. Fortunately in this case, Jazrac didn't even notice the warrior's
mocking tone. Perhaps he assumed Vil was simply dense.
Martine had been around the warrior enough to know that
wasn't true.

It was time to intervene, though, just in case Vil got out
of hand.

"Jazrac, can't this wait until tomorrow?" Martine pleaded
as she pushed herself wearily from the wall she'd been
slumping against. "These last several days have been really
hard on me. Nothing's going to change by tomorrow."

The mage's eyes wrinkled at her suggestion. "I think we
should talk now. I'd like to know everything that has happened." His tone was all authority.

"I'll go see how the Vani are doing," the warrior volunteered graciously. "I'll be back in about an hour." Vil
sheathed his sword and quickly made his departure.

Although she didn't want the warrior around for what
was certain to be an unpleasant conversation, Martine still
couldn't help feeling she was being abandoned. She waited
stiffly for the wizard to speak. Without a knife in hand, her
fingers knitted and clenched nervously.

Jazrac coolly brushed some invisible dust from his
clothes before he looked at Martine. The mask of affability
he'd maintained since he arrived was gone.

"Now, tell me just what has been happening here," he
demanded calmly. "First I read that clever little 'Captured
by gnolls' message. Then after days of silence, you suddenly report that everything is fine but your prize mount is
dead. What is going on, anyway?"

Martine tried to swallow, then offered meekly, "I closed the rift and I've got your keystone."

"Well, that's good to hear, though I already knew about the rift. Both Elminster and I detected the change in the balance of things up here. What I want to know is the rest." Jazrac stared at her, waiting for her answer.

Martine suddenly remembered a prayer to Lady Tymora she'd learned when she was young. Unfortunately, the memory had come too late for her to use it.

"Astriphie died on the glacier," Martine murmured. Her voice cracked as she thought of the hippogriff lying broken and gutted on the ice.

"Details, Martine, always details. Now, how did the beast die?"

Oh, gods, what do I tell him? That I pushed Astriphie too close to the geyser? Or should I leave that part out?

"Astriphie got caught in a windstorm at the rift and was blown out of the sky. The hippogriff died when we landed. I thought it was important to get as close to the rift as possible in order to get done quickly." Martine found herself wringing her hands, feeling like an apprentice reciting her lessons.

"Hmmm" was Jazrac's only comment. "Then what happened?"

The woman avoided the wizard's unwavering gaze, looking instead at the wood grain in the bare walls. "Then I closed the rift, like you showed me. And then something caught me." Martine hurried through the last part, vainly hoping Vil would overlook it.

"Something?" the senior Harper asked pointedly.

"It was a thing of ice and cold. It called itself Vreesar," Martine explained. "There was another creature with it. A mephit, I think. I killed it."

"Hmmm." This time the pause was longer and more profound. "Some type of elemental, no doubt," the wizard mur-

mured to himself. "And did you kill this creature as well or
send it back where it came from as you were instructed?"

"I couldn't send it back, Jazrac. The rift was already
closed." Feeling frustrated at the impossibility of the question and the need to defend her actions, the woman carefully undid the top strings of her blouse and pulled it open
to reveal her shoulder. Livid unhealed scars were etched
lightninglike across her skin. "That's what the little one did
to me. I'd crashed, I was half frozen, and I had broken a
couple of ribs. I couldn't fight it. It's only by the luck of
Tymora that I'm still alive. At least I closed your rift for you.
And," she added as she closed her blouse and furiously dug
through her pouch, "I brought back your damned stone!
Isn't that enough?" Biting back her words so she didn't
completely lose her temper, she slapped the stone onto a
bare patch of the bed.

Jazrac shook his head. "I'm sorry, Martine," he offered,
though he didn't sound particularly sorry. "I'm sorry, my
dear, if this is unpleasant for you, but if you want to be a
true Harper, then you must realize that the bare minimum
is not enough. This creature—Vreesar, was it?—should
have been dealt with. You should have called for help."

"I didn't have the chance," she protested. "I was captured
by the gnolls." In her nervous state, she started to pace the
small room like a caged cat.

"You were able to get me a message, young woman," the
wizard reminded her. "You could have added one word:
'Help.'"

" 'Captured by gnolls' wasn't clear enough? It was all I
could think of at the time."

Jazrac grabbed her by the arm as she paced by. "You're
supposed to be a Harper. I can't go running every time you
have a little problem. You're supposed to be able to take
care of yourself."

"You just said I should have called for help." The wizard's

inconsistencies were maddening.

"To deal with this Vreesar, not the gnolls. You *did* escape, after all. So what happened? And please remember the details."

"I got away from Vreesar, but I was hurt and freezing. When I came across the gnolls, I decided the best thing to do was surrender." She found herself twisting her fingers again.

"Wise choice."

"I managed to convince them not to kill me," the woman continued, though she decided to leave out the business of her marriage.

Jazrac twiddled his beard. "So you tricked one into writing that message. . . ."

"Their shaman—Krote Word-Maker. He's my prisoner now."

"A gnoll shaman prisoner . . . very interesting." The wizard tapped the side of his sharp nose thoughtfully. "So how did you escape?"

Martine felt her shoulders tense. "The creature—Vreesar—came off the glacier and kind of took over the tribe."

"Kind of?"

Martine took a deep breath. "He killed the chief and took his place. It's a gnoll law. But then he wanted me to reopen the gate for him. I knew I couldn't, so I escaped as soon as I could."

The wizard scowled so that his fine goatee waggled sharply at her. "So now he leads these gnolls? I assumed you used good judgment and could recognize true dangers from inconvenience," he said with cutting coolness. "This is bad. Your second letter didn't say a thing about the elemental, did it?"

Martine turned away. "No, it didn't," she admitted.

"Why not, Martine?"

Now was the painful part, she knew. "I was afraid to," she

whispered as she turned back to face him. "I really wanted
to do well, for everything to work out. I didn't want you to
think anything had gone wrong. Besides, it's only one creature, and he can't get back because you've got the keystone."

"It's never that simple, Martine," Jazrac snapped. "We
can't leave things like this."

"Why not? Aren't you the one who always told me that
the Harpers can't get involved in everything?" The ranger
flipped her black bangs from her eyes. "This is just the sort
of situation you used to tell me about. Vreesar doesn't
threaten the safety of the Dales, or even the Heartlands. It's
a local problem, and we don't get involved in local problems—at least that's what you used to tell me."

Jazrac stood up tall with his arms crossed so that he towered over her. "It's not a local matter anymore, Martine.
You don't understand," he said flatly. "You're involved,
which means the Harpers are involved. We didn't let this
Vreesar into our world, but because of you, the creature's a
threat to the safety of everyone who lives here. These
gnomes, for example. True, you closed the rift, but what
good is that if the results still destroy everyone in the
vicinity?"

"Not much, I guess," the ranger answered sheepishly.

"You shouldn't have tried to hide things." Jazrac's chest
rolled with a sigh. "Simply put, this has jeopardized your
career. Yes, you've handled the mission, but not well. Not
only that, I vouched for you before the others, and now
you're making me look like a fool." He thrust a long finger
in her direction irritably. "Now we have no choice. We've
got to straighten out this mess and, gods forbid, hope there
isn't any more trouble."

Feeling miserable and humiliated, Martine sank onto the
bedding in the middle of the floor. "There is—more trouble,
I mean," she moaned, holding her face in her hands. "The

gnolls have attacked, and now the Vani are going to war."

"Wonderful!" Jazrac exclaimed, his voice filled with sarcasm. "Well, then, my dear, we'd better get busy." Assuming there was no more to discuss, the wizard began sorting through his unpacked possessions. "I'd like to talk with this shaman. Can that be arranged?"

Without looking up, Martine nodded numbly. "Someone—Vil or Turi maybe—can show you the way."

"Vil, is it?" Jazrac murmured.

"He's not my lover, if that's what you're thinking," Martine said indignantly, her back stiffening. "Vil saved my life and has let me stay with him since."

"Indeed."

"Jazrac, don't be such a prig." The woman was too angry to be polite.

"You're right. I'm being rude," Jazrac said. "What kind of man is he?"

Martine considered the question before offering an opinion. "Trustworthy . . . decent . . . He says he was a paladin of Torm."

"Was? What happened?"

"Something about his god abandoning him. It was during the Time of Troubles."

"Hmmm . . . yes, that would make sense." Jazrac fastidiously straightened his doublet as he went to the door. "Well, grab one of those chairs," he instructed, pointing to the furniture heaped on the bed. "If we're all going stay in one room, we'd better clear off that bed."

Martine set to work numbly. By the time Vil returned, the tables and chairs were neatly placed against the wall of the hallway outside the room. The linens and quilts were divided into thirds. Two beds were laid out on the floor, while the small gnome bed was made up for the third. Vil took these new accommodations in stride.

For what little remained of the night, the trio slept, the

two men sleeping on the floor while Martine curled up on
the bed. It wasn't gallantry that gave her the mattress; both
men were far too tall to squeeze between the cramped
head- and footboards. Even for Martine, it was hardly rest-
ful. Although she was only five feet tall, that was still nearly
two feet taller than the average gnome. It was only by curling up like a kitten that she was able fit on the bed.

By morning, the ranger had cramps from her neck to the
base of her spine. Stretching, she heard the bones in her
back pop and crack with every move, but she was grateful
to stand upright. She watched enviously as Jazrac laced up
his clean linen shirt, trimmed with Chessentian lacework.
The smell of town-laundered clothes was unmistakable
after weeks of having to wash her own clothes in cold
streams or not at all.

Catching her eye, the wizard nodded toward a pile of fabric near his bag. "I thought you might want those," he said
with deceptive casualness.

Curious, Martine went to investigate. "Jazrac, how could
you know?" she exclaimed. First she held up a quilted
smock, then a pair of woolen breeches, then linen blouses,
and finally a long, thick gown. "Why, these are my own
clothes! Where did you—" She stopped suddenly and her
eyes narrowed. "You *have* been spying on me, haven't you?
Somehow, with that crystal ball of yours, you've been
watching me."

Jazrac only laughed while Vil looked at the two of them
in sleepy confusion.

"How much spying does it take to guess you'd need
clothes?" the wizard asked innocently. "I just asked Jhaele if
you'd left anything at the inn that I could bring you."

"Oh," the woman said, her face reddening. "Would both
of you please turn around so I can change?" As they faced
the door, Martine took her time selecting an outfit. After so
long, clean, proper-fitting clothes were almost a novelty;

she was resolved to savor dressing in them.

"All done," Martine finally called. When he saw her, Vil cocked his head in surprise. "Is that—uh—functional for fighting?" he queried, clearly suspect of her choice but at the same time taken aback by her appearance. After so many days wearing the same stained jerkins, Martine had deliberately chosen a tightly tailored smock that hugged her figure yet kept her warm.

"I'll be fine, Vil. You're just not used to women's clothes." She smiled at the former paladin's reaction, secretly flattered. "Thank you for being concerned, though." Impulsively she swooped over and gave him a quick kiss on the cheek, flustering the man. "Now we'd better introduce Jazrac to our hosts."

Finding their hosts didn't take very long. Just outside the door, Martine saw two pairs of eyes that looked up with her appearance. Round Turi and his leaner brother Jouka sat in the hallway on the two chairs Martine had removed from the room the night before. Turi's glossy black braids swung loosely as he stared at them. Feet clomped as the pair stood to greet them.

"Masters Jouka and Turi," Vilheim said as he ducked through the door and entered the hall. "I want you to meet Jazrac of—"

"Mage of Saerloon," the wizard offered as he emerged from the room. The two gnomes blinked with surprise at seeing yet another human in their midst.

"I apologize for appearing unannounced, but the hour was late when I arrived last night," Jazrac said in a rich gnomish accent, showing his familiarity with the small race. He bowed deeply to the gnomes, his lace sleeve nearly sweeping the floor. "I ask for your tolerance and hospitality and hope that I can repay you with any service at my power."

Jouka and Turi gaped openly at the wizard until the

woodsman finally stammered, "Master Vil, will you-uh—
give assurance for this person?"

Vil sucked his cheek as he considered the request, not
particularly eager to stake his word on someone unknown
to him.

"I will be the model of behavior," Jazrac assured them.

With no small reluctance, Vilheim nodded. The gnomes
seemed satisfied.

"I understand there is a gnoll prisoner being held here,"
Jazrac said, not one to be timid. "I would appreciate it if I
could see him. Can someone show me the way?"

Behind the wizard, Martine could only marvel at how
quickly the wizard made himself at home. "I know the way,
Jazrac," she offered, but the wizard shook his head.

"It would be best if you reflected on your actions up to
now, my dear," the wizard whispered. "I think one of the
things you need is more time for contemplation." With that,
the wizard prevailed upon Turi to act as his guide.

The pudgy gnome, a crafter of magical illusions by trade,
was intrigued by the opportunity to talk with the human
wizard and the pair of them disappeared down the hall,
engrossed in conversation.

"I invite you, Master Vilheim, to meet with the council
regarding matters that concern you as well as us," Jouka
gruffly announced once he had regained his composure.
"You have a home in our valley, so it is right that you join
us." It was clear from Jouka's invitation that it extended
only to Vil. The warrior could hardly refuse, and soon he
and the gnomes also left, leaving Martine alone. Upset, she
returned to the room.

Clannnggg!

A steel helm ricocheted off the bedpost and skittered
across the floor, propelled by the sharp kick of a hard-shod
foot.

"Damn that man!" The oath followed hard on the rattling

clank of the still-spinning helmet. "The nerve—the utter gall!" Martine launched into a string of invectives, dredging up the choicest insults she had learned in her years along the coasts of the Inner Sea. It was fortunate the wizard wasn't present to hear her curse his ancestry, his wit, and especially his prowess.

It was so like him, Martine knew. If there was anything that bothered her most among Jazrac's many irritating qualities—his condescension, his smugness, his superiority—it was Jazrac's consummate ability to thrust himself to the forefront in every situation. He was egotistical, overbearing, even childish, but most of all Jazrac had the talent to transform even the most mundane action to a mystery that captivated others even as it infuriated her.

"Wizards!" she fumed, as if that explained everything that bothered her about Jazrac's behavior.

As she sat in imposed contemplation, Martine doubted she was learning whatever lesson it was that Jazrac wanted her to learn. Instead, all she could think about was how close she had come, years ago, to being her mentor's lover. She had been considerably younger then, and Jazrac had seemed urbane and dashing. It seemed as if he had traveled to every exotic place she had longed to see and had tasted, touched, and seen things the young ranger could only imagine. She had been thoroughly infatuated with him. The thought appalled her now.

Still, Martine had to acknowledge a certain basic decency in the man. Naive as she had been, the wizard had always been gentlemanly toward her. He had never taken advantage of her and had always told her honestly what he thought was best for her career. Although his manner was infuriating, the wizard had always cared about her.

The longer she sat, the stranger the turns her contemplation took. Her anger at Jazrac became anger at herself. She had let him down, even though she had completed the mission. The wizard had a right to be angry with her.

Her thoughts were interrupted by a distant blaring noise that sounded dully through the halls. It was a curious noise, one of those sounds that Martine was certain was familiar, yet she couldn't place it. She ignored it until it happened again, proving it wasn't just a freak occurrence. She went out into the hall to investigate.

The blaring note sounded again, tapering off like a wailing child. It sounded like a huntsman calling his hounds, like a huntsman's . . .

"Horn!" Martine blurted suddenly. "Someone's outside sounding a horn." Grabbing her gear from the room, she sprinted down the wooden hall, trying to remember the way to the main chamber. Just as she was beginning to think she was lost, the ranger rounded a corner and almost tripped over Jouka, rushing in her direction. Instinctively the two sprang back, both reaching for their blades, before realizing exactly what was happening. Hurrying behind the gnome came Vil, towering over the rest of the gnomes of the council.

The fierce look fled from Jouka's bearded face as he recognized the human. "The south doors, everyone! Quickly!" Without waiting for a reply, Jouka sprinted past Martine and down the hall.

The Harper seized on the chance to follow before anyone could object to her presence. She knew she wasn't supposed to be part of this council assembly, but she assumed his words just now negated that restriction.

Led by Jouka, Martine, and Vil, the gnomes hurried through corridors lit by cold flames and passed through doors so low that even Martine, hardly tall by human standards, had to duck her head. Other gnomes they encountered, startled by this strange entourage, shouted questions as they passed. Martine couldn't make out the hurried replies. Elder Sumalo soon fell far back, his legs showing his age. As they ran, more Vani men joined them, spears and short swords in hand.

At last they poured into the great foyer at the south entrance to the warren. The passage was built without regard for humans, and Martine found it impossible to stand upright. The low ceiling made her feel uncomfortable. She noted that Vil was forced to crouch on the floor.

Sumalo, with Turi in his wake, pushed his way through the throng to join Jouka at the front of the group. Looking back, Martine saw the colorful flash of Jazrac's doublet. "Jazrac!" she shouted, trying to let the wizard know she was here.

From the inside, the exit was an elegant work of simplicity, consisting of closely fitted panels of polished pine, once blond though now golden-brown with age. Looking at the cracks in the doorposts and the worn floorboards, Martine judged they were in one of the oldest sections of the warren.

By now, a half-dozen gnomes had formed a rough line in response to Jouka's shouted commands. Their weapons were a mismatched assortment of whatever had been at hand. Martine noticed swords, spears, and axes, and one gnome even flourished a meat cleaver as he chattered eagerly in an accent so thick the Harper couldn't follow it. Jouka's sharp commands formed them into a rough rank that blocked the door. Curious children who had followed the group were herded back behind the line in case there was some danger.

While the gnomes were getting organized, Martine slid to the front to take the opportunity to scan the surface. Kneeling, she slid open the small peephole in the door. Dazzling light burst through the square opening and splayed across the worn floor, reflecting off the golden pine to brighten the entire chamber. A freezing draft accompanied the sunbeam, as if to mock its warmth.

"Human, get away from there!" Jouka snapped. Mindful she was only a guest, but still curious, Martine started to close the shutter but kept her eye glued to the peephole. Squinting, she strained against the sun-dazzled snow to make out anything clearly. A frosty morning haze hung over the berry canes at the meadow's edge.

Martine could hear Jouka's grumbling grow louder with every passing second, and she was about to give up when she spotted a movement among the canes. "Jouka, look there," she whispered eagerly as she stepped aside. "By that uprooted pine."

The gnome pressed his eye to the slot. "I don't see—you mean the big white thing?"

The ranger nodded. "Vreesar."

The rasping horn blew again, sounding louder through the opening. Standing next to the distant elemental was a gnoll blowing a curved horn. The winter wind whipped the gnoll's ragged clothes.

"It followed you here!" Jouka accused Martine as Elder Sumalo stepped forward to have a look.

"Not me," Martine said with a shake of her head. "I've never used this entrance. Buri, perhaps."

Jouka grunted, unwilling to divert the blame. "You brought them to this valley," he insisted.

The Harper couldn't deny that. The accusation reminded her of Jazrac's words last night. In solving one problem for the Harpers, she'd created another, and it was just as much her duty to solve this one.

"We should hear what Vreesar has to say," the woman said when Jouka gave no orders to open the gate.

The dour little man snorted. "There is nothing to say. I say we kill it when it comes closer."

Martine's first reaction to the gnome's suggestion was that it would solve the problem, and in the instant when words come before thought, she almost agreed aloud. However, second thoughts followed, and she recoiled at what she had almost done.

"No, Jouka. The woman speaks wisely. We must hear the creature out," Elder Sumalo said disapprovingly. "Heikko, open the door."

The golden-bearded warrior nodded and shot back the massive bolt in its track. Martine, Jouka, and Sumalo fell back among the ranks of gnomes as the gate swung inward, releasing a shower of icy chunks from the bank overhead. The hardened snow shattered on the wooden floor and lay there to crackle underfoot. Warmth fled the hallway, fluttering the long beards of the little warriors braced for attack.

Across the snowfield, the elemental stood hunched and motionless at the edge of the woods. Behind him, in clusters of two or three, Martine saw in the haze the phantoms of Burnt Fur warriors among the brambles and trees. Like the elemental, they did not move.

"People of the dirt!" the elemental croaked in its peculiar buzzing accent. "I am Vreesar, prince of ice and master of the Burnt Fur. Who speakz for the little dirt people?"

Without hesitation, Elder Sumalo stepped from the line of militia advanced to the doorway. "I am Elder Sumalo. I speak for the Vani." The old gnome's normally thin voice penetrated the distance across the clearing with authority.

The elemental's icicled brow flared in the sunlight, and it cocked its head to survey the small figure that faced him. "Su-ma-lo," the creature said with difficulty, shaping the soft syllables with its harsh lips. "Su-ma-lo," it repeated, striding across the snow. "Come out and we will talk."

"Watch for any sign of treachery," the priest said softly to Jouka. The warrior nodded, then motioned several spearmen to the edge of the door where they had a clear view.

The old priest waded through the drifted path to the center of the small field between the warren and the woods, where the elemental already stood. Barely had they met when the elemental pointed toward the entrance. "The female comez, too," it shrilled. Martine realized its icy finger was pointed at her. Jouka eyed her darkly, suspicious of the link between the woman and the fiend.

Unbuckling her sword, Martine joined Sumalo on the frozen meadow. Away from the shelter of the doors, the wind blasted her cheeks and cut through the light clothing she wore.

"Speaker of the Vani, listen to me," Vreesar was saying as Martine approached. "Give me the woman and the stone she haz stolen, and I will leave you in peace. She waz Hakk'z mate, and now she iz mine. She stole the stone from Hakk."

Sumalo stared up at the towering elemental. "There are far more stones in the earth than Vani. I do not know which one you mean."

"The woman knowz! Ask her," Vreesar hissed, voice crackling with frost. The creature squatted down till its angular face was level with the old priest's.

The tired veins on Sumalo's neck traced blue-black lines as the priest tensed. His eyes narrowed, the gnome turned to the Harper. "What does he mean, Martine of Sembia?"

"It was a rock I found on the glacier," the Harper lied. "I don't have it now. Last I saw it was in the chieftain's lodge." Suddenly she was thankful for the cold, for her shivering disguised her trembles of fear.

"Liez! I know it iz the key! That iz why you stole it, human!" The elemental almost reached for her, then restrained itself, perhaps deterred by the line of spear points behind her.

Martine trembled. Damn! The creature knows! I was too obvious. I can't let it get the stone. "I don't have it," she repeated fiercely.

Vreesar changed his tactics. "My slavez say, 'People of the dirt hate the Burnt Fur. You must lead uz in war against them.' But I, Vreesar, do not want war. You do not want war. I give you thiz chance to make peace, Su-ma-lo. Do not be tricked by thiz human. She haz the stone. Give them both to me." The creature's icy face crackled in expectation.

"The woman is our guest. I will not break the laws of the warren."

"She liez!" Vreesar's razor edges glinted in the sunlight. "She haz stolen the stone. She must be punished!"

"Your law is not our law, creature," Sumalo snapped back, his anger rising with each threat. "We did not start this war. You invaded our valley."

The elemental drew itself up. "We see no totemz, no claim stakez," Vreesar said with a sneer.

"Our homes are our claims," Sumalo replied. "You murdered Elder Hudni! The crimes are yours, not the Vani's."

The fiend buzzed in a mockery of laughter, its needled mouth cracking in a perversion of a smile. "When all of you are dead, I will bring my brotherz to amuse themselvez here. No more talk! I kill some of your people. Then we talk again."

The elemental turned and strode back toward the woods and the waiting gnolls. At the edge of the forest, it stopped and looked back. "People of the dirt, remember who started thiz war!" With that, the wind embraced the pale creature in a cloak of driven snow, swirling him out of sight.

"Shut the doors," Sumalo rasped as they entered the warren. The puffs of his breath hung like cold charms in the air. Martine held out one arm to help the old gnome along, but he paid her no attention. When they reached the foyer, the others quickly labored to close the broad wooden gates. The doors met with a loud *thump,* and the bar rattled into place.

Sumalo pointed at the gnomes nearest the door. "Stay here and guard. Three others each guard the cliffside and the east entrances. Vani, arm yourselves and prepare for war!"

Twelve

The rumble of heavy feet sounded through the thick, earth-banked walls of the warren as the Vani hurried to carry out their priest's commands. Farmers and hunters alike sprang to their new duties.

"Harper, wait," Sumalo called, using the same tone of command he used with the gnomes. Martine, Vil, and Jazrac slowed until the priest, with Jouka close behind, joined them.

"What was that all about, Harper? What is this stone the creature wants?" The normally understanding priest looked at her sternly, rather like her father the blacksmith had when he caught her playing with the swords he made.

Feeling she was caught in yet another web, the huntress explained. "It's the key to the rift—the one I closed. If that creature got possession of it, it could break the seal and reopen the gap it came through."

"And do you have the stone?"

With Jazrac there, Martine could hardly avoid the truth.

If she were to deny existence of the stone, the wizard would surely contradict her. "Yes. I lied to Vreesar."

Sumalo's face clenched with anger. "You have the stone it wants? Didn't you hear the creature? It will kill the Vani for your stone, yet you refuse to give it up? You have no right to condemn us, human. Give me this stone, and I will put an end to this thing."

"No . . . she can't do that," Jazrac said as he stepped forward to support his fellow Harper. He adjusted his cape and planted himself firmly at her side. "If this creature opens the rift, do you think he will go home and leave you alone? No. Instead, more will come, and then what will you do? Can you defeat ten, twenty, a hundred of his kind?"

"So you say we must fight?"

"You already chose that last night," Martine snapped.

Sumalo's face reddened and he chose to ignore the illogic of his arguments. "*We* chose, not you. You are not Vani. You do not have the right to choose for us!"

"Elder Sumalo," Martine snapped back, her patience almost at an end. "You heard the creature talk of its brothers. If it gets the stone, that will be the death of the Vani. As long as we have the stone, the creature fights alone."

"Not alone—with the gnolls," Jouka growled.

The woman wheeled on the other gnome. "You're a hunter, Master Jouka. Which way are your odds better? Against one bear or three?"

The gnome swore under his breath. "One," he said reluctantly.

Vil spoke up for the first time. "The Harpers are right." His voice was even and calm, in marked contrast to the growing passions on both sides. "They have acted badly, but they are right. Now is not the time to argue among ourselves. We must act as one or we will all lose."

Standing as straight as the low hall ceiling allowed him to, Vil stepped between the two groups. "Jouka," the former paladin said in a way that neither cajoled nor dictated, "we must act now—together. What do you recommend?"

"Organize a raid," Jouka said, glowering. "Attack them first, before they attack us." Beside him, Sumalo nodded in agreement.

"But your strength is your warren," protested Jazrac.

"The Vani do not hide in their homes!"

"What do you say, Elder Sumalo?" Vil interrupted before passions once more got out of hand.

"I agree with Jourka. We must attack!"

"Martine?"

"I also agree. Let's hit them before they attack us and put a quick end to it."

"Then I think we're in agreement," Vil said, placing his hands on Jouka's and Martine's shoulders. "We will help you in this, Master Jouka, if you will have us."

"Meet us at the east gate, then," Jouka said, his voice somewhat surly. "We'll pick up their trail from there."

With the course of action decided, the two groups split. Sumalo and Jouka went to organize their people while the three humans headed for their room. All the way there, Jazrac argued against the wisdom of the raid and his part in it. He wasn't prepared, he didn't have the right spells, they needed more information, he didn't have fighting gear . . . the litany went on and on until Martine was sure Jazrac was looking for some excuse to back out.

At their room, the wizard, who had nothing to prepare, waited outside while the other two made ready for battle. Working quickly, the pair struggled into what armor each had brought from Vil's cabin. Martine wore a resilient tunic of chain mail, intricately woven by elves under the light of the full moon—or so the merchant who had sold it to her claimed. Whatever the circumstances of its creation, the suit had served her well for many years, helped by careful patching and a fine sheen of oil. As she pulled it on, the

metal felt bone cold even through the clothing she wore
beneath it. Her open helm fit tightly over her fur cap, so she
finally opted to set the helmet aside. She missed the light
touch of her sword, the one she'd christened Sea Dog, but
the weapon she'd borrowed from Vil was solid enough. She
still had her bow and quiver, which she slung over her
shoulder. "Ready?" she asked finally.

"You can help me with this clasp." Vil grunted. The warrior was almost finished buckling on his battered old
breastplate, the final piece of his armor, an unmatched collection of leather, chain, and metal plates. It was an old suit
and well matched to the wearer, the armor shaping itself to
his body over the years. The big man moved easily in it,
and without the sometimes annoying squeaks and creaks of
poorly made plate mail. Sword and hanger in arm, he nodded he was ready to go.

In the hall, Jazrac waited. Borrowing one of the old
quilts, he had bundled it around himself till his face barely
peeked through a small gap at the top. "I still think we need
more information," the wizard complained even as they
started down the hall.

Just as the three neared the east gate, a fantastic figure,
encrusted from head to toe in a suit of iron and jutting
spikes, ambled around the corner and almost walked into
Martine. The Harper could barely recognize the grim
Jouka beneath the bizarre armor. The gnome's black beard
was bound with ribbons and tucked around his neck so it
didn't snag on the spikes bristling across his breastplate.
His armor consisted of three pieces of black iron, jointed at
his chest to follow the curvature of his muscles. Shaped
iron covered his arms, thighs, and calves.

That alone would have made the armor more than serviceable for war, but Jouka's plates were studded with thick,
rusting iron spikes that almost looked as if they had been
driven through from the underside so that the sharp points

wavered dangerously with every movement of the wearer. The suit was complete—nail-studded gauntlets, tack-covered arms, even a metal helm, a full-skull mask of hammered iron, gingerly tucked under one arm. The helm sported features of smooth anonymity, with barely the trace of a mouth, nose, and chin. The whole thing was marked by the needle-sharp points that projected to an even length about the skull, like some strange cultist's mask.

"What is *that?*" The question, full of disbelief, exploded unconsciously from Martine's lips.

"This, human, is my badger-fighting suit," Jouka said proudly, almost thumping a thorny fist against his spiky chest.

"A what?" She knelt to have a better look.

"My badger-fighting suit," came the fierce reply. "Sometimes badgers dig into the warren and we have to kill them."

"In that?"

"It is an old Vani tradition, Martine," Vil answered, coming up behind the pair. "The Vani corner the badger or wolverine, usually by penning it inside a room. Then one of the warriors goes in and tries to kill it. By custom, the lucky fighter is armed with just a knife and that outfit." The man nodded toward Jouka's armor.

"Lucky?"

"It is a great honor to kill a badger," Jouka huffed. "I have killed two badgers already."

"It's how their men become true warriors," Vil pointed out.

"But why the suit?" Martine asked as she gingerly touched one of the spikes.

"Badgers do not like the spikes, human. It gives the fighter a fair chance."

"A chance? Against a badger?"

Jouka glared up at her as if she had questioned his

manhood. "Have you ever fought a badger, woman? Do not—"

"The Vani call him *tukkavaaskivo*—'little mean one,'" Vil cut in quickly. "The animals are not be trifled with. I've seen a wolverine take on a bear twenty or more times its size and win," the man added.

The gnome nodded sagely. "A bear will run where a badger turns and fights. The Vani fight like badgers, too." Having arrived at the east gate, he cut the conversation short.

In the chill hall, an assemblage of gnomes were gathered into rough-and-ready companies. The militia broke ranks the minute Jouka and the others entered the hall and besieged the spiky gnome with questions, demands, and suggestions. In the cramped chamber, Vil and Jazrac towered over the clustered gnomes packed around them. The little warriors bristled with an assortment of weapons, mostly stubby spears. Short swords, their hilt grips well worn with use, hung in the undecorated scabbards of many others. There was a suggestion of armor under the shapeless layers of their dirty white parkas. Armets, pot helms, skullcaps, and other wondrously incongruous headdresses bobbed among them. The air reeked of gnome sweat, oil, and stale beer, the latter no doubt consumed to fortify more than a few before they set out.

With all the voices raised at once, Martine did her best to listen, but the tumult was a blend of shouting so thickly accented that the Harper gave up all hope of understanding.

At last Jouka, who would serve as commander of the raid, restored order. Organized back into their companies, the gnomes stood tensely expectant while Jouka huddled with his chosen captains.

"I didn't think the gnomes had this many warriors," Martine said to Vil. There were about forty of the Vani packed into the little hall.

"They don't," Vil said softly. "You can't count most of
these fellows as warriors. Most of them are farmers. A few
are hunters who know the valley well, but fighters like
Jouka are precious few."

The aforesaid gnome, in the middle of his captains, nodded toward the humans. "The humans are welcome, too.
Master Vil you know. The woman can use a sword as well."
There was a murmur of surprise from some of the more traditional farmers. "The thin one is a wizard . . . or so he
claims."

Martine felt that Jouka's introductions were somewhat
strained, as if he were unwilling to admit their skills. However, the gnome added finally, "They know how to fight,
brothers, and every sword will help us. They will travel
with me. That way they cannot get lost." A weak chuckle
rose at their expense from the gnomes.

"Elder Sumalo is no longer as young as he once was,"
Jouka continued, "so we will have no priest. If your brothers are hurt, you will have to bring them back to the warren
for healing. Sumalo will be ready for you. My brother, Turi,
and the human wizard are our only magi."

"Is Turi a good mage?" Martine whispered to Vil.

The warrior shrugged. "Good enough, if you need illusions—tricks of light and shadow, phantoms—those sorts
of things. Better get yourself ready to go," Vil added with
the barest nod to Jazrac. "Does he need skis?" Jouka was
already herding his chattering fellows outside as Vil took
his skis from the pegs.

"Not at all," Jazrac cheerily replied, overhearing the
question.

Stamping their ski-clad feet to drive out the cold, the
gnomes waited impatiently outside for the humans. In the
morning chill, their frosty breath caught in their beards
and mustaches, coating them with a snow-whitened glaze.
The waiting gnomes said little, their gazes fixed grimly on

the woods. Their old eyes held no fear, only determination for the mission before them.

Jouka gave the signal to move out. The outer doors parted. "We go!" barked Jouka, barely waiting for the humans. Expert skiers, the Vani set a brisk pace, each following in the track of the gnome before him. Martine was surprised how quickly the short-legged folk could shoot across the snow as she and Vil labored to keep pace. Only Jazrac traveled without the long boards, instead drifting over the surface of the snow, held magically aloft, floating alongside Martine and Vil.

"I thought such magic could be used only for brief periods," the former paladin rumbled. "We're likely to be traveling all day."

The wizard ignored Vil's evident irritation. "That's true of spells, yes, but a ring of flying is much more useful." To demonstrate, the wizard made a pass by the skiing warrior, rising slowly until his feet were level with the man's helmeted head.

Singularly unimpressed, Vil growled, "I've seen flying wizards before. Archers call them flying pincushions."

Martine chuckled, for wizards tended to be pretty useless as fighters. It was their spells and not their fighting prowess that made them powerful.

Appropriately chastised, Jazrac resumed skimming over the snow, stirring up a thin cloud of ice crystals as he went. As she pulled alongside her skiing companion, Martine couldn't help but notice a sardonic smile on Vil's lips.

After half an hour of nonstop travel, Jouka whispered back the command to halt. Her throat rasped raw by the fierce cold, Martine was thankful for the slightest break in their march. She wanted to spit, but her mouth was parched by the arid winter air. Her sides burned and her legs felt ready to buckle, reminding her of just how little experience she had had on skis. Knowing the gnome hadn't halted the column just for her benefit, Martine somehow resisted collapsing into an exhausted heap. Instead, she slowly drew her sword for battle, her fingers muffling the scrape where the scabbard's metal lip rubbed the blade. The sword's edge nipped her finger, a sharp sting that she ignored as several drops of blood rolled down her finger and plopped, overlapping, on the snow. The white crystals melted and then spread into a pink areola at her feet.

Jouka carefully issued orders to form a search line. The instructions that followed were simple; the gnome knew he couldn't expect anything too complicated from his militia. They were to fan out in a line. If they saw anything, they should freeze and stay hidden, then signal those to their left and right, who would pass the signal down the line. Most of all—as the gnome said it, he looked pointedly at the three humans—no one was to act on his own. No individuals were to rush to the attack, but rather wait until the command was given. To be certain they understood, Jouka had his warriors repeat the instructions. Only when he was completely satisfied that all the farmhands and carpenters understood did Jouka begin posting the gnomes to their positions.

"Do you know where the gnolls are?" Martine asked Jouka privately once everyone had received his instructions. She wondered if the gnome was privy to some information, perhaps brought in by a scout or outlying farmer.

Jouka shook his head from side to side, then pointed toward the northwest. "No reports, but Hudni's place lies off that way. There's sheltered ground and fresh water between us and the farm. That's where I'd camp if I were the gnolls. We'll search there first."

The search line formed a long irregular arc along the edge of the woods. Martine kept Jazrac to her left, and Jouka took up position on her right, forming the center of the line. Vil was somewhere farther to the right, lost to her sight by the paper-white trunks of birch trees. Beyond him was Turi. Martine guessed Jouka was being careful, keeping his ablest fighters close at hand. That way he could quickly change directions when the enemy was spotted.

The gnome waved his ski poles to both sides, a signal Martine dutifully passed down the line. Tentatively, as if expecting a gnoll behind every tree, the scouting line entered the woods like beaters on a king's hunt.

After breaking through the thicket-lined edge of the woods, no easy feat on skis, the Harper cast about for her flankers. Jazrac was abreast of her, about ten feet off the ground, gliding easily over the last of the bramble wall she had just labored through. A more experienced skier, Jouka was already well ahead of her. "Damn!" Martine hissed under her breath as she floundered awkwardly on her skis, determined not to be shown up.

Now the trip became considerably more difficult than before. There was no clean track broken by the others for her to follow. The search did not move along any easy paths like game trails, so her route was constantly impeded by thickets and deadfalls that forced her into slow detours. To make it worse, sometime in the last day or two a brief thaw had transformed what had been soft powder into a glazed sheet of ice that slid under her skis like a greased pig. One ski or the other kept unexpectedly shooting forward, only to have it break through the crust and disappear completely into the powder beneath. It wasn't long before she had worked herself into a lathered sweat.

Eventually the thickets thinned and the forest floor became more open as the raiders plunged deeper into the ancient forest. Regaining her position, Martine continued to scan the woods ahead for signs of their enemy.

They continued unimpeded for several hours, the searchers moving with deadly slowness. Occasionally the interlaced pine boughs gave way to leafless aspens, and Martine could see the sun hanging well above the tallest peak of the mountain wall, making ice and bare rock glint brilliantly. Streamers of windswept snow flumed off the jagged slopes and made the distant sky sparkle like a magical star shower. Such glimpses were brief, for as soon as the openings appeared, the forest closed back in around them.

On another day, the wild beauty of the winter woods would have undoubtedly thrilled the ranger. There was no such enjoyment today, however. Martine's concentration was too fixed on the dark spaces that lurked between the creaking trees. Bird calls, rabbit tracks, wind-fallen trees, and the bloodstains of a lynx's kill all acquired and then lost ominous meanings. The eerie silence of the other searchers unnerved her.

A whispered signal brought the line to a halt. While everyone else waited, Jouka silently disappeared down the line to investigate. Martine was impressed by the gnome's stealth.

It quickly became difficult to remain still. Curiosity and intense cold both made her want to keep moving.

At last the small figure returned. The gnome skied past his own position to confer with her. "We found tracks angling to the northwest. Signal the message down the line." No more explanation was needed.

From there on, the skiers moved with even greater stealth. Although the valley was certainly well known to the gnomes, they were now in essence entering an unknown region prowled by hidden terrors. While everyone that morning had been placid, if grim, they were now tense. Jouka skied with sword and poles in hand, a technique Martine was not ready to master.

It wasn't until the sun had started on its long descent toward the western treetops that the searchers ground to a stop. A terse word rippled down the line. "We've found them, woman. Come," Jouka glided over to say. With that, he plunged deeper into the woods. The Harper signaled to the wizard behind her. She waited only long enough for Jazrac to confirm her hand signs before breaking position to follow Jouka's trail.

The pace now became extraordinarily slow as the ranger scanned every inch for signs of the enemy. Matching her advance were the shadows of the others, flickering among the pines, the thickets, and the hummocks of snow. These farmers were better than she thought, moving as if they were stalking nervous squirrels for the dinner pot.

Gradually the raiders converged on a point where Jouka lay, belly down, in the snow at the base of a large drift. Beyond his position, the stalking was over and the strike would be at hand. Jouka softly issued a string of commands, sometimes drawing the more detailed instructions in the snow. The tired warriors, tight-lipped and tense, listened and then stealthily moved down the drift, each drawing his weapon and wending into the woods to his assigned post. Jouka laid a hand on Martine, signaling her and Vil to stay close.

"What should I do?" Jazrac whispered at her side.

"Don't you know?" Martine hissed back, astonished by the question. She had assumed that the wizard, older than she and skilled in magic, was naturally experienced at this sort of thing. The look of uncertainty in his eyes said otherwise.

"I abhor fighting," he explained. "I never was any good in battles. Research and study are my strengths."

Martine bit back a curse, especially since Jazrac was her superior, but she certainly wished he'd said something before. "Stay back and be ready then," she snapped, unable to keep a hint of scorn out of her voice. The wizard stiffened but, perhaps knowing his place, accepted her command.

With Jouka's warriors in position, Martine expected the

commander to immediately plunge over the drift and into battle. Instead, Jouka waited and listened for any sounds of their foe. After several minutes with no indication his advancing warriors had been discovered, he undid his skis, jammed them upright into the snow, and then slithered up the bank. Vil and Martine quickly followed suit.

At the top of the drift, the trio took position behind the cover of a thin stand of young birch that broke through the snow. They lay aflank several other gnomes hunkered down in the snow. Snarling voices came from beyond the ridge.

The gnome reached up and cut away a small gap in the drift for the trio to peer through. "There they are," he whispered. "The brutes."

Nestled in a bowl of drifts was the gnoll camp. Small dark leather tents dotted the ground. In a quick count, the Harper estimated there were about twenty of them. Along the base of a large drift opposite were the tunneled openings to snow caves like the one she and Krote had shared. About fifteen gnolls, bundled in furs and rags, were in the camp, most of them squatted around the large bonfire at the center of the clearing. With the habit born of combat, Martine noted three guards, none particularly attentive, widely spaced around the camp's edges. They seemed more concerned about their freezing feet and fingers than the dark woods beyond the drifts.

Carefully the trio slid back just below the top of the drift. "Did you see any sign of Vreesar?" the ranger softly quizzed the other two, wondering if she'd missed the creature. Both gnoll and man shook their heads. The creature's absence was both a disappointment and a relief. Martine had hoped they would catch the elemental here and end it all, but at the same time, with the fiend gone, their chances were much better.

"What's the plan?" Vil asked.

"We outnumber them," Jouka pointed out. "On my signal, we rush them from all sides. Kill everyone and destroy the camp. Those who are not in camp now can freeze or starve."

"Not much of a plan," Martine commented.

"We are not an army. It must be simple."

"He's right, Martine," Vil concurred.

Martine peeked back over the ridge. "We should hold some of our forces back, just in case Vreesar shows up."

The gnome shook his head, the spikes of his armor wavering as he did so. "No. We can't weaken the attack, and the others would not be enough against the creature anyway. If the monster appears, we and your wizard will fight it."

The Harper didn't like the looseness of the idea but, upon consideration, knew that Jouka was right. Even the entire raiding party might not be enough against the elemental. She drew her sword to show she was ready.

Jouka looked down both sides of the line, signaling his warriors to prepare themselves. As the silent signal passed from gnome to gnome, their leader fitted his spiked helm in place. His fierce eyes raged from behind the bizarre smoothness of the black mask.

With a loud battle cry, the gnome heaved to his feet and charged the unsuspecting gnolls, plowing through the waist-deep snow with dreadful abandon. His fellow gnomes caught up the signal and hurled themselves upon the foe, leaping and bounding through the drifts as best as their short legs could carry them. Some twirled swords over their heads, while others hammered their blades against wooden shields. The air was filled with a horrible din, the convoluted call of bloodlust accompanied by the deadly hum and clash of steel.

The unsuspecting gnolls froze in confusion near the fire pit, their savage eyes staring with shock. One recovered quickly, disengaging itself from its stunned fellows to scramble frantically for a bare-bladed sword stuck into the snow. The others sat staring, unable to move for a crucial instant as the gnomes descended upon them.

Almost as surprised as the gnolls, Martine sprang to her feet only moments after Jouka led the charge, but even with her longer legs, she couldn't keep pace with the enraged gnome. Then suddenly Martine was brought low when her feet hit a patch of hidden ice and dropped her solidly to the ground.

The nearest guard stood transfixed with astonishment. When it finally realized the situation, all it could do was futilely fling a fistful of snow before attempting to run. Bounding down the slope with extraordinary speed, Jouka whirled his sword over his head and caught the fleeing gnoll across the neck with the full force of his swing. The meaty *thunk* of blade slicing through muscle and bone rose above the bloodthirsty din of his fellow raiders. Fresh blood streamed in an executioner's arc as the blow cleanly severed the gnoll's neck, its mange-marked head plopping softly into the snow. The gnoll's decapitated body staggered two lifeless steps forward, the arms jabbing at the air in spasmodic twitches. Then, although its legs moved no more, momentum flung the body forward, spraying warm blood across the pristine winter ground.

A second gnoll, a battle-scarred veteran distinguished by a lopped-off ear, wasn't going to fall so easily. With canny verve, it dove upon the nearest charging gnome and clamped its fangs into the Vani's sword arm. The warrior shrieked, his blade slipping from his grasp, and the gnoll callously hurled him aside and scrambled after the weapon. Momentarily beyond the reach of its enemies, the gnoll tensed to fight, the rags it wore flapping wildly about it.

Yet even as the gnoll battled to gain a fighting stance, the Vani were slashing through its fellows. Barely breaking stride, Jouka shrilled out a series of orders that his fellow gnomes were quick to implement. The ring quickly closed about the gnolls trapped beside the fire pit, cut off from their weapons. When they drove forward, the gnomes ahead gave ground while their brothers rushed up from behind to catch the stragglers unprepared. One by one the gnolls fell to the overwhelming numbers of the Vani, until only a small knot remained, surrounded by the dead and the blindly thrashing wounded.

With the main force pinned, Martine and Vil found themselves facing the veteran. It was quick and canny, whirling constantly to face off against first one, then the other. The creature's face was contorted, its black lips pulled back in a tight, skeletal rictus. Martine could hear its breath come in rasping gasps, and its legs wobbled from exhaustion, but the primal glare in the gnoll's eyes showed its determination not to give up. The dance between hunter and prey, the roles shifting constantly between gnoll and human, slowly continued toward its inevitable conclusion.

Huffing from the effort of breaking through the snow, Vil growled, "I must be getting old. I can't keep this up anymore." Nonetheless, he lunged again, the point of his blade tearing into the gnoll's side. The creature swept its sword about in a hapless effort to parry, and in that instant, Martine slashed at the opening the creature left in its guard. Her blade hit the beast in the midsection. With fury driven by pain, the gnoll parried Vil's second thrust with a vicious clang of metal and whirled to face the Harper, driving her back with a mad series of slashes. As she stumbled out of reach, the creature staggered to a stop. Woman and beast stood staring at each other, both too intent on their foe to feel fear.

It was the gnoll who ended the standoff. With a wild leap, it hurled itself toward Martine. The gnoll's ululating cry rang through the woods as the wind shook the branches in sympathy. The long sword slashed out viciously.

In a single, graceful move, Martine dropped flat, thrusting upward at the same time. Her sword tip caught the charging gnoll just above its sternum and sliced downward. Warm blood sprayed her face as the gnoll toppled past her to die, twitching, on the ground.

Martine didn't waste any time but was already moving to rejoin the main battle. Five gnolls remained, glaring at their enemies who thronged around them on all sides.

At the forefront of the gnomes, Jouka picked up an axe from the litter of a trampled tent and, with a snap of his wrist, hurled it spinning into the gnolls' midst. Immediately behind it, he plunged into their ranks, bloody sword in hand. The closest gnoll threw its furry arms up. It could have been no more than a cub, barely trained in combat and hopelessly outmatched. Jouka's single darting lunge was enough to plunge his blade past the futilely warding arms and into the gnoll's gut. The creature staggered to its knees with a look of terrified astonishment across its drawn muzzle. Savagely Jouka slashed the blade free, ripping the wound open to complete the job, his eyes already alighting on another gnoll.

Their leader's onslaught released the other Vani warriors from their hesitation. With a communal rush, the band hurled itself upon the gnolls in a flood of savagery. Hopelessly overwhelmed, the creatures staggered and reeled under the Vani charge, futilely trying to lash out even as they fell with a howl of agonized terror. A chorus of blades flashed, first silver, then bloodstained, as the gnomes hacked blindly at their enemies even after the beasts were long dead.

Martine turned away, sickened by the sight. Up to now, the Vani had seemed a fierce but nevertheless compassionate people. Now, crazed by bloodlust, they acted with unbridled savagery. Echoes of Krote asking who was better, gnoll or Vani, flooded her thoughts. The words made the shaman seem like a remarkably accurate seer.

"Look out!" Vil's hand shoved Martine forcefully to one side. There was a loud *thunk* from roughly where she had stood. The shaft of a spear vibrated in the snow beside her. Her battle instincts springing to life, Martine maneuvered as quickly as she could manage in the broken drift.

"Kill them! Kill the little people!" a buzzing voice shrilled from behind them.

Wheeling about, Martine looked up in horror at the snowy ridge. There, towering over them all, flanked by more gnolls, was Vreesar, glinting cruel and silver in the afternoon light. Jazrac, who had been waiting on the ridge, was nowhere in sight.

"The trap haz worked, my slavez! Kill them . . . all but the female! She must live to give me the stone!"

Thirteen

"Over there . . . more of them!" Vil shifted Martine's attention to the west side of the bowl. The Harper was distracted as another spear arced over their heads to tunnel into the drift behind them. "Damn their mangy hides! It looks like a war party!" the former paladin cursed.

A baying rose from the woods in the direction where Vil pointed. Surging from the trees was a lanky line of fur-clad, snowshoe-shod gnolls, wreathed in a swirl of white snow. Yipping and howling, the beasts charged in ragged waves, some breaking stride to let fly steel spears. As the six-foot shafts hissed through the cold air, a screech of anguish proved one had hit its mark. Suddenly the air was filled with spears that flew like lightning on the tightly packed gnomes. One scream became a chorus as a full score of the Vani fell under the iron-tipped bolts.

"Jouka, fall back—now!" Vil bellowed, his hands cupped around his mouth. Already the gnomes were aware of the danger and had begun to retreat in confusion. Fear and panic became their enemies now as much as the gnolls themselves.

"This way! Stay in order and don't panic!" Martine found herself calling to the fleeing gnomes. The trap was not completely sprung, she saw. A gap in the line of gnolls lay open to the east. Some luck held with them, for the gnolls held their position on the ridge, either in confusion or because they were content to merely drive the gnomes away. With Vreesar screeching in rage at his own warriors, it wasn't an opportunity that was likely to last.

"You, you, and you—into the bush and keep watch in all directions so they don't flank us," the Harper snapped, grabbing the three nearest gnomes and pushing them toward the gap. Their skis abandoned, the little men floundered through the snow. "The rest of you, fall back through there."

Vil added his voice to her commands, and under the direction of the two humans, the Vani tumbled madly for the woods. It was barely in time, for the elemental finally compelled the gnolls forward.

"Jouka!" Vil bellowed again. The Vani leader still stood in the center of the camp, trying to drag a wounded gnome with him. Seeing that sense was not going to overcome passion, Vil hurtled back through the camp and grabbed the gnome by the collar and shoved him toward the others. With a manic heave, the man threw the injured gnome over his shoulder and sprinted after Jouka.

A gray-haired gnoll lunged forward from the rest of his pack, closing on the burdened former paladin, but by then Martine had already unslung her bow. A feathered shaft shot through her fingers and pierced the beast's shoulder. Squealing in pain, it toppled to the ground, giving Vil the time he needed to reach safety. Several gnolls, sprinting forward, hurled their spears. One glanced off the man's plate armor, but he continued to run. Martine quickly released a volley of ill-aimed shots that, while they caused little harm, slowed the gnoll advance.

Clearing the last drift with wild leaps, Jouka and Vil rejoined the others. Without hesitation, Jouka barked out a quick series of orders.

"You know the way," Martine shouted to the gnomish commander. "You lead. Vil and I will guard the rear."

Amazingly enough, Jouka did not argue, but let himself be caught up in the arms of Ojakangas, who had managed to recover his skis. Vil declined the set offered him, and Martine did the same. Of those gnomes who had escaped, less than half still had skis. Those that did doubled up, awkwardly balancing another gnome on the boards with them. Vil passed the wounded gnome off to one of them. "Where was your wizard during the fighting?" Jouka demanded angrily as they set out.

Martine said nothing as she floundered through the waist-deep snow, trying to match the speed of the gnomes. Over her rasping breath, the Harper strained to hear sounds of pursuit. She heard the mingled cries of the gnolls, some like wolves on the scent, others barking and quarreling as the creatures fell to looting the dead. Over it all, Martine distinctly heard the shrill voice of Vreesar. The pursuit was on, with only herself and Vil to act as the rear guard.

Martine took position behind a pair of tree trunks that formed a V, a good shelter for her archery. With arrows staked in the snow around her, she waited while Vil stayed close by, his sword at the ready.

The first three gnolls that broke the crest of the ridge received two arrows each. Five of the six were hits, Martine noted, and two of her targets squealed and flopped into the snow. The third gnoll did neither, for the shafts had transfixed him to the trunk of a tree. There he hung, making gurgling noises while his arms swung feebly like a broken puppet!

"On your left!" Vil hissed in her ear.

Another shaft hissed from between her fingers, speeding toward a shadow that darted across a sunlit patch. Martine didn't see the arrow hit, but a yowl from the woods confirmed the accuracy of her aim.

"Any more?" she demanded, relying on Vil as her spotter.

"Nothing yet," he whispered.

The pair waited, trying not to start at every shadow. They could hear the gnolls barking crude insults at the gnomes, though no more of the dogmen showed their faces.

"What do you suppose they're planning to do?" the ranger asked.

"They're scared. They'll shout insults for a while, and then they'll rush us."

Martine nodded. "That's what I was thinking."

"What do you suggest?"

"Good time to move," she offered.

"Right," the man said. "Give me some of those arrows." Without wondering why, she grabbed a handful from her quiver and passed them to the former paladin. "Cover me." Vil said. The warrior struggled to his feet and set out toward a fallen log in a doubled-over run. He disappeared behind the log in a frantic, ungraceful dive.

Panic started to rise in Martine, an unreasoning fear that she had been abandoned. When the man didn't reappear immediately, she shifted about nervously and hissed, "Vil!"

Nothing. The shouts of the gnolls were growing fiercer.

"Vil!" she repeated, a little louder.

Vil's black-haired head popped up over the log. "Quiet! Throw me the bow. I'll cover you."

Unnocking her arrow, the Harper threw the bow like a spear. The throw came up short, and a for a fearful instant, she thought it would end up stranded between the two of them, but the curve of the bow acted like a sleigh's skid, and it slid across the snow till it was just within Vil's grasp.

Suddenly the woods rang with Vreesar's buzzing rage, echoed by a chorus of howls from the gnolls.

Martine waited for the man's signal, and when it came, she launched herself into a blind sprint. "Quick—this way!" Vil ordered, shoving her farther into the woods almost as soon as she hurtled over the log. Blindly obedient, she sprinted on to fling herself down beside a frozen stream.

"Ready!" she panted.

The bow came sailing across the gap. Catching it before it crashed into the brush on the far side, the ranger moved down the bank a bit till she was behind their original position. She saw moving shapes, and without waiting to find out just what they were, she fired off a series of quick shots. A chorus of yelps and confused shouts came from the general direction of the movement. Then the shadows scattered once more into the woods.

Working from cover to cover, the pair finally managed to put some distance between themselves and their pursuers. There was no doubt the gnolls were still on the trail—the sound of their savage voices was evidence enough of that—but the creatures no longer could risk open movement, thanks to the stinging warnings from Vil and Martine.

Both humans were breathing hard and soaked with sweat, while their coats were sticky with pine resin from clinging to the cover of the tree trunks. However, neither was conscious of fatigue, being far too occupied with the chase.

It was Martine's turn to leapfrog. She darted across a half-shaded clearing, moving from shadow to shadow in an effort to remain unseen. Her efforts almost came to naught when a tall figure moved out from the shadow of a tree trunk directly ahead of her. It was a gnoll, his attention focused just slightly off to her side. Martine froze in the shadow of a rock ledge like a rabbit caught in the open.

The creature moved slowly, its canine head hung low as its body hunched over with the unmistakable poise of a hunter. In one paw, it held a cleaverlike sword; in the other, a small shield poised half at the ready.

Outflanked! The ranger instantly reassessed the situation, and indeed a quick scan of what she could see nearby told the Harper the beast was not alone. Dim, hulking shapes crept through the snow-draped woods to either side, barely visible yet close enough to respond to an alarm. Easing farther back into the shadow of the rock, she signaled Vil to stay down. They couldn't risk a missed shot or a howl of pain that might alert the other gnolls. The dogman before her would have to be taken out by hand. Martine silently drew her sword and waited for the stalker.

The woman breathed only slightly faster than the gnoll stalked, waiting for him to close the gap between them. Not only did she watch him, but she also kept a wary eye on his brothers. When at last he had moved close enough to be jumped in a single sprint, the Harper raised her sword, only to hold back from the final lunge that would close the gap. She wasn't concerned about losing her advantage over him, only whether she could drop him before an alarm was raised. She had to wait until the moment was right, a moment when the beast could die unnoticed by his companions.

The opportunity came when the gnoll passed on one side of a drift formed from a fence of tall, dried grass. With the drift on one side and a rock outcropping on the other, there was no better opportunity. Holding her breath, Martine waited until the gnoll had angled past her and then sprinted the last few steps between them to spring on the gnoll's back. With a single motion, she rammed the sword into its lower back, thrusting the blade under the ribs and up toward the creature's heart, while at the same time seizing the front of its helm. Her fingers closed on the metal, and she savagely wrenched the armor downward. Stooped forward for the hunt, the stalker crashed headlong into the snow even as its snout was jammed into its chest. The pair plunged through the frozen crust, where the gnoll's howl of alarm was muffled in the thick powder. Martine threw her weight onto the beast's back, jamming its face into the snow while she thrust again and again with her sword. The creature kicked and squirmed, choking on mouthfuls of snow when it tried to scream, but she clung on, pressing herself close till she breathed the gnoll's animal stench.

At last the creature writhed no more, though the Harper gave one last stab to be certain. Remaining in a crouched position, she watched for signs of any rescuers, flicking her head from side to side like a cornered mountain lion, but nothing appeared. The drift had screened her from sight of the others. Creeping forward, she reached the point where the snowy mound tapered down. There she could see the stalkers fade in and out of sight, still intent on their goal ahead. She had broken the line without their knowing. By hand signals, she let Vil know what she had done and then, ignoring the cold, wriggled on her belly through the gap. Vil followed suit, taking care not to be seen.

The pair burrowed like field mice for several minutes till they were sure there were no stragglers who might discover them. With a gasp of relief, the Harper sat up, the dying light of day shining on her as if she had surfaced from some deep, dark world.

Momentarily free of their hunters, the pair made the most of the opportunity, running through the snow as fast as they could. They crashed down slopes, bounding half out of control, and skidded across frozen patches between the trees.

"Where'd Jouka go?" Martine panted as they finally

slowed their pace along the banks of a stream.

Vil bent double, his shoulders heaving. "Probably . . . made for . . . the river," he gasped between huge breaths. "The going should be easier there."

"Which way?" Martine asked, staggering so she didn't fall. She kept her arms wrapped round her sides so they wouldn't burst from the pain.

"That way." Vil didn't point but set off in a stumbling jog. Sucking in a lungful of raw air, Martine followed after him.

Vil's guess proved right, and it didn't take long for the two groups to join up at the frozen grass hummocks that marked the edge of the river meadows.

Martine noted that no more than twelve gnomes were with Jouka . . . twelve out of forty who had started the day. There were probably a few stragglers in the woods, but there was no doubt that many of the Vani had fallen at the gnoll camp. Twelve gnomes, tired and dispirited, stood among the hummocks with the same dejected blankness beggars develop when they have lost all hope.

"Is Turi with you? Or that wizard?" were Jouka's first questions, the first asked eagerly, the second dark with the edge of threat.

Both humans shook their heads. To his credit, the gnome took the news well, displaying none of the anger or fear he must certainly have felt. The other news was quickly shared, and word of the gnolls' pursuit gave new life to the weary band of Vani. They laid into their skis in a desperate race for the warren.

At every brief break, the gnomes strained their ears as they listened for sounds of pursuit. Their efforts were not unrewarded. From the wooded ridge along the river came the barking exchanges of gnoll trackers as they picked up the trail. The intention of the marauders was clear to all in the group. That knowledge gave further strength to the little homesteaders, a strength Martine could not match.

The Harper toiled to keep up, ignoring the fire in her sides as she slogged along in the flat-pressed tracks of their skis. Her fingers and toes were numb from cold, a cold that was steadily sapping her drive. Only Vil's strong arm, which sometimes pulled her up the steep grades, at other times guided her across half-frozen streams, enabled her to keep up with the pack.

By dusk, the race was in its final lap as the survivors neared the east gate. The snarling howls that rang through the eerily still woods told them the gnolls, fired by the lust of the hunt, were close at hand. Shrill barks were punctuated by the thick chop of metal against wood and the clang of beaten shields. Through the woods, the Harper caught glimpses of dark moving figures, awkwardly loping through the drifts. At staggered intervals, the creatures turned their muzzles up to bay at the fading sun.

The panting group finally crashed through the last of the brush, all pretense of caution and silence forgotten, and plunged toward the hillside that held the gate. Human and gnome floundered across the familiar ground, each drawing reserves from deep inside. At the front of the exhausted and dispirited party, Jouka hailed those inside with a gasping cry, his voice rattling with breathlessness.

The Vani ahead of Martine shrieked in pain and abruptly sank to the snow. A feathered shaft jutted from his shoulder. Martine heard the hiss of another arrow passing close by her ear. A quick glance back revealed a tall, ragged bowman, its wolfish ears perked up with excitement, clumsily nocking another arrow with its mittened hands.

"Archers!" the woman squawked in hoarse warning. It was hardly necessary; another arrow dug into the snow close beside the bobbing line of retreating gnomes.

Ahead, the door cracked open cautiously as the gnomes inside peered out fearfully, alarmed by the cries and howls descending on them. Jouka's barked commands urged them to greater speed, his voice harsh and coarse.

Martine thrust a hand under the arm of the fallen gnome. "Help me, Vil!" The big man grabbed the other arm, and the pair heaved the gnome upright. The bearded warrior choked off a scream as the protruding arrow twisted in his shoulder. The two humans dragged the gnome across the last few yards. Vil's shield arm, held high as a screen to protect them from the gnoll archer, jumped when a deadly shaft pierced its wooden face and jutted out the back side.

The door gaped just wide enough for the trio to tumble through, slipping as they hit the polished wooden floor. Craning her head around, Martine saw a line of perhaps twenty gnolls already spread along the edge of the woods. The sudden *thunk* of arrows against the wooden gates testified to the presence of more than one archer.

Martine tugged her ice-encrusted mittens free with her teeth while a throng of Vani threw their shoulders against the doors. The sight of the gate shuddering shut and their chances slipping away caused the gnolls to charge with savage abandon. The doors met just as the first of the huge beasts thudded against the heavy wood. A frustrated chorus of animal howls rose from beyond the gate, and then the pressure grew, while inside the Vani grunted and heaved against the surge.

Slowly the Vani gave ground to the greater strength of the gnolls outside.

"Look out!" Vil shouted as metal scraped against wood and a sword thrust through the gap. The former paladin sprang to the portal and hurled his mass against the parting gates. "Martine—the bar! Help them!" he shouted, rolling his head in the direction of a trio of old Vani who were struggling to raise a heavy wooden crossbeam over their heads and slam it home to lock the gate. The Harper sized up the situation quickly and bent to the task. With a heave, she got a shoulder under the bar. Small Vani hands groped behind her, scraping the beam over her injured shoulder till it felt like gravelly fire. With a loud *bang*, the bolt dropped into the metal brackets.

The door shook and shuddered at the gnolls' assaults but held firm. Everyone inside seemed to wilt with relief. Beside Martine, Vil sagged back against the gate in his wet clothes, his beard streaming with melting ice and perspiration. Her own her black hair was soaked with sweat. Her hands shook when she tried to steady them, and her breath came in uneven pants. At her back, the gates continued to shake as the gnolls futilely tried to batter them down.

Throughout the hall, the Vani, numb with relief, made their way through the tangle of discarded skis and swords to collapse in the quiet, dark corners of the hall. Sumalo hunched over the injured, his hands bloody from healing the worst of the wounded. A pair of spinsters in black dresses dictated the work of a team of womenfolk, who scurried after Sumalo with buckets of steaming water and linen bandages. Hot water and blood slopped across the shining floor, running in pink streams through the cracks between the boards.

"Vil," Martine said urgently, "we can't afford to rest yet." Refusing to surrender to exhaustion, the Harper got her wobbly legs under her and strode among the spent gnomes, shaking them to action "Get up! Come on, don't just lie there! You're not safe yet. Pick up your weapons." Grumbling, the gnomes rose and tottered about, gathering their gear. Vil heaved to his feet and put those who were able to the task of bracing the door. Runners went in search of beams, hammers, and pegs to reinforce it.

"Where's your damned wizard friend, woman?" Jouka shouted as he pulled at Martine's sleeve. "He killed my brother!"

Infuriated by the gnome's tone, Martine wrenched herself free from his grasp, almost impaling her arm on the gnome's spiked breastplate. "Let go of me! I haven't seen Jazrac, and he didn't kill your brother!"

"Fiend's fires he didn't," Jouka swore, his prominent nose flaming red, his eyes wild with passion. "Turi's not back yet. Nobody even saw him make it to the woods. Your friend should have warned us Vreesar was coming. He was in the rear."

"I haven't seen him, you—you stupid little midget!" the Harper exploded. The fear and exhaustion of the day stoked her irritation with the gnome into fury until she had to lash out.

"Martine, Jouka! Now is not the time for this!" Vil thundered as he pushed himself between the two. "Master Jouka, direct your people. They'll listen to you better than they will to me." Separated from the Harper by the former paladin, the gnome growled angrily and bustled off.

"As for you, Martine, back off," Vil said, grabbing her shoulders and steering her toward the inner doors. She quivered fiercely against his grasp. "Turi's still out there. Jouka cares a lot for him."

"Damn him!" the woman spat out, still not completely under control. "I mean, damn it all. He's right. Where *was* Jazrac when we needed him?" The question hung without an answer.

"You need rest," Vil said. "Things seem under control here. Go get some sleep. I'll alert you if anything happens."

"I'll stay here."

"Go!" This time Vil's words were not a suggestion. "Staying here will only provoke Jouka. Give him time to cool down. Get out of his sight."

"What about Jazrac?"

"If you mean looking for him, forget it. We can't risk losing anyone else. He's on his own, just like Turi." Vil didn't wait for her to agree but walked the woman a short way down the hall, heading in the direction of their room.

Eventually Martine found herself standing alone outside the small guest room. Although it wasn't her choice, sleep was a good idea right now. Opening the door, she ducked her head and stepped over the threshold. Inside, the magical tapers had been covered and only the faintest light leaked through the hoods.

"Hello, Martine," said Jazrac, his melancholy voice whispering softly from the gloom.

Martine slammed the door in shock. "Jazrac, where in Cyric's hells have you been? What are you doing here?" Martine clenched the door handle, furious to see the wizard huddled on the bed before her.

Jazrac looked at her. His once imperious gaze was lost in the gray hollows of his eyes. The regally manicured goatee and perfect coiffure were in disarray; bits of pine needles clung to his graying hair and beard. Streaks of sweat and pine resin covered his face. With clothes stained and only half-laced, Jazrac looked more like a drunkard than the proud Harper she knew.

"Does anybody know you're here?" the woman hissed, her back against the door.

"No. I used a spell to get in," the mage mumbled.

Martine slowly crossed the room, still moving like a huntress. "Jouka wants your hide. I'm not sure I blame him," she said. "What happened out there? The gnolls came right up behind us—right where you were supposed to be."

With a pained expression, the wizard leaned back and looked at the ceiling, avoiding Martine's unforgiving gaze. "I . . . panicked."

"What do you mean, you panicked?" she shouted in disbelief. There had to be a better reason, she knew. Jazrac was a powerful Harper, a wizard. He didn't panic.

"I mean I panicked, that's all! I ran!" Jazrac bellowed back, unleashing all his self-loathing on Martine. "When I saw them coming, I couldn't do anything! I was afraid . . .

afraid of Vreesar and dying and all that, so I forgot everything and ran. Do you understand now? Is that clear enough for you? Didn't anybody ever run in your world—or did they all die gloriously?"

"You ran? How could you? You're a Harper—"

"I didn't want to die!"

"—and Harpers don't run!"

"They just never tell anyone!"

Jazrac's last statement stunned Martine into silence. The pair glared at each other across the room. Each shivered with passion, struggling to control the rage within.

Finally Jazrac spoke, his voice a pleading whisper. "Martine, I could have been here in a day with my spells. Why do you think I sent you here?"

She shook her head furiously, as if to deny him any understanding.

"I'm not a warrior," the man continued with a touch of sorrow in his voice. "I'm not even a war wizard. I've spent my years reading scrolls and making magical artifacts, like the stones you used. I don't fight. So when something needs doing, I make whatever device is called for and then I send someone like you to take the risk."

"You . . . you do that, and then you have the nerve to come up here and lecture me about what a true Harper should do?" Impulsively Martine stepped forward and slapped Jazrac hard across the face. Even as she did it, she cringed in horror at the realization of what she'd done. "Oh, gods," she breathed. Lingering respect mingled with the knowledge the wizard could still break her career.

A little of the imperious fire returned to the wizard as he sat up straight on the edge of the bed. "And I was right, too. You know it." His pride faded as the energy to hold it drained from him. He was no longer Jazrac, her mentor, or Jazrac, the Harper, but just Jazrac, drained and flawed. Inside, Martine's anger cooled along with her old fearful respect.

"As I said before, Jouka wants your hide." The ranger's voice was no longer angry but cold and flat. "A lot of gnomes died in that ambush."

"I know. I just don't know what to do."

In silence, each sought an answer. Finally Martine held out her hand. "Do you still have the stone? Give it to me."

His eyes furrowed in puzzled suspicion, Jazrac hesitated. Then, pulling a leather sack from under the bed, he produced the keystone and laid it in her hand. The rock appeared no different from before. It was still pitted and veined with its own internal fires.

The woman went to the door. "Stay here till I come for you."

Outside, the ranger hurried down the halls, hoping she could remember the way. At last she arrived in the cold, dirt-floored section that contained the animal pens. As she knelt beside a cage, she noticed Hakk's doll, still lying in the dirt where'd she thrown it. Carefully she brushed it off and pushed it back through the bars.

"Word-Maker?"

"I hear you, human," echoed the shaman's hollow voice from the other side.

"Do your people want war with the Vani?" she asked.

"Ask the new chieftain of the Burnt Fur," Krote replied bitterly.

"The pit fiends take Vreesar! I mean *your* tribe . . . would they make peace?"

"The pack has no quarrel with the little people." Martine heard a scuffling in the straw, and then the dog-man slid into the light.

"If I give you the chance, can you convince your people—your pack—to make peace?" Martine squatted down to look Krote in the eyes.

"What do you want, female?" the gnoll growled.

"Will you?"

"The price is my freedom," the shaman insisted.

"Only if they agree," Martine countered. "Well?"

Krote licked his chops. "I will try. They may not listen to me."

"Good enough. Now slide to the back again." Despite the gnoll's promise, the Harper didn't trust him completely. As Krote crouched at the pen's far wall, Martine cut the ropes that bound the door shut. Once the door opened, she signaled him out and then followed the stooped gnoll through the halls.

The pair retraced her path through the windowless corridors to the room where Jazrac waited. Krote bared his fangs at the gnomish women they passed along the way, taking delight in the way they shrank in terror against the passage walls.

"Jazrac, I need you," Martine called from outside the door. "Now," she added when the wizard did not respond immediately.

The door clattered open and the Harper wizard came out, tidying his disheveled clothing in a weak attempt to regain some smattering of his dignity. He paused, hands hovering over his doublet, when he saw Krote. "What's he doing here?"

"I've got an idea," was all Martine said. She was still angry with the wizard, uncomfortable even talking to him. Most of all, though, she couldn't abide the thought that he might criticize what she intended to do. "You said Harpers should fix things. Well, I'm going to fix something." She motioned Krote and Jazrac down the hall.

"Where are we going?" Jazrac asked as he fell in beside her.

"To the council chamber. I'm guessing that's where Sumalo and the others are—making plans."

When they approached the council hall, the somber tone of voices inside confirmed Martine's guess. On entering the outer chamber, where the dance had been held, the three passed through a silent crowd. Wives of council members and some older gnomish children were clustered near the council doors, trying to catch every word of what was said inside. Around them orbited the smaller children, who didn't really understand what had happened but sensed its importance from the reaction of their elders.

Now the Harper herself could hear the grim litany that echoed from inside.

"Buri?"

"He's hurt but he made it back."

"And Heikko?"

"I think he fell at the gnolls' camp."

"That makes seventeen."

"Ojakangas?"

"He's helping to guard the south gate."

Martine pushed into the edge of the crowd blocking the door, with Krote and Jazrac following. A ripple of alarm spread through the crowd, and the gnomes parted like water before them. The women eyed Krote with fear, but their expressions changed to hostile scowls when they saw Jazrac. Stories of his role in the massacre were no doubt among the whispers that they passed from ear to ear.

The commotion at the door alerted those inside of their arrival. The hall, always before well filled with elders, was half empty, particularly the upper tiers. Those who were present sat near Sumalo's chair, where the priest was carefully making notes on a birchbark scroll. All work stopped the instant Martine guided Krote into the hall.

"What are they doing here?" Jouka demanded of Sumalo, as if the priest had something to do with Martine's arrival.

The priest set his quill aside. "Harpers, you were not summoned here," he said sternly, "and you are not welcome. It's because of you and your plots that I must add these names to the record of the dead." The whitebeards around the priest loudly grumbled their agreement.

"It's because of him!" Jouka cried accusingly, spying Jazrac. The gnome hopped down from the bench and stood with hands on hips. "Where were you during the battle, wizard? Where was your magic? My brother and friends died because of—"

"Elder Sumalo, I ask permission to speak," Martine asked, trying to prevent the meeting from becoming a shouting match.

"—because of you, you craven—"

"Elder Sumalo, please!" Martine persisted.

Thump! The speaker's rod banged on the hollow bench. "Jouka Tunkelo! Hold for a moment!" The force of Sumalo's words silenced the gnome, though he remained rooted to the spot, glaring at Jazrac.

"Martine of Sembia, what do you have to say to us?"

Martine prodded Krote, and the gnoll moved stiffly to one side. The shaman's lips curled with a slight trace of a fanged smile as he listened to the squabbling among his enemies.

"I have a plan to stop the fighting and get Vreesar out of the valley," the woman began as she stepped into the center of the hall.

"What is it, human?" Jouka sneered. "Are you and the brave wizard there going to kill this fiend yourselves?"

Martine turned stiffly to face the belligerent gnome. "No . . . I'm going to give him this." From her pocket, she pulled out Jazrac's stone and held it up for the gnomes to see. "This is the stone Vreesar wanted."

"Martine, you can't!" Jazrac blurted in alarm as he stepped forward to try and reclaim the stone.

The ranger snatched her hand back. "I can and will, Jazrac. Harpers have a duty to solve problems, not let others do it for them."

"But that thing will reopen the gate! What happens to

these people then?"

Sumalo and the others shifted uneasily when they heard this news.

"I said I have a plan. Jazrac, do you have a spell that can get you back to Shadowdale quickly?" Martine pressed. She could see that the council was wavering, and she needed to make her point quickly.

"I can teleport with this," the wizard said, meaningfully tapping the ring on his finger.

The woman breathed an inward sigh of relief, for her idea hinged on the wizard's magical abilities. "Then my plan is this," she pronounced, turning back to the council. "Vreesar wants the stone. Once the creature gets it, it'll head back to the glacier. The elemental isn't interested in you Vani or your warren. I'll give him the stone and then he'll leave."

Jouka snorted. "What about the gnolls?"

"And the rift?" Jazrac added.

Martine had her answer ready. "That's why I brought Word-Maker with me. He says he'll get the gnolls to make peace—"

"I will try, human," Krote growled, "in exchange for my freedom."

Martine winced at the gnoll's correction. Her plan was risky enough; she didn't need to have the shaman make it sound any worse.

Elder Sumalo stirred on his chair, his iron charms clinking. "As the wizard said, this creature called Vreesar will reopen this gate, and then there will be even more of them."

Martine hesitated. The time had come when she finally had to give up her pride. Pointing to the wizard, she explained, "That's where he comes in. Jazrac uses his ring to get more help from the Harpers because the job's too big for me. We take the chance that reinforcements come in time."

"Him? The coward?" Jouka scoffed. He turned his back and clambered back onto his bench in disgust.

"Yes, him." Martine had no choice but to leap to Jazrac's defense. "He simply goes home and gets help. You won't have to rely on him to fight. And he doesn't even have to come back." Martine knew the words must have stung Jazrac, but when she looked at him, his face showed no sign of any reaction.

The elders stroked their white beards thoughtfully.

"And if Vreesar kills you and takes this—this thing?" Jouka demanded, still seeking fault with her plan.

The ranger was ready for this question, too. "I plan to hide it before we meet. That way he can't just kill me and get the stone."

Sumalo turned to Jouka and said, "If the woman is killed, her plan can still go forward. She is not needed after that."

Martine had not considered that. Thinking about it now was hardly comforting. She noticed that Jouka was smiling grimly.

Now it was Jouka's turn to stroke at his beard as he leaned back on his bench and considered. The others on the council waited expectantly for him to announce his decision. Clearly, as one of the Vani's few warriors, Jouka's word carried great weight.

Finally the gnome leaned forward, placing his small hands on his small knees. "Since the woman wants to take the risk, I say we let her. Let the Harpers fix their problems. We risk nothing."

Except a hundred more creatures like Vreesar if we fail, Martine thought grimly.

Fourteen

Back in their tiny quarters after several more hours of planning with the gnomes, Martine finished going over the particulars with Jazrac. The woman was overflowing with details—the likeliest places to find the gnolls, where to hide the stone, even what gate she'd use to leave. Vil listened with interest, saying nothing all the while she outlined the plan. He sat on the edge of the bed, still in his armor, his hair stiff with dried sweat. Streaks of brown-red blood soiled his tabard.

"Could I see it?" the ex-paladin asked, pointing to the stone.

Martine shrugged and passed it to him.

"This is what he wants, eh?"

She nodded.

Vil held it up to the light, turning it like a jeweler looking for a flaw in a diamond. "It seems awfully small to have cost so many lives." He carefully handed it back to the Harper. "But then it always does."

"With that stone, Vreesar and its kind could overrun the north," Jazrac said ominously.

"I'm coming along with you," the warrior announced. He rose and buckled on his hanger as if the matter was already decided.

"No," Martine protested. "This is my plan, Vil. I can't have you taking such a risk."

"But you need me." His voice was filled with self-confidence.

Martine did a slow burn. She'd already admitted she would need help to defeat Vreesar, but it wasn't as if she couldn't handle the meeting. "I can handle myself, thank you, Vilheim Baltson."

"I know you can, but you shouldn't be alone. You'll need someone to watch the gnoll while you talk, just in case he tries something." Vil adjusted the straps on his helm.

"The man makes sense, Martine," Jazrac observed, even though Martine couldn't help considering the wizard's counsel suspect in such matters.

"You're going to insist on this, aren't you?" Sensing there was no winning, the ranger rose awkwardly from the floor, the weight of her armor making the move difficult.

Vil nodded in the affirmative as he tipped his chin back to finish buckling the helmet's straps. "Call it my old paladin self. You need help and I'm duty bound to give it." The words sounded a little choked as he fussed with the strap.

"Are you sure you're not still a paladin?" she asked with mock suspicion.

Vil rocked the helmet on his head, testing the soundness of the buckles. "I can't help it if I still think like one."

"All right. It's your choice. But I'm not responsible for you," Martine relented as she strung her bow.

"Don't worry. I can take care of myself."

Inwardly, Martine was relieved at the chance to have his company. None of the Vani could be spared to come along, so it would be just she and Vil.

Armored and outfitted, the pair took their leave of the wizard. Jazrac remained behind in the room, too mortified to face the gnomes alone. "Jazrac, don't leave before I get back," Martine said as they started through the door.

"I know—just to make sure everything has gone as planned," the wizard concluded wearily as he closed the door.

It felt uncomfortable giving the mage orders like a child, but Martine was keenly aware that this was her responsibility. Uncomfortable or not, she couldn't allow any mistakes.

Bound and guarded, Krote was waiting for them in the hall. The gnomes had produced his ragged arm wrappings from somewhere. Seeing how filthy they were, Martine was amazed the gnomes hadn't burned them. Even the studded crossed belts had been returned.

"Untie him," the woman ordered as one of the guards handed over the shaman's charms.

"You can do that outside," the gnome replied.

It wasn't important, so Martine let it drop. The gnomes led the way. The warren's hallways were empty and quiet, somehow missing the normal bustle of everyday life.

A great yawn swept over the ranger.

"When did you last sleep?" Vil asked.

"I don't really know. Is it day or night?" Cut off from the cycles of light and dark inside the windowless burrow, the ranger had lost all track of time. Was it quiet because it was nighttime? Did the gnomes even care?

"It's almost dawn," their guide offered. The gnome led them to a section of the warren Martine had never seen before. How big is this den? she wondered. She'd heard of immense underground complexes in the wild regions of the Heartlands, but those were almost always inhabited by fell orcs and the like. Could it be that the gnomes were even greater tunnelers than she ever suspected?

Their arrival at a small doorway at the end of a long passage ended these considerations. There was a small alcove carved at the very end, and here two gnomes guarded the portal. The pair sprang to their feet guiltily, shoving the draughts board out of sight and clenching their stubby spears tightly. They eyed the party nervously.

"The cliffside entrance," explained the guide with a nod toward the small door. The gate couldn't have been more than four feet high and half as wide and was constructed of heavy beams bound by iron. A set of double bars lay firmly in heavy brackets at the top and bottom. Everything at this end of the hall was black and polished smooth by the touch of the years.

Their skis hung beside the door on pegs. The gnome quickly passed them to Martine and Vil. There were no skis for the gnoll, but the Harper had already arranged for a pair of snowshoes. The hall was too cramped for them to don their gear, so Martine motioned for the door to be opened while Vil's lips moved in a silent prayer.

He's still a paladin at heart, Martine realized suddenly.

The three gnomes set their shoulders to the top bar, and the scarred black beam grated as it slid aside. Next they dragged the lower beam from its brackets. When they worked the iron latch, the gate swung inward with a leaden *thunk* to open onto a small square of predawn light held in a frame of thick snow, a short tunnel-like passage to the surface.

"It must not be used much," Martine noted as she peered at the patch of light at the end. The gnomes noted her words, but offered no comment.

"It's a bolt hole . . . an escape route. We'll strap on our skis outside," Vil said.

Bent almost double, the three of them half-walked, half-crawled up the four steps and onto the surface. Cliffside was aptly named, for the gate deposited them on a small

ledge of a bluff overlooking the river. In the predawn
gloom, Martine could see that the slope dropped away
quickly and was thick with young birches that had gained a
purchase on its steep sides. Below and beyond the dim
light, she heard the creak and groan of river ice, while
behind them, the gate thudded shut, followed by the
rumble of the bars as they were slid back in place.

Drawing her bone-handled knife, Martine cut the shaman's bonds. The gnoll eagerly flexed his wrists and
rubbed them to get circulation back into his hands. With
his superior night vision, the gnoll flicked his yellow eyes
over the woods while his black nose crinkled, searching for
scents the humans could never discern.

"Wear these," the ranger ordered, thrusting the snowshoes into Krote's hands. Vil held his sword ready while
Martine strapped her skis on; then she did the same for
him. Ice crackled softly under their feet as the party broke
a path along the trail. The skis hissed through the powder,
grinding on the hard chunks of ice that roiled up like waves
on a frozen sea.

The trail wound along the river bluff, hairpinning several
times before it finally reached level ground well away from
the warren.

Upon reaching the flat, Martine signaled the silent group
to a stop. "Wait here," she whispered as if there were gnolls
all about. "I've got to hide the stone." She slid away into the
frost-filled gloom of the forest.

"Take off your snowshoes and sit," the former paladin
ordered, motioning to the gnoll with his sword. As the shaman obeyed, Vil settled down for a long wait.

The pair spent what seemed like an hour in silence, listening to the hunting calls of the owls along the river, the
last before their coming daytime silence. Once they heard a
barking cough that alerted them both, but then the yellow
gleam of eyes showed it to be a lynx irritated with their

presence. The gnoll growled and bared his teeth at the wildcat to send it scampering into the woods. It was as close to talking as the man and gnoll got.

The slide of skis heralded Martine's return. She said nothing about where she had been, believing it best that only she knew the stone's hiding place. Vil was happy to get moving again and work out the chill that had seeped into his body. The dawn sun was breaking over the eastern mountains, but its rays only created bright glare and long shadows without providing any warmth.

"So where do we find Vreesar?" Vil asked as they skirted the snow-choked borders of a frozen pond, an extension of the low-banked river. A mountain fog, moisture freezing in the air, hung in the trees along the shore's edge.

"We'll try their camp first," Martine answered. "I don't think they've had time to move any closer to the warren. The gnomes didn't see any signs of major activity—no smoke from campfires or anything. My best guess is that they're still at the camp we raided."

Krote spoke up. "They will not stay there."

"Why not?" Martine demanded.

"Many died there. The ground is *paavak*—a place for evil spirits. Even Vreesar cannot get my people to stay."

Martine trusted the shaman's words because they made sense. Places of death, especially battlegrounds, were always dangerous, and not only because the dead might walk again. There was always the risk of being possessed by a vengeful spirit still haunting such areas. "All right. Then we'll assume Vreesar's somewhere between his old camp and the warren. With all those gnolls, the camp can't be hard to find."

Keeping alert for any tracks, Martine plunged into the woods, following a path that would form a loop around the warren's east side. Sooner than she expected, they found the broken snow of a trail made by a number of creatures, all more or less following the same direction.

"Definitely gnolls," the ranger whispered after a brief inspection of the tracks. "About twenty of them. See the snow in the prints? They can't be more than a few hours old."

"How about the elemental?" Vil asked.

Martine shook her head. "Not among these. Let's go." The woman didn't like standing still. The gnolls could be anywhere. They might have looped back, or they could be stopped just over the next ridge. There was a thrill to the uncertainty of stalking that made her want to keep moving, especially when the prey was as cunning and dangerous as the gnolls were.

"Be ready, shaman," she added. "In case we find them."

The gnoll growled. Martine wasn't sure what that signified. Word-Maker had assured her that he could get them a parley. She would rather have used a white flag, assuming such things were universal, but the gnolls, according to the shaman, didn't understand the meaning of that gesture. Thus she found herself forced to rely on the shaman more than she liked. It made her all the happier to have Vil along, in case Krote decided to betray her trust.

The trail split around some tree trunks and branched off, with several lone tracks trailing off into the woods, but the main trail kept a steady course, angling toward a ridge that overlooked the east gate. The ridge was formed by a mountain spur that forced the river into a wide loop and formed the small bluff upon which the warren sat. The high end of the ridge, to the east, crested in a series of granite outcroppings that thrust through the snow like the exposed vertebrae of the mountain's spine. A gnoll perched atop the rocks would have a clear view of the east and south gates of the Vani warren. Making a sensible guess, Martine figured the camp was somewhere just below the crest.

From ahead, there came a raven's mournful protest.

After that, it became completely silent. There were no sounds of forest animals foraging for their breakfasts, no bird calls of any type. Without speaking, Martine signaled caution. Vil drew his sword and held it close to the gnoll's back, making sure the shaman saw his move. The Harper kept her weapons sheathed. She wanted to parley and could not afford any misunderstanding that might lead to battle.

Stealthily the ranger led them on, using all her woodland skill to avoid any noise. She winced with every crackle of Krote's snowshoes. Soon they heard harsh voices through the trees, and then they saw their goal.

It was a new camp, as Martine had hoped. Though the ground was trampled with the tribe's coming and going, only a few rude tents had been put up. The gnolls huddled in small groups, bundled in their furs, their weapons thrust in the snow beside them. A few were making an anemic effort to chop wood, but no fires smoked. It must have been a cold and hard night for the gnolls, she thought. They looked exhausted, which probably explained the lack of guards around the camp's perimeter.

Martine beckoned Krote forward. "Remember, we've come to talk, not fight. You'll die first if you betray us," she whispered. The gnoll's ears twitched, the only sign that he heard.

Stepping from the background of the trees, Krote raised his hands high. Several faces glanced his way, and those that saw him spread the alarm, creating a flurry that swept through the camp.

"Brothers of the Burnt Fur!" Krote shouted, his voice harsh against the coldness of the morning.

Growled barks rippled through the small packs of warriors.

"Brothers of the Burnt Fur, I bring the humans with me. They come to speak with the chieftain of the Burnt Fur. I

call the chieftain of the Burnt Fur to come forth and speak
for his tribe." Krote crossed his arms, looking as regal and
proud as his thin, haggard body allowed.

The gnolls swayed with indecision. Some took several
steps forward, only to falter hesitantly as the rest of the
pack hung back. Their eyes scanned the wood on all sides,
looking for a trap. Swords and spears were cautiously
drawn from the snow. It was obvious they did not welcome
the shaman, but no tribesman acted with enough boldness
to tip the balance one way or the other. They were confused, since the two humans were not enough for an attack,
but there was no sign of an ambush. Yet the concept of talking was foreign to them.

"Varka," Krote demanded of a small gnoll near the center
of the camp, "is your chieftain here? Where is the one
called Vreesar?"

Eyes blazing, Varka pointed toward the far end of the
camp. Krote noticed something stir near the farthest tent.
Movement defined the camouflaged shape of the elemental, reclined against a mound of snow. "I am here, traitor," it
droned in a leaden buzz. "You are not welcome."

"I bring humans to talk," Krote shouted across the camp.

"Humanz . . . more than one? I see the female. Who iz the
other?" The elemental pushed itself up from the snow and
slowly came forward in its stiff-legged walk. The gnolls
drew aside and then followed their chieftain, bolder and
more belligerent behind the fiend.

"He does not matter," Krote said.

Martine stepped ahead of the shaman. "I come to end
this fighting, Vreesar." The wind swept away the quaver in
her voice.

"End fighting? Why?" The creature cocked its head, as if
curious. "It iz fun. I will kill you all, and then I will get my
brotherz."

The Harper took a deep breath. "No, you won't. You

won't have the stone."

Vreesar moved closer. Behind Martine, Vil slipped out of his skis, getting ready for whatever might happen next. "When you are dead, I will take the stone. It iz simple."

"If you kill me, you'll never get it. I've hidden it."

Vreesar stopped at her words, its iciclelike facial ridges flexing in thought. Then its pinched face seemed to brighten. "I will make you tell me where it iz."

Martine had expected this. She hoped her voice sounded as firm as her conviction. "It won't work."

Once again the elemental's face flexed as it considered her words. Its claws tapped together like frozen chimes. "Why did you come?" it purred.

Martine's shoulders softened as every contracted muscle in her body relaxed. "To make a deal—peace in exchange for the stone."

"Peace?"

"Leave the Vani alone and I'll tell you where the stone is."

"Why?"

This question was also expected, and it was crucial. The elemental had to believe and accept her answer. Martine had already thought out several replies, but now it seemed that only the truth would do.

"Because I don't want them to die. This is not their fight, and I shouldn't gotten them involved."

"You did not choose anything, human. I fight them because I want to," Vreesar said with a sneer.

"Then there's nothing to talk about. We'll fight you, and you'll never get the stone, creature." The Harper turned to go. She signaled for Vil and Krote to follow. The gnoll looked at her dumbly, but Vil nodded and also turned to leave.

"Wait, human," Vreesar barked before the pair had gone two steps. "Perhapz we can reach an agreement."

Still facing away, Martine smiled. Her bluff had worked.

"Like what?"

"My slavez will not attack the little people." With its alien drone of a voice, Martine had no way to gauge the depth of the elemental's sincerity.

"How do I know I can trust you?" she asked, turning back.

"I am Vreesar." This time she could hear the creature's shock that the ranger would doubt its word.

"So?" Martine caught Vil looking at her, as if to warn her not to push things too far.

"An oath to the prince of ice!" it spat, frustrated at her rejection.

"So you swear?"

"Yez," it answered venomously. "Now, human, there iz one thing I want."

"What?"

The elemental pointed at the Word-Maker. "Leave me the traitor."

Martine had no ready answer for this unexpected turn of events. A quick look at the shaman told her his opinion; the gnoll's ears were flattened back in the fighting response. Beyond him, Vil shook his head almost imperceptibly from side to side.

"He's a living creature," the former paladin hissed. "You can't barter his life."

The Harper steeled herself to face the elemental squarely, her eyes focusing on its ice-veiled face. The thing's tiny mouth rasped eagerly as it waited for her reply. Slowly she shook her head. "Krote is my prisoner. He's not part of my bargain. He stays with me." She still needed the shaman to forge a peace with the gnolls once this was all done.

"He iz mine! He iz one of the Burnt Fur, and I am hiz chieftain!" Vreesar shrilled. It started to lunge forward, claws outstretched. . . .

"The stone! Not if you want the stone!" Martine shouted

even as Krote leaped backward to avoid the elemental's icy grasp.

Vreesar stopped suddenly, held by her words.

"Harm him and the deal's off," Martine announced. Her sword was in her hand as if it sprang magically from its sheath.

Vil stepped forward to flank Martine, with Krote between them. Behind Vreesar, the gathered gnolls bristled, awaiting their chieftain's word. The clearing was cloudy with their steaming breath.

Vreesar looked hungrily at the three before him. Its clawed hands flexed slowly. Finally it eased its body back until it was no longer in a hunter's crouch. "You can have him, human. He iz worthlez." The elemental stepped back and twisted its gleaming head around to address the rest of the tribe. "Let them leave thiz time, but if you see the traitor again, kill him."

Several eager yowls of bloodlust rose from the pack, but most kept silent, as if judging the worth of their chieftain against that of their shaman.

Vreesar turned back to Martine and under its gaze, she suddenly felt cold. "Now, human, where iz the stone?"

The Harper was trembling so hard she wasn't sure she could remain standing. "On the big island in the river. You'll find a blazed trail that will lead you to it." All three of them stopped breathing, waiting to see if Vreesar would kill them now.

The tiny mouth cracked in the slightest of smiles, as if sensing their fears. "Leave, humanz," the elemental hummed. It pointed to a packed trail across the camp. "Take the short trail. No one will harm you."

Martine didn't wait for a second offer, but neither did she let her fears make her bolt. Warily she trudged through the camp, her gaze constantly moving from enemy to enemy. As they passed, each gnoll stepped aside slightly, although none were submissive. Neck hairs bristled, ears flattened, and growls rumbled in the throats of the dog-men. At first Martine thought they were directed at her, but then she realized most of their attention was directed at Krote, who was immediately behind her. The shaman walked stiff and tall, never once even glancing at those who threatened him. He seemed almost icy calm in the midst of their animalistic hatred.

As soon as the three entered the forest, they buckled on their skis and snowshoes. The only one who spoke was Krote. "I come with you until Vreesar leaves my people," he growled, "but I am free."

Martine shook her head. "That wasn't the agreement. You're free when you make peace with your tribe."

Krote spat. "When I try, you said! I cannot try now. They will kill me."

Martine shook her head. "Find a way if you want your freedom." Her voice was firm. Vil, with his sword drawn, pressed it gently against the gnoll's back.

The measured march through the camp became a hurried flight now that they were out of sight. The trail was well used, but coarsely broken. The skiers bumped and skidded over the trampled footprints of their enemies. In the packed snow, Krote had little difficulty keeping up as they hurried through the tightly packed trees of the slope.

The caws of ravens alerted them that something was up. Before the skiers could slow their pace, a coven of black forms swirled up, screeching, from a line of posts in the trail just ahead of them. A few of the brave birds stayed behind, unwilling to surrender their meaty prizes. The ravens pecked at a row of bloodless heads, jammed onto the ends of crudely sharpened stakes. They were small heads, smaller than a human's.

"Oh, gods!" Martine swore. She couldn't stand to look.

"Claim stakes. We Burnt Fur mark our territory with the

heads of our enemies." Krote's voice echoed with fierce pride.

"We? You're our prisoner now, Word-Maker," Martine snapped.

As they sparred, Vil knelt to examine the gruesome display. He paused before one in the middle. "This is Turi," Vil said softly.

Martine forced herself to look. The birds had done thorough work. The eye sockets of the head were empty, and most of the face was gone, except for a few frozen bits of flesh and the bloody strings of a beard. "How can you tell?" she asked quickly, trying to hold in her rage.

The man spoke with pain. He gently touched the beads woven into the beard of the little face. "Turi's braids," he explained.

"The little people will remember not to attack the Burnt Fur," Krote predicted as they set out once more.

Fifteen

Aghast at what she had seen, Martine shoved the shaman back onto the trail. Krote snarled a warning as she shouldered past to resume lead. "Be careful, human. Someday I will not be your prisoner." The Harper drew her sword quickly and, twisting about, let the blade flash in the sunlight. She said nothing but sheathed the weapon and laid into her skis, setting a brutal pace. After a mile of winding through the wood, even Vil, a better skier than Martine, was panting hard.

Just ahead, the trail broke out of the woods and plunged and plunged down a steep slope to the clear meadows of a marshy stream. Just as Martine was about launch over the edge, Vil pulled up short. "Let's rest here a minute," he insisted. Fiercely determined to match the Harper's pace, Krote breathed shuddering clouds of steam from the exertion.

Martine stood poised on the brink of the descent, upset at the delay. The longer she stood, the less irritated she became as she finally felt the effects of her pace. The sweat of exertion quickly cooled in the bitter wind that swept up the slope, drawing the heat from her flushed skin.

Calm down, she urged herself. You can't exhaust yourself here. There's still too much to be done.

As she stood gathering her strength, Vil sheltered his eyes to scan the slope for the best route down. "That's odd," he murmured suddenly. "What do you make of that?"

The warrior pointed a mittened hand toward a thick gray-white cloud that settled over the warren less than a mile ahead. Coiling arms of snow rose upward on spirals of wind, only to fall back to earth. It was like a storm blown down fresh from the mountains, but everywhere else the sky was clear. As the pair watched, the gray mass swirled and spread to swallow the adjacent trees within its white depths.

"It seems to be spreading in a circle," the Harper noted with a sense of dread.

"Does your friend have any weather magic in his gear?"

The question caught the woman off guard. "Jazrac? I wouldn't know."

"It's definitely not natural."

Krote snorted. "Storms are things of cold."

"Vreesar! You don't suppose . . . ?"

Vil nodded, his lips pursed tight beneath his ice-encrusted mustache. "Vreesar's an elemental. He just might be able to stir up a storm like that."

"Come on!" Martine launched herself down the steep slope. Rocks and trees sped past as she plowed through the icy snow. The Harper skied blindly, barely managing to stay erect. Suddenly the slope ended and the Harper hit the flat meadow, still on her feet. Skidding to a stop, she barely evaded Vil as the man shot past. Right behind the man came Krote. Martine quickly drew her sword and advanced toward the shaman.

"I must come with you or freeze," the dog-man snarled as he struggled to stand at the bottom. "If you kill me now, there is no peace with the Burnt Fur."

The Harper barely heard his threat. Seizing his arm, she shoved him toward Vil and then started across the frozen bog. Cursing, the gnoll delayed until Vil goaded him into a shuffling sprint, the fastest pace the gnoll could maintain.

The forest ahead of them abruptly changed. A billowing gray-white wall swallowed the forest one tree at a time. The swirling vortex seemed to reach out cloudlike arms and embrace each tree before dragging its victim into its dark depths.

They pulled to a stop, uncertain whether they should plunge into the whirling mass. The line between sunlight and storm was clearly demarcated. "What do you think's happening inside?" Vil asked.

Martine peered into the gloom as she pulled back the thick hood of her parka and adjusted her helmet for battle. The storm facing them presented a gray wall that swallowed up the forest after only a few feet. "I don't know," she shouted over the howling wind, "but I don't like it. That bastard Vreesar's up to something."

"If we go in there, we'll be traveling blind."

"So what do we do? Just stand here?" the Harper asked in exasperation. "Help me tie him up." She nodded at Krote.

Unarmed, Krote could only submit. Vil played out a length of rope to serve as a leash to prevent the gnoll from disappearing once they were inside the storm. The gnoll turned to the warrior with bitter smile. "Vreesar plans to attack. My people may be warm tonight in your warren after all."

"Not if I can help it," Vil promised. "And if they do, where will you sleep, outcast?"

The gnoll snarled at the words, but he followed Martine as she stepped across the line between sunshine and storm.

The biting blizzard greedily devoured the three, wrapping them in its embrace. Barely ten feet inside, all sunlight had disappeared, leaving only a stinging white glare into which everything dissolved. The thick forest vanished and was replaced by individual trunks that faded as the group passed.

In her limited experience with winter, Martine had never been in a blizzard before, much less one summoned by magical force. Almost instantly she stumbled back, driven by the stinging gale. The wind-whipped snow tore at her face until she had to squeeze her eyes to mere slits, and the tears that formed barely started to run down her cheeks before they froze. A push from Vil, bent double against the gale, kept her moving forward.

"What now?" she shouted, her words snatched from her mouth by the wind.

Vil pulled close, dragging the shaman with him, and pressed his helmeted forehead close to hers. "Keep moving forward. Watch for anything that looks familiar," he advised, ice and snow cracking from his beard as his lips moved. Even though he was shouting in her face, she could barely hear him over the roar. She waved her understanding and struck out again.

What direction, though? Already she had no idea whether she was plunging deeper inside or moving back toward the outside edge of the storm. The trail had all but vanished, leaving only maddening traces that never seemed to go in directions the ranger expected. Finally she sighted a tree she thought looked familiar. It was hard to be certain because it seemed to keep changing in the storm. She decided to head toward the pine tree she thought she recognized. From there, she targeted for the faint outline of another tree no more than ten feet ahead.

Intent on her goal, Martine bumped into the hummock lying across her path. As she did, her skis jolted to a

sudden stop, and the ranger tumbled forward into the
mound.

She struck something hard rather than soft snow. It must
be a log, she thought, until she saw the red ice beneath the
blowing snow. "Vil!" she shouted as she frantically scraped
away the powdery blanket. Underneath, already cool and
growing pale, was a gnome. His helm was split, his face
shattered by a massive blow that had left no hope of his survival.

"Who—who is he?" the Harper asked haltingly.

"I don't know. One of the gnomes from yesterday's raid?"

Martine pulled a mitten off and pressed her hand to the
gnome's cheek. "No. He's still a little warm," she shouted.
"A scout, I'd bet. What about the others?"

Suddenly a howl rang hauntingly on the wind. A gnoll?
Martine couldn't tell. The ranger looked quickly at the
Word-Maker, to make sure the dog-man did not reply.
Krote's expression was blank.

She decided to head in the direction of the sounds. Any
goal was preferable to aimless wandering. "Leave the
gnome here. He's dead," the ranger shouted as she
struggled to her feet against the wind. Vil lingered a few
moments while he murmured a quick prayer. She didn't
wait and plunged ahead.

With every tree that loomed out of the snowy haze, with
every hummock and deadfall, Martine expected to be con-
fronted by a snarling rush of gnoll warriors. There was no
way to tell if the enemy was near or far or even present at
all, although the Harper was sure by now that Vreesar had
not sent the humans back on the shortest trail.

It was luck, a fortunate turn on Tymora's wheel, that
guided them through the howling storm. They met no
gnolls, even though both Vil and Martine seemed to see
the beasts in everything. Suddenly the trees vanished and
the tracks became more definite—well-cut grooves in the

hardened crust. The three only had to follow these a little way before they came to the heavy doors of the east gate. Their pounding on the wooden gate could barely be heard over the wail of the storm.

The peephole shot open, framing a pair of weary, bloodshot eyes. "We're back!" Martine shouted. "Let us in!"

The heavy bolts rattled on the other side, and the gate parted cautiously. The Harper pushed the cracked doors open and hurried inside. Vil herded Krote in and got himself through the door as quickly as possible.

Two small guards, old Tikkanen and another, stood tense and hesitant as the trio entered. "Get those doors shut!" the Harper snapped. "There are gnolls outside."

The old gatekeeper's rheumy eyes widened. "Impossible!" he blustered. "Luski would have come back to warn us."

"Shut the doors, damn it!" the ranger demanded as she kicked off her skis. The fierceness of her command set them in motion. "This one you called Luski—did you send him outside?"

"Not me. The council posted him as a scout."

Martine cursed as she stamped her feet to warm them. Vil already had his skis off. He forced the gnoll onto a small bench to remove the beast's snowshoes. He looked up from his work. "Your scout's dead, Tikkanen."

That news motivated the gnomes. The gate was quickly swung closed and shot with bolts and bars. "Elder Sumalo must be told," Tikkanen said excitedly once the work was done. Leaving his companion peering through the peephole at the storm, the ancient gnome waddled down the hall as fast as his short legs could take him, scurrying away to warn the others.

"Vil," Martine said wearily as she sank onto one of the small benches, "can you take Krote back to his cell?"

The warrior nodded and roused the shaman, who rose

resentfully. "Meet you back here?"

Eyes closed, she nodded, then listened as the former paladin trundled their prisoner away. Her mind was already drifting.

Twenty minutes and a short catnap later, the foyer of the east gate was crowded with gnomes. Jouka stood at the forefront in his spined armor. The survivors of the previous raid milled nervously about. Sumalo stayed to the rear, his charms tinkling with tuneless rythym.

"Are you sure about the gnolls, humans?" Jouka demanded again as he stepped away from the window slot. "I see nothing but the storm out there."

"And the storm doesn't seem odd to you?" the Harper asked.

"It is winter. Storms come up quickly here."

"No, Jouka," Vil interceded. "This storm's not natural."

"And what about Luski?" Martine added.

"Brother Jouka," the guard at the door shouted excitedly, "there's something moving out there!"

Crrrack!

The gate exploded in a sudden crescendo of noise. A screaming rain of sharp wooden projectiles rode the shock wave of the blast, splintered from the shattered doors with all the fury of a hurricane wind. The jagged wood ripped clothes and flesh alike, tangled in Martine's hair, and tore at her skin. The blow slammed the slight woman against the side wall, bruising her good shoulder.

Rising to her feet, the Harper drew her sword and took quick stock of the situation. A shrieking gnome stumbled past, half his ruddy face gouged by the wood. Other screams filled the air. At the back of the hall, the ranger could barely see Jouka amid the upheaval, thrown to the rear by the force of the blast. Vil was sprawled onto a bench opposite her, startled but apparently all right. The gnomes between them reeled in confusion.

The gate itself hung half shattered in the doorway, splintered boards held up by the heavy wooden bar that lay askew in the portal, partially blocking the opening. Cold air whistled through the gaps, one of which was large enough to see through clearly. Beyond, in the eerie golden light of the storm, stood the elemental, its slick body gleaming with the same whitish gold that bathed the ground. There was a look of intense satisfaction on its bestial face as it raised its hands before it. Silver white energy flashed between its fingertips, rapidly spinning into a hardened ball of glowing ice. The creature threw back its wedgelike head with a cry of triumph, a sanguinary howl taken up by the gnolls Martine now saw clustered behind him. It echoed and reechoed through the chamber.

Deliberately the elemental turned his attention to the gate once more, raising the sphere that hovered between his hands.

"Get down, everybody!" Martine bellowed in the loudest voice she could, while at the same instant translating words to action. The Harper had barely flattened herself on the floor before the second explosion rocketed from the elemental's hands. The ice ball smashed into the partially shattered gate like a stone from a catapult and exploded in a hail of icy, needlelike shards. This second blast felt harder than the first, since the broken gate afforded little protection. The hall shook, and fresh screams rang out as the razorlike ice ripped through gnomes still staggering from the first assault. Dirt sifted through new gaps in the ceiling boards. The gate bar flexed, then snapped with an explosive crack. The remaining door planks burst from the frame and flew across the hall like projectiles. The lintel over the door buckled and groaned, long splits rippling through the carved beam. Snow quickly filled the air through the gaping opening.

Even before the dirt and snow had settled, the gnolls

were charging forward. The gate was a shattered tangle, a barrier no more. The first line of the warren's defenses had been destroyed in a matter of seconds.

"What was that?" Vil shouted as he scrambled forward to fill the breach. Martine jerked her sword free and stumbled up to join him, stepping amid the mewling bodies of the gnomes who'd been closest to the door.

"How should I know?" the woman gasped. "With Vreesar's powers, maybe—"

The rush of the Burnt Fur cut short any further talk as the dog-men sprang through the wreckage. The first gnoll through the gap took both their swords full in the chest and died before it even had a chance to clear the threshold. It had not yet fallen when another wild-eyed gnoll elbowed the dying body out of the way, jabbing with a spike-headed axe as it kicked away the broken boards. The wolf-man was quick, beating back their blades as it bulled forward. Another gnoll with a maul battered the still-standing frame to widen the gap.

Jouka, his face blood-streaked and eyes ablaze, slipped between the two humans and darted beneath the gnoll's axe to stab the beast in the thigh with his thick-bladed spear. Howling, the gnoll swung downward at its new tormentor, lowering its guard in the process. Martine hacked furiously at it, and the gnoll's hand suddenly flew free of the beast's body. The gnoll staggered back, screeching as blood jetted from the stump. Just as Vil moved in for the kill, the maul-wielder crashed through the remaining splinters and swung madly at the former paladin. Vil shifted targets in midswing and chopped the second gnoll across the face. The maul crashed down helplessly as the gnoll flopped forward with a gurgling spray of blood, its lower jaw and windpipe sliced away.

For a second, Martine thought the three of them just might be able to hold the tide at the gate. The gnolls in the front rank had been killed, and the reinforcements were already falling back, fleeing from the bloodbath in the doorway.

Then, too late to do anything about it, Martine saw Vreesar raising its hands for yet another blast. The elemental's tiny mouth twisted in triumph as it callously condemned the gnolls in the sphere's path to destruction.

"Gods—"

The rest of Martine's oath was extinguished by an explosive roar. The shock wave, an invisible bubble of force, hit like a battering ram, jerking the Harper from the floor and flinging her slight body toward the back wall. The dying axe-wielder had caught the full force of the magical blast in its back. Now its body flopped forward with a flattish, splayed look, riddled by ice-torn holes. Its insides spilled through the huge gashes. Jouka was hurled across the debris-cluttered floor, bouncing against the overturned benches that blocked his way. Vil, whom she could barely see, reeled against a side wall as he awkwardly avoided falling ceiling timbers.

The ground came up hard, even though Martine's fall was cushioned by a tangle of Vani. Her side, blistered and torn, took the brunt of her slide, so that Martine's knees buckled as she crawled free from the struggling mass.

There was no rush into the gaping breach. The gnolls were apparently unwilling to charge lest their chieftain launch another strike. That delay was all the Vani had going for them. Reaching out, the woman seized dazed Jouka by the collar and dragged him from the center of the floor. "Get them out of here! We can't hold out any longer!"

Jouka didn't argue. Instead, he merely nodded weakly. "Fall back!" he gasped, shoving nearby warriors toward the inner door. They required no further urging.

A strong hand grabbed Martine's shoulder and hoisted her up. "Thank Torm, you're alive!" Vil breathed huskily. "I fear the warren is lost." He pulled her toward the temporary safety of the inner hall, for they both knew the respite granted by the gnolls would not last.

"We can still defeat them," Martine objected. They were the last two through the inner gates. The doors quickly closed behind them. Tables and benches were braced against the doors—anything that could absorb the brunt of Vreesar's icy blasts.

"At what cost, Harper? There are women and children here." A Vani scream from the outer chamber, drawn out and agonizing riveted everyone's attention. The gnolls were celebrating their victory. At least it will buy us more time, Martine noted grimly.

"Would you sacrifice them, too?" Vil demanded, speaking not only to the woman but also to Jouka, whose face was set hard. "It's time to evacuate the warren."

"This is our home! This dirt is in our blood," Jouka snarled contemptuously. "We will not run. Maybe you would be chased out of your home and idly watch it burn, human, but we make our stand here." Jouka looked fiercely to his fellows for support, but instead of a passionate band of warriors, he saw a handful of tired and frightened family men who held no false illusions of honor. The dwindling screams from beyond their sight reminded all of the fate that might be in store for their wives and children.

"Jouka, the human is right," Elder Sumalo gasped. The priest had been wounded in the first blast and now lay on a litter, bloody blankets bound around his side. "We cannot stand against their magic. Every door we close will be blasted like the first. We must think of our families."

"Where will we go, Elder Sumalo? If we leave the warren, we'll freeze," Jouka protested. "It's all the fault of this human—her and her plan."

"Who is at fault is not the issue, Jouka. Survival is," Martine countered. "Look, we can hole up at Vil's cabin."

"Unfortunately it lies that way." Vil pointed toward the doors leading to the east gate. "We'll never make it from another gate in this storm."

Martine sagged against the wall. She just wanted to give up. Why had Jazrac even offered her . . .

"Jazrac! Gods, I forgot about him completely. He hasn't left yet!" The Harper's face brightened, and she turned to Sumalo and Jouka with renewed hope. "Gather the women and children in one of these rooms on the eastern side. Make sure they're well away from the fighting and send someone to have the wizard join them. He can get us out."

"The wizard is useless." Jouka spat contemptuously.

"He's our only chance."

A loud thud sounded against the doors, and everyone glanced at them nervously. "Gather everyone at the granary," Jouka said stiffly as he relented reluctantly.

* * * * *

When the inner door shattered under two ringing blasts from Vreesar, the gnolls charged into an empty chamber. Confused, the warriors ripped through the meager furnishings of the hall, howling in triumph. They were certain of victory. The gnolls broke into hunting packs and scattered down the empty halls.

"Now!" Vil cried out as the marauders cleared the first corner. The passage echoed with the sharp twang of crossbows fired by the small cadre of Vani accompanying him. A loud shriek proved at least one quarrel had struck home, but Vil didn't wait to see. "To the next position—go!" he bellowed. The gnomes sprang from their hiding places and ran down the hall, past where Martine lurked with another small band of warriors.

After several minutes, the gnolls reappeared cautiously, peering around the corner. "Hold your fire," the Harper hissed. The Vani next to her trembled slightly. The head disappeared, and then a single gnoll slowly stepped forward, nervous and wary. Martine waited as he advanced two cautious steps forward. "Fire!" she shouted. The gnoll shrieked and slumped to the floor. "Back, everyone!" she barked as the gnomes pulled out quickly. They had barely reached Vil's new position around the next corner when a handful of magical ice hurtled down the passage and burst in a small explosion right where they had been.

"Be careful, Vil. Vreesar's up there somewhere," Martine said softly.

"You too, Martine," he said with unmistakable concern. "You sure you don't need help?"

"Krote's only one gnoll. You'll need every available gnome. Don't worry about me."

"I'm—I'm only afraid I'll never see you again," the big man said awkwardly.

"They're coming, Master Vilheim!" the Vani lookout cried.

"Go, Martine—and let the blessed gods go with you." The former paladin turned his back to her as if he welcomed the interruption, so Martine left him to his command, feeling touched by the man's sudden concern.

Martine limped through the dim halls, wary because of the chance the gnolls might break through the defenders. The distant noise of battle mingled with fainter sounds—a baby crying, a confused murmur of voices. The normally warm warren was cold, the warmth lost to the night air through shattered doors.

At last she reached Krote's pen, and she gave small thanks to Tymora. She had secretly feared that one of the Vani—Jouka, perhaps—might have taken it upon himself to rid the valley of one more gnoll, but that apparently had not happened.

"Word-Maker!" she called into the pen. "Come out here."

The mound of matted straw at the back stirred, and a pair of feral eyes glinted in the dim light. "My brothers come. Is true, human?"

The woman undid the lock and quickly stepped back, her sword held ready. The lanky gnoll eased slowly from the pen, stiffly unworking his cramped joints, even though the ceiling was too low for the seven-foot tall shaman to stand straight.

Martine motioned him to start down the passage. "I don't want to kill you, Word-Maker, but I will if I you force me to. Do I have your word you won't attack?" The question was almost a demand.

Krote stopped his canine stretching to look at the Harper and then ask with silken cynicism, "Why should I believe your words? You said you would free me."

"I will."

"Why?"

Martine tossed back her stringy, short hair. "Because you're the Word-Maker and you believe in your words— don't you?"

Krote stood silent, ears twitching to the echoes that rolled down the corridor. "I give you my word, human. I will not attack. My people will kill me anyway."

"Good enough. Now go—quickly."

They hurried down the corridor, gradually increasing their speed to an easy lope. They moved through the dark passages toward the nervous din of the Vani. The hallways were deserted, not surprising considering the battle that raged through the underground halls, but it felt strange nonetheless.

Finally they reached the granary Jouka had chosen. The last of the refugees were just arriving. The way quickly became jammed with cloaked older Vani women, young wives cradling their newborns in swaddling, and children clinging to their mothers' skirts. The council elders, too old

to fight but carrying canes and swords, were directing the
last preparations for escape, urging families to hurry as
they finished bundling packs of food and blankets. Hostile
eyes followed the gnoll, an enemy in their midst.

"Martine!" a deep bass rumbled from the hallway. It was
Vil, with the last of the rear guard, sprinting down the hall.
The gnomes of his command slipped into the room and
immediately struggled to slip into the few remaining supply
packs already prepared, all the while keeping an eye on the
corridor.

"Now what?" Vil asked.

"We hope Jazrac can cast the spells needed to get us out
of here."

"You don't know?" Vil's face suddenly creased with concern. "I thought you had this planned."

"Almost. We just need a little luck." With that, the Harper
pushed her way through the crowd, peering over their
heads for Jazrac's tall form. At last she found him, looking
somewhat confused.

Martine was shocked to see the normally resplendent
wizard, a man who valued immaculate grooming as much
as his spells, looking so haggard. His lean face sagged; his
eyes made hollow depressions underscored by gray bags.
Even the carefully groomed goatee that Jazrac could almost
use like another finger jutted soullessly downward.

"Jazrac, over here!" She raised her hand high above the
milling crowd. The wizard stumbled over to where she
stood near the outside wall. He'd clearly slept no more than
she had, though he lacked the energy the surge of battle
had renewed in her.

"What are we doing here? Shouldn't we be doing something?" the wizard asked in confusion.

"We are. I have an important question to ask you. When
you sneaked back into our room after the raid, you used a
spell, right?"

Pain crossed the wizard's face. "Yes . . . a passwall spell."

"Can you cast it right here and now?" The Harper pointed toward the nearby outside wall.

"As a matter of fact, I have memorized it again. But why—"

"Just do it! We don't have time to talk," Martine blurted with relief. "Just open a passage to the outside and get these people out of here!"

The wizard's worn expression brightened slightly. "I am, as you have reminded me, a senior Harper."

"Jazrac, you don't have to playact for me."

"Perhaps I can atone, if only in part, for past sins. . . . Please stand back, everyone."

As Martine helped to clear a space around the wizard, Jazrac straightened his clothing. Then, his hands stroking the wall, the wizard uttered a series of garbled phrases. As he spoke, the wooden wall seemed to evaporate like water. Then the dirt, and finally a layer of snow, all faded into nothing. A hallway, broad by gnome standards, had been cut straight through the hillside. The howl of wind and a blast of cold air proved it was not an illusion.

"It won't stay open for long," the wizard said urgently.

"Jouka! Vil!" Martine shouted. "Guide everyone to the cabin."

With a calmness bred by fear, the gnomes formed into lines and hurriedly filed through the magical passage toward the storm that raged outside.

Sixteen

The granary was empty except for Martine, Jazrac, and a handful of Vani who had volunteered to cover the retreat. They'd already barred the door with barrels of supplies and bags of flour. Martine knew the barrier couldn't hold up to Vreesar's icy blasts, but she had no doubt it would slow down the Burnt Fur. At their backs, snow blew into the room through Jazrac's magical passageway.

"Get going, Jazrac. Use your ring to go and get more help," Martine said once she was satisfied that everyone else was gone. "We'll cover you."

"I'm staying with you."

Martine grimaced. "Look, this could get bloody. I don't need any fake heroics now. Besides, we need you to go back to Shadowdale and get help dealing with Vreesar."

"That can wait. Vreesar is here right now, and I don't think he'll leave until he's done with us all. Like you, my dear, I choose my troubles," Jazrac said with his old confidence. "I'm not running away this time. You need me." He pushed her up the magical passage. "If we don't get moving now, we'll all be trapped."

Martine threw her hands up in despair. "Fine. Play hero then." She turned to face the Vani. "It's time to leave, everybody!" The gnomes quickly scurried up the hall Jazrac had parted through the hillside.

As the wizard followed the little warriors, Martine said, "I appreciate your offer, Jazrac, but do me a favor. Be careful out there."

Jazrac struck an attitude of mock pride, with one hand pressed to his chest. "Me? I shall be in no danger, my dear. I am still quite capable of taking on a few ignorant gnolls."

Martine had to smile at the wizard's display of confidence. "Just don't get carried away—for old friendship's sake, okay?"

"For . . . old friendship's sake." The wizard savored the words like a Chessentian wine merchant before giving his grandest bow and departing. Martine wistfully watched him go up the passage. She was surprised to realize she still felt some respect for the man. After one last check of the storeroom, she, too, hurried up the passage.

Jazrac's spell had opened a route cleanly through to the outside, where the storm still raged, its fury unabated. The trampled path of the refugees was already half drifted over. Martine paused.

"Do we follow the others?" shouted Ojakangas, her second-in-command, pointing to the trail.

Martine shook her head. "Not yet. There's a rope in my pack. Get it out." She stooped to allow Ojakangas to reach inside and draw out the looped coils. Taking the rope, the ranger passed the length along to each warrior. "Hang on to it," she said, "so you don't get lost." With that, she drew her sword, ready for the fight she knew would come.

"I'll go ahead. When you feel a pull, follow me and stay

close!" Without wasting any more precious seconds, she plunged into storm, feeding out line as she went.

Without skis, the Harper blundered through the snow, stumbling in the footprints made by those who had passed through previously. At last she reached the end of the rope and tugged to signal the others forward. After several minutes, the rest of the rear guard had all joined her. "Any sign of the gnolls?" she asked Ojakangas.

"None."

"The gods must still like us a little bit," the Harper said with a frozen grin.

"Indeed. Thanks be to the Great Crafter," answered the black-bearded Vani.

Three times the group repeated the procedure. Each time, Ojakangas reported no sign of pursuit. Then the storm stopped with eerie suddenness. At first Martine thought she had finally reached the blizzard's edge, but that wasn't it. The storm had simply stopped.

"Our escape has been discovered!" Martine called to those behind her. "Come here and find cover!" The gnomes lumbered through the snow to join her. As each arrived, she silently pointed out a position to keep watch. Jazrac she kept close at hand. If the wizard didn't break again, his spells were her best asset.

"When this is over, you get yourself back to Shadowdale. Understand?" It was simply too much risk having the wizard out here fighting. They needed him to bring reinforcements.

Jazrac held up his hands. "Don't worry. I have no desire to do this more than once."

Hiss . . . thunk! An arrow tore at the sleeve of Martine's parka, spiraling madly into the thick trunk behind her. There it hummed angrily as the shaft quivered in the wood.

"Down!" she shouted, throwing her shoulder into her companion's side. She acted instinctively, with no thought of the man's dignity. The pair flopped ludicrously into the snow.

"What in the hells—"

Hiss! Hiss! Several more shafts whipped overhead, right where they had been standing. One struck the same tree with a solid *thwack*, while the others clattered off into the branches beyond. A gout of snow kicked up as another arrow tunneled into the snowbank beside them.

In a twinkling, Martine tumbled off to one side. She saw Jazrac roll the other way, not a moment before the icy ground was churned by a fusillade of arrows. No more than twenty yards distant knelt three lanky gnolls, already drawing a bead on her.

Eschewing caution, the warrior woman sprang to her feet and charged the doglike archers, high-stepping through the snow as she screamed a war cry. With one hand, she whirled her sword over her head; in the other, her knife flashed in the dusky light. She heard the harsh music of a bowstring being released, but the shot went wide. The second and third fired, and Martine gave a start when an arrow hit her gut just below her sternum. The metal armor she wore saved her, glancing the rough-forged arrowhead off to the side.

Her seeming invulnerability was enough to shatter the resolve of the gnolls. The lead archer threw down its bow and ran, bolting an instant before her sword swiped through the air where it had stood. The other two broke rank with barking yips of terror as the wildly howling woman descended upon them. The tip of her blade carved a long slash through the ragged cloak of one, but the creatures managed to escape. Her battle lust departed with them, leaving her feeling drained and bewildered.

There was a huffing behind her, and Martine nearly thrust her blade into Jazrac's stomach before she realized who it was. "Hold!" the man cried. "Save it for the gnolls!"

Pushing her aside, the wizard traced a figure in the air, and from his fingers leapt a series of sparkling motes of light. They rocketed toward the knolls, sizzling the air as they went. Two struck the nearest dog-man in the back, spewing out gouts of blood as if it had been struck by arrows. Two more struck the second, reeling it around in a circle, but the creature staggered on. The last dodged and darted through a stand of saplings to strike the third full in the face just as it turned to fire another shot. The beast howled and dropped its bow, fingers clutching blindly at its shattered muzzle.

"Jazrac, get back!" Martine blurted, her battle instincts alerted by the sound of sprinting footsteps through snow. In a single move, she spun to face a charging gnoll, little more than a shadow against the snow. With one arm, she thrust out in a long lunge while her body ducked low beneath the creature's high swing. *Thwack!* The dog-man's blade hewed into wood, hacking splinters from the tree trunk beside the wizard's head. The Harper's sword drove into the beast's chest, and the gnoll's momentum almost toppled her before the blade slithered through its ribs.

The gnoll's muzzle dropped open to show a fanged maw. There was a gurgling hiss as the flopping body slid down the length of her blade. Even impaled clear through, the creature wasn't finished. One scabrous arm, reeking like sewage, swung out awkwardly for her, clipping the woman in the side of her helmet. Thick claws gouged futilely at the metal.

With a quick flip of her other hand, the ranger slashed out with a dagger. She aimed high, just under the dog-man's muzzle, and was rewarded when warmth soaked her sleeve and the gnoll's head lolled stupidly. Twisting, she let the creature fall. With one foot on its chest, she tried to pull her sword free, but the blade was stuck fast for the moment.

Even as Martine dispatched her foe, the others were

embroiled in battle. Though she held only a knife, Martine unhesitatingly threw herself at the nearest creature, a big brute who had cornered Jazrac. The wizard didn't stand a chance in close combat and had only managed to survive by dodging behind a tree trunk. Preoccupied with Jazrac, the dog-man was blindsided by Martine's rush. With a pushing stroke, she drew her blade across the beast's belly, slicing through layers of fur to the flesh beneath it. The startled gnoll tipped back its wolfish head and howled in astonished pain, leaving itself wide open to attack. Before Martine could strike again, Jazrac lashed out with his dagger. His grip was awkward, and the wizard left himself wide open to a counterstrike, but it didn't matter. The blade dug into the gnoll's chest, and the creature sank to its knees, gasping for life. Martine seized its helm and twisted its head back to deliver a quick *coup de grace*.

Swallowing, Martine stood a moment until her heart stopped pounding. Breaths of raw air burned her throat, but until the panic of the moment passed, gasping gulps of air were all she could manage.

Almost as quickly as it began, the battle was over. By the time the two humans were able to join the gnomes, the Vani's skirmishes were ended. A quick assessment revealed three wounded, two minor and one serious one. He was a youth named Yannis, who had been hit in the gut by two arrows. That was bad enough, but worse still by Martine's estimation was the fact that at least one gnoll had gotten away. Already the baying of the hunters was closing through the wood.

"We're not going to make it," a little bearded warrior grunted. "Not with Yannis wounded. You and the others make for the *mustikka*." He pointed toward a thicket of blueberry bushes off to the left.

"And you?"

"I will delay them."

"No, not you. Me." Jazrac stepped forward.

"You, human?" Ojakangas said. He spat into the snow. "You ran from battle."

"I'm not running this time, and I have a better chance than you. My spells can take out more gnolls than your sword can."

"Ojakangas," Martine said impulsively, "take Yannis and the others to the cabin. I'll stay here. The wizard goes with you."

"No, Martine—"

"I'm going to get you back alive, Jazrac," Martine promised as she wiped her blade clean. "We still need you to get help. Ojakangas, Jazrac . . . get going."

Jazrac didn't move. "No. You go. I'm staying here."

Martine was about to protest, then hesitated. It was Jazrac's choice and the noblest thing he had done so far. For all his faults, the man was still her superior, and she couldn't deny him this chance to regain his own self-esteem.

The Vani had already completed a makeshift drag for the wounded Yannis.

"Get going," she ordered.

"Good luck, wizard," Ojakangas called back as he started off.

"Remember, I need you alive, Jazrac," the junior Harper said simply. "That was the plan."

"Plans change. A Harper has to be flexible. Now go."

The gnomes had barely entered the edge of the thicket when the baying started up, close at hand. At the rear of the group, Martine lingered at the edge of the clearing, knowing she should stay with Jazrac. She saw the wizard turn, and for an instant, the ranger thought he was going to change his mind, but instead Jazrac turned toward the sounds of baying in the woods beyond and raised his arms. Twisted words flew from his lips, and a small flaming sphere formed between his fingers, then rocketed between the trees. Jazrac didn't wait to see it hit but ducked low. Deep in the woods, the sphere burst into a fiery globe. The woods rattled with the crackling hiss of fire, and the air was permeated with the scent of burnt pine needles.

The searing flames roiled outward, catching several gnolls in its fiery wash. Fur and cloth, heated to the flash point, erupted in fire, and the screaming creatures flailed helplessly about like macabre torches. Then, as suddenly as it had appeared, the fire faded, leaving only a round melted scorch in the earth.

Even as the wizard was preparing to cast another spell, Martine caught a glimpse of silvery white movement through the trees off to the left. Madly she abandoned the gnomes and charged across the snow, trying to angle between Jazrac and the icy white form she knew was Vreesar.

"Jazrac! Look out!"

Martine barely had time to see the elemental raise its hands before a blue-white sparkle flashed from its fingers straight for her. The Harper dodged to the right without thinking, and the air cracked loudly as a beam of bitter frost crackled across the gap between them. Intense cold coursed like galvanizing fire along her limbs and lanced at her joints till her body curled and spasmed. A violent shock wave and a deafening thunderclap followed immediately, the air shattered by the precipitous drop in temperature. The Harper crashed into the snow, her body paralyzed, her ears screaming from the reverberations of the blast.

Wheeling away from the icy streak the bolt had carved across the snowfield, the elemental turned on Jazrac. The wizard snarled something unintelligible to Martine's ringing ears, and another series of fiery sparks flew from his hand straight toward the fiend. The buzz of the creature's laughter filled the forest as the dazzling sparks faded before they reached their target.

"Your magic iz uselez against me, human," the elemental buzzed evilly.

It was as if the words were a signal, for out of the woods advanced a line of gnolls. Their clothes were ragged furs. Some wore conical caps with dangling earflaps; a fortunate few had helms. Jaws agape and panting steamy air, they closed in for the kill.

Martine heaved to her feet and drew her sword. She still felt weak and unsettled from the icy bolt she'd barely avoided. She knew she couldn't afford to be struck by another one of those, but that didn't matter. All that mattered was that Jazrac needed her help. She stumbled toward him unsteadily.

Two gnolls closed on her, hoping to trap the Harper between them. Her attackers quickly discovered they had miscalculated. Even with her nerves still twitching, Martine easily evaded their unschooled blows, although she couldn't prevent them from flanking her on two sides. Even then she managed to hold them off, alternating lightning-quick thrusts from one side to the other. A swift lunge sliced the arm of one, sending him reeling back. That break in tempo gave her a chance to cast a look back toward Jazrac. The stalking line of gnolls had begun to charge, leaping through snowy drifts with yipping cries. Vreesar held back, apparently preferring to let the gnolls do its fighting. The dogmen knew their prey and sought to close the distance so their swords would have the advantage over the mage's spells.

"Jazrac, look out!" Martine screeched.

The wizard looked up and then jabbed a finger of warning off toward her left. Concerned about Jazrac, she'd ignored her own predicament. The unwounded gnoll was crashing through the knee-deep snow, axe swung back to the side like a bare-knuckle fighter about to throw a two-fisted roundhouse. The Harper dropped to one knee as the axehead whistled over her head, ruffling her hair. With a quick flip, she turned her sword and rammed it backhand into the gnoll's gut. The blade drove in with virtually no resistance till it hit bone.

The gnoll shrieked and continued its charge, blind momentum carrying it forward. Martine leaned backward to avoid the blundering beast, fiercely clinging to the sword hilt as the creature tumbled forward. She wrenched the blade sideways and twisted until the dog-man had spun almost completely around. Rolling back into the snow, she then planted one foot up against the gnoll's midsection, just below her blade, and kicked outward. The gutted gnoll tumbled backward, axe flailing, and her blade slid free, hot blood steaming in the frigid winter air. Her attacker writhed in the snow, yowling mindlessly.

Martine's other attacker, clutching its bloodied arm, broke and fled as she rose to her feet, chosing not to face her again.

Somehow Jazrac seemed to be holding his own, but the gnolls were pressing him hard on three sides. Suddenly the wizard put his hands to his mouth and uttered a tremendous roar, inconceivably loud. All along a spreading line, ice in the trees shattered and fell through the branches. Two of the dog-men, injured by the magical blast, clutched at their bloodied ears and flopped helplessly to the ground, while another staggered back, dazed.

Neither Martine nor the wizard waited to assess the results. As she plowed forward to dispatch the gnoll Jazrac had staggered, the wizard abruptly took flight just in time to avoid Vreesar's slashing claws.

To Martine's relief, the wizard shot upward. With Jazrac out of danger, she could concentrate on her own battles. She was alone now, facing Vreesar and half a dozen of the enemy. One was dying, one had fled, and two were crippled, at least for the time being. That left the one staggering from the effects of the magical sound blast and another somewhere off to her left. The fiend was the greatest threat, but he seemed more obsessed with Jazrac than her.

Hovering in midair, the wizard's hands flew as he worked another spell. This time flaming darts appeared in his hands, and he hurled these at the elemental. Unlike his earlier effort, these did not fade but struck the fiend solidly. The icy creature shrilled in pain as the fire burned into it, and the unfinished magic it had been forming crackled uselessly in the air.

Martine was like the cold reaper collecting its due. A quick slash at the hamstrings of the staggering foe removed him from the fight. Moving past one of those the wizard had bloodied, Martine delivered a swift kick to its jaw, rocking its head with a satisfying snap, even as she faced off against the remaining uninjured foe. "Jazrac!" she bellowed, her hearing finally starting to return to normal. "How are you doing?"

"Holding my own!" The wizard twirled in midair, his arm raised to cast a spell even as Vreesar finished forming another of its potent ice spheres.

"Jazrac, look out!"

The icy sphere shot toward its target with a whoosh and struck the hovering wizard full in the chest. Without an anchor to hold him, Jazrac hurtled backward, encased in a blue, crackling aura, trailing frostlike sparks until he slammed into a thick pine with a sickening thud. Even as he ricocheted limply from the trunk, another sphere rocketed forth, grazing the wizard and throwing him into a tumble before tearing away half of the thick tree trunk. Wood and ice splinters showered into the snow, stinging Martine as they hit.

The wizard crashed to earth with an inert flop, gouging the icy ground in a smear of black ash and red blood.

"Jazrac!"

Heedless of the gnolls, heedless of falling shards, heedless of Vreesar, even heedless of the teetering pine tree wavering dangerously on its half-shattered trunk, Martine crashed through the drifts to the fallen wizard's side. The Harper lay in a broken tangle, his back twisted in a way that was totally unnatural. His clothes were white and frost-coated, his finery brittle. The air smelled of blood and death. Martine didn't bother checking further. She knew there was no point.

"Son of a bitch!" she screamed in the direction of the elemental. Her view of the fiend was blocked by the trees, but that had probably saved her up to this point. Martine quickly scanned the distance to where she thought she saw Vreesar, trying to guess the best route to close on the monster.

Crack! Crack! Crack! All thoughts of attack were cut short by a rapid series of splintering sounds overhead as the cold-blasted pine sheared loose. The shattered trunk swung outward, ripping away other branches as it fell. Another tree cracked and groaned as its shallow roots gave way, unable to support the weight of the fallen giant. The forest rang with the echoes of splintering wood. A mass of dark green and snowy white descended into the gap between the two adversaries, driving Martine back from Jazrac's corpse. The two trees crashed to earth in flumes of pine needles and snow. The grit of broken bark stung her eyes.

"Woman!" Vreesar's voice buzzed over the fading roar. "Thank you for the stone! I leave you now to get my broth-erz!" From far off, she heard Vreesar's buzzing laughter as the elemental faded into the night. "Tell the little onez I will be back!"

Seventeen

 Everything's gone wrong, Martine thought miserably. Jazrac's dead, Vreesar has the key, and I can't do anything about it. I should never have come. I'm not cut out to be a Harper, and now I've killed them all. The gnomes, Jazrac, Vil, me—we're all either dead or as good as dead.

Martine sat in the snow next to her mentor's corpse in silent despair. The pain in her side, the arctic chill, the days without sleep—all added to her feeling of utter hopelessness. All she had to do was sit here among the drifts and slowly let herself sink into death. It would be so easy.

It was the yipping calls of the gnolls that roused her. She and Jazrac had beaten back one wave of them, but already another was forming. Soon they would sweep through, following the trail of the refugees.

This isn't right, a voice within her said. This isn't the way Jazrac died. He died fighting for his beliefs. Get up, woman. Die fighting, like Jazrac. Die like a Harper's supposed to die, the voice urged.

Blindly, automatically, the Harper lurched to her feet. Her hands felt as if they belonged to some other creature, and her side tingled with the cold. Feeling it was her duty, she futilely tried to drag the wizard's body with her, but his chest was wedged beneath a fallen branch. The body wouldn't budge. In her daze, the ranger managed to remember the ring, the one Jazrac had planned to teleport with, but even that was buried beyond her reach. Cold hands scrabbled at the snow, trying to reach the wizard's lifeless hand, but it was to no avail. The gnoll calls were coming closer; Martine couldn't wait any longer.

Sword in hand, the Harper crashed through the thicket, alternately ignoring the thorns that scratched her face, then cursing them when they caught her clothing and slowed her down. Smaller than even Martine, the gnomes had chosen paths that were nearly impossible for her to follow. More than once she dropped to her hands and knees to crawl through a gap in the thick thorns. Her only consolation was that the route would be even more difficult for the gnolls who followed.

When she was finally out of the brambled ravine, it still took the Harper almost an hour to reach Vil's cabin. Snow borne on a stiff night wind helped to cover her tracks, but the same wind froze her blood-dampened clothes stiff.

"Martine! Jazrac!" a voice cried ahead of her and slightly off to the left.

"Over here!" the ranger tried to shout back, but the words choked in her cold-parched throat. Even speaking hurt through her chapped wind-cracked lips.

They must have heard her, however, for within moments, tall Vilheim, accompanied by a pair of diminutive gnomes, stormed into sight, weapons held ready for battle. Spotting the Harper wading through the snow, the man rushed to her side while the gnomes fanned out in both directions.

"What happened?" he demanded, his voice a mixture of

relief and concern. "Where's the wizard?"

"Jazrac's dead," she mumbled. "What are you doing here?"

"Scouting."

A wolflike cry echoed through the woods.

One of the two gnomes skied to a stop alongside the humans. "They're coming, Master Vilheim." Fear filled his voice.

"Lean on me, Martine." The warrior pulled the woman's arm over his shoulder, holding it in place with one hand while he wrapped his other arm around her waist. He was still on his skis, and she was surprised he could remain balanced, the way her weight tipped him off center. Nonetheless, Vil managed to half drag her along with him.

When the cabin came into view, a dim glimmer of light in the darkness of the woods, Martine was relieved to see the gnolls had not yet discovered the place. Heads bobbed back in forth in the flicker of torchlight. The woman thought the clearing around the building seemed slightly larger than before, but she couldn't decipher why. As they neared, Martine saw a good deal of activity outside and then realized what had changed. A crude barricade filled the center of the clearing, surrounding the cabin. It was constructed of thin-trunked trees chopped from the clearing's edge and heaved into place. In spots at the edge of the clearing, the concealing underbrush was cut or trampled for several yards into the woods. The gnomes had been industrious in the short time since their arrival.

Panting, the group reached the solid logs of the barricade and began scrambling over it. The howls of pursuit were clear now, and the Harper could catch glimpses of movement through the trees. Outlined by the glow from the cabin windows and the torches, she knew they were easy targets. The hiss and thunk of an arrow into one of the logs confirmed her fears. Two, then three more whistled out of the night. One of the Vani screamed as an arrow struck him squarely in the shoulder. The little man toppled into the compound.

"Get him!" the Harper croaked to the gnomes guarding the perimeter, pointing to the injured gnome, who sat dazed in the snow at the base of the barricade. "Vil, are there any archers?"

"Not enough." Noticing that the Harper did not carry her bow, the man thrust his wooden longbow into her hands. "Take mine. You're probably a better shot."

The wood was cool and smooth under her fingers. Instinctively Martine field-checked it, sliding the bowstring between her fingers, checking the mounts at top and bottom. The bow was supple, the string a little overstretched, but it would do. Vil stepped behind her and gripped her shoulders in his gnarled hands, guiding her sight toward the trees. "See those shadows over by the bent pine?" he whispered, as if the gnolls would hear. His scratchy cheek pressed against her neck as he sighted down her temple.

Focusing her attention on the area Vil had indicated, Martine finally saw a shadowy shape, tall and feral, then two, then three move out from under the sheltering trees and into the moonlight, stalking. Martine judged the distance and the light.

"I see them."

"Then send them this present. If we kill a few, that should encourage the others to stay out of range." The warrior pressed a slim shaft into her hand. With experienced precision, the ranger nocked the arrow and drew back without looking. As she brought the bowstring to her cheek, she noticed that the leaf-headed tip glowed a silvery blue, radiating its own light. She paused; the tip wavered.

"Yes, it's magical," Vil assured her, reading her thoughts. "I've been saving these, but I think now's the time to put them to use."

Martine focused on the target. Behind her, Vil slid away to direct the shooting of the others, like a master of archers guiding his unit through a drill.

The bowstring released with a *twang*, and a silvery streak shot through the darkness. The Harper didn't wait to follow its flight, but busily nocked another arrow.

A spitting howl was proof of her aim. Sighting in again, the Harper spotted her target, twisting and staggering, one clawed hand clutching at a shoulder. *Twang!* A second shot sped through the air. She had another arrow nocked and drawn before the creature screamed a second time. The third shaft hissed away at another target before Martine paused to check her work. The first gnoll clutched spasmodically at the moon, its torso heaving. The third arrow struck its target just above the clavicle and below the throat. As the second gnoll reeled and tried to stumble away, moonlight flashed off the arrowhead projecting from the back of its neck. The beast took a jerky step and then sagged against its milling companions. The dying gnoll slid facedown into the snow. Another gnoll jumped, struck by another arrow, and then the area around them erupted in little fountains of snow as the few Vani archers released a fusillade. The gnolls broke for the shelter of the deeper woods, leaving behind their wounded companions.

"Hold fire! They're retreating!" Martine shouted triumphantly.

A clatter of arrows hailed the shelter of their barricade. The Harper ducked for the cover of the fallen trees. A thick gnomish curse sounded near her as an arrow grazed one of the defenders. The gnome clamped back the pain, determined to stay at his post at all costs.

"Good work!" Vil praised. "That'll hold them for now. Put the torches out, keep watch through the logs, and don't stick your heads up." The warrior commanded the Vani with easy confidence. This was clearly not his first big battle. The fires hissed in the snow as the gnomes put his commands into action.

Vil crawled to where Martine sat, cradling the bow in her arms. "What happened out there?"

Martine looked at him dully, for a moment not comprehending the question. "Jazrac's dead," she said finally. "Vreesar killed him."

"What about Vreesar?"

"It's gone—off to get the stone. Jaz hurt it, badly I think, before he died."

"Praise Torm for small favors," Vil breathed. "At least we won't be fighting Vreesar tonight."

"It's coming back, Vil, with more creatures like it! I've got to stop him. It's my duty," she mumbled.

Vil put a firm hand on her shoulder and pulled her gently toward the cabin door. "Right now you need some rest. Get yourself inside and find a place to bed down if you can. It's pretty crowded. I'll get some shifts set up out here and join you in a little while."

The cabin was more than a little crowded, Martine saw immediately. There was barely sufficient space for all the refugees from the warren. The storeroom entryway was filled with the handful of Vani men who remained. Despite their small numbers, they were packed into the tiny area so tightly that there was only space to sleep sitting up leaning against each other. Most either slept or sat round a smoky pine fire built in the center of the floor. Wives came to sit with their husbands before returning to the task of comforting the new widows. Others tended to the walking injured among them, bandaging their wounds with embroidered scarves and once-precious lacework. Krote sat in the coldest corner, bound hand and foot. He watched Martine with yellow eyes as she stepped through the crowded group.

The main room of the cabin was filled to bursting, with

mothers, their babies and other children, and older Vani.
Nearly all of Vil's scant furniture had been piled outside
onto the barricade. Only the bed remained, and it was
loaded with infants. The rest of the floor was covered with
makeshift beds of blankets and mats. There was barely
space to step across the room. Steam from the tightly
packed bodies condensed in the doorway when the outer
door was opened.

Vil's treasured bath was no better. Peeking inside, Martine saw that the small space was filled with about eight
wounded Vani, being tended by the womenfolk. The ranger
noted with relief that most of the injured didn't seem to be
seriously hurt. If necessary, they could be put back on the
line. Most of their wounds were cuts or gashes from splinters of wood and ice received in the initial assault on the
warren. The bad news was that one of the few who were
hurt was Elder Sumalo. The old priest was sleeping fitfully
on a hard wooden pallet, a blood-encrusted bandage
wrapped round his bare chest. Without him, without the
gifts of the Great Crafter, there was no healing for the
others.

It was clear from the cramped conditions that Martine
and Vil could not stay there. The only space that seemed
possible was in the crowded entry, with the Vani warriors.
Returning there, the Harper, with much shifting and
squeezing, cleared a space for herself and Vil. With her
knees tucked up under her chin, she claimed a blanket and
almost immediately dozed off.

The rattling of the door roused the Harper, and she
opened her eyes just in time to see Vil and a few others slip
inside the room. There was a brief flurry of movement as
the next shift of guards stepped over everyone to get outside. The cold from outside caught them in its frigid
embrace, as if welcoming the heat it would leech from their
bodies. After the door was closed, trapping a fresh glitter of

frost within, Martine could hear the cabin groan while the timbers redistributed their heat.

Vil settled next to Martine and huddled close so the small blanket could cover them both. The other gnomes wormed in among their companions—except for Jouka. Still wearing his spiked badger suit, he couldn't very well squeeze into the tight spaces next to the others. His only choice was to join Krote in his cold corner near the outside door. The gnome glared up at his bound enemy, and Martine swore the gnoll bared his fangs.

"I do not like this, Master Vilheim. We should have more guards posted. How do you know the gnolls will not attack?" Jouka grumbled, all the time staring balefully at the prisoner next to him.

Vil sighed. "The gnolls won't attack tonight. Think it through. Right now they're probably looting your homes. With any luck, they're getting drunk and maybe even fighting among themselves. Second, they're not that desperate. They've got food and shelter, so I don't think they see any need to hurry. Third, the moon's just past full. The gnolls are too smart to rush this place on a bright, moonlit night. The only thing that could get them to change their minds is Vreesar, and he's gone." He shifted his long legs, trying to find a comfortable position. "I've fought plenty of gnolls over the years, so you'll just have to trust me. What do you think, Martine?"

"That sounds reasonable."

"Why ask her? It was her mission, her plan that got us into this mess." His black beard bristling, Jouka puffed up his chest, ready to argue. His fellow gnomes were silent, many watching him with interest. "This is all the fault of interfering humans," he growled, glaring at Martine. "She came here and caused this trouble. If we had been left alone, none of this would have happened. Now she hides here with that." The gnome pointed toward Krote, sitting

beside him. The gnoll snapped at Jouka's finger, but the
gnome pulled it back quickly.

"And she brought Vreesar here, too, seeking her magical
stone. First she risks all our lives by hiding it, and now
we're all in danger because she gave Vreesar the stone as
part of some plan of hers." Martine shifted uneasily. Jouka's
grumblings were starting to get nasty, and the other
gnomes were listening to him.

"Such a good plan it was . . . now we no longer have a
home," he ended sarcastically. The other Vani said nothing,
their expressions wrapped in thoughtful concentration.
With no one else speaking in her favor, Martine prepared
to defend herself. Just then Vil's firm hand steadied the
Harper.

"Let him rage," the former paladin advised. "He's lost a
great deal."

Martine bit her lip and nodded. Even though she knew
Vil was right, it was difficult to accept the man's wisdom
this time. Seeing that she would not rise to the bait, the
sullen gnome slowly let his accusations fade into a murmur
of discontent. Someone poked up the fire and laid on more
wood, stirring up a cloud of sparks. The weary Vani murmured among themselves, softly debating the wisdom of
Jouka's words.

"Is he right?" Martine whispered to Vil.

Vil leaned his face close to hers. "No."

The answer came too quickly to satisfy Martine. "He
could be. If I hadn't come here, then Vreesar would never
have come here either. The Vani would still be safe in their
warren."

"Or dead in the snow," the man countered. "Vreesar
would have crossed the rift whether you arrived or not."

"But I came to help, and now look at everything."

"So you think all this is your fault?"

"Damn it, Vil, I'm a Harper. Helping is what I'm supposed

to do."

"Martine, you are only one person. What did you expect?" Martine felt the deep concern in the man's voice. "What do you think would have happened if you hadn't come?"

"I don't know," she answered slowly. With her dagger, the woman poked at the packed dirt just beyond the edge of the blanket.

"Vreesar would have come through unchallenged, bringing more and more of his kind with him," Vil speculated as he shifted into a more comfortable position. "Sooner or later a whole army of them would have moved south, probably with the gnolls. The Vani wouldn't have stood a chance then. You've already made a difference. At least there's only one of Vreesar's kind. The gnomes have a chance to fight."

Vil's words didn't exactly console Martine. "It was supposed to be an easy mission. I tried so hard to impress the other Harpers, and now look at the mess everything is in. A fine Harper I make. I don't know what to do, and then when I do something, everything goes wrong." She stabbed at the dirt. The gnome next to her shifted his feet uneasily.

Vil sighed. "Do you think if the job was easy they'd have sent a Harper?"

Martine studied the man's face in the gloomy firelight. The stubble on his chin was becoming a full-fledged beard, streaked through with gray. Lines of sweat and dirt clung in the creases of his weather-beaten skin. "I don't know. Jazrac said it was like a test."

Vil shook his head. "If nothing else, Jazrac was cautious. He wouldn't have sent you if he didn't think you could do the job. Quit worrying about what others think and do what's right."

"That's not the way Jouka sees things." Martine had managed to gouge a small hole in the dirt floor by now.

"Martine, Jouka seeks only to blame." Vil paused, trying to find a way to make his point clear. "There's an old story.

A fox catches a mouse out gathering acorns. 'Cursed be the oak,' moans the mouse beneath the fox's paw. The fox says, 'Foolish mouse, why do you curse the tree? It didn't hurt you.' And the mouse answers, 'If the oak hadn't dropped the acorns, I wouldn't have been gathering them, and you would never have caught me.' Hearing the little mouse complain, the fox laughs and laughs so much that he lets his paw slip, and the mouse pulls his tail free. Off runs the mouse, only to be caught in the jaws of a snake. 'Oh, cursed be the fox,' moans the mouse, 'for letting me go, else I would not have been caught.'"

"So what happened to the mouse?"

"I don't know. Maybe the snake ate him."

Martine leaned wearily against the former paladin's shoulder. "So if Jouka's the mouse, what am I? The fox or the snake?"

"Well, I sort of thought of you as another mouse," Vil said with a dry chuckle.

Martine snorted. "Are you sure you're not still a paladin? You always seem to be worried about others."

Vil tried to shrug the question off. "I don't know."

"Huh?"

"I've been feeling more . . . paladinish lately. Maybe it was a mistake; maybe I should seek Torm's forgiveness." Vil shifted again, still trying to find a comfortable position for his lanky legs.

"What about the freedom you have now . . . you know, like you told me?"

Vil smirked. "An illusion. I have all this freedom, and what do I do? I hide up here in the north, doing nothing but chopping wood. I've been hiding up here, hiding from everything I lost—the people I knew, the things I did. Maybe I thought they'd all forget who I once was, and then I could go home. What kind of freedom is that?" He turned to look at her. "I didn't realize it until all this happened. I've

just been moldering up here. Now I feel as if there's a purpose again."

Just in time to die in a senseless war, Martine thought to
herself. She couldn't think of a quick, understanding reply
to Vil's sudden confession. "You're tired. Get some sleep,"
she said instead.

Realizing that perhaps he'd said too much, Vil nodded
and settled back against the wall. Within minutes, his
snores joined those of the gnomes around her while the
cold wind whistling between the boards provided a mournful accompaniment.

Martine lay awake, cradled in the man's arms. She was
tired, but her mind was churning as she thought about
what Vil had said, about Jazrac's death, about Jouka, about
the threat of Vreesar. Slowly thoughts formed as she forced
herself to think like a Harper and not some hesitant apprentice. A new plan was forming in her mind, bold and dangerous. It held no guarantee of success, but it was, she thought,
a plan worthy of a Harper.

Gingerly Martine slid free of Vil's arms. The man snorted
and stirred, and Martine thought he might wake, but he
only rolled over to fill the space she'd abandoned. The
woman picked her way across the small room to where
Krote huddled, his rags pulled tight round his furry body,
trying to keep in every bit of warmth.

The glint of the gnoll's eyes greeted her. Knowing he
could see her, Martine signaled him to keep silent and
knelt in front of him, light glinting off the knife she carried.
She looked at Jouka carefully to make absolutely sure the
gnome was asleep. His spiked breastplate rose and fell in
the slow rhythm of slumber.

"Word-Maker, listen to me," she barely breathed, turning
her attention back to the shaman. The gnoll shifted uneasily
when he saw the knife. "Hold out your hands." Suspiciously
Krote raised his bound wrists, and she set to sawing the

ropes apart. "I'm letting you go."

"Why?" the gnoll demanded in a hoarse whisper.

"I want you to help me kill Vreesar." There was no point in trying to be clever.

The gnoll's eyes widened in disbelief. "What did you say, human?"

"You're free. I'm letting you go—and I'm asking you to stay," Martine said as she continued to saw at the ropes. "I need your help to kill Vreesar. If you don't choose to give it, you can go out the door right now. I'll make sure the gnomes don't hurt you."

As the ropes fell away, the gnoll flexed his clawed fingers, which were purple and numb under his brown fur. "You trust me?" His voice was an incredulous snarling hiss.

"Yes." Martine did trust the gnoll, but for no reason that she could name. "You live for your honor, don't you?"

"Yes," the shaman rumbled. "Why should I help you?"

The Harper turned her attention to the ropes around his ankles. "I'm guessing you don't have much choice. As long as Vreesar lives, you can't go home."

The gnoll's lips parted in a wolfish grin. "Mahr-tin, you not like little ones. You think like gnolls. You are right. I help."

Martine nodded as she undid the coils around his feet. It was the closest thing to a compliment she'd likely ever get from the shaman.

Helping Krote to his feet, Martine cleared her throat loudly until the noise roused the slumbering gnomes. As they stared up in astonishment at the unbound gnoll towering over them, Martine made her pronouncement. "I'm going to kill Vreesar and put an end to this. Who wants to come with me?"

Eighteen

An array of startled large-nosed faces stared up at her. Fiery Jouka, his hand clutching the severed ropes, jumped to his feet.

"Are you mad, woman? You've cut this beast free!" the gnome raged, his face florid in the dim light.

"I've set him free," the Harper announced, staring down at the irate gnome. "He's chosen to help me."

A gasp of astonishment rose from the little men. Jouka sputtered. "That beast? How can it help?"

Martine laid a restraining hand on the gnoll. "For one thing, he's going to get me to the glacier. I have a plan."

"Another of your plans! Will this one work any better than your other ones?" The gnome sneered.

"I don't know," Martine snapped. Disgusted, she turned to the others. "I don't absolutely need your help, but I'm asking anyway. If this works, Vreesar's dead and you can go home. If it fails—well, then I'm dead, but at least you're no worse off than you are now."

Vil pushed his way to his feet. "I'll go. What's the plan?"

Martine looked down at her audience. "Vreesar's gone back to the glacier to open the gate. We'll ambush it when it gets there."

Jouka kicked a bucket in disgust. "An excellent plan! And how will you get there—fly? It takes a full day and night of hard skiing to reach the glacier, and this fiend has a full night's head start on you."

"We'll teleport."

"What?"

"We'll teleport there," she repeated firmly. "Jazrac had a ring. I can't use it, and you can't use it," Martine explained, pointing to Jouka, "but I'm betting that Krote can. He uses magic like Jazrac did, so the ring should work for him."

"If you give him the ring, he'll just run away."

The woman stepped aside, giving Krote a clear route to the door. "He could leave now if he wanted to."

The shaman seemed to relish being the subject of their argument. He smiled broadly. "Maybe I not help. Maybe I let little people all die."

The faces of the gnomes seemed to change color magically at his words. Some grew pale, while others turned red with indignation. The shaman's words triggered a wave of discussion among the gnomes. In the heat of argument, the Vani all but forgot the presence of the humans or the gnoll. It was as if they were back in their council chambers at the warren. Only Jouka, indignant and inflexible, remained silent. He stood in his corner, spiked arms carefully folded over his spiked chest.

After some time, Ojakangas, the broad-chested carpenter, finally rose pretentiously and, in his best imitation of Elder Sumalo, pronounced the decision.

"You propose a great risk, Harper," Ojakangas announced, stroking his trim black beard. The gnome's voice was high and nasal, and if the situation had not been so serious,

Martine would have found it comical.

"But if you are willing to take this risk, we will allow it," the gnome continued. Martine wasn't aware the gnomes had any real say in the matter, but she kept her opinions to herself. "There are conditions, however."

The woman set her hands on her hips. This was her plan, and she didn't care for the idea of the gnomes imposing any conditions. "Like what?"

"The gnolls may still attack. If they do, we think it will be at dawn. We ask you to wait until after the sun has risen before leaving. Your enemy will still be far from the glacier then."

Martine pondered Okajangas's words, wondering if there was any trick. "Agreed," she finally said.

"Second, one of our people will go with you, to be sure that someone"—Ojakangas looked meaningfully at Krote—"does not betray you."

"I welcome the aid, but who will it be?" Martine suspected the answer, but she couldn't refuse the gnomes on this.

"Jouka Tunkelo."

The Harper winced. Jouka looked up in furious surprise. "Me?"

"That is right, Brother Jouka," Ojakangas said sternly. "The council has decided."

The black-armored warrior fumed but couldn't very well challenge the authority of his fellow gnomes. Instead, he snatched his thorny helm and stormed out of the cabin into the frozen compound.

With Jouka's departure, the gnomes began to chatter excitedly, warily circling their new ally. Krote stood stock still, his rag-wrapped arms folded over his chest, the sardonic smile still on his lips.

Martine pushed through the confusion of gnomes to Vil. "Why did they choose him? He hates the whole plan." The gnome logic was completely lost on her.

"Martine," Vil said with a chuckle, almost as amused as Krote by the outcome, "what other choice did they have? Think a minute. It allows Jouka to save face, and it gives you the best warrior they've got. Still, the look on Jouka's face . . ."

"Wonderful . . . just wonderful," Martine snapped, far from happy. "Excuse me, but we have some preparing to do. Come on." She led the way into the heart of Vil's cabin.

Inside, the pair picked their way through the carpet of gnomes, gathering supplies. Occasionally babies bawled and whimpered, only to be quickly hushed by their mothers, and here and there widows wept softly in the arms of a comforting relative or friend, but in general the room remained grimly silent. Silence settled over the two humans as they worked, contemplating the task that lay before them. Clearing a little floor space, they assembled their gear. The warrior produced two wicker packs and a mound of blankets from the small planked loft overhead, followed by sausages, hardtack, bundles of sugar, dried fruits, wax, whetstones, and a host of minor but necessary items. Vil fussed over the preparations, paying careful attention to each item selected. Only when he was satisfied did he finally pause to warm himself by the fire. "That should be enough," he said as he rubbed his chilled hands together. "We don't want to overload the packs."

Shouldering their gear, they carried the loads outside. Martine was startled to see a faint trace of dawn limning the mountain ridges. The whole night had passed by unnoticed. When was the last time she had slept more than a catnap? Two days ago? Three? She couldn't even remember.

"We sleep now," the man advised, noticing her grogginess as she stumbled over the frozen ground. "The gnomes will wake us if anything happens."

Martine nodded and let him steer her back inside for what she hoped would not be another futile attempt at rest.

* * * * *

A firm shake roused the Harper from a world of warmth and comfort. Martine tried to tell the landlady to let her sleep by the fire for an hour more, but the shaking was insistent until finally the woman opened her groggy eyes. "No more ale, Jhaele," she mumbled, trying to focus her eyes.

"Ale?" squeaked a nasal voice.

The Harper shook her head and her vision cleared. Ojakangas leaned over her, his expression unamused by her blathering. "They're coming, human. You're needed on the line."

The Harper lurched to her feet, suddenly clearheaded. Her side throbbed, her cuts and scratches burned, and her skin chafed, raw from days in armor, but the woman hardly felt these pains. Quickly buckling on her sword, she opened the door and stumbled into the glare of early morning, the sun's reflection blinding off the snow.

Stilll in a semidazed condition from sleep, she heard Vil shout, "Get down, Martine!" in a tone that demanded immediate attention. An instant after she'd let her knees buckle in response to his order, she heard the whistle of an arrow just overhead. It ended in a solid *thunk* against the cabin wall, its head driving several inches into the solid pine.

"Be careful, for Torm's sake! They've targeted the doorway!" Vil was crouched in the snow against the fallen trees, gnomes to either side of him. Black-feathered shafts jutted from the log barricade, testimony to the events of the dawn.

Fully awake now, the Harper scuttled across the snow to join Vil. "Anything happen?" she asked, dismissing the archery as unimportant.

Vil shook his head. "Not yet. I think they're building up their courage for a charge. Their archers have us pinned down, so my guess is it shouldn't be too much longer."

"What's the plan?"

"Plan? Fight them." Vil gestured toward the cabin. "Ojakangas has gathered the wounded who can still fight. They're our reserves. Everybody else who can fight, about fifteen in all, is out here. Good plan, eh?"

A whooping cry came from the woods. Before the echoes had finished, a lone gnoll charged from between the mist-cloaked trees, running madly toward the barricade. The beast sprinted with its wicker shield held high and its sword low, covering the open ground at a startling pace.

"Stay down . . . wait!" Vil bellowed. A volley of gnoll arrows punctuated his warning.

With a last spring, the gnoll scrambled onto the barricade, trying to hack a gap through the tangled pine branches. "Stop him!" Vil shouted, and a small squad of gnomes hurried to the position. They jabbed their spears up between the trunks, but the gnoll furiously blocked the thrusts aside with his shield, meantime trying to poke his sword back at them through the gaps. The clatter and clang of the skirmish resounded through the clearing.

In the midst of that fight the woods erupted in a chorus of howls. The ravens gathered at the fringe of the woods squawked and took flight all at once.

"Jouka, Oja—here they come!" Vil warned.

A ragged line of gnolls, shrieking savagely, burst from the woods and sprinted madly across the gap. Martine guessed there were about twenty of them. The pack headed for a different section of the wall, one unprotected now that their pack mate had drawn off the defenders.

Moving in a crouching run along the line, Martine and Vil reached the new position just as the first of the gnolls scrambled onto the logs. Swords drawn, Martine and Vil madly slashed and thrust at the mass of Burnt Fur warriors. Fresh blood on her blade told the Harper at least one of her blows had been successful, but there was no time to pick targets. The barricade hampered the attackers, but even so, the pair could not hold off the massed assault. Arrows winged into the snow between the humans and the cabin as the gnoll archers tried to pick off the two defenders.

First one gnoll, then another, leaped over the top of the wall to land inside the compound. They wheeled madly to fend off the few gnome reinforcements rushing to the humans' aid. Martine caught one in the back with the point her sword, cutting it about where its kidney should be, but even as the dog-man fell, another leaped over the wall to take its place. She watched in amazement as Jouka, a dagger in each hand, sprang from the top of the logs and landed spread-eagled on the chest of another gnoll, hugging the creature in his spiked embrace. The gnoll squealed as the nailed armor shredded through leather and fur to tear the flesh underneath. As the creature flailed, Jouka finished it off with a double thrust of his daggers to its throat.

Jouka untangled himself from the corpse, bits of cloth and fur clinging to his bloodstained spikes just as Martine and Vil were forced to give ground. "Ojakangas—now!" Vil yelled as he hacked the legs out from under a gnoll who attempted to break past.

The cabin door banged open, and a stream of little men poured out, screaming shrilly. Their charge hit the startled gnolls in the flank. Seeing the makings of a trap, Martine shifted to the far side, hacking her way past the opposition until she stood alongside Jouka and several other gnomes who had joined him.

Now the attackers were pressed on both sides. In addition, the cabin wall blocked the gnolls in front of them, while the barricade would severely hamper any retreat. The twang of a bowstring behind her told Martine that the

Vani were returning fire on the gnoll archers, forcing them to concentrate on the bowmen.

With a wild cry, Jouka charged forward once more, and the gnolls instinctively retreated from the porcupine-like warrior. They backed into their pack mates trying to hold back Ojakangas's crew on the other side. The resulting confusion was all that was needed. Believing they were being abandoned by their brothers, the front ranks started to clamber over the barricade and make for the trees.

The Harper was determined to keep the gnolls in full retreat and not to let them reorganize. "Rush them!" she ordered even as she charged forward. Screeching her best banshee yell, the woman whirled her sword in broad arcs, heedless of her own danger.

At the sight of a wild woman and a spiked midget fearlessly rushing them, the dog-men in the front rank broke and clawed at those behind them in a frantic bid to get away. The spark of panic fanned into a flame, and the retreat turned into a rout. The Vani fell upon the backs of the fleeing enemy as they tried to get over the barricade.

As the last of the Burnt Fur warriors finally broke free and fled for the woods, Martine and Vil moved quickly to restore order. Several Vani had to be restrained from scaling the logs and setting off in pursuit. A quick count of the bodies showed two gnomes dead, plus several with minor wounds. Not bad, Martine thought, noting the bodies of twelve dead gnolls. It was anyone's guess how many of the dog-men had been injured, but the number was significant.

"That should hold them for a while," Vil murmured as he and Martine sprawled against the logs to rest. The man's relief was obvious.

"Can you be sure?" the woman asked.

"It would stop me. They'll fall back out of bow range and then dig in, but I don't think they'll try another direct assault."

With the fierce skirmish ended, a gnomish woman was cautiously making the rounds with bowls of hot porridge. The Harper had almost forgotten what hot food—*any* food—was like. Pulling off her mittens, she greedily scooped the warm gruel into her mouth with her fingers. She could feel her energy returning.

As the defenders sat in the snow eating, an echo of gnoll voices reached them. Nervous, the Vani put down their bowls and scurried to battle positions, awaiting another attack.

Nothing happened, however. In vain, they watched the tree line for the gnolls to rush into view. Even the sporadic rain of arrows stopped.

"Little people!" a voice barked suddenly from somewhere beyond the barricade. "You fight well today. You make worthy enemies.

"Listen, little people. Our chieftain is gone, and we do not want to kill any more of you. We leave now in peace. Do not try to follow us. We will know if you do. No more war between us, little people. Agreed?" The words faded, leaving only the silence of the trees creaking in the wind.

The Vani clung to their barricade in stunned disbelief. Then Ojakangas cut short any debate by standing up and shouting, "Go back to your valley, dog-men, and we will make peace!"

"We go. It is cold here, and your little tunnels are too small for us. We leave a guard to make sure you keep peace. Do not leave cabin, or we kill you all."

"It's a trick," Jouka said grimly.

"No trick, little one," said Krote. The gnoll stood in the cabin doorway where he had listened to the exchange. The shaman looked at the bodies of the Burnt Fur, still sprawled over the barricade where they had been cut down. "You have killed many warriors," the gnoll said with a touch of sadness. "There will be many females without mates."

The Word-Maker went from body to body, turning each so he could see it. "Blind-Eye. Rakk. Broken-Tooth. Fat Belly." Krote recited the roll of the dead. "That was Varka who spoke," he said finally. "He must be new Word-Maker. If he says peace, there will be peace."

Martine took a chance and stood up. No arrows flew. "That still leaves Vreesar. How are we going to get out of here without breaking this peace?"

"I don't know about you, Martine, but I figured we'd use the back door," Vil commented casually as he stood.

"Back door?"

The former paladin flashed a smile. "Only a fool makes a stand without a means to escape. I built another way out."

"Where is it?" she asked quickly.

"Under my bath. All we have to do is knock a hole in the bottom of my tub and crawl out the tunnel. It comes out at the edge of the woods." Vil grinned impishly.

The Harper impulsively stood on tiptoe and kissed the warrior firmly on the lips. Vil was too startled to do anything. His face colored under his graying beard. Martine quickly pulled away.

She looked at her companions' faces, surprised, amused, weary. "Jouka, Krote, Vil . . . are you ready to go?"

Vil hefted an axe and purposefully strode into the cabin, looking taller and even more gaunt than usual.

Nineteen

Martine, Vil, Krote, and Jouka crowded into Vil's already cramped bathroom. As soon as the wounded Vani were moved carefully aside, Jouka jumped into the bottom of the big wooden tub Vil had set into the floor. Taking a hand axe, the gnome set to work. As he watched the destruction of his craftsmanship, Vil winced each time the axe descended. Outside the room, the gnomes pressed around the door of the chamber and watched curiously.

When the axe finally broke through, Jouka lost his balance and nearly dropped it down the gaping hole beneath. The musky smell of damp earth filled the small room. Jouka moved several feet to one side, then began to chop at the other end of the broken board.

"No more hot baths," Vil moaned. "I'll miss them."

More wood splintered, and the gnome passed a three-foot section of board out. The group passed it down the line as if it were something to treasure.

"It took me weeks to build this," Vil lamented mournfully.

A barking cough of a gnoll echoed faintly from outside. It sounded as if it came from near the front of the house. Martine stiffened, her hand reaching instictively for an arrow from her quiver.

"Do not end our peace, humans," Krote Word-Maker cautioned as he saw her move.

Several more planks were passed out of the tub before Jouka clambered out. "It's done," he announced, slipping his axe back into the sheath he wore.

Martine stepped forward and gazed downward. The jagged hole in the bottom of the tub yawned into blackness. "Does everyone understand what to do?"

The group nodded.

"All right. I'll go first."

From the way Vil had explained it, the tunnel dropped about four feet and then wormed around toward the rear of the cabin. Vil had described it as a "tight fit," but Martine figured she'd be able to wriggle through without difficulty. She slid carefully past the jagged edges, and her feet touched bottom.

"Candle."

Vil passed a taper down. Guided by the small flame, she lowered herself to lie on her belly. The dim light did not carry far, blocked by a thick mass of cobwebs across the tunnel. With her sword, she brushed the webbing aside, but it still hung in dusty tendrils from the top of the passage.

The Harper wriggled across the cold ground into the darkness. There was barely space to raise her head up to look ahead. Vil hadn't been kidding when he said it was cramped. The ceiling rubbed at her back in places. Tiny shapes scurried away frantically as she roused a den of field mice.

It wasn't long before she began to feel the dark tunnel was endless. Pushing the candle ahead of her, the Harper crept along slowly. At last she saw a faint glow that marked the end of the tunnel. Beyond another curtain of cobwebs, the shaft was lit by opaque light.

"Made it," the woman called back to the others.

Struggling with her sword in the tight space, she carefully jabbed at the icy crust that sealed the opening. It was thicker than she guessed, and by the time the blade had broken through it, Jouka was bumping up against her feet. At last she succeeded in clearing a hole in the ice large enough to wriggle through. Halfway out, she paused, watching for anything suspicious.

By daylight, the woods at the back of the cabin appeared unwatched, but the morning fog concealed everything beyond the first row of trees. Martine waited cautiously for any sign of the enemy. "Hurry up," the gnome behind her hissed impatiently. Finally, still uncertain it was clear, the black-haired woman scrambled through the gap, signaled for Jouka to hand out her gear, and then sprinted into the nearby woods. Gulping the fresh air and pleased to be in daylight once more, the woman flopped onto an icy snowbank and strung Vil's bow.

One by one, as Martine kept watch with nocked arrow, the others wriggled out and melted into the forest. First came Jouka, followed by a long pause before Krote appeared. The gnoll had to tear at the ice with his claws to widen the hole before he could squirm his broad shoulders through.

Just as Vil was emerging from the hole, gnoll voices rang from the front of the house.

"My brothers come after their dead," Krote said.

"Will they notice we're gone?" Martine worried aloud.

"How can they know, human?" Krote asked.

"Whatever," Vil added. "Let's not linger here. Martine, you know where Jazrac's body is. We'll need his ring to catch Vreesar in time. You lead."

Without benefit of skis, the group's progress through the

snow was difficult. The birds were all silent, whether as a reaction to the chaos of battle or their presence, Martine did not know. They slipped through the sepulchral woods, hip-deep in white snow. The low fog, somewhere between ice and mist, swallowed the noise of their exertions, distorting calls and echoes till it was impossible for Martine to gauge the distance of any sound.

The fog provided traitorous comfort, for it came and went unexpectedly, one minute concealing, the next leaving them horribly exposed. "Cyric's damnation!" Martine swore each time the fog lifted and revealed their position. There was already too much risk of being discovered without the tricks of winter conspiring to make things worse.

As the four neared the conquered warren, progress became slower and slower as mistrust and caution played on their fears. Martine could only pray she was right about Krote; she had no reason to trust him other than an irrational instinct about the gnoll. Some might have called it woman's intuition, but it wasn't that. She had long ago learned to dismiss such reactions. No, her faith was grounded on the vague kinship between warriors, the bond between men, women, even brutes who lived according to the dictates of the sword. It was this bond that allowed her to work with the unruly, the mercenary, or the detestable, whose motives and goals she could not conscionably abide anywhere else. It was this fraternity that made her trust Krote. Even though he was a shaman, the gnoll understood the life of the sword.

Would Krote betray her? No more, she felt, than the gnome at her side. Both were fierce in their beliefs, adamant in their pride and honor.

At last Martine guided them to the edge of the ravine. She remembered the stand of massed birch that flourished in a sunlit break between the trees. She remembered it being at her back. Using that to orient herself, the Harper quickly found the wind-drifted tracks of the night before. From there, it was a simple matter to backtrack to the battle site.

In bright daylight, the place looked different. What seemed ominous by dusk was clear and peaceful this morning. Not innocent, though, Martine thought. Few forests were innocent, but their daytime secrets were less sinister than those that lurked in the depths of the night.

Broken trees, frozen bodies, and pink snow was evidence they had found the site. The gnolls had made no effort to collect their dead, although the bodies had evidently been quickly stripped of everything useful. The naked corpses were frozen hard, their skin ice blue beneath the tawny fur. Vil and Jouka examined the battlefield with the curiosity of warriors, quietly impressed by the woman's handiwork. Krote moved from body to body, commending each by name to his fierce god Gorellik.

Seeing signs of the looting, Martine realized her plan would come to naught if the gnolls had stripped Jazrac clean. Not wanting to look, she had to force herself to examine the site. It was with sick relief that she saw a booted foot jutting out from beneath a tangle of branches. A quick cry summoned the others.

The two humans and the gnome dug away the drifted snow. Krote stood back, his arms wrapped around himself for warmth, refusing to assist. "It is not clean," he insisted adamantly. "I will not touch it." Martine wondered if his conviction were true or if it was just an excuse.

Gradually the snow was cleared from the corpse. Jazrac's skin was an awful bloodless white with traces of frozen blue veins under the skin. Martine forced herself to think of the corpse as a thing. Remembering it as Jazrac salted too many wounds in her memory, and she couldn't afford to break down now.

"The ring was on his left hand, I think. There, under . . .

that tree trunk." The Harper pointed deep into the tangle of wood.

Vil surveyed the deadfall and shook his head. "We'll never be able to move this. Jouka, can you get in there?"

The gnome wormed his way through the branches until he reached the heart of the tangle. After a moment, he swore bitterly. "The ring won't come off. The finger's swollen."

"Cut it off," Krote suggested without hesitation. He glared at the humans to see if they had any objection.

"Should I, woman?" Jouka asked.

Martine flinched at the thought, but she could think of no other solution. "Do it," she said before stepping away. She didn't want to see or know anything about this part of the gruesome job.

When Jouka resurfaced, he looked tight-lipped and grim. He held out a plain silver ring toward the ranger. "The blessings of the Great Crafter on you in this age of sorrow," he consoled stiffly. "I commend you on his release from toil."

"What?"

Vil intervened. "The Vani live for centuries," he explained. "In their opinion, death frees the spirit from centuries of drudgery."

Jouka nodded. "It is just our way to steal some joy from Death and his minions."

"Thank you, Master Jouka." Martine held the ring in her fingers. "Word-Maker . . . the ring."

The shaman reached with his clawed fingers to accept the magical ring. His eyes were wide and eager, his jaw open wolfishly.

"I do not like this," Jouka said softly. Even as the gnoll moved forward to claim the prize, Jouka and Vil stepped in close behind him, their swords tensely poised.

The gnoll plucked the ring from Martine's fingers, his

face twisting. Was it wonder? Triumph? Martine looked up into his face but could not tell. He was a gnoll. Who knew what emotions filled his mind?

With deliberate movements, Krote slipped the ring over his clawed finger. The silver circlet slid over his bony knuckle and settled into place. The shaman let out a rasping breath and closed his eyes as if in bliss.

"Can you use it, Krote? Can you use it?" the Harper asked eagerly. Everything depended on his answer.

Behind the gnoll, like the slave who warned the king of his own mortality, Jouka softly added his own words: "Remember, dog-man. My sword is faster than—"

Whaaaam!

All at once every ounce of air in Martine's lungs felt as if it had been sucked out of her. The shock knocked her legs completely out from under her. The next thing she knew, she and the others were sprawled across a hard sheet of ice, nearly blinded by the glaring reflection of sunlight. The morning air felt colder than it had been mere seconds ago.

"Gods!" the Harper swore.

"What happened?"

"Where are—"

"There," Krote rasped, pointing his long arm toward a ridge of upheaved ice, the edge of a great frozen crater in the center of a frozen plain.

"The glacier," Martine mouthed in an awed whisper. "We're here." Slowly she stood up, like a sailor home from the sea adjusting his legs to shore. The others rose, their expressions awed. Krote stared at the ring on his finger. Vil kept his eyes on the ridge and adjusted his gear, while little Jouka felt himself over, as if checking to see that all his parts had survived in one piece.

"I bring you here as I said I would," the shaman said.

"Now what?" Vil queried.

Martine shaded her eyes and scanned the ridge. "Now

we find Vreesar. Up there, I think."

"Where?" Jouka asked.

Vil studied the waste. "That's a lot of territory, Martine."

"We'll just have to look," Martine said helplessly. She started trudging in the crater's direction.

Krote growled. "I do not waste time searching. Woman, where are my charms?"

"What are you talking about?"

Word-Maker snapped his teeth in irritation. "My signs of Gorellik . . . where are they?"

"I have them, dog-man," Jouka answered unexpectedly.

"Give them to me."

"Do it, Jouka," Martine ordered.

The gnome grudgingly handed over a leather pouch. Taking out the iron fetish of his god, the shaman held it in his hands while he mumbled a prayer. When he had finished, the gnoll held the charm out and carefully turned around in a circle. Halfway through, he stopped and pointed farther up the crater wall. "There—not far. Gorellik has given me a sign."

Martine guessed the shaman had used a spell to find things. She'd seen priests use them before, though only for simple searches such as finding a peasant's lost axe or a merchant's stolen purse. It had worked then, and she didn't doubt its effectiveness now. "Let's go." Shouldering a pack, the Harper began scrambling over the uneven ice as fast as she could manage.

After only fifty yards, the group came to a fresh trail concealed beyond a pressure ridge. The tracks, large and clawed, were unmistakably Vreesar's, and they were headed toward the crater's rim.

"Too late!" Jouka cried.

Martine seized the little warrior and pushed him forward. "Not yet—the tracks are fresh. If we hurry—"

"Up there!" Vil shouted, scanning the slope. The

elemental wasn't more than a hundred yards away, almost to the lip of the shattered rift. There was no indication it had seen the group, although there was nothing to prevent it from turning and seeing them at any time.

The man broke into a sprint, leaving the others behind. Martine followed at a dead run, but her shorter legs could not keep up with the long-striding warrior. Jouka lagged even farther behind, struggling in the snow and ice, while the gnoll hung to the rear.

"Vil, wait!" the Harper shouted. "We should attack together."

The man kept running. "We've got to stop it now, before it can break the stone," he shouted back.

"Damn it, Vil," the woman huffed as she thrashed after him, "don't be so . . . paladinish!"

The elemental evidently heard something, and it turned to steal a look in their direction.

"You!" Vreesar shrilled as the charging warriors bounded across the icy field toward their enemy. Although the fiend could have meant Vil, Martine felt the creature's gaze fixed on her. "Too late, humanz!"

The Harper was still several long strides behind Vil when the elemental held up Jazrac's blood-black stone, clutched in the viselike grip of its fingers. There was no time left, no hope of snatching the key from Vreesar's grasp before it could crush the fragile rock.

"No!" Martine shouted as she flung her sword in desperation. The long sword tumbled awkwardly toward the fiend. "Please, Tymora—" she started to pray.

The goddess of luck must have heard her plea, for the iron hilt of her tumbling blade struck the elemental solidly across the shoulder, knocking its arm wide. The stone, clamped in Vreesar's fingertips, jarred loose and tumbled into the snow.

Before the fiend could recover, Vil sprang upon it, the

man's sword cutting a brilliant arc of sunlight as he slashed.
Steel rang as the warrior struck the elemental's hard carapace. Vreesar shrieked as the sword pierced the ice creature's shell with a noise like the popping of a lobster being
shelled.

"Vil! Look out!" the woman screamed.

The warning came too late. Vil was drawing back his
sword for another swing when the elemental slashed its
glittering claws across the man's head. Martine heard the
sound of tearing flesh, and Vil's head snapped back. His
muscles rubbery, the former paladin staggered a few steps
before collapsing to the ice, the long sword dropping from
his grasp and skittering across the ice. Blood streamed
from a long gash in his helm and the shredded flesh of his
cheek. The slash had laid his jaw open to teeth and bone, so
that when he tried to scream, the cries only made gurgling
noises with no mouth to shape them. Nonetheless the warrior lunged for the elemental, desperately hugging the
freezing creature in his grasp.

Martine groped for Vil's sword, the only weapon close at
hand. As she searched futilely, afraid to take her eyes off
the fiend, the creature shaped its tiny mouth in a mockery
of a smile. Sparkling fire formed into a ball between Vreesar's fingertips even as Vil tried in vain to pull the creature
down.

"Let go, Vil!" Martine shouted, helpless to stop the fiend.

"It endz, human," Vreesar snarled. With a sudden jab, it
shoved the frozen ball down Vil's breastplate and hurled
the man aside. Vil's torn face barely had a chance to regis-
ter confused surprise before he was pitched agonizingly
against an icy upthrust. A repercussive roar filled the air.
Metal shrieked as Vil's breastplate burst in bloody rup-
tures, blasted by the ice-splintered explosion it contained.
The man heaved with a single twitch, then flopped, his shattered body barely contained by the twisted metal shell.

"*Vil!*" Martine screamed again. Tears blinded her eyes. She scrambled forward, anguish giving her strength. The swirling snow kicked up by the blast uncovered a glint of metal, and her hand settled on the cool steel of Vil's sword.

Using the weapon like a cane, Martine heaved unsteadily to her feet. Rage fought with tears as she faced the fiend. Martine wanted to vent her hatred of the creature more than she had ever wanted to strike out at anything in all the world. Stumbling over the snow, the Harper pulled her arm back to thrust. The elemental was distracted by its own wound, a clean split in its hardened shell, so Martine managed to get close enough to hear its heaving gasps and smell the murderer's freezing aura.

She wanted to see its eyes, to see if there would be fear in them. She hoped the elemental would be afraid, afraid of its own death.

"Vreesar," she whispered.

The fiend looked up, and their eyes met, its orbs tiny and almost hidden behind an icy fringe. The elemental thrust its hand forward, already crackling with energy, but Martine knew that trick and batted it away with a fast swat. Before the creature could recover, the Harper slammed her sword forward, throwing all her weight behind it. The sword tip skidded and then found a gap where the hip met the torso and sliced inward. The creature reeled back, and Martine, still staring eye to eye, fell forward with it. They hit the ground with a bone-breaking impact that threw the Harper to the side. Vreesar's magical ice ball slipped from its grasp and rolled down the slope.

Crackle-booom!

The blast's shock wave stunned Martine, and the ice needles tore at her back, but her prone position saved her from the worst of the blast. Vreesar's knee hit her in the gut, and she flipped away to land painfully in a jagged bed of hard ice.

As both struggled to their feet, Krote's tawny form flashed past the Harper. Martine thought the gnoll was lunging to attack, but instead the shaman dove at a patch of snow. When he emerged, Word-Maker held Jazrac's stone in his paw. The gnoll panted clouds of steam as he savored the power in his grasp.

Vreesar froze, torn between the stone and the threat of Martine's sword. It couldn't turn on the shaman without exposing itself to the ranger. Its wounds, leaking a clear fluid, were testimony to the effectiveness of its attackers.

Even with both hands wrapped around the hilt, the Harper barely could hold the sword. The ground seemed to tilt and roll as she tried to shake off the reverberations pounding inside her head. Every gulp of breath lanced her with fiery pain.

Greedy eyes coveted the artifact. "Shaman," Vreesar droned soothingly, "I will make you chieftain—chieftain of all the tribez of the north. My brotherz will be your army. Give me the stone and we will destroy the humanz and the little onez." The elemental slowly held out its hand, waiting to receive Krote's gift.

The shaman crouched. His eyes were filled with feral light as he looked from human to monster. His jaw hung open, salivating like a hound hunched over its kill.

"Krote, don't do it!" Martine managed to croak in desperation.

"Word-Maker, you can be chieftain."

"Your word—you live by your word," she reminded him.

"Chieftain of the Burnt Fur," Vreesar tempted.

The wild light vanished from the shaman's eyes. "Burnt Fur all dead!" he snarled. "And *you* killed them. You not get stone!" With a sudden move, the gnoll tossed the cinder to Martine.

"Now you die!" Vreesar shrieked. With a halting step, it lunged toward the woman. Martine dropped her guard as she reached out to catch the stone. Suddenly a hand pushed her aside, and Jouka's small black-spiked figure sprang between her and Vreesar. Sunlight blazed in a hundred sparks off the steel points on Jouka's outspread arms. Before the charging elemental could evade him, the gnome seized the monster's legs in his porcupine embrace, triggering a series of cracks as the spikes drove through the fiend's shell. Vreesar kicked its leg frantically, trying to throw the little warrior off, but the gnome clung like a burr, all the time banging his spiked face mask against the elemental's thigh. Cold white ichor streamed down the featureless curves of the gnome's helm.

Forgotten by Vreesar, Krote rose up behind the elemental. Almost as tall as the monster, the gaunt gnoll seized the fiend's shoulders and twisted its body backward. The air rang with the beast's alarmed shriek. Its long arms flailed as it tried to reach the tormentor at its back. Claws raked Krote's arms, slicing his wrapping until it dangled in bloody strips, and the gnoll's face writhed with pain, but still he clung to the creature.

"Now, human!" the Word-Maker roared. Releasing one hand, he grabbed Vreesar's jagged brow, ignoring the needlelike points, and stretched its head back. "Kill it!"

Though the world still spun, Martine staggered forward and raised her sword with both arms till it pointed down like a spike. Vreesar's little eyes widened in fear. "Nooo!" the shrill voice pleaded.

Martine slammed her sword point first into the fiend's exposed throat.

When the monster finally stopped thrashing, Martine left Krote, left Jouka, left her sword, and stumbled to where Vil lay. She knelt beside the man, knowing already all hope was lost. He sagged against the canted ice, eye half closed and dull, his head turned so that she could not see his shredded face. Blood trickled from his mouth and became lost in the

black and gray of his beard. More soaked through the rents
in his armor, the steel bloated out by the blast. When she
raised his arms to fold them over his chest, his limbs
flopped with the impossible limpness that only death
brings.

There was no breath, no last words of farewell, no
chance for one last speech as in the tales of the bards.
There was only his body, still warm, but lost forever.

"Good-bye, Vil," she murmured, saying what he could
not hear.

Behind her, Krote stood silent, ignoring the streams of
blood that trickled from his arms while Jouka undid the
dark-spiked mask that hid his face. Krote turned to face
him, and in another place and time, the two might have
traded blows, but now Jouka only kept a wary distance, perhaps finally deciding that this one gnoll deserved to live.

"It's over, Mistress Martine. The battle's done. Your plan
worked." Jouka paused and mustered up what little compassion he could. "He did not fail, Mistress Martine. He did
not die in vain."

The words slowly returned her to the world, and she
gently closed the man's one remaining eye. With a weary
effort, filled with pain, she rose to her feet. "Praise be to
Torm, Jouka," the woman intoned, looking at the stone in
her hand. "Praise be to Torm."

Epilogue

 The woman walked across the spring meadow, boots sinking in the icy mud. Her black hair was a little longer now, and she moved a little stiffly, too, although her wounds were fully healed. She would always be a little stiff as an aftereffect of Vreesar's icy blast; such things were part of her life now.

On her back the woman carried a stout wicker pack. It was heavy with gear—armor, weapons, blankets, and food—that she would need to cross the southern mountains. Vil's sword swung at her side, along with a pouch full of magical oddments recovered from Jazrac's hoard. So many things were new to her, gifts from the gnomes, that it almost seemed as if she were carrying a new life away from the valley of Samek. She wished it were so, for that would mean release from old pains and sorrows.

Eventually she joined the man and beast who waited at the center of the meadow. The man was young, handsome enough in a rugged way and brimming with self-assurance.

The beast was a hippogriff, a fine steed filled with fire and strength.

"Are you sure you won't reconsider?" the young man asked solicitously.

"And ride with you?" She looked from the golden-plumed hippogriff to the sky. It was amazing how his mount had the look and lines of Astriphie. "Thank you, but no. I'm sure the Harpers can do without me for a few more weeks."

"So they told me when I asked," the young man allowed. "Silverhand wondered if you were planning to pass through Mulmaster on your way back. There are rumors the High Blade is growing more powerful than seems right. He didn't say you had to, though."

Martine smiled ruefully. "More reports. Well, they said I need more seasoning."

"Actually, I'm supposed to make the report. He said you should 'assess and act as you see fit.'" The young man looked past her toward the grassy mound of the warren. "You spent all winter there?"

"Most of it. There's a cabin in the woods." The old pains returned.

Martine looked back to see if any of the gnomes had come to see her off—not that she expected them to. Jouka and Ojakangas were busy rebuilding now that warm weather had come, and Sumalo was feeling his age. She'd said good-bye to them already anyway.

The youth was a fresh young Harper, a messenger for those higher up, sent north to find her and Jazrac. It took the Harpers some time, but eventually someone had gotten concerned enough to send someone to look for them. News of Jazrac's loss was met with sorrow, but no one blamed her. Instead, they read her reports and asked her to stay a little longer to ensure the peace and help rebuild. At first Martine thought it was a punishment, but as the weeks went by she wondered if they hadn't meant it as a reward.

With spring, though, she was rested and eager to move on.

Martine watched as the messenger mounted and strapped his harness in. "Farewell," he said. "Remember Mulmaster."

"May the gods—especially Torm—go with you. As for Mulmaster, tell Silverhand I won't be saving the world anymore."

"What does that mean? Are you going or not?"

"Just tell him. I think he'll understand."

The messenger shrugged and gave his hippogriff a gentle spur. Martine watched them leave, remembering Astriphie as the mount soared through the sky. In a short time, it was only a dwindling speck near the horizon.

Feeling a little wistful about the long journey, Martine shouldered her pack and started walking. From the directions the Vani had given, she thought she could be through the pass by nightfall, but only if she did not dally.

It was sometime around noon when she heard other footsteps on the trail. Not expecting company, the woman drew her sword and waited, ready for the worst. Her vigil ended when a tall, gaunt figure came into view.

"Woman," said the rasping voice, "I will go with you." From the shadows stepped Krote, Word-Maker no more, bow and spear in hand. He still looked as skeletal and haggard as before—more so, perhaps, because of his scarred arms and shredded ears.

Martine paused in surprise. Since the fight on the glacier, she had seen the gnoll only a few times, when he'd come to speak with the gnomes. She understood he wasn't chieftain and that Varka had usurped his role as shaman. The tribe hadn't killed him, as Vreesar had demanded, but every time she saw him, Krote had always been alone.

"Go with me? What about your people?"

"I have no people," the gnoll answered coldly. "They have no use for me."

"Why come with me?"

"I owe you my life."

"And I you. Why, Krote . . . really?"

The Word-Maker drew himself up with dignity. "Because you trust the words of gnolls."

Martine studied the gnoll, trying to make up her mind. As much as he had been the enemy, she still respected and trusted him in ways not fully explainable. The journey would be long, and a companion would be welcome.

"You have my word I will not harm you," Krote said simply.

"Or any others?"

"That depends, woman."

It was good enough. Martine shrugged her pack into position once more. "You may join me, Word-Maker," she offered.

"That is good, human," Krote fell in step behind her, and they began the long hike over the pass.

"I can't wait till we get to Mulmaster," the woman called out cheerily as she disappeared into the woods.

"Mul-massster" the gnoll echoed curiously. "What is that?"

TALES OF GOTHIC HORROR
BEYOND YOUR WILDEST SCREAMS!

Tapestry of Dark Souls
Elaine Bergstrom
ISBN 1-56076-571-2
The monks' hold over the Gathering Cloth, containing some of the vilest evils in Ravenloft, is slipping. The only hope is a strange youth, who will become either the monks' champion . . . or their doom.

Heart of Midnight
J. Robert King
ISBN 1-56076-355-8
Even before he'd drawn his first breath, Casimir had inherited his father's lycanthropic curse. Now the young werewolf must embrace his powers to ward off his own murder and gain revenge.

MORE TALES OF TERROR

Vampire of the Mists
Christie Golden
ISBN 1-56076-155-5

Knight of the Black Rose
James Lowder
ISBN 1-56076-156-3

Dance of the Dead
Christie Golden
ISBN 1-56076-352-3

Available now at book and hobby stores everywhere!

Each $4.95/CAN $5.95/U.K. £3.99

Ravenloft
Books